Praise for E. A. Markham
Meet Me in Mozambique
(2005)

'This is a very funny and sometimes moving book, its dead-pan wit embedded in almost every line'   *Independent*

'In defying the rules, Markham has produced a book which has a wonderfully original, eccentric charm . . . His prose is often quirkily conversational, rather like the musings of an absent-minded professor whose speech is full of playful literary references, private jokes and little epiphanies, and whose memory shifts back and forth . . . All [these stories] serve to build up a picture of Pewter's complex life: a life which defies easy racial stereotyping and oversimplified categorisation. And this is the real achievement of this excellent book'   *Guardian*

'E. A. Markham moves freely between unserious topical references and the serious comedy of metafiction. Which-ever it is, it is always beautifully written and, in the end, oriented towards the unknown, the lure of what lies beyond'   *TLS*

'All are observed with dry humour and eye for detail, and each offers a different account of that most contemporary of experiences – being an exile. Reminiscent of the writings of V. S. Naipaul, these stories are both less literary in form and more relaxed in tone than his work, but are none the worse for that'   *The Times*

Praise for E. A. Markham
At Home with Miss Vanesa
(2006)

'Welcome to the narrative veranda! For it is here that Miss Vanesa holds court on her Caribbean island, playing hostess to the literary returnees – West Indians from various islands and cultures, who have lived abroad all their working lives. E. A. Markham's absorbing, speculative, digressive new work belongs to no known genre'   *Guardian*

'This is another unclassifiable gem of a book from E. A. Markham. Time and viewpoint shift effortlessly between characters. *At Home with Miss Vanesa* is a very clever and immensely warm book'   *Independent*

'If you want originality these days, look to the independent presses. E. A. Markham was born in the Caribbean island of Montserrat, and these linked stories explore the lives of returning exiles. Boisterous, eccentric and playful'
The Times

'Markham includes fascinating morsels which touch on pressing issues of socio-political importance, without trying to push the reader to any particular conclusion . . . the sporadic and evasive nature of *At Home with Miss Vanesa* makes for a clever, witty illustration of the disconnectedness of modern life'   *Irish Times*

'E. A. Markham's most recent collection of linked stories spills out of Miss Vanesa's Caribbean veranda with charming originality'   *Romesh Gunesekera*

The Three Suitors
of Fred Belair

E. A. MARKHAM
1939–2008

E. A. MARKHAM was born in 1939 on the volcanic Caribbean island of Montserrat, the model for his fictional territory of St Caesare. In 1956 his family moved to London, where he went to school. He was an undergraduate student at the University of Wales in Lampeter. After working in theatre in London and the Eastern Caribbean, he lived mainly in continental Europe in the 1970s, where he was a member of the *Coopérative Ouvrière du Bâtiment,* building and restoring houses in the Alpes Maritimes.

Markham moved to Paris in 2005. He was Professor Emeritus of Creative Writing at Sheffield Hallam University, where he headed the Creative Writing programme for fourteen years, introducing the highly successful MA in Writing. He was elected a member of the Royal Society of Literature and in 2006 Markham was International Writing Fellow at Trinity College Dublin. He died in Paris in March 2008.

E. A. Markham worked in all the literary genres; his publications include nine collections of poetry, six collections of short stories, a novel and two memoirs. His 2002 book of verse, *A Rough Climate,* was shortlisted for the T. S. Eliot Prize for Poetry. In 2005 Tindal Street Press published his critically acclaimed collections of linked stories, *Meet Me in Mozambique* and *At Home with Miss Vanesa.*

Since his death in 2008, a memoir of the 1950s, *Against the Grain,* has been published by Peepal Tree Press; this collection of stories, *The Three Suitors of Fred Belair* has appeared from Tindal Street Press; and a selection of his poetry is forthcoming from Anvil Press.

The Three Suitors
of Fred Belair

E. A. Markham

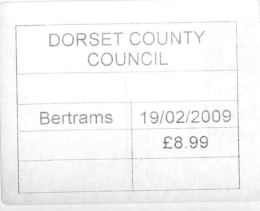

First published in January 2009
by Tindal Street Press Ltd
217 The Custard Factory, Gibb Street,
Birmingham, B9 4AA
www.tindalstreet.co.uk

2 4 6 8 10 9 7 5 3 1

A CIP catalogue reference for this book is available
from the British Library

ISBN: 978 0 9556476 3 5

Typeset by Country Setting, Kingsdown, Kent
Printed and bound in Great Britain by Clays Ltd, St Ives PLC

FSC
Mixed Sources
Product group from well-managed
forests and other controlled sources
Cert no. SGS - COC - 2061
www.fsc.org
© 1996 Forest Stewardship Council

Birmingham City Council

In Memoriam

Edward Archibald Markham

Born Harris, Montserrat, 1939
Died Paris, 2008

Contents

PART ONE

Too Big for
Your Little Island?

I

Eden

I

There were only five in the party, day visitors, and they were running a bit late, and the heat was already overpowering; and they were looking forward to an early lunch at Miss Odilie's, which was all part of the package. After that, of course, it would be too hot for sightseeing, so after a rest at the Tourist Office, and buying small things on display there to remind them of the visit, they'd head for the plane back to Antigua. All but Paul, that is, who was resident on the island.

The buried capital was officially out of bounds; though the danger of sinking in the phreatic ash was long past – years of rain had impacted the soil – the officials weren't taking chances, particularly with tourists. So as they stood at the edge of what used to be the capital, snapping sand, the guide had tried to give them a sense of orientation, to recreate something of the town: the hospital used to be near here; then, on the same line, going down towards the harbour, were the War Memorial and the Customs House. Halfway down was Mr X's bottling factory (store and sweet-drinks factory) and Miss Y lived on the same street, opposite. Further over to the left – on the line of that gas tower you can see in the distance – you could just see the top of it (the jail was beyond that, other side of the bridge) – you had some nice houses of the merchants who lived in town and not further up the hill where it was cooler. And beyond that, of course, was the market. Surprisingly busy for a small place.

One woman from England wanted to know what had happened to the people during the disaster; she had met someone from St Caesare, a writer, in England – a familiar name – was he from these parts?

So the guide reassured them that though a few people had died it was in the aftermath, not in the eruption itself; and that the person whom the woman from England knew was not one of them.

Paul had a question about archaeological digs in the capital. The guide said that it wasn't archaeologists who had been digging, it was a writer (the same writer that the woman from England knew), and the diggings had been suspended because of some sort of dispute; and the writer had gone off again.

And, pictures taken of more sand, they moved on. Paul – who wasn't taking pictures – was slightly surprised at the colour of the sand – or ash: it was a dull grey colour rather than the pristine white he had imagined it to be.

The woman from England wanted a bit more information about those people who had died, and was told that they were mainly old people who had refused to be moved from their homes, even though the authorities had tried to persuade them they were in danger.

So it was a relief when, just before heading back to lunch, they paused at a little cottage, the first one to be obviously inhabited, on the edge of the capital. There was no sign or name on the house but the guide referred to it as North Terrace. At which point Paul put up his hand and proudly-bashfully admitted that he was the new resident. Immediately, pictures were being taken of Paul.

Why was it called North Terrace? Was this the north end of the town?

The guide didn't really know. Though, working it out, this way, behind us, would be heading east. North would be that way. Over there. And really, the villa was known locally as Fred's cottage, after the woman who had lived there.

And where was she now, this Fred?

She was in Martinique. Or maybe in France. She had family in both places.

Could Paul enlighten them?

Paul couldn't. He hadn't been in on the transaction to purchase the cottage. That was all taken care of by his partner; he had never met the widow. The partner also hadn't met her, but had dealt with her relatives.

Fred Belair, the guide said, was very mysterious. Remarkable but mysterious; and greatly loved throughout the island. The island could ill afford to lose people like Fred. Particularly women. It was their loss.

So that was the end of the tour, and the other four tourists took pictures of the cottage, of themselves and Paul, with Paul in front of the cottage, and then headed off to Miss Odilie's with the guide, leaving Paul, with much shaking of hands and wishes of good luck.

*

Late afternoon Paul was on the terrace reading his book.

Simon came out of the villa, giving a quick glance at Paul's progress while he walked past. He went to the railing and looked out. He sighed like a man content.

Paul looked up with interest, and after a pause, said, 'You really are in the Garden of Eden.'

'Better. An improvement. No apple tree. No serpent. No Eve.'

'I see.' He seemed uncertain how to proceed. Paul was considerably younger than Simon; they were both casually dressed, but each befitting his own age.

Paul closed his book and got up, and approached Simon at the railing, also looking out. 'So, what do you see?' he asked quietly.

Simon didn't respond. Eventually, he said, 'Oh. End of a journey, really.'

'Come on.'

'I don't know. I'd like to say . . . I see the sea, I smell the Mediterranean, I . . . can bid goodbye at last to the . . . to the, what we euphemistically call the grown-up constraints of England.'

'Grown-up? You want to regress?'

'Wrong word, possibly.'

'Don't tell me that now you'll be making epic films and planting your own vineyards and – leasing your own bit of Amalfi coast.'

'You have a critic's wit, *mon ami*. Have you read that little play of Bernard Shaw's where the critics do their thing?'

'No.'

'"Trotter, Vaughan and Gunn", he calls them.'

'So, you're not letting on.'

'Um?'

'I asked what you saw. When you looked out from your new estate.'

'Difficult. Difficult at the moment to see beyond volcanic ash. I see an abandoned building next door.'

'Abandoned but not vandalized. Good sign.'

'Yes . . . yes. Very good sign. These details matter. How's your book?'

'Not getting on with it, really.'

A pause.

Simon spoke. 'Any . . . further thoughts on "Eden"?'

'"Eden"'s OK by me.'

'I like it. Centre of the world. Neither east, west, south or . . . Just Eden. All we need is a garden.'

'I see . . . ' and the gesture showed he was about to be ironic. 'I see *oliviers*. Olive, pine and oak . . . I see . . . '

'OK, you win.' A slight pause. 'Though there's no reason why vines shouldn't grow here, is there? There's a line by Emerson . . . '

'Don't use up all your quotes, *mon ami*, we might need them later.' He taps him lightly on the arm and goes back into the house.

Simon Hutton has finally got his house in the sun; and at a good price, too. He never met the owner but dealt with her representatives; but he thinks of her as a kindred spirit; and somehow he feels closer to her than he does to those other people who bought his original house in the south of France; she's left some gardening books that he will explore: he is content to be here, where there are no great buildings to emulate. (He'll keep the gardening books, and throw out the soft toys.)

Of course, he missed the old garden in London, that really was the only wrench, the only pause in exchanging that life for this; not that he would try to reproduce Bayswater here. The hedge would be of something local. Crocus, maybe. He'd love a better variety of apple in the garden. Indeed, the sugar-apple variety; how about that? And instead of lily and iris (why, oh why, must they all have girls' names?), instead of that, something more *à la mode*. A plum tree. Bananas. Pigeon peas. There's water after the event; this is not a desert island. Sweetcorn, too. Ah, the possibilities were endless.

II

Pewter met Nora in London. They were both away from home. They met at a hotel in the middle of town; Nora had her own house in London, but the young people were living in it, and unless she was staying for a few weeks, it was too much of a hassle to get the house back in the shape she liked, and if she didn't do that she was uncomfortable, uneasy. She had lived in too many makeshift places to accept that arrangement in her own home. Also, she couldn't countenance the thought that the young people were accommodating her – with good grace, they were good kids – but clearly just waiting for the moment she was off to rearrange the house to their taste. So she preferred to put herself up in a hotel for a few days before setting off on her mission.

Pewter said he knew what she meant about being comfortable in her own place. Once, he had rented a flat from a friend, middle of town. This was London in the sixties. A splendid flat. Convenient. Sharing with two marvellous people, just down from university. Only problem was this landlord friend of his was a bit of an artist, a painter, and practically covered the walls with his paintings.

Naturally, they took them down and stored them, and put up proper prints that suited the taste at the time. But once in a while the landlord visited – he and Pewter taught at the same college – visited, giving due warning. On the first two or three occasions Pewter and his friends duly took their preferred prints off the walls and rehung the landlord's daubings. Then one day they decided not to bother. It was a little bit more deliberate than that: they decided not to play the game. And the landlord's expression of being crushed was something Pewter didn't get over for a long time: *to what extent was it your responsibility to look after the feelings of people not close to you?* Those close to him, over the years, reminded him he had not done that there, either. This was a roundabout way of telling Nora that he would do whatever was required to rescue Fred from the difficulty she was in. Was it true that Nora and Vanesa had had a falling-out over the issue?

8

Not a falling-out, Nora said; just a difference of opinion of how next to proceed, after the mishap in Fort-de-France. But Vanesa would do her bit. Fred was living in a gite in the Dordogne, not with family, but with other people; and the plan was just to go down and check out these other people and make sure they were legit, and that what they were saying about Fred – what Fred was saying about herself – added up; that she was there of her own free will and had given up her plan to adopt; and that her money supply hadn't been cut off. Nora had already made the arrangements. It was a pity that Pewter no longer had his house in the south; that could have been the base for operations; but living in Paris was good, too, Nora had enjoyed visiting him there. In Paris Pewter had hatched a plan for Fred to adopt, when he had seen a couple of vulnerable young girls, one holding her younger sister tightly by the hand, guiltily browsing among the stalls, bravely crossing the traffic, no parent in sight; but that seemed far-fetched to him now, and he didn't tell Nora about it. What he did reveal was having been to this very hotel before, maybe thirty years ago, to meet a man who wanted to be a writer. The man was from a country with an appalling human rights record; and wanted to be a writer. In those days Pewter thought that the act of writing humanized a man. So, he read the stories and met the man here; Pewter lived in London then. When he was shown up to the room he found that the man had been reading Proust. There were maybe three volumes of *A la recherche . . .* on the coffee table, one with a bookmark well into the volume. A good sign. He stopped at this point as Nora was showing signs of inattention.

'And did it work?' she asked him.

'No, it didn't work.' In one of the stories, the rich man, a millionaire, comes over very sentimental about a woman servant in his house; all the fine feelings expressed, and when Pewter pointed out that the relationship didn't ring true because the man didn't seem to know the servant's name, his writer host thought that that was just a detail.

'So much for Proust,' Nora said.

Pewter was conscious that he was annoying Nora somewhat, and he didn't blame her. Nora had clearly seen through the fact that Pewter's mind wasn't on the job. He was pretending to focus on Fred but really his mission had been different. Here, in London, he was in the middle of seeing to other business, of repairing a fracture even older than Fred; and he had a feeling that this time it might work; but he was too superstitious to speak to Nora about these matters; hence the waffle about the hotel man and Proust.

Looked at from the outside, he would wonder at the pointlessness of himself and Nora going down to the Dordogne to rescue Fred Belair.

III

Simon and Paul are about to have their first dinner party on the island. They have been preparing for it for days. First impressions, and all that. There is a laid table in the cool of the terrace, but the main table is inside. Everything is ready and they are making a big show of relaxing; Simon still in his apron. (Gentle music can be heard from somewhere.) Though Paul glances at his watch.

'Mustn't try and impose our sense of time,' Simon says lightly. But he gets up and goes into the house. There is a bowl of green and brown olives on the table. Paul reaches for an olive, thinks better of it and goes to the railing and looks out. Simon comes back with a thick book, minus the apron, sits and makes a show of leafing through it.

'Don't tell me,' Paul says, without looking round. 'Your book of architectural delights . . . Salamanca. The Aztec place, whatyoucallit . . . Oscar Niemeyer's building in São Paulo . . .'

'Have an olive,' Simon says, without looking up. But he snaps the book shut and joins Paul at the railing, looking out.

'Ah!'

The Very Reverend Doctor is the first to arrive.

'I think it's so pretentious,' he says, on greeting his hosts, 'to come late to the party. Like saying to your hosts, "I'm the important man. All that happens before I arrive, that's just a prelude to the real event." So, my friends, welcome to the island.'

2

The Three Suitors
of Fred Belair

I

Fred Belair has nightmares and she's frightened; because even though she hasn't read Freud and those sorts of people, she knows that it's something she'd done in her waking life that's bringing on these dreams that's making so many people in this world angry. And when she chanced to fall asleep with the radio on and it brought all sorts of wars and bombing and pornographic goings-on in the world into her home, she wakes up not knowing if it's she who has caused this. Because of the men and women who are angry and blaming her, blaming her because she has rejected them: she's just one woman, she wants to tell them, not even a country; she can't accommodate them all; why don't they go somewhere else, there are enough women, enough countries in the world. It's because of this dream, these dreams, that she's quite happy to talk to her friend Vanesa today because there's no point in being coy about these things, especially when you can't sleep at night.

So she's frightened; almost as frightened as when she was waiting for the doctor's verdict. And the fact of having to wait and wait, while they sent abroad to have other doctors decide whether she was to live or die, turned terror into something else – her friend Nora would use words like 'rage' – but Fred didn't rise to rage, with her it was more like resentment, that living here on the island, with the verdict on your health in the balance, you had to send abroad and wait, and wait. And maybe that is what accounted for her little bit of madness in the end.

And even for that she was being punished: she was thinking now of Maas Tommy White from St Anthony's village who spent all those years in England driving a bus, nothing to boast about back home, driving a bus; but the man did well for himself, looked after his family, and then he came home to settle down, more to grieve the fact that his wife had died in England than anything; and there he is settled back in the old house, done up over the years; and one day he's sitting down in the little drawing room listening to his music; and he looks up and notices something like a bump running along the wall, nothing big; so out of curiosity he prods and scratches it with his finger, with his fingernail, and his finger goes right through the surface; and what he discovers is wood ants, woodlice, woodlice eating down the house; and that was enough to send the poor man into the madhouse in Antigua; a man who had survived hard times in England and his wife's death, a woman that he loved; the fact that the woodlice consumed the house, but still left it standing, sent the man straight to the madhouse in Antigua. Well, that is how Fred felt after meeting two of the men who were to help her restore confidence in herself after the shock of waiting for the verdict of the doctors. And here was Vanesa, partner in crime, pretending to cheer her up.

So she said to Vanesa again, after her experience with the Frenchman and the man who beat her, beat her with his mental brilliance, she was back where she started, like a bowl of jelly she was inside; and she was definitely going to call the whole thing off, for it was her sanity they were dealing with now, and say what you like it was no skin off Vanesa's nose.

Vanesa said she was glad that Fred was using imagery; that meant things weren't as bad as all that. (Vanesa was a literary person, so most of the time you put up with her foolishness.)

Now Fred reminded Vanesa that Vanesa was sitting here in her house, on her verandah, like an unaffected visitor, talking about a thing that was important to Fred; and that Vanesa mustn't treat her as if this was a meeting of her reading group where they were discussing a book, at the end of which nothing changed, because the book was already written and published. Vanesa felt maybe she deserved the put-down, so she tried not to be flippant with her friend.

She reminded Fred that she, too, was a woman, and a woman knew what courage was. True, a woman's middle name was humiliation, but she knew what courage was, and if women gave up after one setback, however major, there wouldn't be anybody left in the world today to carry on the struggle and Fred had to remember she wasn't just a woman, she was a Belair; so where was that old Belair spirit, then? And that's the line that Vanesa took to persuade Fred to see her next suitor.

Fred was not convinced; but she sort of trusted Vanesa, who herself had not had an easy life.

'I only doing this to show I not shame, is only a game,' she said, maybe to Vanesa, maybe out loud to herself. 'Just to show all you that after the shock I experience, I just wasn't going to give up and crawl into my shell; and start praying in church, or something.'

'Fred, you're absolutely right; that's the spirit. You're alive, you're healthy and – as Nora keeps telling you – you're one of the best-looking women on the island . . . '

'There's people beginning to talk about Nora.'

Vanesa ignored that. 'If you put your mind to it, you could still give these thirty-something bitches a run for their money. I say go for it, Fred.'

Fred didn't substantially disagree with what Vanesa was saying, but she also knew the meaning of hubris; they thought she didn't know these words, but she went to school.

'All you just want me to make poppy show of meself,' she said, yielding. 'You not the only ones about the place who have your dignity, you know.'

'I am not asking you to do anything, Fred, that you don't want to do. Advertising in the paper for a man was your idea, not mine.'

Fred was hurt by the phrasing. 'I didn't advertise for a man,' she corrected this woman who was maybe not her friend after all. 'I . . . put a discreet ad in a foreign paper and asked . . . if there was a professional person of breeding and superior manners who would like to come to tea, and be served by a lady of wit and charm . . . then I might be prepared to serve the tea.' And then, sharply, 'And in any case, is Nora who suggested the paper. And you, too.'

'"How're you going to fend off those American lesbians?" That's what Nora said to the final wording of the ad, remember?' But Nora was supportive of Fred, and Fred wasn't going to take this opportunity to badmouth Nora.

Vanesa said: 'I notice all you didn't invite any of the women for interview – to share your ladylike charm and wit.'

'Vanesa, I don't know why I tell you my business at all, you and Nora; your mind altogether too coarse for my liking; just because you stand by me when I thought I was . . . when I had my little scare, don't mean you can start taking advantage now. Anyway, the Frenchman seal it; and that other ejaculating jackarse. But after the Frenchman, I not interested at all, at all.'

'It's the ambiguous nature of the ad that confuse everybody.'

'Ambivalent.'

'What?'

'I prefer to use the word "ambivalent". Not "ambiguous". Just because there's no finesse left in the world any more, I don't see why I should blame meself for people not reading between the lines. My daddy used to say: there's two types of people in this world. Is not rich and poor or black and white. Is people who understand nuance and people who don't understand nuance; you better look that up in your dictionary.'

'Your daddy was an intellectual.'

'But he didn't like to show off, like some that pass through here. But if we talking 'bout confusing, I give you confusing: a Frenchman . . . who call himself a Frenchman and live in France, and turn out to be a jackarse from Guadeloupe who end up talking some foolishness that even I don't recognize as French.'

'You thought he would have flown in straight from Paris.'

'Why not?'

'Living on the rue du Faubourg Saint-Honoré.'

Fred had a think about that. Vanesa wouldn't know that that was the address of the Elysée Palace if Fred hadn't told her, so she accepted that Vanesa wasn't trying to pull rank.

'He doesn't have to live at fifty-five rue du Faubourg Saint-Honoré.' And then she added mischievously, 'Though is not a crime to see yourself sitting down here on your verandah next to a man who has a certain routine. You know, striding along the avenue this. Or the boulevard that. Oh, it don't have to be in the middle of Paris. He could be down at Montparnasse before it get spoil. Or even up there out in the Eighteenth. On the rue Ordener, rue Damremont; it don't matter. He's still going to pass the Crédit Agricole and the *pharmacie* and the Arab shop selling vegetables, and to get to his paper shop for *Le Monde,* and the *boulangerie* for the croissants and baguette. Instead of that we get that jackarse.'

'Well, he didn't lie to you when he said he lived in France; he came from Guadeloupe.'

'Jackarse.'

'You would have said something different if it was Martinique.'

'My family don't apologize that they come from Martinique, you know. They don't pretend they're from France. Anyway, Vanesa, I don't want to talk about this man any more. I absolutely not going let you wind up any more over this thing. How about a little drink now?'

'"You know I don't drink",' Vanesa said, quoting their mutual friend. So they had a little smile at that; and went indoors to make themselves a drink.

II

With Nora, the conversation was different. Nora was, if anything, more responsible for this thing than Vanesa was. For it was on Nora's advice that Fred avoided using her own address (as if she was stupid, as if she was born yesterday) and operated out of Nora's Internet café. Not that the process was online, the café just served as a return address. Nora was the one who knew about this business – media, advertising – and identified a couple of discreet and far-from-the-island journals in Canada and France – because Fred wanted a French connection – where they could place the ad. (The third one was an up-market literary magazine in England that Vanesa knew.) But Fred isn't into blaming Nora; no recriminations, though of course she blamed Nora for the quality of vetting, letting through first the rogue Frenchman and then the jackarse with his book learning – *a man from this very island*, though he pretended to be from abroad: if that was the best Nora could come up with from the thousands of responses, Fred wasn't going to play this game any more.

'The men are devious,' Nora said. 'We have to be more watchful.'

(Thank you, Nora.)

You always ended up deferring to Nora because she was a confident woman who had done well abroad, in business. She was one of those power women who had prospered in Thatcher's Britain, beating the men at their own game; and she was recognized for it too. Because Nora had a little badge that had been pinned on her ample titty by Prince Charles himself, which she could take out and dress herself with, if she was going to a function and wanted to turn the conversation her way.

She'd been back home for less than five years and already she had a string of Internet cafés down the islands. So apart from crediting Nora for being a man in a man's world, you didn't want to make yourself look pathetic in her presence. That's why Fred wouldn't discuss the dream with Nora. Instead – to put her a little on the defensive – Fred would talk about the intellectual jackarse who had tried to pull rank with her.

'He should have concentrated on pulling the woman before pulling rank,' was Nora's verdict; Nora wasn't a prude.

The man had started talking about the English language in a way that made Fred conscious of her own speech, her accent; because even though he himself came from these parts his accent wasn't of these parts any more; and for a brief moment Fred had let herself go and wondered if the man would keep up that accent when he was making love. Though she was jumping the gun thinking of making love when they were still, if you like, at the first-stage interview. But she wasn't going to admit this to Nora in case Nora thought she was pathetic. So, talking of the intellectual jackarse, the conversation had proceeded in its nervy way for a while, because the man wasn't really talking about accent but about the English language in a wider, maybe colonial sense; he talked about how foreigners were conned, at international gatherings, into making statements in English (ignoring their own language) that showed them to be imperfect speakers; something the English and American listeners liked. For with that degree of foreignness, it put them one step removed from the thing they were talking about, as if they were living in a second-hand world. And he used examples from the United Nations to make his point.

'I don't have any problem with the philosophizing,' Nora said. 'But what's that got to do with getting into a woman's bed?'

'He called himself a feminist.'

'That's nice.'

'Said he respected a woman's mind.'

'Maybe these feminist men should allow a woman to respect her own mind,' Nora said. 'I am glad you sent him packing.'

So it was easy talking to Nora about sending the intellectual jackarse packing; all the while Fred was replaying the latest nightmare in her mind.

She's alone in a boat, a little boat, on the water, and it's the middle of the sea, nowhere near land, and there're all these distressed men in the water; and she's about to reach out to help some of them into the boat; and she suddenly realizes that they're not distressed, they're angry: they're shouting at her, screaming at her – their faces all contorted – because it's she who caused the shipwreck where most of them are going to drown; and it suddenly dawns on Fred that these men don't want her help, they're not trying to get into the boat, they're determined to drag her into the sea to punish her. And she could hear them; they're telling her why: because she's rejected their application, their proposal; they are rejected suitors and they're going to get her, they're going to punish her, they're going to see her drown.

But instead she hears herself talking to Nora about the Fool in Shakespeare and the Maid in Molière, and asking if that is really how lovers talk to each other nowadays.

III

The Reverend Alex Taylor is on his way to Winifred Belair's. He's several islands away – being three days early – in Barbados. He wants to acclimatize himself for the encounter; he believes in paying attention to detail; he's in no hurry. At the airport he fixes up the last leg of the journey, to St Caesare, in two days' time. Then he books himself into a guesthouse recommended at the airport; and tries to take in the local colour as the taxi driver fills him in on what's happening. He reveals nothing of himself.

Ensconced in his room, he's thinking of the etiquette of descending on the lady. He's come a long way; maybe she thinks he wouldn't come this far just for 'tea'.

Better send her another e-mail. Just to confirm his arrival. No, this calls for something a bit more intimate and near at hand; the e-mail is too impersonal: with e-mail how's she to know he's not a dwarf? Or a bearded fanatic? He'll send her a fax; there's a fax number on the address: the fax won't reveal that he's not a dwarf or a bearded fanatic; but at least it would display the quality of his handwriting, the nakedness of it. He's proud of his handwriting; handwriting of this quality would reassure the lady of breeding. Yes, the guesthouse has a fax machine.

He gets a reply by fax, almost before he knows it. He'll need to deconstruct that. It says he'll be met in St Caesare but that's not what he wants to decode; he has to get behind the grammar.

After dinner he goes back to his room and, with the help of the Internet, analyses the contents of the meal he's just had. Nothing sinister here. The aim is simply to be ready for any eventuality; to be able to keep the conversation going on the meal you've just had, on its nutritional value (the woman was some sort of scientist), its rightness for the metabolism of the person concerned, and for the climate, to show that he's a man who hasn't spent his life in frivolity and brutishness. (He ponders the rhyme or assonance of 'brutishness' with 'Britishness', and wonders if the lady would be impressed by that sort of 'wit'.) Then he settles down to watch some television for the evening. During the night – he is not particularly insomniac, but he's slept a bit that afternoon – he returns to reflecting on the lady's name. During the night, also, he listens to the radio.

Fred Belair, Fred for Winifred. But why Fred? Was she bi? Did she acquire it at school; at university, where those close to her would know something the parents wouldn't? So why did she stick with it? Wilfulness? Perversity? Is she one of those women asking to be punished? To be done things to? An extrovert, certainly; but did she also know how to protect herself? Belair was an old name. Old family. So there'll be protection there. Family in the background; off-island, even, but always watchful. The woman would be allowed so much rope, but not enough to hang herself: if you crossed that line which you're not to know, then the big guns would come in, the cavalry. But there's no fun in this life without risk.

She wouldn't mind marrying down; but not too far down; so the denomination of the church was important; a little more work was needed on that. So far so good.

The next day was well spent, checking things at the university library, checking things on the Internet – as if there was anything new to be learnt of the Belair family. And he listened to the radio at night. The waves of religion washed over him. (What coast was he on? The Atlantic?) He had forgotten, growing up in these parts, that it could be so insistent. If the sermonizing and piety was so open, so naked, he might have to tune up his own delivery. Some of the voices were local, some were American, but the message was the same: take no responsibility for your lives; it's all in the hands of someone else. Accident is to be ruled out. The kindness of strangers. And neighbours. The lucky throw, the skill of surgeons, none of this worked – if it worked – except by the aegis of prayer. The islands had suffered hurricane and volcano. Praise the Lord. Nice. Nice one. By day three, on his way to the airport, he felt better prepared for the meeting. Just one small thing nagged.

Otherwise everything was resolved. On the radio, the sermons tended to favour St Peter: the fisher of men image kept coming up; maybe because they were dealing with islands the sea imagery seemed appropriate, although most of the sermons were coming from America. So he would steer clear of St Peter and fishing imagery.

Also, the feeder of lambs. Jesus called him *cephas*, rock. '*Tu es Petrus et super hanc petram*', etc. 'I will build my church . . . ' He would take his text from a lesser-known saint – the lady was unconventional – someone like St John Chrysostom of Constantinople; or St Monica, the mother of Augustine, patron saint of mothers and wives. (He had done his homework.) And he had sorted out the church. The fax from the lady had helped to clarify the mind; it had been unexpectedly cool and businesslike. As if he were looking over her shoulder while writing it, not daring to give herself away; the strong bold letters contributing to that effect. But he liked that in a woman: he liked a challenge.

So, to run through it all again: what did he have? A nice middle-class woman. Divorced. Nice-looking, he knew she was nice-looking even though he didn't have a photograph, because only a nice-looking woman would have that kind of confidence. A nice-looking woman or a desperate one. (Ms Belair was wilful but not desperate.)

She wouldn't be impressed by some storefront, low-level church; no Saturday church, either; something more mainstream. But not too mainstream, something slightly out of the ordinary. The woman may have charm but she also had wit. So the choice of church would have to seem 'witty'. No little nonsense garage space in Finsbury Park or Stoke Newington, First Church of Christ, whatever. So he had made a decision about that.

He spent some time thinking of an American alternative – and rejected it. For here you were dealing with a pampered woman; the memory of civil rights would probably frighten her off. And all those massed soul-singing choirs in their rent-a-choir gowns wouldn't appeal to a lady of 'wit and charm'. So the church would be in Canada. Canada didn't have the down-at-heel associations of England or the vulgar connotations of America; Canada was just right. His church would not be in Montreal, as originally intended, but in Toronto. How high in the British Methodist Episcopal Church of Toronto he was, is open to debate.

*

When they met, the Reverend Alex Taylor seemed hot and bothered; somewhat out of sorts. He wore a clerical collar and a suit; but he had sustained an accident: there was a small bruise on his forehead; and the collar seemed not quite to fit; and he was dusty and sweaty and ill at ease.

The lady apologized for the mishap, blamed the driver, blamed the roads. Blamed the fact that, though this was not a lawless land, people went about their business as if it were a lawless land.

He had helped to mend the vehicle, he said, after the accident; he was pleased to be of service.

She thanked him. Yes, Skerrit, the driver, was useless. All muscle and menace; but useless. Would the Reverend like to have a rest before . . . ?

No, no, no, he was a man of the world, he . . .

A man of the world!

Man of the cloth, of course, but . . . man of the world, too. (*This was not going as planned: he had been thinking of a saint, the saint of accidents, he should take the opportunity to quote, to show how a man could think on his feet; and he had the information in his case, but he couldn't remember which one it was – St Mary Magdalene was the patron saint of repentant prostitutes; and St Martin of Porres patron of those of mixed race; but he couldn't remember, for the life of him, who the patron saint of accidents was. And he couldn't very well open his case to find out. Never mind. Concentrate on the present; forget the jackarse of a driver who didn't seem able even to change a tyre. But to this lady, who was not as expected. Let's hope other things were to be as expected.*)

A couple of miles away Fred sits on her verandah waiting for her visitor. She's had a message from Nora saying the man's been delayed. Maybe the plane, maybe something else; what's new? Third World. Fourth World. Though she's a bit relieved as well. A clergyman in a clerical collar. She imagines him sitting opposite her and, without warning, tearing off the collar to reveal a T-shirt which has something written on it like: I LIKE SUN SEX AND MONEY, *and leaping on her and having her right there in the open.*

'So what brings you to these parts?' she'd ask him, the

ingénue, stimulating him into playfulness. (She'd be looking over the railing at her garden, knowing the Latin names of her plants, but not owning up to it.)

'So what brings you to these parts?' Nora asked the bruised and battered clergyman sitting opposite her in the cybercafé.

(Go for it, he says for himself; show you're not discomfited by the situation.)

'What brings me to these parts? Plane. The aeroplane.' *(Risk it.)*

'Witty. Are your sermons witty?'

(He doesn't like this woman. She's not smiling. He must get a grip. If it weren't for the prize at the end of it he'd give it up right now. He was toying with the punishments he'd administer, after the event. He had prepared for this, and would have dropped John Donne into the conversation at this point; he would have said that he was sure Dr Donne's sermons were witty, but as he hadn't had the pleasure of reading them since he was young, he was only guessing. That way she would not accuse him of being a know-all. Now he felt the woman wasn't worth that type of energy. Just get the conquest over and done with.)

'I sense you're disappointed in me,' Nora said.

(She's not stupid.)

'You expected Fred Belair to be lithe and petite, flickering in the wind and . . . fair . . . '

(He had to deny it, but at that point the lumbering clown of a driver appeared, wanting something.)

'Excuse me,' the lady said. 'Skerrit?'

'It have a problem in there, you know, with number five. It not turning on, it . . . Like the thing gone dead, again.'

'Oh, Skerrit, do I have to do everything in this place?' She is about to get up, and then stops; turns to Reverend. 'You wouldn't know anything about computers, would you . . . ? No, I suppose this is out of order; you're here on other business.'

But he couldn't let that challenge go; so he offered to see to the computer.

After the computer, it was to see a drunk off the premises, a man who managed to foul the clergyman's clothes. (But he had to do something to prevent Skerrit beating the man up); and now it was a bucket and mop. The place had to be cleaned up, and Skerrit had disappeared; so the lady would have to do the job herself, with no man around: there were the customers to consider. So the Reverend, having long discarded his jacket and clerical collar, took the mop and bucket. Then something reasserted itself. He threw down the mop and bucket.

'What's your game?' he asked Nora.

And by now he had spread a whole series of papers on her table.

'That's my line,' Nora said, looking fully at him. 'We know all about you, *Reverend*. You can tell me about it; or you can tell Skerrit about it. Your choice. No hurry; you're not going anywhere.'

And when he looked up, Skerrit had reappeared, with a weapon.

*

Later, the three women were having a drink on Fred's verandah.

'You know I don't drink; I'm just accompanying you,' Nora said.

'So what did this preacher man have to say?' Fred wanted to know.

'Oh . . . ' Nora seemed bored. 'He was all right; as far as preacher men go. Lots of quotes and stuff from scriptures. He's looking for a soulmate to help him with the Good Works. And save the world.'

'Well, I glad you screened him out because I sick of being politically correct and all the boring things that people want me to be.'

'We didn't bring him round,' Nora said, 'because he would have bored you.' Then she switched attention to her glass. 'I hope you didn't put any alcohol in this,' she said, sipping the water like an expert.

'No, Nora, is only water.'

'And afterwards, if you feel like it,' Nora said, 'there are a couple of new ones you might like to look at. One is from England. A poet. He was knighted by the Finnish state.'

3

Eucalyptus

PEWTER STAPLETON

He was not particularly relieved to be here in danger-ous country; flagellation and penance were for those with more robust belief. The vulcanologists, though, said this was dangerous; and they claimed to be accurate bet-ween sixty and sixty-five per cent of the time. So he could trade on that. The danger may have been out there, in the port area. Escaped prisoners. Though the escaped prisoners denied they were any such, just people laying claim to abandoned houses and the international aid, turned back to other islands. And the government, claiming to be just a committee organizing the relief. So who knows?

Who cares? Pewter assumed 'Nurse Jones' to be a hoaxer, like Felix, the 'African', was before him; but what did he know. He was living in the unsafe zone. That carried privi-leges, though. One of which was having Fred Belair as a neighbour.

FRED BELAIR

Winifred. Everyone said how canny he was to arrange it so that Fred could be his neighbour. So Pewter took credit for that.

He had admitted to talking dirty to Fred; and that was a mistake, because he had assumed a degree of irony in his listeners, which you usually got post disaster. But here it seemed to have gone the other way. Pewter remembered the time he had sent Fred 'pornographic' cuttings wittily wrapped up in brown paper, of things done in this or that country where he lived, or might have lived, including a case history of cannibalism in Germany. In Hamburg, if he remembered. And there were the Sunday supplements about goings-on in Serbia, Sierra Leone, Palestine. Unfazed, she had demanded pictures of Rwanda.

Before you knew it he had been targeted by the lady as her 'dealer' in pornography, while she responded with real sex with the trivial men, described as deprived of too much mind and imagination: 'I only sleep with stupid men,' she boasted, using her own inflection to make it sound like something he might want to hear. And she had, by all accounts, reassured many men of their stupidity. Anyway, Fred said she could talk to Pewter about things she couldn't talk to other men about; things that only her women friends would understand. So now he was enrolled as her woman friend. It was another of her ways of unmanning him. With her other men – the rumour goes – she played no game of dare, she felt no need for finesse: when they unzipped themselves, she said: come in, come in; what's keeping you? Despite his rage Pewter would be polite to Fred, and treat her as a neighbour should.

'NURSE'
('I COULD HAVE BEEN CALLED JEREMIAH') JONES

It is said by his spokespeople that 'Nurse' might not exist, might just be a tantalizing possibility; but that it is necessary, nonetheless, to counter certain vulgar assumptions about Jones. That he is the tyrant of the gullible imagination. That he is like a bloodstained dictator with his jacket weighted down with medals, and that his brand of champagne is Taittinger. That he appears as a baddy in a James Bond film. Cartoon stuff.

On a positive note, they could confirm that Jones is deeply human and caring, having worked in A and E in various NHS hospitals and now, in this new campaign, has pledged to honour the vote; that he reads novels and used to play the church organ (alas, destroyed), and has never been to Russia. (Incidentally, the destruction of the church organ is a source of disappointment for him.) His wife is off-island, temporarily, for her health, and his daughter, during her gap year, is said to be walking in the Andes. A regular guy, is Jones. Far removed from the Eugene O'Neill caricature of a crazed, buffoonish black man in the Irishman's pornographic play. Different, also, from the madman who killed all those gullible people (and their children) in the Guyana bush in the 1970s.

'Jeremiah'? Oh, a joke only for the initiated. Suffice it to say: Jeremiah, too, got a bad press for his efforts at conflict resolution, bringing Egypt and Babylon together, long ago. *Plus ça change.*

FRED

She no longer talked to people, to Pewter, even, about her garden: once she had made the mistake of saying that she didn't miss her old garden; why miss a life that would end up reminding you of your avatar, anyway. When a garden, something you had grown up with, grown to maturity with, was lost, the next one would be like something bought to order. Next time round it wouldn't be the same garden; things there would no longer be older than you, would not remind you of an indulgent parent; all those mistakes that turned out right in the end. Even if the plants in it had the same name as before. *E. rameliana,* for instance. Or *E. australiana.* She's beginning not to remember if she had them in her garden. Or fantasized about having them in her garden. To put them in her garden now just because . . . well, that would be a desperate thing to do. So there would be a shadow on this garden, a shadow of the garden of memory, the garden lost; and so that would bring a sadness to this new scene.

It was at that point that Pewter, her new neighbour, called her a philosopher for pretending that there was a difference between 'shadow' and 'shade'. More to the point, for suggesting that when she said 'shadow' she was deliberately not saying 'shade'. How could you sleep with such a man! (Who, moreover, wore his glasses on his forehead rather than on his eyes, like a creature that hadn't quite got the hang of evolving the right way.) Oh, but you granted men their funny ways; though you tried not to be the butt of their jokes. So she decided to speak no more about her garden, but to sit on her verandah when the heat wasn't too fierce and the ash wasn't falling; and read her book; and do some sketches for her grandchild; when it depressed her to go on potting new cuttings.

PEWTER

Pewter used Fred as an illustration of an idea he had long held. (She had not taken the 'shadow/shade' bait, so he didn't pursue it.) He resorted to Plan B, to an idea he had toyed with for years but hadn't developed to his satisfaction: it was about a woman on the verandah reading a book. There were so many paintings of women reading; he had written about this, he had given a lecture on it. The point he had made was that (apart from the odd exception of Rembrandt's mother and the joke picture of Marilyn Monroe in a bikini on a beach chair reading the last pages of *Ulysses*) nearly all the women reading in portraits were stuck at or near the *start* of their book. What was noticeable, then, was that the expressions of the readers hadn't had time to absorb the *contents* of the book, and hence the experience of reading (thinking and reflecting) hadn't been communicated in the expression of the women sitters.

So Pewter observed 'Fred' from his bathroom window

(pornographic?), not happy in her work, potting, sketching; and he observed her openly from the verandah, reading her book. (She reads magazines, she sketches, she could claim not to be reading without interruption: she might be doing this consciously to frustrate an observer.) She was up-hill, he was down-hill, a detail he knew not to be significant, yet, in his mind, it was worth toying with. He hung on to these stirrings in case they were substantial enough to become thoughts. In an earlier life, a life partly dedicated to teasing out such notions, to weighing them, as it were, he would consign the lighter reflections to something not quite attaining the 'body' of thought: they often needed another bundle of feathers on the scales. But this didn't help with Fred. Oh, for the stupid men and their reliable zips!

Yet the book she was reading was not in a foreign language: that was a *thought*. The doodlings she made, the drawings, *were* pornographic. And when she dressed in her hat and gloves, and wore her walking boots, he had it in mind to follow her trail up in the hills.

Then one day a clergyman appeared in the garden asking about French lessons.

Here we go. The man looked like an athlete forced into formal clothes. They talked about this and that; and then the man lectured Pewter on the benefits of eucalyptus. (He stood by the makeshift sign outside Fred's garden, and held forth on eucalypti.)

FRED

No one on the island escaped the rumour mill, so why should she? Winifred Belair was always going to take a beating. Because she was good-looking. Because she spoke French with thin lips, and encouraged others, whose lips weren't thin, to speak the language, to their embarrassment; they hated her. Because of her family, too: she was from one of those families that people used to associate with ruling the islands, though hers had never ruled – they didn't even have land to talk of – and lived off-island for long periods when her father was alive and worked in Martinique. But the trouble with Fred, they said, was with her wilfulness, which had made the break-up of her marriage a certainty.

There were, as you would expect, the experts who knew the details of this, and said they would never talk if you paid them. Among those who would never talk were an ex-maid in the house, and a boy who used to help with the garden. What they related was how Miss Fred had mocked the husband's churchgoing even in front of their young son, the boy down in Martinique, till the poor man, the husband, couldn't take it any more and went off abroad to wherever the girlfriend was living in one of the American Virgin Islands (though no one knew about the girlfriend then). Now, as everyone knows, it's rare for the man to take the child when the marriage goes wrong. Unheard of in those days. Even if the man had a little lady waiting in the background, she would want to have a go at making her own family, her own children, rather than taking on the child of the previous wife. So everything said of Fred was to be believed. It was said that she preferred her garden to the man she was married to, and to the child of her womb; and that she considered her plants that she cared for and grafted and watered as something more holy than the writ of the holy book. It was said that she mocked the husband and his church. Not in a crude way, of course, but mocking is mocking. That's why no one blamed the man, the night before he went off to the alternative life, taking the boy with him – no one blamed him when he went out into the prized garden with a cutlass or garden shears, or maybe with a hatchet or axe, and caused *havoc*.

Fred replanted her garden; and then the hurricane came and wrecked it a second time, and the volcano soon completed the job. Something biblical, you might say. Now, if the most sophisticated warplanes from you-know-where can't hit their far-off target without collateral damage, what chances do you give a blind thing of a hurricane, like an army of men full of lust; or a volcano, to silt up Fred Belair's garden without taking out the rest of island life with it! There are some, to this day, who blame the whole devastation of the region on the wilfulness and godlessness of Winifred Belair.

PEWTER

Pewter and Fred were two of a kind; no wonder they ended up neighbours in what was the unsafe zone. There were some who said they lived together at night, and only came back to their separate homes during daylight to make it look good; but that was just the rumour. (Once, early in the morning, he had heard her, clearly distressed, and had gone up to investigate, and eventually had comforted her. She had had a dream that her habit of pruning plants had been picked up and was being used by a committee in America, to clone animals; the US Food and Drug Administration, no less, was using her as justification to clone cattle and pigs and goats. And she was powerless to stop it. And Pewter had reassured her that that was a fantasy, that she had nothing to fear; that it was all rumour. And Fred got into the spirit of it and said she was all right now, she'd be all right: the panic had come about because she suddenly realized that without her plants, her old garden, the butterflies wouldn't know where to come any more. That day Pewter promised himself he would cook for her.)

Pewter, it was said, was under some sort of voluntary exile, for something he had done in his life; an arrogant sort of self-punishment. (He liked to hint that this was for something he had *not* done in his life, but that was typical of Pewter, confusing the issue unnecessarily. Though a woman had visited him. An elegant, pretty woman from overseas, whom some claimed to be an ex-wife. Others said she was an official come to make sure that the terms of the sentence weren't being breached, and – this is a fact – she spent the night.) Anyway, the priest who had stood outside Fred's garden of ash spouting Latin names for eucalyptus came back while Fred had gone down to Martinique for the weekend to visit her son, and Pewter was the only one around; he invited the clergyman in for a drink. They were having it on the verandah, and the clergyman looked pointedly at the little radio on the table, which wasn't turned on, as if he were urging a cricket commentary out of it. Pewter relayed an earlier score and declined to turn on the radio. As the clergyman couldn't manage to engage Pewter in gossip about Jones or Fred, or eucalypti – and Pewter admitted that his private thoughts left him confused – the clergyman concluded that his friend was depressed, thanked him for the drink and soon left.

Back in the makeshift town he reported that Pewter was not just depressed but indeed contrite. Though he might still renounce the Good Book in a mechanical sort of way. *In the beginning chemists created the* pharmacie *and the living was good* sort of thing. But what Pewter was renouncing was his old life, lived among a library of books that revealed nothing of the true life. While he might be dismissive of those who worked on the behalf of all that was holy, he was mourning the emptiness of his own life. As a woman in the Russian play was said to have done, a play that the clergyman had neither seen nor read, the reference coming, like a confession, from Pewter. So the good news was that Pewter had renounced the pornography of many books and big-city life for the simplicity of volcanic ash, albeit to lie, side by side, as it were, with a godless neighbour and her drawings of copulating plants.

When Pewter had talked to Fred earlier about gardens

they had talked about formal gardens in Italy and France. Fred had said that a garden told you whether you were right for it, that sometimes when you tried to suggest this or that pattern, it refused to go that way, refused to *grow* that way, and in the end you would take the hint and accept that the garden had one way with its life and you had another. On that occasion she had produced a picture from an English magazine of a man, a *couple*, and their garden – Roy Strong and his wife in their country-house garden somewhere in England. And garden and couple looked so right together. Indeed, the couple looked like something the gardener might have planted and tended, trained and trimmed, over the years, into human shape. And then the wife goes and dies (and this is without hurricane and volcano in England); and the poor man is now reduced, baffled at the loss of something that had had the right shape; and he doesn't know if he has the energy or the will to start again.

Always careful to avoid unnecessary emotion, Pewter didn't let the conversation stray into the details of Fred's own lost-to-the-elements garden.

FRED

Fred would adopt a child. Fred wasn't needy; she had had a full life. (Husband, child, garden, men of every class and colour – even schoolboys who didn't know their dative from their ablative case in Latin now wanted to practise their French. They all told her, in whatever language they managed to speak, that she was the reason for creation, the miracle of miracles: that was no compensation for the loss of her cat, Riley, but it was something.) Fred's father had loved her, her mother had tried to understand her (she'd have nothing said against her mother). She had a son who – despite the brainwashing – had turned out OK, and was earning something of a living down in Martinique. In time he would manage to support his family, without her help;

he was doing as well as could be expected. Fred and her daughter-in-law were on good terms, though she was relieved that they lived on different islands. And she adored her grandson, her Shoy, whom she went down to Martinique to see as often as was proper. That she and her cat, Riley, had prospered at a time before the hurricane and volcano, in the days when her garden bloomed and her plants were correctly labelled, made people whisper witchcraft; and Fred said if it was witchcraft, then witchcraft wasn't so bad. She missed Riley.

She still had friends, of course; from the good time that was pre-volcano. Now – well, now, was it something in the air; was it the volcanic ash that was addling their brains? Was it the sense that suddenly so much that you valued was taken from you, and you not exactly living in a war zone, you not being subject to some brutal human dictator with the sexual habits of a prophet? Suddenly, you had to reassess your life lived above the ash.

Her friends were still her friends, though Vanesa was reluctant to come back to the wreckage, and Nora was off, like a young woman again, full of Spam, rebuilding her IT business empire down the islands. They had tried to marry her off as if she was a young girl got pregnant from her piano teacher. (Or from a man in her own family; though you couldn't talk about this sort of thing except with friends who were not on-island any more. Not that that saved you from the rumour mill. And Gossip, as everyone knew, was a Serb and a Hutu man with his weapon doing what he liked to a woman he had conquered.) So she wouldn't settle for a life of compromise; she would adopt a child before it was too late.

RUMOUR

Fred Belair was a woman of a certain age: Winifred. Miss Belair. Ms Belair. Another sort of woman would accept the logic of her position; and her age. She's a grandmother. She's got a son and a grandchild down in Martinique. She visits them. They come from time to time to visit her. So, despite everything that's said, they're on good terms. The son has forgiven her for trying to turn him into an atheist.

But, to stress again, she's a woman of a certain age; a grandmother. OK, she's lost her garden, and her cat, Riley. (Funny, that a woman should be so attached to her cat, even after she's had the experience of husband and lovers. That was the sort of higher restlessness you expected of people in big, restless places like England and America and Nigeria, where sexual perversions were more or less required.) That sort of thing is not part of our St Caesare tradition; we are broad-minded people, but there are limits. When you breach those limits, you have to pay a penalty. A big country with lots of space can survive the foolishness that would destroy a small island: look how India survived its millions killed at independence. Russia and Germany, too, could survive Stalin and Hitler. (Though the rest of the world didn't survive Stalin and Hitler.) Not the same with a small country, a little island: the god-fearing and the godless get trashed to the same degree, innit. It rains on the just and unjust equally. Don't it!

NEIGHBOUR

Pewter is a good neighbour. When you fail at being a good son, father, husband; when you fail at being a good uncle, even – though you can fake that, more or less – at least try to be a good neighbour. Watch the house. Fend off stray prowlers, the boy wanting to cut the grass where there is no grass, the postman bringing the post though that particular service hasn't been resumed. Watch out for the priest come to improve his French, and then convert you to an interest in eucalyptus.

But this seems a small ambition for a man, privately not yet given up on ambition. For though he had renounced writing, he still liked to work out some of the puzzles crammed in his head: *these additional ways do the power-less give to the powerful.* Or: *how without a compass or a map or a sun do you distinguish the sensation of travelling east from travelling west?* Or: *how to protect privacy and not find your privacy unbearable?* But today there's a partner somewhere in the world still to be communicated with, to be placated. Another ex-partner; old friends to be prevented from falling ill. Recently, a letter from a couple, always ill, long dead in his memory, tracks him down through two abandoned addresses.

So they must be replied to. A card, recalling times past in a city long distant, in *her* handwriting, all well spelt, as if nothing has gone wrong in the world. These two, past eighty, now in sheltered accommodation, their life after illness, illness, illness not corrupting her memory or her handwriting. These are lines to be reconnected. There is no escape.

Meanwhile, Fred has gone down to Martinique to convince her son and daughter-in-law that the decision to adopt a child won't harm their prospects; they will be provided for, new child or no new child; Shoy won't be done out of his inheritance. Fred has rehearsed her arguments (with Pewter and others) and is confident of winning her case. The child will be from Africa, yes, not because she has a thing about Africa; in an earlier time it might well have been from Vietnam, or . . . a child from a war zone we all know. The child would not mind the fact that Fred is a grandmother and misses her garden. And doesn't know about football. So maybe a girl would be best. (The family would argue against a boy, particularly a boy of a certain age, accustomed to the ways of the bush.) A soft house for a girl. Handed-down toys. A cat. Maybe a new garden. French lessons in the drawing room. Piano practice. In time the child would recognize *E. globulus* in the garden. She would learn the proper use for weapons in the kitchen.

And, no, there'll be no man in the house to frighten her. Fred will convince her son, who is still not robust, that his future is secure, that Shoy's future is secure, adoptee or no adoptee. She would not tell him of her plans to travel to a far continent to carry out her plan; for he would fear for her, he is her son.

Pewter is jealous of Fred's son, of the new child soon to be in Fred's life; of her garden, of Shoy, of her cat. But he is good at keeping these slaps in the face playful.

THE FICTION

He had once offered her a garden, a gift not taken up. Others had admired but declined the garden. It was another country, far from where the person lived; it was on the other side of the moon, though the weather was perfect. And she spoke the language of that place. Montauroux. *Montauroux*, with that inviting pout of the lips. It was sunny, a Christmas day. An away-from-family day.

So there they were. On his way back from the village with the croissants, he found her up, outside, coffee in hand, surveying the garden; so he put her to work naming the plants that he should have named years ago. But she had misunderstood. The daffodils and asparagus and geraniums, yes – with their pink and red flowers – shamed him into recognition. But what he called grass she has names for. He let that pass and focused on, ah, the rose bush next to the front door that needed cutting back; and the asparagus that apparently sent out shoots far from the parent plant.

Interesting, that, with asparagus growing in the boxes hanging on the railing of the pool: shoots in the middle of the pool? And so to the north terrace; for the wide expanse of terrace at the front of the house offered too much to name; *messugue, poign de sorcière* (you heard it here first: that fellow, Adam. Must have been quite a poet). *Genévrier* was said to be dangerous; and thyme, thyme, thyme, what would we do without you in the kitchen? Or is the scent of thyme vaguely hospitally? The *chênes verts* gave their name to the house. *Pissinlit, lierre* and *salse-pareille* are destined to be forgotten.

(On the way to the north terrace she said she missed her grandson, Shoy.)

TWO MEN

The Very Reverend Doctor – that's his proper title – and Pewter are having a drink on the verandah. (Until today Pewter had thought of the man, privately, as 'the Boxer'. Hard to know what suggested that, probably a slight feint when Pewter unexpectedly counterattacked a proposition, or the way the shoulder seemed to dip before hitting back with a joke. And one day Pewter mentioned boxing, and before you knew it the man was up on his hind legs demonstrating Ali in his prime. The phrase 'muscular Christianity' came to Pewter's mind.) Today, Pewter's back is to Fred's house, the Very Reverend Doctor is facing it. They are talking nonsense to each other, like tolerant brothers signalling a truce. Nurse Jones had been a pastry chef (the white coat wasn't medical), not unlike Uncle Ho, back then. Jones was a theology student in Dublin, and a drop-out, like Stalin was in Russia, etc. Now the Very Reverend Doctor is saying something else. He's saying there is a comparison to be made between cricket and the universe, the fact that cricket pitches all over the world are getting slower is significant. (He looks pointedly at the silent radio, but doesn't ask the score.) From Perth in Western Australia, he says, to Sabina Park in Jamaica, the earth is showing her tiredness, his tiredness, its tiredness, whatever. The earth is exhausted because it's taken such a beating over the years, over the centuries, over millennia, over its, yes, more than six thousand years.

That makes Pewter perk up and warm to the fraud; his mind stops trying to formulate a question about the difference between a Very Reverend and a Nearly Reverend Doctor. So the earth is tired, the waterways silting up, the mighty Yellow River in China, the biblical Jordan: we have to find ways to renewal. *Sport, sex, new forms of evolution*: will that do it? There's a religious movement, the Very Reverend Doctor says – there's always a religious movement somewhere – that fits the bill.

There was the English Church of Country Sports, dedicated to hunting, which captured something of the English spirit. The image of vigorous ladies in wellingtons, squashing the mud, is a bracing one. Pewter could agree with that. There is, of course, the Church of Satan, that also appealed to the vigorous. That one originating from the ancient Egyptian god of chaos and evil, the god they called Set, popular in Europe of the Enlightenment. Oh, the names they give to things! The Hellfire Clubs of England were relatively non-racist, he said. In the eighteenth century: they drew strength from the Christian Bible. Matthew 25:33: 'Sheep to the right, goats to the left.' All that vigour. So maybe now a period of tiredness, like the cricket pitches, is to be welcomed.

When they talked about Fred the Reverend Doctor asked if Pewter had noticed the lady's sketches. From the Book of Eucalyptus. The Very Reverend Doctor said that Eucalyptus was a religion he could warm to. It ought not to be suppressed. He had studied all the sects, from the Roman to the New Guinean, and had a good feeling about this one.

Eucalyptus was a religion without a defined hierarchy (and therefore not injurious to women and children); it was diffused and understated, and he reckoned that Ms Belair was one of its secret priests; that's why he had a mind to help her. He had a plan, which, in confidence, he couldn't divulge. (Pewter couldn't help recalling hearing Fred talking of her eucalyptus as if it was something sacred; he could see her, see those inviting lips fashion *Eucalyptus pulverulenta, Eucalyptus camaldulensis.* And then there were the drawings.)

It was not well known, the Very Reverend Doctor was saying, that the founder of the religion was an Australian called Holland. Holland had a daughter but no wife. (Nothing should be made of that.) Holland had a farm on which he planted eucalypti. Come the time for the daughter to be given in marriage, the father advertises for a man to win his daughter's hand, a man who could name every one of the eucalypti on his farm, no mistake allowed.

In Latin, of course?

Of course. But despite appearances, it's another male religion, no women suitors admitted. This is Australia, of cricket and sport. But the conceit puts it on a par with the higher religions. The naming of eucalypti, hundreds of species of them, and in Latin, and with an Australian accent, is as near as dammit an impossible task; infinite. In conceptual terms not infinite, a smaller task, perhaps, than contemplating the Milky Way. But reduced to human scale, near-infinite. So it's the human scale of this religion of Holland's that will win the day in this unsafe zone. With a beautiful woman practising it here in the sand. A religion tastefully erotic. Erotic, in a spiritual sense. She must be a fine botanist, looking at those pictures of consenting eucalypti.

This image of Fred the botanist turned priestess was attractive to Pewter. Already five of his friends who should be alive had been buried or cremated. That sort of humiliation would never stop; would increase. Instead of that,

E. globulus and *E. salmonophloia*, out of a sensuous mouth reserved for stupid men, was appealing.

And then he realized he had been trumped again by a stupid man. He was only partially listening now as the Very Reverend Doctor talked about the shortcomings of the various religions of Rome and New Guinea; of the Aetherius Society of Sir John King, the Taxi Driver; of Zoroaster of ancient Persia and India and of the First Presleytarian Church of Elvis the Divine, of modern America.

They call it the moment of epiphany, but he saw it coming. Fred's garden was a religion to Fred. Fred would buy this because it was unlike the religions she had no time for. This man would find his way to Fred's bed through Fred's garden. Ah, well, Pewter said to himself in defeat. Try to be gracious about it; so he turned on the radio, in case there was a cricket commentary coming from somewhere, suggested another drink; and the men settled down, hoping for magic from the little box.

4

North Terrace

I

Just as he was about to set out, the phone rang. He hesitated: might as well answer it, he had time. It took only an hour to the airport and he had given himself a good hour and a half. He didn't like the sound of the phone ringing, or rather, it made him uneasy; but he remembered to tell himself that he was not superstitious.

He was calm on the phone, thinking that these things happen, reminding himself not to press, for things were more likely to resolve themselves in a normal way if you didn't press; and when he put down the phone he knew he had done all the wrong things. So what to do?

What was he doing? He pulled up sharply; he was still setting out for the airport after the call saying she would not be coming. But you didn't do this; you didn't do this to people. You didn't throw weeks of preparation (and expense) out of the window, back in someone's face, just on a whim.

But it wasn't a whim; she was at the airport. She was at the airport in England. At Luton. (An airport she had never liked, so it must have shown intent to get her to Luton.) You didn't invest all that, get packed, pay the fare, travel to Luton and then lightly decide not to come, not to get on the plane.

How did he know she was at Luton? Oh, she didn't play those games, she didn't lie. *But how did he know she was at Luton?* He thought of ringing the flat, ringing her London number to see if she answered. He'd ring the landline. But no; this was the sort of thing that other people did; and they had long prided themselves that they were not like other people. He trusted her. She didn't, of course, trust him; but he trusted her. He was the one to dissemble, to ring from some place and pretend he was at another place. Unless she was doing this to punish him. No, she was at Luton. And he remembered to spare a thought for her stuck at Luton, a place she had never liked. And the thought of her heading back for London made him accuse himself of every sort of brutality.

And there was distress in her voice. Perhaps not quite distress, but concern. Not overdoing it, not putting on an act. She spoke slightly slower than usual, indicating that she knew the effect her words were having on him. She said she had left it till the last moment. But that she had to ring now, before he set out for the airport. (*Even then she was thinking of him.*) It was the least bad of the options, to catch him before he set out, rather than to have him drive to the airport (and she knew he didn't enjoy the drive to the airport), and then find her not there, and have to turn around, and be cross.

He didn't like that last phrase of being cross. That was the only false note he detected: to think of him being cross in these circumstances was to dismiss him as something less than he was. Of course he was cross, but that was the least of the things he would describe himself as being at the moment.

Yes, he respected her care of his . . . his pride: she didn't want him to go to the airport and wait around for hours and be made to look foolish. To go to the airport and take the blame for having the flight details wrong, and make the phone calls when, maybe, his mobile wasn't working; and be flustered and made to look foolish; then he'd legitimately be cross. So was the phone call merely to prevent him getting cross? *And what sort of animal was he when he was cross? Was he violent? Was he a danger to life and limb?* He resented being characterized as someone who had to be placated in case he got cross. He was not cross; *he was in a much worse way than being cross.*

But she wasn't gloating. She wasn't *pretending* to save him from humiliation and distress. She just wanted to save him from going all the way to Nice for nothing, and being cross. He would remind himself that she was trying to save his feelings.

And that made him think about her. Turning back halfway; all the plans of reconciliation and starting again shelved, thought better of, abandoned; the feelings of maybe hopelessness, certainly tiredness coming as a relief, cases to be unpacked, contents unused, on a train back to London, a sort of relief: who would console her for this? He preferred not to think about that.

So what to do? He felt a fool in this clean, suddenly large, echoing house in the Var, the fridge full of things that he liked less well than she did; and somewhere at the back of his mind he heard the suggestion of a laugh, a giggle, as if he was being watched by people he had disappointed over the years; and they were enjoying his humiliation. Without thinking, he flicked on the switch of the kettle for tea. His alcohol drinking was controlled: this would be a good time to let go of the constraints, to be less fussy about health; but he was still intact: what was the point of excess if there was no enjoyment in it! So he'd stick to tea. He was suddenly very tired. He realized later that he was so tired he had forgotten to make the tea.

But he did the mechanical things, opened up the shutters from the dining area, unloaded the washing machine, and then he thought: stupid STUPID *STUPID: why didn't I persuade her on to the plane?* Why didn't I take charge of the situation and order her on to the plane? It was pathetic; it was a character failing. It was what she was punishing him for. 'Don't be silly, get on the plane. I've done the shopping; been to Leclerc; I've planned supper for tonight.' And as she was weakening, he'd go on to say, in a lighter vein, 'The house is spotless, the weather is beautiful. Madame Roustan came today and did the cleaning. The fridge is full of things you like. There's lots of wood for the fire, pine and oak, even though it's not cold. Somewhere outside, the man with the sheep with the bells on is crossing from the forest; you'd love the sheep. Last time there were a few goats among the sheep. Big, black ones. And then came the donkeys, all laid on. And inside, we have lined up the videos we've never watched together. *Get on the plane. Pronto.*'

If that was all too meandering and indirect, he would simply say, 'I'll kill you. I'll kill you as they do in fiction.'

But why should he believe her? She was not a literal person; she was not banal. Why should he believe that she was not on the plane? So he was stung into action; he didn't bother to close shutters but grabbed the car keys and headed out of the door. He couldn't afford to keep her waiting at the airport.

As he drove through the village he had an image of her, at Luton, distressed instead of smiling. He quickly put that image out of his mind. The lone and abandoned people waiting in houses, waiting at airports, had nothing to do with them; had their sympathy, of course, but had nothing to do with them; with people of imagination.

*

And there they were, sharing the house for a few days, Fred Belair and Pewter Stapleton. And despite everything, they had had a good time. Pewter learned to like the forest, to recognize plants; and Fred affected to be more relieved than anxious to be away from her family: why come all the way to France to make yourself miserable? She could be miserable at home; she decided for once not to be won over by the situation in Martinique, not to be responsible, even though her son needed the support, and someone had to limit the damage they were inflicting on little Shoy – who was already announcing to everyone that he was a Christian. The compromise was a visit to family in France, in the Dordogne, who could keep an eye on her. It was from there that she rang a number not expecting an answer; and Pewter Stapleton invited her to come down for Christmas. Fred had to pretend to her relations that this was a long-standing arrangement, and that she had somehow forgotten to mention it. They were not impressed: typical Fred, when will she grow up! They knew she was holding something back; but then they weren't really responsible for her, were they?

It was obvious that she was third or fourth or fifth – or tenth – name on his list of people that the man had invited to share his house over the holidays. But for Fred it was survival against pride.

So she was happy to go off in the car with him to visit his friends, and eat oysters and whatnot, and hear about his building exploits; and she pretended not to notice that her French was better than his.

When someone asked point-blank if they were together they cheerfully admitted that they were not; but subtly suggested otherwise. And then a year on, here they were again, on the other side of the world; neighbours.

They were having a drink on her verandah.

'The taxi driver calls your place the North Terrace!' He looked around, as if expecting a sign.

'I'm sorry, Pewter. I just couldn't think of another name. It's temporary.'

'No, it's fine . . . fine.'

'Everything have to have a name. If there's no street name, the house has to have a name; I hope you don't mind.'

Pewter was flattered. A bit disconcerted, but flattered. He had talked a lot about the North Terrace when Fred had spent Christmas in the Var, the year before; he suspected now that much of what he said then was nonsense; and that made him a bit defensive now: he wasn't used to people being so . . . suggestible. *This* North Terrace was set in volcanic ash.

'Your friend. Did she ever come?'

It took him a little while to register; to think back to last Christmas; and he tried to play down his confusion.

'Ah.' He didn't know how much to reveal.

'Sorry, is none of me business.'

'No, no. Bad timing,' Pewter said. 'I eventually got rid of the house. I started the process, anyway.'

'Oh, I sorry. It was a nice house.'

'It *was* a nice house. Built it meself. Near enough.'

Fred knew the story.

'And you come to live here. In volcanic sand.'

'The company's good.'

'I was expecting James Mason meself. But you'll do.'

'He's dead. James Mason.'

'The lengths these men will go to to . . . ' And then she turned serious. 'Me can't offer you any, what was it? *Messugue* and *cade* and . . . '

'Ah, well . . . '

They drank to that.

II

When the relative came Pewter wasn't prepared for it. The people removing Fred's stuff from her house obviously weren't relatives; but this one was. Pewter had never met him before but he knew him: you couldn't misjudge this man. There was nothing of the clownishness that he liked to associate with the Very Reverend Doctors; and, anyway, he wasn't dressed like a Very Reverend Doctor, and he probably wasn't a Very Reverend Doctor. It was hard to pick up his accent. He did the talking while his friends violated the woman's house. But they had a key, and they claimed to be Fred's relatives, come to collect some of her things to take them down to Martinique, where she had decided to spend more time with her family. Till the situation on the island here got a little better.

It was all so plausible and yet he didn't trust it; he felt he was being outmanoeuvred. He had lost a bit of credibility when he had asked if Fred had sent any message for him.

What kind of message?

And then he was trapped. He wasn't her lover, and he didn't want to give the impression that he was. But clearly, that was precisely the conclusion the man drew; and Pewter immediately saw, from the pursing of the lips, that he, Pewter, was cast, in the relative's mind, with the reported rogues and vagabonds who had sought to abuse Fred Belair; to take advantage of her for sex or money or social advancement. So he had to lift himself back up on his high horse and claim Winifred (less intimate than 'Fred') as an old friend and new neighbour, someone who was resilient and not self-pitying; someone you could talk to, yes, a sort of *intellectual* soul sister; but one who knew about plants and gardens.

'Winifred has a good brain,' the man agreed. 'There's no denying that. It's her judgement that's in question.'

Pewter refused to be intimidated by this man. There was something about him that was too . . . self-consciously calm and studied to be really threatening – though the phrase 'Southern Baptist' came to mind. It wasn't the calm, it was the body language, the expression with the features not set, but *practisedly* relaxed: when he spoke to Pewter it was as if – that slight pause – as if he took time to decide what idiom to employ. He spoke a near-enough unaccented English, and yet . . . he gave the impression that it wasn't his first language. The message was: *I am invulnerable. I am unbreachable. I am in charge.* A message that some said Pewter himself had employed in situations like this. *How would Fred fare against this man, her family?*

'Is Fred all right?' Pewter asked, quickly, lightly, as if to discomfort him; and then realized he should have said 'Winifred'.

'Yeah. She needs rest, that's all. A bit of calm. She's down there with her family, where . . . '

' . . . she belongs?'

' . . . where she will get a bit of rest. Calm.'

The boundaries were being set down by other people; Pewter was learning that he had perhaps reached them. He had phoned the Martinique number once and someone had answered and said that Miss Winifred was resting (*rest, resting . . . Miss Winifred*) and would call back; and she didn't call back . . . He phoned a few days later to say that he was watering the plants, and was told that Winifred was out in the park with her daughter-in-law and Shoy, and would call back when she got home; and she didn't, of course, call back. So Pewter got the message; the one thing he didn't want to do was to put pressure on Fred, wherever she was, by making nuisance calls, and having her suffer the consequences. So he hadn't called again. And now here was this man, her relative, standing on Pewter's verandah. He was holding some books. He had declined a seat (forcing Pewter, who had sat down again, to look up at him, at the books), confirming his worst fears.

Reverting to bad habits, Pewter's instinct was to protect himself, so he wanted to spell it out in case it was not understood.

'We were never lovers, you know, Fred and . . . Winifred and me. Just friends. And of course, now, neighbours.
She taught me a lot about flowers, y'know, her garden.
Made me want to be a scientist. Botanist.' *Was the message getting through?* 'We never slept together.'

'You're one of those who, shall we say, messed with her
head.' *Messed with her head? One of those . . . ?* The man
offered the three or four books he had brought from
Fred's house. 'These . . . may belong to you.'

Pewter glanced at them. They weren't his. But the man
clearly didn't care; he was making some sort of statement.
And Pewter wouldn't fall into the trap to say the books
weren't his. In any case he couldn't see why they would be
said to have interfered with anybody's head. He would not
engage with the notion that Fred was crazy. So he accepted
the books and quietly praised himself for not being drawn
into a pointless argument: if the books were the worst that
he was being accused of, he could live with that, fight it.
But not now. *But these were cruel people. Fred had to be
rescued.*

Afterwards, experiencing his usual feeling of abandonment, having inherited books he didn't particularly want
to read, Pewter reflected that, yes, it was right what he had
said about Fred, about their relationship: if to call them
intellectual soulmates was a bit strong, they had a healthy
respect for each other; out of that they had both renamed
their dwelling quarters, each mindful of the other. Fred's
renaming of her bleak, gardenless, expanse of ash as 'North
Terrace' was in recognition of the Christmas spent with
Pewter in the south of France, in the Var: the fact that
nothing thrived under Fred's volcanic ash was not a criticism of Pewter's house, was not even an ironic comment
on Fred's present circumstance; it was just an impulsive
gesture on Fred's part. And Pewter was touched by it.

Pewter had renamed his own North Terrace after the intervention of Ms Belair, a year ago.

When they had been standing there that Christmas morning, Fred with her mug of coffee, Pewter with his fresh croissants from the village – *au beurre* for her, *nature* for himself – after she had identified the flowers and the weeds, first at the front of the house and then at that terrace, he began to explain to her the difference between this new North Terrace and the original North Terrace a few yards away behind the original structure, the main house.

That one over there, with the clotheslines, was conventional; that went with the house, the territory; that, if you like, served the north bedroom – the one in which he traditionally slept, reserving the master/mistress bedroom with its en suite for his special guest, in this case, Fred. He associated the old North Terrace with the holidaymaker's house, sun and the Mediterranean, a house you visited with friends. You would show off the special features, the challenges of conversation, the few mistakes, talk of the hassle of building in those days, demonize (or praise) your workers – Muhammad, the Tunisian – your main suppliers of materials, Gaziello and Costamagna, like a brace of Italian lawyers, still on the main road. That was part of the rhetoric, the narrative of the old house, which was sometimes let; and a praise diary of satisfied customers, kept on a low table, to be read out to guests.

But then there was *this* new North Terrace, where Fred and Pewter stood that Christmas morning: they were on the flat roof of what might be a garage, but was, in fact, a secret apartment, carved out of rock and sand, and buried, to outwit the planning mafia. Pewter was explaining to Fred (for whom this was the first visit) that this spot, under the great oak tree, fringed by all those plants and bushes that she named, resting on a perfectly, elegantly lettable apartment, was now his favourite 'thinking space'.

'Because you have something hiding underneath there.'
Fred was always down-to-earth; Fred pricked his pretensions.

Even then he misunderstood her; he thought she was referring to the game with French bureaucracy. But no, she was ahead of him: *she was imagining what he would shelter in his thinking space* – the genesis of poems and stories and plays, whole 'novel' worlds would come into being just by his sitting/standing here. He recalled a debate with a man at a university concerning the creation of mental images, the difference between the artist creating mental images and God – the God of Bishop Berkeley – creating mental images, both of nothing. The difference, according to the Philosopher, was that the artist was trapped within his creation; the God standing outside his. *True or false?*

No evidence that that was true.

No evidence that the God was not trapped in *its* creation.

Though both could be outside or inside its creation.

Both could be outside *and* inside its creation.

Or a bigger God, a bigger Artist standing outside the creation of a lesser god, a lesser artist.

The debate, becoming endless, becomes uninteresting.

And now Fred was challenging him to share his thoughts.

He admitted that his thinking space might sometimes provoke something shameful. But that most of the time it provoked nothing shameful; rather, it transformed him beyond his usual level of caution to a larger level of courage, of risk.

'Like hiding them poor women from the Bible.'

'Eh! What?'

'From Sodom.'

(He thought, stupidly, of Saddam.) But Fred was explaining.

'The man who give his daughters to the good men of

Sodom. So that they wouldn't sodomize – that's where the word come from, you know? So that they wouldn't sodomize the two visiting angels. The father was a pimp for his own daughters. Telling the man and them, "I have two daughters which have not known man; let me, I pray you, bring them unto you, and do ye to them as is good in your eyes." Is not easy being a daughter or a woman in the Bible. Like in Judges nineteen, twenty-three to twenty-four. And you have it again in Genesis nineteen, verses thirty-one to thirty-six. And then the man wife turn into a pillar of salt because she turn round and take a look at what happening. And I say, your secret hiding place underneath there would be a good place to hide the woman before she turn to salt. And the daughters. Till things calm down a bit in Sodom.'

He didn't have his Bible with him, inherited from his mother; but it all rang true. At that moment he had decided to rename the new North Terrace apartment 'Lot's Cabin'. The main house would still be *Les Chênes verts*. But now we had Lot's Cabin, a refuge for the wife and daughters. Later, in attempting to get rid of the house, Pewter felt that he was betraying his friend in London who hadn't come that Christmas, who had got as far as Luton airport and had turned round and gone home. In getting rid of Lot's Cabin, he felt he was betraying Fred Belair.

*

When the idiot came – this was the original Very Reverend Doctor – Pewter was not minded to be inhospitable. They had by now struck up something of a passing acquaintanceship, maybe even a relationship, talking about nothing in particular much of the time; and as Pewter had said to himself: when you've got nobody much to talk to, you talk to whoever presents himself. He recalled an essay by

C. L. R. James, about England during World War I, and the coarsening effects on the civilian population of that adventure, in this case the way it allowed men to treat women with scant respect, there being a shortage of men with, what? a wider range of sensibility on offer. Well, the present environment was equally blighted.

He had talked about this and that with the visitor (who was, in effect, in pursuit of Fred Belair), talked theology at a lowish level, then talked cricket and boxing, and talked more guardedly about gardens, about varieties of eucalyptus as a metaphor for something or other, a garden of earthly delights to be enjoyed in this life. They meditated, of course, on the eucalyptus book that Fred had been reading so obsessively, and agreed that it was a religious text, in its essential maleness. So Pewter brought out a beer, as usual, which he didn't drink now for health reasons, but kept a stock for visitors; and settled down on the verandah with his uninvited guest.

And after the usual meandering talk, the conversation came to Fred.

Neither man had any news. From Martinique.

'So we have to pray for her,' the man said.

'What d'you mean, pray?'

'Ask God to take a hand.' This was the man who, over how many visits, had lured Pewter into a sort of curiosity. He had got Pewter to agree that he was a believer in *something*. And they ran through the various possibilities. In the end they found common cause: a Church of England Cricket Commentators (CECC). From the sainted John Arlott, the Founder, through the Cardinal and High Priest Brian Johnston to the young Altar Boys, Jonathan Agnew and Gus Fraser. Not forgetting the old Retainers, the preppy Blowers (Henry Blofeld) and the doctrinally conservative Geoff Boycott. So, increasingly, they talked not cricket, but cricket commentary; and deconstructed the relative absence of national chauvinism (Boycott excepted) and lack of racism (Boycott included) in the commentaries. And after all that this jackarse has reverted to his familiar role, feeling free to patronize Fred Belair.

'Well . . . ' Pewter said: 'Fred wouldn't thank you for that.'

'We don't always know our best interest.'

This was intolerable. 'So you know Fred's best interest better than Fred. An educated woman. A scientist.'

'She might be confused.'

'Confused. *Confused.*' The jackarse. '*You* clear-thinking, and she confused!'

'I didn't mean . . . '

'Don't you think the woman has enough to put up with than to have every – *Very Reverend Doctor – Boxerman –* come here to abuse her in this way!'

'We each serve the cause in the way we know best, Professor. No doubt you –'

'*Confused.* What is this? A conspiracy. You're lucky I don't believe in conspiracy theories.'

'I . . . I must have struck a wrong nerve, I . . . ' (he was on his feet) 'I . . . bid you a good day, professor. We're all upset. We both wish for the same outcome.'

'The lady is not confused,' Pewter said evenly. 'I suggest you use that statement for your text. From your pulpit.' And he called after him, conscious even then that this was a bit excessive. 'And we don't. We don't wish for the same outcome!'

III

'It's a mess. A joke. Is poppy show time.' Miss Vanesa was not amused. 'Any wonder nobody can come back and live in this poppyshow place again.'

'No use crying over spilt milk now, Vanesa, what's

done's done. I wonder if they're serving supper. If we've missed it.'

'Nora, you thinking of food at a time like this!'

It was Fred's rescue party and they had fallen at the first hurdle. The helicopter was out of service and Vanesa absolutely refused to take the launch to Antigua because of the roughness of the ride. If it was *down* from Antigua to St Caesare, she explained to everyone, that would be different – the ride was a lot smoother; but no way was she going to brave the tempest up to Antigua on that boat, and be sick.

So they'd put up at the hotel here with the electricians from England and make an early start out in the morning. It was a good idea that Pewter agreed to come over to the hotel for the night so they could talk things over and coordinate their plan; and all set out together in the morning.

Pewter didn't see the point of leaving his place and going over to the hotel, but he was stung by the fact that while he had sat there wringing his hands and watering her plants, unbeknown to him, Fred's real friends had decided to *act*. They had shown him up to that point that he would have done anything they asked.

The plan was not clear to him, except that they would go down to Martinique and liberate Fred. Vanesa claimed to have had experience of women being trapped by their families, not only here, not only in the islands, but in England; and she reminded them all about those women who went to England in the fifties and sixties in the prime of life only to be 'castrated' by their men, husbands, partners and, finally, by their sons. The husbands and partners, who had preceded them, and had formed new alliances, new relationships, often found the original women an embarrassment, and instead of getting rid of them decided to punish them sexually. This is one thing the sons learnt from their fathers, how to punish their mothers: they kept watch over them so the women were sexually neutered: that was a punishment much greater than the racism they all went on about.

After Miss Vanesa had had her say Nora agreed that, yes, the philosophy was always to be considered, but then you had to move on to something *practical*, and that would concentrate minds all round. Her reading of the situation was this: Fred and the family had had a falling-out over the bringing up of her grandchild, Shoy. (Fred was on weak ground here because she was only the grand-mother.) Fred finally decides to adopt a child from war-torn Africa, threatening Shoy's inheritance from Fred, who had inherited her own father's estate. The family makes a big thing of Fred's emotional instability, but really, what they were concerned about was money. So why not get Fred to make a settlement now, on Shoy; and maybe become a godmother to some distant family's child: you could be emotionally attached to your godchild without it costing you money.

To Pewter's suggestion that the family – odd as they were – might be genuinely concerned about Fred's emotional welfare, both women thought he was being sentimental, just like a man. Plan B was to persuade Fred to give up the idea of adoption – of her own free will: adoption was, anyway, a hassle – but not let the family benefit financially. She could come and stay with Nora or Vanesa for as long as it took to clear her head; and then they'd see.

Pewter had a horrible thought that neither Nora nor Vanesa had had dealings with the family, and he didn't fancy their chances facing down the man with the books. Or were certain people right about him: did he simply lack the courage to be effective in a crisis? Some time earlier, when he had been having those conversations with that jackarse, the Very Reverend Doctor fellow, they had talked about overcoming the odds in sport, like those weak English cricket teams in the 1970s – those that Illingworth, 'the racist', captained. Even though they were weak they refused to succumb to the stronger opposition. They didn't often win, but they usually held out for a draw. Then there was talk about Muhammad Ali. Ali and Foreman in that 'rumble in the jungle' in Zaire, in 1975. Ali ageing. Foreman, in his prime, an unstoppable force. Ali, in the end, overcoming Foreman with wit and poetry and *strategy*, leading with that right hand. *He's hitting him with rights!* they screamed excitedly from the ringside. And there on Pewter's verandah, the Very Reverend Doctor had got up and demonstrated the audacity of leading with the right, 'a punch difficult to deliver and dangerous to yourself', as Norman Mailer had explained in his book. Difficult to deliver because in most boxing positions the right has longer to travel. Maybe a foot more than the left. And you're open to the counter-jab. And in that match Ali led from the right *from round one*, and gave a display in round five that boxing has never seen before or since.

So now Pewter reflected, in the quiet of his room in the reopened hotel: that's the strategy he would use against the relative, to get Fred released: *the unexpected lead with the right*.

And if it worked – why not – he would use it to try and get his house back, his house in the Var. And armed with that double success, he would, this time, talk his friend on to that plane at Luton airport.

5

The Casting Vote

I

Pewter, in this role, preferred to be looked at in the third person; it would make the thing less subjective.

Yes, the money for the sculpture was being put up by the Retford Foundation, which was being financed from Africa, not America; and he was their representative; but that didn't mean he had the casting vote; he wouldn't have wanted that anyway. But he was pretty comfortable representing the Foundation, which had a good environmental record, originally built round recycling bottles and jars and whatnot for reuse over there. He had for years been saving his corks from the wine bottles and shipping them over to help people keep dead insects and other unwanted stuff out of their medicine and cooking oil. Now, of course, the Foundation was big business. Pewter was saying all this to reassure another member of the panel who had a sort of ideological distrust of foundations, whatever part of the world they came from.

Everyone had accepted that the musicians and the writers, particularly the poets, had been given a good run. Or, at least, had been allowed to make the running; and the reason the visual arts were in such a bad way was lack of public support: patronage coming neither from private nor official sources. That was all there was to it, nothing complicated like the artists' failures to measure up to the challenge of representation. If that were the case how do you account for da Firenze's 'late period', where he took risks with 'representation' to the point of making himself unpopular at home. At least he had tried to make St Caesareans face up – 'face' being the operative word – face up to the reality rather than the fancy image of themselves. It was more in loyalty to da Firenze than to the Foundation that Pewter felt they mustn't play it safe here. Not that honouring C. J. Harris was playing it safe.

They had short-listed five artists whom they would commission for studies, three in England, one in Martinique and one, well, one said to be travelling. So the thing now was to put together some sort of profile of CJ for circulation to the sculptors – and also for the general public. For even though CJ was to be the man, the decision wasn't unanimous. So, to run through, again, CJ's claims to distinction:

1. *His encyclopedic memory* and total recall deep into his nineties gave the lie to those people who felt that a man's usefulness was limited to his working life, more or less. People in these parts thought there was something vaguely comic, almost shameful, about a person of a certain age still striving to achieve, like acquiring a university degree, say, when you're already in your seventies or eighties. Harris's vigour in extreme old age puts one in mind of those Rembrandt old men and women whose dignity and conspicuous humanity make you proud to be of the same species.

And then there were the usual anecdotes about CJ's sharpness, all those years in the home, which made visitors there come away with the feeling that people in fifth-century Athens must have had on encountering Socrates.

2. *His wit and wisdom.* They weren't just talking of a long life; a long life was interesting but it wasn't everything, and indeed, there were lots of people in the Bible,

say, who had lived longer lives than CJ and nobody would propose immortalizing them in paint or in bronze because of that; they were talking here about what Martin Luther King would have called a long *and productive* life, and the life of C. J. Harris was *intellectually* productive, if nothing else. And it was important here, where people more or less worshipped the cult of youth and sport, to celebrate someone whose gymnastic prowess was of the mind. Indeed, wasn't it significant that with all the books coming out of the region no one had yet written an intellectual history of the people who lived here.

And as they say, a long life was valuable, but too much stress shouldn't be put on that because there were people who had lived valuable *short* lives, people throughout history, the likes of James Dean and Joan of Arc, who did their business and died before they were twenty. Dean was a bit older, in his twenties, but you get the point.

Anyway, to the wit: less, perhaps, about the Harris *bons mots*. These abound, of course, and CJ's son, in England, had made a little collection and published them privately; and Pewter had had occasion to point out that one, at least, of those sayings could more accurately have been attributed to his own grandmother and not to CJ; but never mind. What attracted Pewter there was the more generalized 'wit and wisdom' of CJ, his advice to young people, say, about to leave the island for study abroad. 'Is all right to go to America and England,' CJ used to say. 'Nothing wrong with that. They have the learning factories over there that we can work in. But the trade mustn't be all one way. I don't agree with that. You have to show that you need the training but you're not needy in other ways. They're giving something to you so what do you have to offer *them* in return? And the way I look at it, is quite simple. Here we are with a respect for education because we don't have it. There they are bored with it because it's part of the landscape and they don't see it any more. They don't understand what used to make them special. It had a man in England which used to make that place special; I call him Shakespeare. And the same in America: you must read Mr Emerson before you go over to America. Ralph Waldo Emerson. Yes, sir. So when you can go over there and tell them what they forget about Shakespeare, and what they forget about Mr Emerson – then after you come away with your degree and thing you don't owe them anything.'

3. *His writing.* There was the feeling, even among his admirers, that CJ had not published enough. Indeed, the essential line on C. J. Harris all along was that he was a valued, indeed, an essential resource for those who came after; and that his influence could be traced through two, maybe three generations of writers from the Caribbean and beyond. And Pewter shared that view. Until recently.

The rethink really came about when one day he happened to be browsing in his favourite bookshop in Paris, where he lived. Shakespeare & Company, next to the cathedral, on the rue de la Bûcherie, was a regular haunt. It was one of those dull, drizzly days in Paris and he was outside scanning the second-hand racks, and came across the special offers at one euro each. Hardback, so he looked to see if there was anything of interest. One of the books was by an odd man who had been prime minister in England in the 1960s. Briefly. Lord Home. Sir Alec Douglas-Home. Well, there was this book of letters to Home's grandson, and Pewter found himself flicking through it; and the very first paragraph put him in mind of C. J. Harris. Home recalls a time when the young boy – the grandson to whom the letters were supposedly written – was staying with them at the ancestral home and they were looking through the eighty-eight volumes of the boy's grandmother's scrapbooks. *Eighty-eight volumes of scrapbooks!* Suddenly Pewter thought of C. J. Harris's jottings, notes, sayings, false starts, rejected plays and essays, unpublished speeches, conversations, unrecorded but acknowledged here and there by the persons who had benefited from them; and he thought: *what C. J. Harris needs is an editor!* And when he was next on the island he did have a go at trying to dig up some of the material. Literally. It was all under tons of volcanic ash. But it wasn't easy to locate CJ's old house in the capital. The boy who was helping him was fairly useless, and the authorities weren't keen on the project in the first place, because of the safety issue. So that was the end of that, as CJ would have said.

But on a positive note, CJ's deliberations on the naming of the new capital were scrupulously recorded; and the quality of his imagination had been demonstrated there.

4. *The naming of the capital.* CJ had argued, in his amused way, for the name of Concord, and didn't seem to mind that his suggestion wasn't taken up in the end. He was even able to share the joke with those who said that Concord sounded more like a supersonic aeroplane flying to Bahrain and Abu Dhabi and New York than a place where people in this part of the world lived. CJ did point out that they must be right, that maybe he was dreaming – the way these West Indian cricketers do when they get to the crease – dreaming, certainly, when he peopled his imaginary Concord with the likes of Henry David Thoreau and Nathaniel Hawthorne and Ralph Waldo Emerson. Pewter, missing out on that scene, was keen to champion CJ's cause now. Then, of course, there was CJ's battle against the churches, the priesthood: that had to be stressed.

5. *'Free-thinking'* was what his supporters called it. Others put their own name to it. Whether it was his mischievous adding to the established list of saints and icons who performed miracles worthy of having a following – in

this case names like Walter Chrysler and Henry Ford, whoever – that, or his refusal to say 'DV' (*Deo volente* = God willing) when he made plans for himself and his family – that put him on the wrong side of 'respectable' folk, including Pewter's grandmother. That made him a man of some interest.

So, would Pewter write the profile of C. J. Harris? (Not that it was plain sailing. One persistent criticism of CJ's literary *oeuvre* was its lack of . . . what shall we say? . . . *heart*. CJ was said to come over as the critic even when he was writing of the people's distress during natural disaster. So the quality that Pewter admired in CJ was precisely what was said to be suspect by others – including one member of the panel. So in defending C. J. Harris, Pewter was, in a sense, defending himself – not, he hoped (as someone crudely hinted), preparing a new bed.

II

As always, it was a question of context. He was doodling, making little shapes, not thinking of anything much, thinking of coming in on the little plane a couple of days ago, nine people on the plane, willing now to argue that they had lives as rich as his or as thin as his. All of which could be written up. Only knowing when to stop before a thin life was stretched beyond the point of decency; so you had to come back to the belief that some lives were richer than others, or what was the point of honouring some people rather than others?

He was bored with the little shapes he was making on the paper, shapes that wouldn't come to anything recognizable. Finally, he drew a circle, and jotted down three or four names round the edge of the circle, the first of which was C. J. Harris. Running through the other candidates: those who wouldn't get a statue made of them on this – or maybe on any other – occasion deserved some recognition, too. So, really, mention of them in connection with CJ was, in a sense, making their claims visible. That's part of what he meant by context. He would, of course, mention the poets and the calypso singers, one soca singer in particular, with an international reputation, who had pressed CJ hard. Not forgetting the boy with the shoulder armour to ward off crowds on the streets of London; and cousin Horace, who had invented the round tea bag.

The conversation at the judging table was about materials, whether one shouldn't reject the notion of bronze which (despite Benin) seemed 'European' rather than African or Caribbean; and shouldn't other materials – mud, wood – be considered? Someone held up as an exemplar the figures of the Jamaican sculptor Ron Moody ('monolithic, silent and strong'), those torsos in wood chiming so perfectly with the colour of the sitters. Unless, of course, something durable and original could be made from volcanic ash. (There was a man down from Canada reputedly making bricks out of the ash; maybe someone should investigate.)

But Pewter had been given his task and, as he said to himself, *context*. He'd been on a local radio programme years ago, to choose his favourite book. This was in England. It was just after the Booker or the Nobel was announced that year, he couldn't remember. And the host (and other guest) had seemed fairly unimpressed with his public wrestling over which of *Ulysses* and *Anna Karenina* to give the prize to; so, shamed into naming something modern, he hastily plumped for *Catcher in the Rye,* and vowed never to put himself through that sort of humiliation again. But this was different, there was really no pressure here, not having to think on your feet. So he was doodling, drawing a bigger circle now, outside the one he'd already drawn. And he jotted down the word 'Shakespeare', and he jotted down the word 'Mozart' and he jotted down the names Monet and Cervantes together (*Monet/Cervantes*); and another name. He wasn't sure if this last name was right, but he had seen it on a plaque on the wall of the science building at a university where he had briefly worked; a man who had won the Nobel Prize for altering 'matter' in some way . . . and Pewter stopped, to prevent this getting away from him. He was here to give some *presence* to the rejected candidates. First, then, Paul St Vincent.

Paul St Vincent.

This wasn't entirely serious.

Paul wrote poetry of a socially committed kind, and the best of his plays was an irreverent look at his seventeenth-century French namesake, Vincent de Paul, and the great man's doings, a drama that earned Paul some minor notoriety. Paul was actually born on another island, but could also lay claim to this one; and grew up, more or less, in England. His claim to being an inventor rested on the protective shoulder pad. Now, if you were talking of things made of iron and steel the names of Isambard Kingdom Brunel and steam ships and suspension bridges come to mind; but Paul made his contribution, too, with his shoulder armour. It didn't work, of course, being a bugger to wear; heavy, and it ate your skin. Even after he made the modifications, you still had to put it down as a weapon of war that was more injurious to the carrier than to the potential enemy. What was interesting about this – remember, Paul was a bit of a poet – was Paul's later justification of the discomfort to the wearer on *moral* grounds, that it reduced (or elevated) both bruiser and bruised to the equal status of victim. (Almost a CJ conceit.)

What was it for, this shoulder armour? Well, as the man said, we've all had the experience of walking along the street, a crowded street impossible to get through. Oxford Street, say, at rush hour. In the summer. Or at Christmas time. That you are going to be jostled is to be expected. But we're not talking here of ordinary bumping and shoving – sorry, *pardon, scuzati-ma* – the way crowds do. We're talking of the odd and determined pavement fascist. He goes charging at you with a shoulder determined to wound. Generally a youngish, loutish thug, the runt of the pack. He never says sorry because he's at war and you're the enemy. The resulting injury is compounded by the look of satisfied arrogance. What can you do? The thug has already gone past, hence the protective shoulder armour.

Even the felted lining didn't work and it was a hassle to fit, and when Paul left the factory in Redditch that summer (some time in the 1970s) where he had been employed to cut up bits of steel, his inventor's mind soon turned to something else. Also, he had been conscious of the risk of injuring innocent people – women and children and unaggressive men in the street – that would probably not justify his attempt to protect his own shoulder. (His plan to develop a metal brassière for women was shelved.)

Doodling – *this was a big circle* – Pewter found himself writing in the name of NAPOLEON. Now this was silly; where were we? We would sculpt the man in wood, which was an appropriate material, semi-permanent, *not* permanent, a bit like man himself, subject to the ravages of time and weather. And it would be head and shoulders only, full torso; for legs and boots were OK for the sorts of people you saw sitting on a horse or bestriding something, and bestriding and island life didn't go easily together; and anyway, towards the end CJ was lame, with a stroke, but that was neither here nor there.

Pewter hadn't forgotten the claims of Cousin Horace, and his tea bag.

Cousin Horace.

He invented the round tea bag on Pewter's mother's kitchen table in Ladbroke Grove, he claims, in the late 1950s;

70

but it was, in fact, a few years later, when Muhammad Ali was knocking out Sonny Liston for the world title. Of course in those days you didn't think of patenting your inventions. The Americans were ahead of us there. And Pewter's mother had a hand in scuppering that one. Horace had made a mess of the kitchen table, wasting tea, using scissors and Sellotape to shape the bags, using the bathroom scissors that had probably been used to clip toenails, so that Pewter's mother pronounced it *nasty*. Not only childish but nasty. His mother was in no way fascinated at the thought of a man-made sachet of tea which would fit the bottom of the cup, or mug, snugly; and Horace compounded his nastiness by trying to win her over with a joke. 'You must try to think like a scientist, Aunt Christine.' *End of a dream of a life of riches*. Thereafter, Cousin Horace confined his mental energies to the interpretation of dreams.

So, was everything in order? When would they make the announcement, sort of thing? And you know how it is, when idleness and boredom set you thinking, and something gets triggered in the brain that overturns all your calculations; and you wonder why something that was so obvious didn't occur to you in the first place; so now you present this idea to all around you, with the zeal of a convert. We've got it all wrong, you say, we're playing it safe, we're too obvious, we're doing what any other committee would have done, our job, our value, is to do it *differently*. We're neglecting a name, you say, that should be at the top of the list: why didn't anyone think of it?

This was a person of rare distinction, as tough-minded as C. J. Harris, as iconoclastic. Bilingual and, despite abuse and cold-shouldering by those she tried to help, she got *some* people on the island to speak understandable French.

This was not well-received. *He's talking of Fred Belair: weren't they an item some time back?*

'You're talking of a woman who made a lot of people on this island uneasy,' was the objection. 'Encouraging them to thicken up their lips to pronounce what she calls France French.'

Pewter knew the charge. He said: 'If people had a problem with lips it doesn't mean they should also have a problem with speaking French.'

'In profile, certain people look good pushing out their lips. But not everybody looks good pushing out their lips. Though, maybe, you must, maybe, make an exception for kissing. But Fred was taking advantage . . . '

Pewter was thinking of a more substantial charge against Fred Belair: it was what you might call philosophical or ideological, maybe even fundamentalist. It was something about Fred confusing a private student of French by first teaching her the verb *nager* (to swim) and then teaching her the companion verb *noyer* (to drown): *now, did 'to drown' follow naturally from 'to swim'?* Wasn't there something in this mindset that was running counter to the spirit of the times? The sense of *uplift? Wasn't this woman too much of a negative influence?* Knowing that this charge would come, Pewter thought he would set the tone by responding to the earlier one, about lips, with the earnestness it didn't deserve.

Of course, he conceded, there were old-time taboos about your nose and your lips. To the extent that the odd person back then went off to America or somewhere to have her nose fixed; and this was years before Michael Jackson. But . . .

But no one went off to have their *lips* fixed till the Belair woman came along with her France French.

Pewter had to prevent this turning into something silly. He would remind them that much the same things were said – and not only on this island – about his old friend Leon da Firenze, an artist everyone now claims to admire, if still, in a sense, censored. That wasn't the case when he first held the people's noses up for inspection. It wasn't till after he had died in tragic circumstances that they acknowledged da Firenze's role in getting people to accept the way they looked without wanting to be different: that must have contributed some way to what the smart people call their psychic health. And maybe Fred Belair had done something similar for lips.

And what he was thinking was of Fred's visit to him on the other side of the world that Christmas; and how when he had asked her to name the flowers she had had a go at naming everything in sight, not making a distinction between flowers and what they call weeds. And that had set him thinking and made him want to question the certainty of his own categories, indeed, his whole aesthetic; and not only with regard to the garden. But that was a private thought.

No one said anything.

Pewter put away his doodles; he would need to concentrate.

6

Meteorologists and Methodists

In the café, Miss Odilie's café, some little distance from the scene of the rehearsals, they greeted the sound of the drums with interest; but it didn't prompt them to speed up their orders or to gulp their lentil soup; for they didn't have to rush over to the rehearsal rooms to review things out there: their discussions on proceedings could take place here as well as elsewhere, while they enjoyed a cool drink with their lentil soup, and then saw what was on offer for afters. At one table the three men were discussing the executions.

It was daring, but risky, to start the play with the executions; for in so doing weren't you aligning yourself with those barbarous places in the world that still carried out executions; what sort of signal did that send out, what did it say about us?

But the executions weren't carried out, someone protested; it's not even that the sentences were commuted – the convicted fellows were *pardoned* in the end; all that was necessary was a statement from each of the criminals that he had mended his ways and would no longer sin against humanity in the ways he had done before.

And what of the criminals who refused to do it, who failed, convincingly, to renounce criminality? (This was posed by the third person at the table.) The criminals who refused to repent or to recant (in a way that convinced the onlookers), who declined to pledge themselves to normal human behaviour in the future; they were the ones holding up the play. This was only the first scene; if you can't get past that first scene, how are you going to manage a full-length production?

Maybe an island this small didn't deserve a full-length play.

That's defeatist talk.

That, maybe, was the theme of the play; the message.

The play wasn't a post office to be delivering messages, a man by the name of Killigrew had said.

Shakespeare and Brecht had delivered messages.

Some messages were delivered with finesse. And ambiguity. An island like ours, having suffered hurricane and volcano, the people surviving demanded at least finesse and ambiguity.

To convict the people traffickers and the scum dealing drugs and the President-for-Life brothers showed a serious commitment to human values: to give them a chance to repent, etc., and then desist from the carrying out of the sentence, was a statement about us as mature and compassionate human beings.

There was silence at the table as they considered this. The men were conscious that at a nearby table, a woman, who reminded at least one of them of an earth mother, was sitting, like a great queen, with her lentil soup, quietly listening to their conversation. This made them self-conscious; so they studied the menu for the choice of sweet, even though the two options of sweet were written up on a board where everyone could see. And despite the call of the drums in the rehearsal rooms over the way, the men decided to hang on here, at Miss Odilie's, and have the sweet.

The earth woman at the other table had crossed them before. And now they thought she was a plant. Maybe one of those characters involved in the early part of the play, now deemed surplus to requirements, who was either sulking or spoiling for a fight. No one quite knew who she was. The one time she spoke up, when the men were having one of their random conversations about the drift of the play in rehearsal, was, apropos of nothing, to say that in order to move forward it was necessary to understand the riddle of 'One me hand finny and the other one swell.' *That* would explain the rise of the Meteorologists.

The Meteorologists?

Religious sect. New but not new. Exploiting astrology and prophecies and other extra-rational phenomena. There was more than a suspicion that the Meteorologists were hiding behind all that. Now that they'd seen off the Relativists at Thirty Thousand Feet.

'And the Jedi,' a wit at the table joined in.

'Not to mention the Seminary of Benign Racism and the True Church of Many Hats.'

'How did they manage to see off the Relativists? That must have been tough.'

And the men laughed at their joke.

*

What's holding the whole thing up – that's what they say, some of them – what's holding the whole thing up is not this or that complicated factor with supplies and shortage of labour: what's holding things up is the entertainment, the ritual; more specifically, the starting point of that wretched play. Everybody else is ready enough, things are more or less in place; services being restored: water, some electricity. People have trickled back, enough to say that the place is inhabited; they've settled in as best they can. There are shops open. Two restaurants, on the edge of what used to be the town; and compromise reached over the religious settlement (the decision to accept the Methodists and the

Meteorologists as religious movements, if for nothing else than to move on to other things like . . . well, pavements and eggs). And the Chief Minister has prepared his speech. It's a good speech; we've all heard it at various stages of composition, and participated in the debate; made suggestions, some of which have been taken up. The question you might like to ask now, of this speech, seeing that we have all heard it, and it is in due course to be delivered back to us – the question you might ask is whether the Chief Minister is going to have the wit to surprise us when the time comes – with any little new emphasis or change of detail – on the day that he finally gets the chance to deliver the speech formally. Unless he does that, there's the risk of staleness. And remember, we're not going back to the past situation from which we've not yet recovered; so the speech has to retain that sense of freshness, of something new, for both speaker and listener. (That's just a tiny detail of the consequences of delay, the danger of staleness and let-down on the grand occasion. The querulous playmakers, holding things up, *say* they have thought of that.)

It was agreed – not unanimously, for that's not the way we work – it was decided by the majority that the return to the island should be accompanied by appropriate ritual. And though it was never established what ritual was appropriate, we looked across the water to our neighbours who had suffered a similar fate of hurricane and volcano and, like us, had had to abandon their home. And we saw with unease how they had returned to their island, perhaps too soon for comfort, and then proceeded as if nothing out of the ordinary had happened, cleaning up in a frenzy, clearing new land, rebuilding, setting up the courts to settle disputes of ownership; and fighting over the result. In the midst of which they regularly trooped off in their heightened state to their chapels and churches and temples to praise God for having made them homeless in the first place. Well, if it's one thing this island had over its neighbours it was to do things a little differently; to think things through; to pause and reflect, and to *adapt* to the new situation. If some of us have brought back some little experience from our sojourn abroad, it is to learn how to adapt. But, conversely – we are talking about ritual, still – you don't just creep back into your old place, unnoticed, like a thief in the night: you have to strike a balance, neither to be the victim, nor to be triumphant.

It's irritating, isn't it? the way people make vulgar assumptions about you. I can hear them say, some of them: what's the big thing about this play, then? If you can organize the clearing of tons of rubble and sand and have traffic back on the roads, and bring in by ship and helicopter all that's necessary to get life started again, why can't a group of pampered over-opinionated actors get their – excuse the pun – *act* together and do the play? But that of course is to miss the point. People here aren't that green; the people returning are folk who have been forced to camp out on four, maybe all five continents since the disaster overtook them: neither the actors nor the people outside are talking about the traffic in Manhattan holding up a Neil Simon play. When you come to think of it, the one thing that theatre all over the world has in common, whether good theatre or bad theatre it doesn't matter, is that it delivers on time. Can you imagine a fellow from the management, the producer or director, coming on and settling down the audience because they've been waiting some time and are getting a bit restless; and can you imagine him coming on and saying, Sorry, folks, thanks for your patience, but the thing is, we are going to have to hang on for another half hour or so before we can get that opening poker scene going because Vinnie or Murray or whoever it is, Roy, is held up in the traffic – something terrible tonight, in downtown Manhattan, the fog or an accident or something. Even during the war in England, the Hitler war, if the Shakespeare play was threatened to be held up at the Old Vic it wasn't because the war was going badly for the Allies that year; it was, maybe, because someone didn't like the idea of Paul Robeson, a black man, playing a black man in Shakespeare's *Othello*. Now, that's another matter altogether, much bigger than the war. At least longer lasting. So, don't make vulgar assumptions about us here on our little island. Did I tell you about the debates that went on and on about the love scene? Or again, those concerning which of the members of the cast should be axed (not literally, of course), not because of lack of cash but because a small island was deemed large enough only to accommodate just so much negative energy, maybe two or three cast members, at the most, that were feared to be problematic in that way. So how to choose between the Returnee Criminal and the Boy with the Too-Large Fantasy who would eventually need expensive hospitalization? Or the Woman Brainwashed by Abroad to sleep only with white men? (And we haven't come to the question of choosing between the Paedophile and the Methodist!) The feeling was that a small island could accommodate, maybe, only two or three of this problem cast at this time. This wasn't a moral judgement, exactly, just an assessment of what was doable, anticipating the effect that things on stage might have on the *tone* of the community, which, being small, was still in a fragile state. (This was in keeping with the early revision of the Chief Minister's text to make him culpable – not personally but his office – for the fact that thinking in his area hadn't moved on, that they were still saying stale things about history and nothing new about geography, no fresh thoughts about the island's positioning on the map: now, after much trial and effort, the Chief Minister's speech is beginning to be *interesting* in that area, though there's still no mention of Stalin or the Creationists. So, let's bear these things in mind as we proceed.)

So maybe what we should be doing is to review the play still in rehearsal (because, who knows, we might be here a long time, and some of us might, well, not be here come the performance). Take the difficulties over the love scene. You start with a man and a woman. Simple enough. Obvious, even. Let's assume for argument's sake that's where you start. A man and a woman. But is it that simple? What age are they to be, this man and woman? These are returnees. Presumably not children. Who's on his second marriage, who's hankering after a preferred partner overseas, and is just making do here because this is a sort of emergency situation, and, in any case, the next disruption, in terms of hurricane and volcano, might not be too far off in coming; so, like a wartime marriage, anything goes.

It's not simple, as I say, because the love interest has got to be one that other people, looking on, might be drawn to without irony or pity. We want someone (like ourselves) in the audience to look at the couple and think: he's a handsome older man; he knows how to handle himself; but his whole . . . way of relating shows that his ex-partners have not been abused; he will do. And again: that woman, the way she carries herself, knowing but not cynical, you could imagine her firm but loving with the children, now grown up: she hasn't just been used for producing the children and is soon to be discarded for a younger (pain-free) model. She'll do. (If at some point in the scene reference is made to a book she might be in the middle of reading, that brings her even closer to someone we know; yes, she could be relied on, say, to defend the birth-control clinic, knowing these battles are never won.) So far so good. Ah, but this is just the start of it. If they – our couple

– are people of a certain age; what is the real state of their health? Does their medicine cabinet hint at minor-ish and manageable failings of the body, or things of real concern? Have we already established that there is a good doctor and a viable chemist on the island? And reliable electricity to keep the medicines at the right temperature, in the fridge! These are not World Bank requirements for structural adjustment, these are the support systems for the love scene in a viable community.

On the other hand, the island is small. Things must be not scaled down to cramp lives, but one must keep a sense of proportion. There was this joke – was it a joke? There was the case of the Irishman who loved his wife too much, who was so much in awe of his new wife, who felt she was so much beyond his dreams of attainment that he insisted on her living in one country and himself living in another country, separate, so that he wouldn't pollute the ground she walked on. Now, that is very nice as a gesture, or as an idea for a poem; but do we want to go that far? Maybe we had something similar – opposite but similar – in these islands in the old days, with the men sailing off to foreign parts, to Panama and the Canal, and to Cuba and Haiti; and latterly to North America and England, leaving the women and children behind. So, to avoid abandonment from an excess of love, as with the Irishman, or abandonment from the opposite tendency, as with the ancestors, that was an issue worthy of debate. That took quite a bit of time before the love scene could be got under way. And some other background things were just as tricky to slot in place. So we have to be patient with the actors.

*

When they came out for a break – when they came out from their rehearsal space, which they naturally did from time to time, partly to show how hard they had been working behind the scenes – they would pretend to be just stretching their legs or having a smoke, or even to patronize the local business by enquiring what Miss Odilie had in store for us today. (Miss Odilie's was sanctioned, though denied its status as a religion. Even though the waitresses were priestesses, really, and had read Theology at university and done Body-piercing as an ancillary; and the chef spoke Latin and Welsh. As for Miss Odilie herself, well, walls have ears.) So there were always people around, to eavesdrop on the conversation, while they pretended to eat their lentil soup, whatever; or play cards and talk football and women. Today the men on their break – what game would they be playing today? – were heard to slip the name Jones into the conversation.

Well, everyone knew about Jones. Say no more. *It is known that while the intellectuals preoccupied themselves with Anancy and the servants distracted themselves with old-fashioned religion, Jones came through unscathed. Jones wasn't a god person who prayed to the air and the sky and fell to his knees without provocation, he confused you in more subtle ways, even by spelling his name the normal way, 'Jones', like his lay namesakes.*

Though when the breakaway sect started spelling it J-O-N-E-S, he didn't renounce them.

Clever. No schism in Jones.

Though there was a hint of mystery in J-O-N-E-S.

Undoubtedly.

The Commentaries. The commentaries. Distinguishing Jones from J-O-N-E-S. There's a fellow at Keele doing a Ph.D. on it.

So, as usual, those who wished for an update would be disappointed. Even more those who confused an update with progress. For what was progress, after all? A man of sixty-four would have lived eighteen years longer than a man of forty-six. That was progress of a sort. There are some countries in the world that would settle for that statistic as their measure of progress. But we were not in those countries of the world. So progress was a tricky thing to access. There was a thesis – thesis, monograph, call it what you will – on the impact of loo breaks on world history. It said that one of the bleak men in the Kremlin in the old days – it may have been Brezhnev, it may have been someone else – at a Warsaw Pact summit meeting denied a certain leader from the old eastern Europe the right to go to the loo until he had signed his country away to the Russian military and to the Kremlin leadership. Whether true or not, it's an interesting theory, and it makes you wonder how the orderings of the world may have been informed by the urologically frail. (Where is the scene in Shakespeare to tell us what Caesar's bladder was like? Maybe if Our Man had written *Pliny* instead of *Coriolanus* . . . OK. And what of those Lancaster House meetings not so many decades ago sorting out southern Africa to British satisfaction? Which boss man was able to hold his water the longest?)

So it was discouraging asking for an update.

There is, as you know, a hanging on the scaffold in the opening scene of the play. Some people still can't get past that act of realism. Is it symbolic, is it a metaphor for what's going on in the world? Or is it corrupting just to *think* of enacting it? Are we so frightened and traumatized that we have to *censor* the imagination? Or are we so brutalized that we are building ritualized murder into our drama of return?

The deal struck with the enemy, someone is bound to take you aside and tell you, for you haven't heard it before (*whisper, whisper: no such thing as a free lunch* . . .), the deal is that we would take some of their social rejects, along with the goodies, from our benefactors. Nothing big, you understand, no massive offshore prisons or banks, just something symbolic, to weigh the balance, to – if you like – recalibrate the moral scales of aid and foreign policy. Put it this way: 'Let's say I am a big country and you are a small country, and you want me to help you out a bit. Cleaning up after the hurricane and volcano and all that. Petrol at affordable prices. Computers, whatever. It's not going to cost me much. Like kitting out a village. Or a big farm. Or ranch. But, as you know, we're not family. You're not even my mistress to threaten blackmail that can hurt me. And the Methodists and the Meteorologists be praised, you're not a terrorist. So I say: what can you do for me in return? Now, I have a problem because I'm a going concern in a world that's falling into chaos, and people don't like that. Doesn't mean they're evil people, just the human condition. That they resent it that you have what they don't have. I understand; I, too, am human. But there are people out there who want to do me serious harm. Human nature. Thing is, I can deal with them. But there are constraints. I have, *we* have, a certain self-image to maintain. (*The pig don't have that, the pig is not human.*) We want to be able to look in the mirror and . . . you know. We know how to deal with the scum out there. But, as I say. Constraints. Now, you are every bit as human as we are, but you have other priorities at the moment. Certain . . . delicacies have to be deferred. While deferring those delicacies you can help us . . . You get my meaning? . . . You're not saying anything.'

'You lost me really early on.'

'How so?'

'With your very first sentence. Let's suppose, you say, you're a big country and I'm a small country. I say, why do we have to start there? Why can't we start the discussion the other way round. Why don't we start with *me* saying:

I am a small country, you're a big country . . . and see where that logic takes us.'

'I see you believe in a free lunch. Even Miss Odilie charges for her lentil soup.'

'Come on. Let's take a break. Let me treat you to some lentil soup.'

*

And for twenty minutes or so they didn't talk about the play, just commiserated with each other that time was confusing them; for it's well known that as a young man you have notions of changing the world, whereas men of a certain age are more concerned with managing their illnesses; and present company weren't sure whether to give up on one ambition and settle for the other. And it was good, perhaps, that they were voicing this fear here, at Miss Odilie's, rather than inside the rehearsal room, or this would just delay the play further.

So as they talked of their luck – one had fish after the soup, the other chicken; and everything was to be praised – they praised everything they could to put off thinking about the characters over there in the play, lined up on the bench – like the subs at a football match, someone had said – to be executed.

It is known that some inside the play space had been talking for some time about the statute of limitations. Nothing grandiose, just to put a limit to discussion, so that they could move on to other matters. You know, it's not only judicial bandits who invoke this, but even in the old days of Tanzania – remember Ujaama – even there, there was a ten-year limit to the public discussion.

Miss Odilie's was a place where you could relax and shake off pressures you had no right to bring to the island society still not yet under way. And if it wasn't for the weight ('*No, no sweet, thank you,' indicating waistline, and saying in a private language*), if it wasn't for the weight, one would have another helping of Miss Odilie's lentil soup. The other kind, this time. (*And the same again for you . . . ?*)

'Ah! Times like this, you remember them old-time fellers who had a way of looking at things which kept them sane, if nothing else. Remember Graham? Old Graham from . . . up the hill, "One me hand" Graham? That's what Graham used to say: "One me hand finny . . . "'

'Graham used to hold out his hand like this. Both hands. Short man, but, you know, not small. And would say something like, "They say I suffer misfortune in my life. They say I have bad luck. But nobody could say. Nobody could look at me and say that one me hand finny and the other one swell." Meaning the arms, of course, not the hand.

'And it's true, you know, there's a certain logic there. Graham's hands were exactly the same size. More or less. Neither one of them finny. Nor swell.'

'Ah, that beats . . . that beats, y'know, the parable of the pavement and the eggs.'

7

An Exercise in Democracy

I

Miss Vanesa rejected *Phoebe Caulfield*. She rejected it as a title, not because she had anything against it as such, or against choosing a woman's name as the title of her magazine, or even a child's name; but she sort of resented the way the men muscled in on it as well, using everything that came to hand to announce their feminist credentials. Or at the very least, their oneness with the woman-thing. It had got so bad that you couldn't get either Pewter or Michael to admit that they liked *any* male writer, except, maybe, Shakespeare, better than a woman. You had to take it for granted, talking to them, that Virginia Woolf was *always* better than James Joyce; that Katherine Mansfield was *always* better than Chekhov, sort of thing. She consoled herself that she had long given up fighting those sorts of battles. She had been accused – not accused, but sort of accused – of being anti-woman, anti-children; or perhaps being anti-women-and-children; and it's true she wasn't a Madonna and Child sort of person: she always went past those old-time fakes in the art galleries abroad. But apart from that she wasn't anti-woman. Or children, for that matter. What she was anti, was the sentimental way these men had when they spoke about children – preferably other people's children, far away. And to come back to the question of Phoebe Caulfield: she *liked* the portrait of the child; she agreed with them all that Salinger had done a good job there; that, overall, he was very good with children – that *Americans,* as everyone said, were good with children. Miss Vanesa had enjoyed some of Salinger's stories with the reading group. But to call her magazine after a girl's name in an American book – at the urging of two expatriate men, who popped in, did their thing, and then went off again to wherever it was they lived – that was an image that didn't fit her requirements on reclaiming the island from disaster. *Phoebe Caulfield* was not the worst on offer; the men in their cleverness served up odd or obvious alternatives like the *St Caesare Review* and *Ash,* hoping they'd be knocked down by the superior claims of *Phoebe Caulfield.* For, after all, the Americans were well ahead out there with catchy titles like *Axe Factory Review* (in Philadelphia), *Rattapallax* somewhere in New York, and the personalized *Vincent Brothers Review* in Ohio.

Pewter Stapleton and Michael Carrington had settled their differences, more or less; had shaken hands and decided not to fight about who had ownership of Papua New Guinea or, more particularly, of the literature of Papua New Guinea. (At least neither of them had claimed to have written *The Crocodile,* PNG's early claim to literary notice.) Pewter had been there first, to that country, media coordinating, oh, twenty or more years ago, and had introduced to the fighting men of the highlands an Anancy-like figure called Lambchops, a creation of his own, someone who was hip and rebellious and wrote poetry. Lambchops being black and having a Caribbean-British background – rather than, say, an Australian one – might be more effective in dispensing some home truths about social and gender matters to the fighting men of the region. So, in piece after piece in *Enga Nius,* the Office of Information newspaper, which Pewter edited, Lambchops could be seen in satirical mode commenting on, oh, everything from, yes, wife-battering and clan fighting to the way you handed over change to customers in the village shop. Not forgetting to note the whiff of body odour that greeted you standing in the queue at the post office.

By the time Michael Carrington had got to New Guinea – same post, Media Coordinator for Enga Province in the highlands – Pewter was no longer minded to frustrate him. He was now living in Paris; he was working on a theory about democracy in fiction; he couldn't really be bothered with other matters. For, really, time had passed, fifteen years or more, and Carrington no longer posed the old threat. Michael was divorced and had been living, refugee-like, apart from his family, now in Canada, now in Trieste. So, yes, Michael could be allowed to bask in the greater success of his spell at VSO-ing in PNG; and in his fifteen minutes of fame, and in impressing the gullible back home. Instead of Lambchops commenting on clan fighting and women-beating, the new media coordinator had introduced Phoebe Caulfield and her brother, Holden, first as an example of good contemporary writing (contemporary, in this case, being the 1950s), *then* as the portrait of young girl as role model: in this case a fighting environment meant tension between her father and elder brother (*not burning of crops and houses in the village, or pitched battles with arrows and whatnot*). There was, it's said, a dedicated group of highland New Guinea writers producing stories, meeting now in the little village of Kandep or Laiagam or Wapenamanda, where 'Phoebe' was the central character with her 'sensibility' to be explored.

What made Pewter stop pressing his own spin-offs from Lambchops – 'Toothbrush', 'Toothpaste' – on Miss Vanesa, for the more market-friendly *Phoebe Caulfield*, were not the arguments lobbed back and forth across the continents, like baseline tennis, alluring though they were. (Top-heaviness in the Caribbean hadn't worked, so why not bottomend it for a change? Or, think of the image of young Phoebe beamed across Africa: now imagine that dramatized on stage after stage across the continent: how could they dare, after that, to continue to employ child soldiers and child brides for the soldiers!)

And was the suggestion really Michael's? It got to the point when Pewter began to believe that *Phoebe Caulfield* had been *his* choice all along. He had told the story, in Miss Vanesa's presence, of how *Phoebe Caulfield* had come to him. It was when he was living in England in the 1960s or '70s, in Shepherd's Bush in that incredible house full of artists and musicians, and he was making his way as a writer, scanning the magazines on offer before submitting his poems and stories. And there you had titles like *Aggie Weston* and *Joe DiMaggio* (Joe DiMaggio was, of course, Marilyn Monroe's husband before Arthur Miller). And then there was *Arnold Bocklin*: when they looked up Arnold Bocklin, they discovered that Arnold Bocklin was a painter. Should they start tailoring their poems to the provenance of the magazines in order to get published? Would a portrait in verse, of Monet at Giverny, say, get them into *Arnold Bocklin*? So, thirty years on, Pewter claims Miss Vanesa's magazine title as his own.

II

Pewter, in reality, was vaguely bored by all this. He went along with it, but his interests were elsewhere. He was distracted by the idea of democracy. More particularly, by his own practice of democracy. He had published a few books, one or two achieving something close to success. The books were all, to a certain extent, autobiographical. (Nothing wrong with that: think of the peerless Philip

Roth.) But one thing about this bothered him, and that was the colonizing tendency of his main character, who, though a creation of fiction, bore his name. Despite Pewter's best efforts this character tended to know, if not more than others, in the end to know the important things. His was the central journey – physical or emotional or intel-lectual – that defined the story. Others had to fit into its shape; so he was complete, not cut off when some other character lost interest in his doings. He didn't necessarily win the girl – indeed, part of his poignancy (in quotes) was that he almost never won the girl. But he tended to win the argument; his was the unifying presence in the tale. So that's why, despite being more interested in his own dis-coveries, Pewter forced himself to give some thought to Miss Vanesa and the naming of her magazine. He was putting himself through a regime where he insisted that other people's obsessions and concerns were at least as important as his own (if not as interesting). Democracy. Did he remember, clearly, the contents of the Salinger book? He remembered the young girl, Phoebe. He remem-bered that scene where, the brother having sneaked into the house after having been expelled from yet another school, and having spent a lot of money on cabs and hotels on the way – sneaked into the parents' house, it must be said, because he wants to see his little sister; and then is confronted by her concern and overwhelming desire to protect him: 'Daddy's going to kill you. *Daddy's going to kill you.*' He had adopted her there and then as his daughter.

Miss Vanesa has been said to be neurotic about two things: the fact that she had had to abandon her graduate studies; and the fact – in some ways a more enduring affront – that she still couldn't get her plays put on to the stage – except when she mounted them herself. She put it down to malice;

she put it down to a PC culture favouring the worthy over the good. For, as she was wont to point out, anyone with a personal problem who could put a shopping list of complaints together in lines short enough to look like a poem is bound to be taken up by the poetry establishment, and to walk away with the prize. That was one of the reasons she left England: she just couldn't take it. And it was the same in America, in the Americas, the English-speaking parts of America. Political correctness. Affirmative action. Black Studies. She was a West Indian, she had her pride; she wanted no part of it.

Though it would be a mistake to interpret Miss Vanesa's mood as nothing but a prolonged literary sulk. She had just come back from the other part of America. Spanish America: why did anyone think they were better than the other lot? And she was not exactly in the mood to compromise. She could give you statistics, if you wanted statistics. Forget the statistics: the impression you got was of a country dedicated to pursuing its war against the women. Women kidnapped. That's what oppressed her. Women raped and sworn to silence. Women killed. Girls. Sometimes of nineteen years of age. Twenty. More often girls of thirteen; raped and beheaded, their throats cut, again, their bodies tossed in the river, or on the rubbish dump. Often, too often, the throats cut, the bodies chopped up and put in a plastic bag, before being tossed on the rubbish heap. And, of course, they used their weapons of mass destruction, the machete, the meat cleaver, the kitchen knife. There was a programme on the television (a BBC programme, on that country) where the rapists – the few rapists and killers apprehended – came on and pleaded innocence and forgot not to swagger. Though even that was better than the faked innocence. For the girls had asked for it, asked for it by leaving the house unprotected, asked for it by wearing short skirts, and not crossing their legs when they sat down; and for having breasts – which some of the killers had to cut off to punish the girls for straying into their path. And the president of the country had come on the television, a buffoonish man – and made you think those ideas you had about those places weren't so far off the mark. Miss Vanesa wished she was something other than she was, so she could go back to that country and silence some of that species of something she couldn't name, in their tight pants and nerveless faces. She would call her magazine *The Murdered Woman*. She would call her magazine *The Headless Body;* and make these other visiting, right-on men who supported women in all their doings, feel good writing for it.

In the light of that, how frivolous of them to think that she was sulking because her latest play was rejected by a theatre in St Thomas. Naturally, it would be rejected, because the organizers couldn't patronize her as they did other black women. In it she had taken on the American PC thing. There was this play by an American about the death of the last black man. Miss Vanesa had no particular comment to make about the death of the last black man; what interested her more was the survival of the black woman. Indeed, of the woman who might not be black. So that's where she picked up on the play. *From* the play. That was obviously not allowed. Her play was rejected. She would be punished, as always, for doing the thing differently.

Pewter Stapleton, in Paris, wants to write to congratulate Miss Vanesa on *Phoebe Caulfield*. But he has one of those sudden rages that he denies he has. He feels undone, undermined, abused. What brings this on is his happening, idly, to be looking through an old copy of a magazine on his shelf; and in it there is, reprinted, a series of letters from T. S. Eliot to friends. These date from 1923 to 1930.

Letters to W. B. Yeats, to Virginia Woolf ('My dear Virginia . . . '), to Pound, Joyce and a Lady Rothermere. In the letter to Yeats, dated 23 January 1923, Eliot thanks Yeats for liking *The Waste Land* 'in the midst of such disturbing circumstances which I hope are now giving you less anxiety'. A footnote informs us that 'The illness of a child and nurses in the house had prevented Mrs Yeats from reading Dante to her husband in the evenings.' Pewter is enraged that his life has been so arranged that nobody had *ever* read Dante to him in the evenings. And he begins to develop a theory of the privileged and the less privileged in this world.

But he snapped out of it, to the point of being able to deny that it ever happened. And when he picked up the thought, he was thinking of features for Miss Vanesa's magazine that would stamp his influence on it. Lots of things came to mind, including a short story, dimly remembered, a Czech or a Bulgarian short story about wallpaper. Of course, written in those days, it had to be symbolic. In the story a great literary heritage is being preserved, in wallpaper. But the designers are clever: no one is quite sure if the design is old or new: you can read it either way. (You can hang it so that it makes no sense.) The design is of books; it's all book jackets; the bigger books you can identify by the writing on the spine, others, perhaps, if you were in the know. But the trick is, you needed, not any old house decorator to hang the paper, to match the joins, you needed a worker of a special kind to hang your wallpaper to show either fracture or continuity in the narrative. A role, then, for the literary critic who may have lost his job elsewhere; a possibility of dialogue of a sophisticated kind between the reading housewife and the dissident worker. Yes, that would have the Stapleton imprint.

And he was thinking now not of Miss Vanesa but of his sister, who lived in the region, but on another island. The two women were not acquainted: he would ask Miss Vanesa to send a copy of the first issue of her magazine to his sister. For some time he had been thinking of a way to make sense of his sister on the island; she was a returnee, having lived most of her life in Britain; but he couldn't place her with the image of the returnee that most people had, indeed, that he sometimes had. His sister admitted to being bored, so he sent her books. From time to time she commented on the books, and that depressed him slightly, for she commented only on the books that he sent her, making him suspect that it was a duty performed for his benefit: she volunteered no comment on other books. That's why he was stuck with an image of her, on her verandah, reading, that depressed him: (how far into the book would this reader be?). There was a whole series of images of women reading that he had researched, over the years. And he was very keen to observe how the woman reading should be 'read'. In the famous Eve Arnold picture, 'Marilyn Reading *Ulysses*', did anyone really believe that Marilyn, dressed for the beach, her breasts loosely held in a checkerboard bra slung from her neck – did anyone really believe that Marilyn was actually reading *Ulysses*? The fact that the photograph showed her three-quarters of the way through the book – held maybe an inch from her credible breasts – adds to the suspicion that this is something 'got up' for the occasion. But forget Marilyn: all those other pictures of women reading through the ages, in paint, from the medieval altarpiece in the Uffizi with the woman in red reading the Bible – to Michelangelo's massively muscular but aged Sybil in the Sistine Chapel. Not forgetting Rembrandt's wonderfully convincing mother close-reading her substantial tome: all those images, substantial though they are, fail to outweigh the glut of other, what he called near-pornography. He didn't really mind the sensual women, which he associated with Toulouse-

Lautrec. Frolicking nudes with the book casually placed as a decoy. Or the one, fully clothed (in fetching black), slumped on the couch, the book in her right hand, a naughty finger marking the page. (*Oh Eucalyptus!*)

But now he was being responsible and thinking of a portrait befitting his sister: the woman at her window reading (for the light), the woman at the fireplace reading (for the heat). Vermeer's woman reading her letter. He would propose such an image for the cover of Miss Vanesa's magazine.

And now he was ready to write to Miss Vanesa, and offer support. He was still thinking of democracy; of how he could further distribute power to the characters in his fiction. Of course you had to be careful. Dr Busia of Ghana – remember him! – came a cropper in the late 1960s–early '70s, because he decentralized to a point where he left himself and the federal government too little power. Overthrown. (Pewter recalled that story of Pirandello's, where a character confronts the author and demands a better part for himself in the novel of which he is a character. The story is called, 'A Character in Distress'. Character power.) So now, the all-knowing Pewter is trying to imagine the distress of people to whom he failed to give their proper presence – his mother that day in Ladbroke Grove, in 1959, at the political rally that insulted her. He did not come to her aid, he failed to transcribe the thoughts running through her head. There was also that glimpse of the woman in a Sheffield supermarket. Ah, but don't make this personal. There is the young woman, Lucy, the caretaker's daughter in James Joyce's 'The Dead': as a feminist reader you owed her her own story. (Oh, you must think that things are possible, like the tennis player at Wimbledon, TWO SETS down. Four games to LOVE down in the third set. *Still in with a chance.*) Two cheers, then, for *Phoebe Caulfield.*

So he writes to Miss Vanesa and admits that he's a bit hazy about *The Catcher in the Rye*, not having read it in X years, but he thinks the magazine title is brilliant. And, yes, he'd certainly contribute something to it. And where does she find her energy? And he hopes she's taking good care of herself. And there are a couple of books that he will put in the post to her. And she must remember to add his sister to the mailing list.

But Miss Vanesa had rejected *Phoebe Caulfield* for her title and, instead, had drawn on another classic portrait of a young woman, that of the child, Sidonia, in Radclyffe Hall's *A Saturday Life*. The men would, of course, love Radclyffe Hall for her homosexuality, and adopt the child for her wilful brilliance, her random genius. But Vanesa wouldn't make it too easy for them to claim paternity; she wouldn't name the child, she wouldn't name the book; she'd simply call her magazine *Saturday*.

8

Passion

In the dream he shot his tormentor and escaped.
When you wake this early in the morning, an escapee
from a situation that's clearly intolerable – one of being incarcerated, of being in a position of such extreme danger or
fear of abuse that the only option is to shoot your way out –
you can't just shrug it off and go to the kitchen and make
yourself a cup of tea. Because this dream is (these dreams
are) different. There's no sense of relief in waking up.

Put it this way: in the old days when you're up there on
the high building, being chased, cartoon-like, by the man
with the gun, and he's gaining on you, and you've come to
the end of the last high building and are stuck, unable to
move forward or back; and your pursuer raises his gun
and shoots; and you wake at that moment, uncertain for a
few seconds, *then* there's a sigh of relief on re-entering the
safety and familiarity of your bed. Not so with this dream.

Why the gun? Why guns? You've never owned a gun,
but we're assured that most of the world is now armed.
They've always been armed with knives and poisons and
whatnot, but not, until recently, with guns, thanks to Mr
Kalashnikov. Now you're part of the minority in this
world without a gun – except in dream: what makes the
dream so distort your waking life?

The stage psychologist might well encourage me to acquire a gun, along with the skills to use it and, having

perfected the art, to demonstrate first on my grandmother, then on my mother, that the gun and I work well together. I, not *au fait* with these counselling sessions, would be tempted to turn my gun on the person who sold it to me in the first place, without the complications of nuance. (The Kalashnikov family are safe with me: Big Daddy recanted, more or less, towards the end of his life.)

It's just past six in the morning; I have a language lesson at nine; I've neglected – for various reasons – to do the prescribed homework. After that there's a meeting at my bank: a casual observer on the rue Ordener might think I work for the Paribas branch there, my visits are so regular. After the bank there's the library: something about the library seems to nag at me but I can't think what now. This period between six and eight-thirty had been designated 'homework' time. The better-organized would say to me (and I've said it to myself, so part of me belongs to the 'better-organized') – they would say: Look, you've had a week to do this homework, you've fluffed and fluffed about all week doing this and that, you've engaged in every kind of displacement activity, you've left the homework – as you knew you would – till the last possible moment: don't now blame a bad dream for getting in the way of carrying out your responsibility.

I grant all that; I am remiss; I will fail the language test in the end. (Ah, yes, I remember the thing about the library; an aesthetic thing, really. Like a bad tooth in the mouth that doesn't really bother you but . . . well, it bothers you. Something there is starting to rot: how do you kiss someone with good grace, knowing . . . ? And then again, if the mouth is starting to go, what of other parts of the body, discreetly threatening not to stay firm any more, as it were. All of this is diverting you from your *Grammaire Progressive du Français*, this obsession with biology. (Here I am thinking I will change my library because I find the name, Bibliothèque Clignancourt, a trifle unaesthetic: why not la Bibliothèque Pigalle, three stops down the line. Or Bibliothèque Abbesses, up the hill, all those 's's like the swishing skirts of passing nuns. But really, all this, in the light of everything, now seems frivolous. None of this helps to clear up the content of the dream.) Why is one's sleeping life so shabby, so lurid and melodramatic? Why, for instance, was there no *debate* between myself and the man – call him my captor – whom I eventually killed? If there were one line of dialogue preceding the act, that would have given me a clue to the particular circumstances of this drama: was it in a public or private prison that I was being held? What did I do to be so incarcerated? What, exactly, was the nature of the humiliations or threats that I suffered – or feared I might suffer in this (going-to-sleep-and-travelling-to-foreign-country-violently-in-the-news) situation? Why was the texture of this experience so *thin*? And, just as important, what did I escape *to*? Who or what did I have waiting for me on the other side?

You could see why it's impossible just to get up, shrug it off and stumble into the kitchen to make a cup of tea.

*

Of course I know what they say. *They* are the great alternative philosophers of the world. They say, you've got off on the wrong track, that's not the way to look at it, these dreams are not logical. *Dreams, innit.* You are in danger of being literal. Enlarge the frame of the dreaming canvas till it takes in daylight landscape where you can confront all the people who come to disturb you in dreams. Talk out the remorse and guilt. If *they* speak in a foreign tongue, then bring along Madame Belair to translate. Better still, make it a session at Madame Belair's down in the 15th. (Sorry, this is disingenuous.) Though I would demand to know why they won't let me live up to the image of myself

I have tried to cultivate over the years. This might seem a dramatic response to a dream, but when you're a certain age you're conscious that time is passing more quickly for you than for some others; and as you have no belief in an afterlife, the shortening puts a certain pressure on you that it might not exert on more willing fantasists. Remember that story of Iris Murdoch coming down to London from Cambridge and getting out at Liverpool Street and suddenly having no idea why she's come to London. Warning signs like that can be suppressed for just so long. It bothers you that you suddenly can't distinguish between the authors Peter Ackroyd and Peter Carey. Or between A. N. Wilson, D. J. Taylor and Saddam Hussein. *They* come to the rescue.

They also say (those who wish to give me a slim way out): look at the state of the world in which we choose to live. Wars. Barbarity. Cruelties no longer to be documented. No indication that a coalition of the willing would mount a war against oppressors of women and children far away, if only to divert attention from the oppression of women and children nearer home: that, they say, might justify your seeking to learn something from the late Comrade Kalashnikov.

Or further still (the daytime canvas is now more peopled): look at the degraded environment, the condition of that other world, to which you have contributed. Pollution, pollution everywhere. The widespread decline in learning: you have been a teacher all these years. If you were a man of sensibility, of honour, your sense of accountability would lead you to take the Roman's way out: you have read Suetonius. You have read Plutarch. All this floods the mind; which makes the option of a cup of tea seem somewhat feeble.

It's coming up to six-thirty: this won't do; this won't do at all.

*

The language class didn't go well. The later meeting with the bank was OK in its surreal way, two men on opposite sides of the desk speaking a different language. But first, the rendezvous with Madame Belair. On emerging from the Métro, I must have been thinking of the dream. (I *had* been thinking of the dream on the Métro, wondering about the setting on those high buildings, curious how my tendency to vertigo doesn't transfer to night-time living: so could there be advantages in dreams? *Is it possible that I might be able to shoot straight without knowing it*; without having to visit the firing range? Anyway, I got off at the Métro Notre-Dame des-Champs and got lost. I'd been here before – a hundred yards or so up boulevard Raspail and then left into rue Mizon, her street. In the end, defeated, I had to ask directions.

(One slightly good thing about this is that the man who put me right was a man from eastern Europe, the category of man I had been encouraged to be suspicious of in the past. He was a delivery man, with his van, and had overheard me asking directions, and promptly volunteered to help, and took out his map. I was initially affronted to be reduced to the status of foreigner who needed a map to negotiate my way round Paris; but as, first, a woman on the corner and then the traffic wardens couldn't help me – doubting I was in the right *arrondisement* – the man with the map was not to be patronized. It soon became clear: instead of going on to Métro Pasteur – three stops on – I had got off at the stop I had used months before for a conversation class at Alliance Française.)

These are not the mistakes that should happen, you told yourself, hot and bothered now, as you walked along boulevard Pasteur (not bouvelard Raspail) up to rue Mizon on the left, and, eventually, to Madame Belair. How similar they are, boulevard Raspail and boulevard Pasteur – 6th and 15th. *Oh, my Baron Haussmann of long ago, you are part of the confusion.* Though if you were a child living here, at some point you might say to your mother: *Maman, qui est Pasteur?* And that could be the start of a line of dialogue between mother and daughter.

But there is no fun ending to this. Madame Belair, despite her natural inclination to passion, remains calm, a sort of punishment; and offers tea; she thinks me unreliable. There'll be no talk today of Degas. Or Renoir. Not even the near-kissing games of pronunciation, the game of protruding lips. Last time it was as close as was decent, and disguised as an exercise from the book. Say *mûr*, not as in 'wall' but *mûr* as in 'ripe'.

On dit mûr comme . . . ?
Mûr comme . . . le fromage.
Très bon. Encore?
Mûr comme . . . les bananes jaunes . . . ou l'ananas . . .
Bon, bon.

None of that today. None of that intimate rigour today. Even the prepared passages on Degas and Renoir must be held over for lack of time. (A quick definition comes to mind: hell is to be late for a rendezvous with your French mistress and having to make do with a grammar exercise from *Grammaire Progressive du Française* instead of *littérature* about painters and the problematic relationship with their models.) Today, I'm not the sort of person to be indulged with the grammar of foreplay. Today, I'm the sort of person who gets lost in Paris and turns up late for the appointment. Like an *ancien* president of the Republic was supposed, comically, to do. (Our planned life together must be revised.)

*

At the bank there were no surprises. The man sat facing his computer, the screen turned away from me, and he talked figures, and rates of interest; and printed off new agreements to be signed by me, by both of us; and I was trying to hang on to certain facts about this and that, about astronomy from the *Teach Yourself Astronomy* I'd been reading; and it seemed to me so curious that this man sat so solidly in his chair, in his office, on rue Ordener, talking to his computer and his printer with a degree of satisfaction, no hint of resentment at not having been painted by Degas or Renoir. Or again, with no apparent desire to relate his position in the bank to the mystery of astronomy and the sky at night. And as I signed the third set of papers fresh from the printer – who knows what they demanded this time? – the man at his computer suddenly switched language and apologized for the waste of paper. Maybe he was something of a mind-reader. Maybe we could start this meeting all over again, and compensate for lost time.

*

I prefer the logic of waking to the logic of dream. The morning that Madame Belair walked into my life was real enough. I was sitting with seven or eight others in the room waiting for the class to begin. Room whatever it was on the third floor of the Alliance Française building just down from Notre-Dame-des-Champs. Mainly women and a pretty boy with a tan, who turned out to be Mexican – so different from the image of Mexican characters in American films you used to see. I was in the middle of the row, a lazy horseshoe, facing the desk, and introduced myself to the women on either side of me, one from Poland and the other from one of the South American countries, not Brazil. Odd, that the young English girl at the end was already yawning – at nine o'clock in the morning. And then Madame Belair blew in, busy and animated, not really late, but with an air of something about her that suggested she was making up for lost time. And yes, in taking the names of the new students, in confirming how long each was registered for, in establishing how we would prefer to be addressed – having introduced herself and written her name and e-mail address on the board – you realized that the conversation session had, indeed, started without our realizing it. The Mexican, a pretty boy, exquisitely dressed, proved both fluent and confident.

After the break – this was a three-hour session; and expensive: I wonder who was paying for the young English girl, who looked bored throughout. Before the break we had gone through sessions listening to recorded conversations to do with searching for an apartment in Paris, and, at the end of each listening, Madame Belair would explain key words, write them on the board, each word seeming to carry with it revealing information of the geography or history of Paris: if Gambetta wasn't your Métro station, or Louis Blanc, the one nearest to you needed to be identified. And you were asked to describe the journey to the Alliance Française building. And to describe something about your street: in what *arrondisement*; whether it was near a park or a little square, or was busy or tranquil. Was it good for shopping; were the restaurants of different nationalities – and now for the names of various nationalities who might have restaurants in Paris – etc. (We'd leave the menu prices and numbers for another lesson.) And were there *clochards* on your street? Or near the Métro? (This was no French chauvinist, Madame Belair; though she wanted to know if there were *clochards* on the streets of London or Bogota, Warsaw or Mexico City: we would prepare, for a later lesson, for a conversation on *clochards,* etc.)

After the break we got together in three groups to select an apartment in Paris for rent: Madame Belair had photocopied details of '*Appartements à Louer*' from one of the papers, and we spent half an hour doing that, then another fifteen minutes in role-play – owner and tenant – *patron et locataire* – negotiating the arrangement. (I was on familiar territory here.) One thing I admired about Madame Belair's method (I'm trying to avoid talking about the unfussy elegance of her outfit, the unfussily appealing way that her hair, parted in the middle, fell in waves [crinkly-wavy] down both sides of her face, the clarity of her diction, etc.): the thing I liked about her *method* was her refusal to let you rest, so to speak. She used the board a lot, but very soon erased what she had written to make room for new information, which meant you had to pay attention and write things down, you couldn't coast – except for the young Englishwoman, who couldn't suppress a yawn from time to time, and the Mexican, his longish legs clad in impeccable white, topped by highly polished brown shoes, matching his brown crushed-velvet jacket, who looked pleased with himself and wrote nothing down. Then two days later, waking (I mean still awake, not asleep), I ran into Madame Belair at the Musée d'Orsay.

Well, what do you say to that?

*

You say that Paris is small. You say that people who have an interest in language are likely to have an interest in art. You say, if Madame Belair works at Alliance Française in the morning she probably has the afternoon free; and what better way (to come down from the exertions of teaching) than to spend an hour or two with familiar art objects in her favourite gallery. You say that I, a foreigner with a certain view of myself, writing stories in the morning when I'm not at the language class, am likely to head for one of the English-language bookshops in the city, or for some iconic place like the Louvre or the Musée d'Orsay. So that it is not a surprise that I should accidentally run into Madame Belair there, at d'Orsay, on that particular afternoon.

I don't want to hear that. Just as I didn't want to hear the stage psychologists earlier on interpreting my dream, I don't want to hear the common-sense rationalist now. So we move on.

*

It's late now, but one must prepare properly for sleep. I've already made a phone call, a wrong number, and had a satisfactory conversation with somebody I can't visualize. So far so . . . encouraging. I've thought well of two or three iffy people I know; and, randomly, of a man at the launderette who was unexpectedly polite. I've had a light salad. No alcohol since lunch. I've commuted the death sentences of a hundred drugs-and-people smugglers round the world, including the honour killers and women-batterers and Presidents for Life. (*But only a hundred.* To go over that number is to encourage the scum to think that they might somehow linger on and die peacefully in their beds at a biblical age. Fewer than a hundred might show a residual meanness, a punitiveness on my part – and I don't want to be punished in dream for that.) What else?

No, this is to slip back into old thinking. We discussed Degas, Madame Belair and I – no, not in the restaurant but in the corridor, moving from one Impressionist room to another. (This was at the Musée d'Orsay.) Degas and Renoir. I saw her as Degas rather than Renoir; her face lacked the Renoir innocence: I didn't yet see her as the dancer or the bather, *Madame Belair Sortant du Bain* (2007), but . . . She took private classes. *Ah, yes?* In the mornings, when she wasn't at the Alliance Française. Interesting. *Intéressant.* This was her number; her address. Métro Pasteur. But sorry, she had to go now. (I already had her e-mail from the Alliance Française class. Now, the number. The address. The Métro station. How could I not sign on for private classes?)

But it's been a long day, and now it's late. Time to read something before bed, something wholesome, a bit of Blake, maybe. Or Wordsworth. That joke poem of Adrian Henri's comes to mind, the one listing his heroes from art and jazz and literature; but it's not on my shelf. (Sad to think that Adrian H. is dead and not on my shelf.) So I drag out some possible reading matter for the occasion: Calvino. Yeats. Khalvati. *Italo* Calvino. *W. B.* Yeats. *Mimi* Khalvati. *Mimi* sounds the least forbidding.

It's two-thirty in the morning. Time, at last, to make that cup of tea.

9

Invitation to the First Astronomist

I heard that those guys, the returnees, had a wicked sort of wit, but I didn't expect it to be employed at my expense. Well, I sort of expected it; they had been criticized for magnifying their achievements abroad, for stressing their economic success in foreign parts which now enabled them to live middle-class existences back on the islands; but there was resentment, too, that they were not accepted *intellectually* as part of the ruling set: they weren't, on the whole, professionals. Some returned with trophy wives; and that helped a bit. But then the *women* who had had no need to migrate weren't overly impressed by the newcomers. In other ex-colonial places, it is said, in India, in Pakistan, even, there were returnees able to reconnect with the scholarly and cultural ambitions of the branch of the family that had stayed at home. This is what the PWC – the Post War Club – was set up to establish. Don't be confused by the name, PWC: all returnees, in a way, who had worked in foreign factories and post offices were, in a sense, prisoners of war. Even those who rose to become shop stewards and local councillors and teachers had still, in a way, laboured psychologically in the camps. There's nothing new in that; the business of the club was to rise above these everyday notions, and bring added value to the reality of what the returnees might truly represent. The returnees came back knowing that their islands, their territories, were small. They had gone away, some of them, thinking that their place of birth was large. That lesson in realism was seen as progress. So even though the imagination may have been smothered in the camps abroad, it wasn't necessarily snuffed out.

I was impressed when they wrote to me. Not that I join clubs, particularly; but the thought does occasionally cross your mind what sort of club you might join should you choose to go down that road. Who would bother to join something called the Writers' Club? Unless you were unsure of your status as a writer. Or were doing it out of a sense of duty. But the Ex-Post Office Workers' Club, that's different. Or the Pronunciation of Chinese Names Club, that would be a challenge. But to be addressed as the First Astronomist, now that was *special*.

There was an 'astronomist' story, way back. I was impressed that they knew about it. It had been published in a fairly obscure English magazine and not subsequently collected; so these fellows did their homework. They read, they researched, they did their homework, they had *wit*. (Even my English editor at the time had wanted to convert 'astronomist' into something more conventional.)

This is the story, then, that started it all. There was this mysterious man from my youth whom I had labelled the First Astronomist. He had come to dinner and we were prepared for him. (This was in the 1940s, in St Caesare.) You wouldn't, of course, have talked to him about the de Laurence *Book of Magic* (obeah) imported from America, which my grandmother kept secure in the cupboard in her room. The story was that the book was consulted, occasionally, for healing purposes, to help protect the family from evil spirits. For even we children didn't need to have it explained that there were envious people about, people who didn't like it that you had things in your house – a piano from Germany in the drawing room, an ice-cream churner and a mortar and pestle in the kitchen, in the bread room – that *they* didn't have in theirs, and owned property here and there; and as a prominent family doing well both on the island and abroad, you had to find some way of protecting yourself from people's jealousy and envy. No need to call it magic, either, just common sense: you had responsibility for the children and grandchildren, you had to guard them against people who wanted them to fail their exams at school and fall sick in the head. (Everyone knew of the case of Millie Corbett on the hill who had this sore on her foot for as long as you could remember; and she was the first to tell you why the sore would never heal: imagine, then, someone messing with your head!)

We wouldn't talk about those sorts of things with the astronomist, of course. He was called, I remember, Astill; and he was from Antigua, but had learnt and developed his craft abroad – in America. I was selected to go over to Teacher Kitty's, on the main road, where Astill would be dropped off from town, and bring him over to our house. It was an important mission because I was already dealing in magic at school, experimenting with the Heathens' gang, and knew how to recite the Twenty-third Psalm backwards, that sort of thing; and I wanted to test how far we had reached in Black Magic, to see if this man could do anything to me. Though my mother, of course, and grandmother had no knowledge of that. They sent me over to collect Astill because I was the youngest and they thought that he, a grown man, who knew people in Antigua that we knew, wouldn't try anything on a young boy. When I brought him back to the house my mother made me wash my hands and face and change my clothes.

I was a bit disappointed meeting Astill as he looked so ordinary, not dressed in any special way, just in shirt and pants, with the shirt hanging out of the pants, sort of sports shirt. And my mother, right away, picked up on that, voicing her disappointment aloud. Anyway, everything passed off without incident, though Astill proved unable to answer any of the family's questions – some of which, it's fair to say, had not been put to him directly; but he clearly couldn't read the *minds* of present company. (What made us a little cautious was that my grandmother didn't come down to lunch from her room. She had a bad leg, and she said that the leg was playing up, and the trip from her room down to the dining room was too much for her to manage today. My grandmother always knew things that the rest of us didn't know, so you learnt to interpret when her bad leg was acting up.)

So, did he say anything at lunch my grandmother should know about?

Not much, really, except telling me that I should ask for a binocular for my birthday or for Christmas; and then my mother corrected him and said it should be a *pair* of binoculars; and he said, Yes, why not two binoculars, until my mother explained that she meant a pair (as in scissors), and he said, Oh yes, quite; and commended her on her use of the King's English. But the embarrassment was obvious.

And then Astill said something about the number of suns in the world and we were surprised that my mother didn't take him on over that. When he had gone she sighed and said she wondered if it was all worth it, the effort of cooking and baking in the middle of the week, the two meat dishes as well as making the special ice cream for afters: the whole house had been turned upside down for a man who came all the way from Antigua looking so ordinary, you wouldn't think he had studied abroad. But still, when he left, and the family suffered no harm, even after a few days, whatever disappointment there had been gradually turned to relief.

'What's a real astronomist, Teacher Harris?' I asked the man who would know. (Teacher Harris taught us History and Spelling at school, but apart from that he drank in the rum shops in the village, where no respectable person went, and talked with men who had spent years travelling the world in ships; and he didn't believe in God. And that meant, yes, that he shouldn't really have been teaching in a church school, but it was obvious that he was protected.)

Teacher Harris always tried to answer a question you put to him, however hard; that's why we liked to test him, and that's why our parents and grandparents discouraged us from 'provoking him into talking foolishness'.

'That's a hard one, Pewter, boy; that's a hard one,' Teacher Harris said. And then he tried to answer. 'There's fellas that say they know plenty things that other people don't know. And they could be right. They could be right. I not saying that they lie. These fellas don't need a pulpit, even though they talking nonsense half the time. Now you have a fella there who look at things in the world, not from the point of view of what he can see on the ground; instead he prefer to look up there in the sky. Well, I'm not an expert in looking up at the sky, boy. If they tell me there's something up there in the sky and I can't see it, maybe I have to believe it. Or maybe I say: In this case I'm a blind man and you're the one that can see. And you have the instruments to see what you see. But when they start telling me that I'm just like a little ant crawling 'bout on the ground down here, that sound too familiar, man; I have to make a judgement on that.'

I didn't know what Teacher Harris was telling me; I wanted to ask him if it was true that Astill had killed nearly all the ants in Antigua, something he had learnt how to do in America; but when I had put that question to

Astill he had just smiled at me and shaken his head, as if I wasn't advanced enough in magic to know about these things. So I approached it in a roundabout way with Teacher Harris.

'And is true they don't have a lot of ants in England and America, Teacher Harris?'

'Did this astronomist fella say anything about ants crawling about down here, on the ground, where the rest of us have to live?'

Astill hadn't said anything about ants; so I didn't answer directly, so that Teacher Harris could take it any way he liked.

Teacher Harris seemed amused at the idea.

'Pewter boy,' he said, 'you can't help growing up in a backward place like this. But if I had to choose ... If I had to choose between a witch doctor like our friend there looking up in the sky at something you can see if they give you the instrument to look at it – if I had to choose between that, and these witch doctor fellas you have down here talking nonsense from they pulpit, I have to go with the astronomist.' Then, as if to relent, as if to answer my question about the ants, he said: 'England and America no different from us; they have ants.'

'They have ants?'

'Yes, they have ants.'

That was the difficulty in talking out of school to Teacher Harris; you never knew if it's the Teacher who was talking, or if it was the 'cane-juice' that had taken over.

I was too embarrassed to ask Teacher Harris the other things on my mind, about Astill's powers to turn us into things, animal-like, that were even worse than ants; so I left it at that, and felt a bit better when I knew that Astill was safely back in Antigua.

*

Not in defence of Astill, because Astill hadn't, really, been that impressive that time, but perhaps partly because of the disappointment of Astill, and the embarrassment of confusing one subject with another – Astronomy with Astrology – I read Astronomy at university. Not as the main thing, which was English and Philosophy – English in deference to Shakespeare and Philosophy in solidarity with Bertrand Russell (whom I saw live, in Trafalgar Square, protesting against the bomb). Though, in the latter case, I was prepared to widen this interest to the study of other philosophers whom I hadn't met. I remember telling Dr Rhys-Jones, who was a bit of a wit (this was in Wales) that my intention was to study Witch Doctory, but as there was no course on offer in the department, I had decided to settle for Astronomy. Rhys-Jones played along and said there was quite a popular course on Witch Doctory at the university, but it was all about the doings of a sad man in Vienna early in the century, and it was called Psychoanalysis. But he was pleased that I had chosen a calmer form of religion in Astronomy.

Yet, that one-term course sitting at the feet of Rhys-Jones at Lampeter (a welcome respite from Anglo-Saxon and Middle English on the one hand and the German man's *Critique of Pure Reason* on the other) will be seen to have stood me in good stead with the returnees on the island, even if they didn't know about it: I would praise them for lighting on that little-known interest of mine.

Naturally, when you're invited to join a club your first instinct is to find out who else is a member. (A military dictator in a ludicrous uniform – *No*; a performance poet on an Arts Council bursary – *No*. But that's just the worst-case scenario.)

There were one or two ordinary-seeming people who had 'expanded their minds' and had become members of the club. Good; the organizers weren't snobbish. In addition,

I was told, there was the Frenchman from Martinique who was a member. Apparently he had attended a couple of the meetings and contributed. He didn't speak English, but Henri was an illusionist who stole money from people's pockets but said that as wealth was theft, taking money from people's pockets was just *redistribution*. And he did it by *illusion*. Henri had written a book, but though nobody could read it (it being in French), he was deemed to have transcended the usual level of thinking in the islands. And as Henri had managed to stay out of jail, he was proposed – and accepted – as a member of the club; he wasn't a common thief. (If one rule of the club was to tease out something of a native intellectual tradition, you couldn't be blindly prejudiced to people like Henri.)

Then there was Anson, another member. Anson was more interesting, in a way, than Henri, being an honest sort of person. 'Anson' Pascoe was from the island. Anson was a woman. Pascoe (unlike a name that's suddenly appeared from nowhere) was a respected island name. The family had lost everything, of course, in the hurricane and subsequent volcano. But that wasn't the interest in Anson. Years ago she had been written out of the family estate, the family business, because she was a woman, the expectation being that she would marry this or that deserving rascal and be taken off their hands. But she fought for her right to be considered up there alongside the *& Son* (*Pascoe & Son*) hopefuls, so she could inherit her share; and when two male members of the family died suddenly from eating fish contaminated with mercury, the family relented and decided to take Anson's claims to the inheritance seriously.

And though there were likely people about – Miss Vanesa of the Reading Club, for instance – who were not members of the PWC – joining it seemed a sort of mad adventure.

I accepted the invitation.

And here I was, at the club, with the president, whose name was Dr Killigrew, who was said to be an archivist. I had brought a present, a portrait. (I had thought long and hard about what to donate, books from my library at home being the initial response; but that smacked too much of charity; and then there was the hassle of transportation. So, in the end, I thought of something different.)

Dr Killigrew, whom I'd met before somewhere, confused me by speaking in a foreign language I didn't know. But then he relented and said they were on the point of inviting a man to join the club, someone I might know from England; his name was Grosvenor.

I admitted that Grosvenor was a familiar name in England, but not one I had associated with West Indians.

Dr Killigrew said he sort of thought Grosvenor and I would have known each other at Cambridge.

I told Dr Killigrew I wasn't a Cambridge man.

He said I was being modest.

At that point I wondered if I had chosen the right sort of present for the club.

Dr Killigrew then talked of the need for us all to transcend those self-imposed boundaries – not always self-imposed except as a form of protection – that we had been forced to adopt while living in stressful circumstances abroad. Once the bird had had its wings clipped, he said, flight was usually constrained, limited. We must learn, he continued lightly, as if he were pointing out the décor of the club – we must learn that it's never too late, whatever our old-man illnesses, never too late to grow our wings again. (Miss Vanesa, my spy on the island, had warned me about this man. She had even hinted that his name might not be Killigrew. But she was sometimes prone to exaggeration.)

Killigrew had something of an upright stance, which made me connect 'wings' and 'flight' with air-force talk; but the conversation gradually settled down into something less worryingly poetic.

There were pictures on the wall of prominent figures from the region: Toussaint L'Ouverture; C. L. R. James and a mixed group of five or six elderly people labelled 'Bearers of Intellectual Property'. He talked me through the group portrait.

I said it all seemed too good to be true.

He said that was the whole point of the exercise.

I decided that my gift, at least (still in its wrapping) was in keeping with the club's house style. But I felt I needed to supply a bit of context to justify the selection.

I thought back to Dr Rhys-Jones and Lampeter, all those decades ago. Rhys-Jones in his long black overcoat, winter and summer; and the hat that made him look like an old-style gangster, mobster. He talked us through Ptolemy and Kepler and Newton that summer, and told jokes. I recalled getting a new take on Aristotle, the great man working out that the earth was a globe before other people sussed it, because of a star that he observed – whatever the star was called. He could see it in the sky when he was in Alexandria, but it disappeared from the heavens when you tried to look for it back home in Athens. Well, stands to reason.

If things were fixed in earth and sky, and you're able to see a bright star from Alexandria and not from Athens, that would mean that the people living in Alexandria were more privileged than people living in Athens. That would mean that in some ways, Alexandria was itself *privileged* over Athens. Monstrous. Outrageous. *That would never do*. Question of deduction. The only possible answer was that the earth was not flat, but a sphere. I remember thinking at the time that living in a place that is acknowledged to be important (Athens) gives you the confidence to interpret the world in a way that's compelling to others.

We enjoyed those sessions – it was almost a continuation of Philosophy by anecdote. We liked the fact that Plato had his own sea or something named after him, on the Moon – a crater, probably (long before the Americans planted their flag up there); and we felt very smug about the fact that Copernicus was wrong about most things, except for putting the Sun at the centre of his 'system'; he was really not unlike those old men who sat in your grandmother's back yard in Coderington in the afternoon waiting for their dinner and talking interesting nonsense – in one case that comes to mind the 'dialogue' was about the ability of stones on the lawn to grow (for the men, though aware of soil-erosion, didn't apply it in this instance). But it was a good (letting-your-wings-grow) sort of education.

So, to the unwrapping of the portrait.

It was of the Astronomer Royal (appointed in 1675), the Reverend John Flamsteed (1646–1719) who was the first Astronomer Royal, appointed to the post by King Charles II, to take care of the Royal Observatory at Greenwich, at a salary of £100 per annum, a post Flamsteed held until his death. Did Dr Killigrew know Greenwich?

He pronounced Greenwich a nice part of town. (It was then that I worked out that the 'foreign' language that Killigrew had greeted me with was a snatch of the Twenty-third Psalm read backwards. Boys' games, this late in life; I liked it. Maybe I was being altogether too literal about things: I was still, perhaps, embarrassed by the Astill connection.)

What, Killigrew asked, throwing out some sort of life-line, as he identified a spot on the wall for the Astronomer Royal, what was I working on now?

I was a writer, he was talking about books.

I said I was working on this and that. Principally, on a story about a mobile phone.

A story about a mobile phone was good thinking, Killigrew said. Because it gave you the opportunity to write about something that the ancients, however illustrious, had had no knowledge of.

(That was one way of looking at it.) I thought of throwing in a comment of our experience of AIDS, which may also have been unknown to the ancients; but I decided not to bother.

Was it a long story? he asked.

I didn't know. I answered a bit hastily, and said something like Who knows? It was hard to anticipate, indeed to follow, Killigrew's train of thought. So I was forced into explanation.

It was a story that happened to me some time ago in Sheffield, I said. At least five years ago. Someone had tried to sell me a mobile over the phone, the usual thing; all this outsourcing to India and wherever, the caller absolutely not taking no for an answer. Anyway, I already had a landline, I didn't need a mobile. But I'd made the mistake of giving the caller my bank account number. Stupid. I didn't buy the mobile, of course; only I discovered some time later they'd been deducting money from my bank account every month.

'It happens,' Dr Killigrew said, matter-of-factly.

'So naturally I cancelled the whole thing, y'know, with the bank; and demanded my money back.'

'You didn't use the phone, of course.'

'The phone was never delivered. Anyway, it turned out later the phone was delivered to the wrong address. I lived in a place called Upperthorpe. Higher Upperthorpe. There were many Upperthorpes in Sheffield. Higher. Lower. They sent it to the wrong one; it was all too complicated. I wasn't entirely pleased with the way I handled it at the time, so I'm aiming to manage it better now in the short story. The revenge of the writer.'

'Why a short story?' Killigrew asked.

Difficult to know what to say to that.

'I would estimate,' he went on, 'say, eighty thousand words to do the job. That might be the size of it.'

(*The size of it!* I remember coming across a man some years ago; his job description I can't recall, but he worked in the building industry. High enough up. His job was to calculate the right number of bricks for a job, a building project. You lay out your plans, etc., for a factory or a housing estate, whatever, and you send them in to this man. And he calculates the number of bricks you need, so you can order them in bulk. Now, there was evidence, he said, that excess bricks were never sent back. Corruption, of course, theft, bricks held over for the next job. *But*, more interestingly, excess bricks occasionally had an effect on the *shape* of the building erected: the added resource often led the enterprising builder (or maybe the owner) to *enlarge* the original concept. Was Killigrew, in his way, saying something interesting here?)

Over lunch (joined by a lady, a mutual friend) Dr Killigrew said he was pleased to welcome me to the club, and hoped I would write the story of the mobile phone there.

The story had to be retold for our dinner guest. Killigrew explained by way of analogy. The references were to America. He talked of Europeans in America, moving west.

'These people, remember, most of them, came from small farms and cramped tenements; they had no sense of personal space. But they were on the move. And then they saw the vastness of the land stretching out in front of them, and it frightened them; and they had to overcome panic and fear, these immigrants, just to survive. In time they gradually outgrew their European smallness: don't be taken in by the spin of their history, written by themselves – all this circumnavigating of the globe. Columbus and Raleigh and da Gama commanded men who had to be whipped across the oceans. How many English generations could fit into the single mind of Shakespeare? In the newly conquered world of America the Europeans gradually outgrew their smallness and started to gobble the land and people and everything in their wake; they grew fat on it. These cramped short-story people were growing into the others' space; were transforming and extending to the point of inhabiting whole *novels*, suddenly living novels.'

My dinner guest, the woman, looked at me meaningfully; we waited for Dr Killigrew to continue.

I, likewise, he said, had mulled over my mobile phone story for five years – a long time. Five years was longer than an American president's term of office. I had been hassled and threatened this way and that, even with the courts, on account of my decision not to buy the mobile phone. There must have been sleepless nights if not bad dreams during that time. There must have been the natural tendency not to open your post in the morning.

I urged him to go on: I was beginning to see in this man a possible collaborator.

There was the business of the wrong address, he said. The Upperthorpe address. When you're in a country, insecure in your possession of that country, the last thing you want to be confused about is your address. You want others to know where you are if their intentions are benign. On the other hand, you want to be able to hide in case those who pursue you are not benign. The muddle of an address is significant. Do you live here, do you live elsewhere: there is something existential in this dilemma. Identity. How could you not give this story eighty thousand words at least? You're no longer in cramped Europe; no need to clip the wings of your story.

Not forgetting – he hadn't finished – not forgetting the storyline of India and outsourcing. First there was Japan all those years ago, forty-odd, fifty years ago, copying this, copying that. Then there was China and shoddy goods; and India and outsourcing and often getting the idiom wrong over the phone. Now forget Japan. Looking at China and India, who's laughing now?

And then the woman at table made a wicked observation designed to keep the conversation going.

'I don't disagree with all that,' she said. 'All the same, you don't want to grow too big for your little island, and make yourself look foolish.'

PART TWO

In Any of the Places
I Call Home

IO

The Artist as an Older Man

It might not be comforting but it's nevertheless romantic to see the artist as an older man, broken, down on his luck, bitter and disillusioned, homeless, begging on the streets of Paris, a *clochard*. The fact that he has enough French to understand the taunts and insults of passers-by would be seen as a vague *plus* (giving this foreigner a back story) – a sort of buoyancy of a character, say, out of *Les Misérables*; he might still come good, you think, in the musical. So the fact that he has taken up his position here, while the weather is fine, on a main street, the well-lit rue Ordener, say, in the 18th, in *la dix-huitième,* outside a doorway with a whiff of patisserie where, in better times, he would perhaps have gone in to buy bread, cakes being ruled out because of his medical condition – that gives you an image of a man not isolated, not quite giving up on the quest, and not divorced from the life of the city. (And, of course, there's the street market, twice a week, to add texture to his reminiscences, to prevent them all being lyrically mawkish and self-justifying.) And, yes, he'll be dead before long, for his physical condition needs regular medication, and his way of life doesn't accord with attention to this detail; and that, in itself – that limited claim to our interest – will enable us to find him fascinating for the short period.

And he's not isolated in another sense; he's got friends, fellow *clochards,* who can be voluble and jolly when roused: they sometimes raise a cheer to the memory of the king of *clochards,* to the inestimable Coluche, who, don't you remember, ran for president of the Republic in '81, against Mitterrand and Giscard, and withdrew when the opinion polls showed he was likely to get too many votes. (Coluche was a clown, not a *clochard,* but never mind: he had the presidential look, well fed and pear-shaped.) Ah, well, it's a long time since Coluche the First. So now the *clochards* get together in twos or threes to secure their place in the capital (on a bench, here, beside an air vent there, next to the cashpoint, the patisserie), and they sometimes raise a cheer on a Friday night, a goodly party of *clochards* outside the Franprix on Damremont, telling stories of misfortune and occasionally subsiding into HAPPY BIRTHDAY TO YOU, in *English,* the only line of the song they know in that language. They do this to remind the smugly housed in their darkened flats all around that there's life in the street after dark.

For this is the end of a day of taunts and insults (though not all taunts and insults, good times are to be had as well). It was market day on rue Ordener, the stalls set out, piled high with goods beyond imagining, though not really beyond imagining, perhaps just beyond reach. Within sight and smell (oh, to be a painter or a sniffer dog at the airport!), the mounds of fresh fruit shaming your raggedness; fresh fruit, so tightly packed in their skins, so cunningly modelled after the breasts of young women, and, *yes,* of not-so-young women; laid out for the paying, the fondling customers only. *The unfairness of it, the immorality of it.* The sniff of cheese (too close to home for comfort); the cooked meats, the crisp shirts and shoes and women's wear – all like a team of temptresses stripping off just out of grasp to taunt you, *taunt you, sitting there in your glass corridor* – this reserved for the *fonctionnaires* walking along the rue Ordener burdened by the ceaseless dialogue of how to balance the just claims of mistress and wife: the supermarket of the street affords these *fonctionnaires* some relief. *Les avocats. Merci. Trois, s'il vous plaît.* You're not a killer, that's not your profession; and it's not even that easy to kill somebody, not like in the *policiers*; you don't even have a gun. *Et les fraises. Trois pour cinq euros. Merci.*

So, it's the night after the day of the street market on rue Ordener. The market is gone but it taunts you still; still you see the piled fruit and vegetables; you smell the cheeses and cooked meats; you see the stacked shirts and bedding and women's things . . . little shoes for the grandchildren – my God, my God, and my grandchildren, you declaim, to keep your spirits up.

A foreigner stopped by earlier today, to browse. Hovered in front of the shirts. *Chemise. 100% coton. 10 euros. neck size 42. neck size 40. neck size 36. But no arm measurements. The foreigner couldn't make himself understood about the arm measurements. So he buys the shirt. He goes home. Arm measurements wrong. He doesn't risk it. Will go maybe to Galeries Lafayette tomorrow instead.* The *clochards* have a little snigger at that, as if it's still happening.

It is possible to have a little laugh. In the night when they gather outside the friendly supermarket on Damremont one of them is reminding the others of the big pot sizzling with assorted vegetables from the stall. Another completes the menu with the meats, meats and . . . of course, fresh bread. Baguettes. *Pain campagne* and something forbidden from the patisserie. They've got something to drink, of course; they're not to be caught dry; they're old pros at this game. So they drink to the feast to come, to the feast remembered. They toast the absent market traders. They toast the now-quiet street. They toast the sleeping neighbourhood. They toast Joan of Arc and Napoleon and the Battle of Austerlitz. They toast France. They declare jihad and crusade; they bequeath the French language to the world; they are generous. They wake up the sleeping on Ordener and Damremont.

So this is the scene that our author likes to present of the artist as an older man, down on his luck. Diverting, surely. And yet – you can't help it – you must wonder what this determined *fiction* is designed to conceal. And in time you come around to the rather tame conclusion that this image of the artist as an older man is a self-portrait. Disguised, of course. But we know his methods. We have read him before; we know when we're being led off the scent.

That he walks about in disguise is normal. He mingles with the able-ish-bodied, claiming their constituency; his clothes are clean, smartish, even. (He will talk to you about the cost of going to the launderette, and of the necessity for silk scarves.) He reads and writes and publishes, *and teaches creative writing at a university*. An insult, an in-between thing, neither dead artist to be canonized, nor living-as-artist to be envied. The old ones were fortunate: *lucky lucky lucky;* they had patrons and support systems, they had an income (his own income makes him a non-artist, a suspect thing, a mule, a eunuch). The Canon lived at a time when the artist was content to defer fame to posterity, and not hanker after the prizes: you're pulled both ways, towards the Canon and the other way, towards instant fame. The end of that play by Brecht comes to mind. Also, that little story by Ray Carver comes to mind; a tiny story, two pages; it's called 'Little Things': have you read it? And then one day the doctor enters your novel, not as a character, but to see to you, as a patient, *mes amis*. Of course, like anyone else of intelligence this writer doesn't want to live for ever. Just long enough to be Napoleon and win at Waterloo and retire to one of the palaces, maybe

Fontainebleau; and settle down to writing the novels. If that's a cliché, then living *after* other people is a cliché. Don't write a book, it's been done. Hence, writing a book (if you're an author) is not allowed. So redefine yourself as a farmer. Or a fish. Or a tree. Now that's original. The first fish to write an epic poem of the sea, the first tree to be conscious that it lives in a forest. (With that in mind he'll put some new dialogue in the mouth of his *clochards* on rue Ordener. The bruised one with the bladder problem will not notice the cracked ribs for some hours, for he will be regaling his companion with the new line in literature, the fish-sensibility view of the world; the tree-centred cosmology that demands worship.)

In this afterlife the *clochard* is seated at a table in a restaurant where every variety of seafood from the stall is laid out for him to sample and identify.

At an earlier stage of the proceedings, the pre-*clochard* phase, they have met for a drink, these potential down-and-outs; this is in another country, but never mind. As they wait for the announcement of a prize that each man present thinks he deserves (two of these men are women), they engage in chitchat, employ understatement and irony; when nerves begin to fray (oh, oh, the phrase fits) they adopt levity. 'Get yer kit off,' says one potential prize-winner to another.

This, too, is more desperate than writing that epic.

Now I'm going to sulk, a man says.

Don't sulk, says the woman. Sulking doesn't turn me on.

What turns you on?

Money. Money and prizes.

The announcement of the winner interrupts all this wit.

They share the disappointment of not winning the prize that each of them deserves. They are too angry and depressed to have dinner together. They vow to return to their separate homes and to burn their manuscripts as a form of protest; that, along with any sacred texts to be found in their library, to draw attention to the act; *and make the world sorry.*

In order to claw something back, our author writes new lines of dialogue for the *clochards*. They're still on the rue Ordener where he left them, though he's forgotten the street; so he just places them vaguely in a Paris many decades after Hemingway and Joyce and Picasso, but before the Sixth Republic comes in to more or less spontaneous riots. So, it's the familiar Paris of dog shit and people smoking Gitanes, and wearing berets and no one much speaking French. And the conversation, on a bench – which might be outside a shopping centre or a Métro station or, yes, a *boulangerie* or patisserie – the talk now is about the latest catastrophe somewhere in the world, which draws a discreet cheer. Now, the scene is clearer; they're outside the patisserie on rue Ordener drinking to the downfall of another icon; and they drink to the good old days of Coluche, president of the Republic.

In the creative writing class they are discussing the perfect murder. Ten minutes of talk establish that the students are familiar with literary detectives. Then the tutor sets an exercise, at the end of which he asks them to put aside their papers. He acknowledges that someone will have taken down Chekhov's old gun from the stage directions in the first scene and fired it to effect before the final curtain, and ended the play before suspicion could arise: the perfect murder. He acknowledges that someone would have rolled out the doctor's operating table and supplied a patient and put instruments of murder in the doctor's hand and have the evidence buried or cremated, etc.: the perfect murder. Others, more ambitious, would simply bring disorder into the community, into the world – bombs, mass killings, etc. Refugee camps in poor countries; creationists stalking rich suburbs, creating cover for individual and inventive acts of thuggery and impulse. He grants them all that.

'So this is what you've created,' he says, ushering a man into the room. The man's face is dirty and grained, and scarred; he wears a hat stained with grease and grime; the scarf is filthy; the clothes impossible to describe; he stinks; his fly is open. He says something in French.

'Is he murderer or murderee?' someone asks.

'But that's just an old tramp from the rue Ordener,' says a bright student, who did her undergraduate study at a good university.

'OK, you win,' says the tutor, and before he dismisses the tramp, has a long and polite conversation with him, in French, to emphasize his familiarity with that language; and to show that he's not a snob.

'Now,' he says to the class, 'here's one I prepared earlier.' And the person who comes into the room could be the secretary in the department, a well-groomed lady, maybe with grandchildren (he calls her Lillian), or the vice-chancellor, looking shifty (he calls him Lillian); or a woman nobody knows, though her eyes are reassuring; or a man asking for asylum in a language no one understands (so maybe he's not asking for asylum); and so on and so forth till there is a critical mass of murderer, so that the experiment can't be compromised.

Meanwhile, back on the rue Ordener, the *clochards* are celebrating, as one of their number has come into money for playing the *clochard* in a creative writing class. They have gathered round the corner outside Franprix on rue Damremont, where there is a warm vent. The successful *clochard* has extra copies of *Métro* and other freebies like *La Vitrine de Paris* and *A Vendre,* which he distributes, for warmth. They pour their wine and are stuck for a suitable toast.

'Down with foreign dictators on the Côte d'Azur.'

'Be generous,' his friend says. They have another think. Then someone says:

'To Anna.'

'To Anna!'

They drink to Anna.

'To Anna of all the Russians.'

'To Anna of all the Russians. Passionate woman, that. Did it with all sorts.'

'To Anna and the horse.'

'And Putin. *Happy Birthday to You . . .* '

'To Coluche,' someone says. '*Restos du Coeur.*' (The *Restos du Coeur*, set up by Coluche, collected food, money and clothes for the homeless and the needy.)

'To Coluche.' Then someone has a bright idea.

'To Anna.'

They are about to drink to Anna; then a pause.

'We've done Anna.'

'We've done Russian Anna. But not Polish Anna.'

'Polish Anna! Fine woman. Great horse.'

Suddenly vistas open up of all the Annas in the world not yet drunk to. They are delirious, the *clochards*.

Happy Birthday to You.

*

Someone, in clean company, indoors, tells the story of the proof-reader. It's the story that, eventually, should get him the prize of *clochard*. He is not yet weeping, but will be weeping when next encountered with his mates, telling the same story, on the rue Ordener.

So, it was of the day when he finally knew the game was up. It was when he gave the first reading from his last book of stories, and he found a mistake, and then another, two mistakes in one paragraph. Later, at home – oh, yes, he had a home, books, lights that switched on and off; a bed; and bills in the post to be tossed aside. Anyway, back to the story of the proof-reader. Later, at home, he reads through another couple of the stories, finds an inelegant sentence here and there, a misspelt name. So what's happening here? He'd proof-read the stuff. Maybe there was something going on in his life to make him miss this. But what of the publishers? Why hadn't they picked up on this? They no longer rated his work; where was the copy-editor, the proof-reader? The person he sometimes dreamt about. He no longer fancies the copy-editor or proof-reader: is that it? A form of punishment. And what with his own proof-reading powers failing . . . That's when the nightmares started. OK, he'd taken a drink or two to calm his nerves, to steady himself; to come to terms with the waning of whatever (less drastic than Mr Hemingway's solution). So you could put the dreams down to that. Or not sticking to his regime. But what did the doctors know? Did they think you would be content to live on regardless when you'd lost your grip on correcting your own work? And when your publisher no longer thought you rated a copy-editor and a proof-reader?

And they were everywhere, to taunt you; the copy-editors and proof-readers, walking the streets, in and out of Piccard, bags bulging with frozen stuff. Nipping into the patisserie, strong legs, neat shoes, ankles endlessly kissable: *you look after the proof-reading, I'll take care of the ankles.* Division of labour. This one, with the young child, would be more relaxed at home, maybe, her feet up, folded under her, severe glasses and pencil, blue pencil, maybe; or red pencil now, changing a tense here, putting the full stop on the outside of a bracket there, making a note to check the name of the disused building on the corner of Mabillon and rue Princesse. *That's in the 6th.*

All the time she is fantasizing the author, not outside with his mates but right here sitting at her feet, caressing her ankle. The word *clochard* doesn't feature in her vocabulary. She thinks instead, *flaneur*. As she makes him stroke her ankle he whispers to her – the child secure in bed – he whispers to her Baudelaire's sentiments about the *flaneur*.

At some point she lays the blue pencil or the red pencil on the page and puts down the manuscript, and turns with interest to the man lightly kissing her ankle; and takes off her glasses. *That's the proof-reader he's never had. That's why he's now friendless on the rue Ordener, the rue Damremont.* He weeps, he weeps for his proof-reader.

He imagines friends joining in, weeping.

*

The reason he is friendless is that he failed the audition for a place on the street. And therefore his story is of no interest to us any more. The fact that he insists on telling it to anyone who will listen (and many who won't) merely earns him our contempt.

So at this interview he's dressed in his casual best. Yes, yes, the secretary comes and gives him a seating plan of the panel, and he's stumped by this because when he finally meets the panel, it's all different because the secretary hadn't briefed him properly on the sex and age of the panellists, and of their dress sense and their physiognomy, and it's clear to him right there and then that there is a murderer on the panel and he must make an arrest; but he doesn't know how to go about making an arrest because he is not a policeman or a spy, and he is squeamish about physical violence. But surely they would expect him to make the arrest or deny him the position, rightly, because of his moral timidity. *Oh, you don't want to hear the rest. There are twenty-three other cases of failure to report,* including inaction after receiving that final, printed note, a

Thank You note sent by someone claiming to have committed the perfect murder; and signed Lillian.

Meanwhile, back on the rue Ordener, the successful candidate, the deserving *clochard,* is entertaining his new friends:

'So I'm sitting there,' he says. 'Neutralized. No ink for the machine. Out of black and colour at the same time.'

'Ah.'

'No money to buy ink. Checked out Darty on the price of ink. *Forty-five* euros.'

'*What!*'

'As I say, out of colour and black at the same time. Colour was *twenty-five sixty-five*. Black, eighteen ninety-five; that's forty-five euros minus forty cents: what couldn't I do with the forty cents.'

'There's a place down at Guy Môquet, on the stalls, like, where you can get a lot for forty cents. Six or seven clementines.'

'Or maybe four apples and pomelos.'

'But just think of all the novels and poems and plays and film scripts lost to the world. And libretti.'

'And forty-five euros would get you nine roast chickens at the Voiallas Halal on rue Ordener.'

'I'm not making myself clear. I'm trying to tell you what the lack of ink means to a writer cut off in his prime. It's like . . . like sitting in your car at the *payage* with no money for the tolls. Food and women waiting at the other end *in a house.*'

'Oh.'

'It's like sitting stranded on the high road, middle of nowhere; no petrol. In a foreign place *where they don't take euros!*'

'Oh, la la.'

'Like a ship in the middle of the ocean. Becalmed. No power.'

'You don't say.'

'Lights in the world gone out. Switched off.'

'*No.*'

'No cake and pies in the patisserie. No brioche, no *tatallette.*'

'*Ce pas vrai, ça.*'

'A cold pavement. Rain. And puddles.'

'Stop it. Stop it.'

'France humiliated by someone.'

'Kill him.'

'France defeated in the games.'

'Kill him instantly.'

'Foreign dictators on the *Corniche du Paradis Terrestre.*'

'*Kill him now.*'

They kill him.

Tired but relieved, they sing HAPPY BIRTHDAY . . .

On the Staircase at Trinity

'*I*'*m going to sue your arse.*'

Startled, they stopped in mid-flow, surprised at his entrance, surprised that he had brought some guests along. The woman sitting on the Bishop's lap looked up and smiled; he recognized her; it was Madeline.

'Hi, Pewter,' she said; 'I see you've got yourself a key. I'm sure you've met everybody by now.' Pewter held up the key in half-triumph, first securing the front of his dressing gown.

He recognized the Bishop though he couldn't place him: the Bishop was dressed in his formal robes. There was a very calm, pretty woman sitting a little apart in the corner, reading; the light from the side table giving her a special veneer of restfulness. Pewter fancied she had been intro-duced to him as a medieval scholar, though now she was reading the Guardian. *There was a massive portrait on the wall at her back that said* PROVOST *on the bottom, and gave the Provost's dates. There were lots of other provosts hanging on the wall. Everywhere now, people were shift-ing seats and adjusting clothes. Madeline had disentangled herself from the Bishop.*

'Are you over the fall now?' she asked Pewter.

'Now, there's a question,' the Bishop said, fluffing his sleeve. 'I take it your friend's from the Bermudas,' he said to Madeline.

'You're all right there,' Madeline answered, not giving him her full attention, though absent-mindedly smoothing down his sleeve, which was silken and voluminous. And then to Pewter: 'You going to introduce your guests?' The guests were two men and a woman.

Someone spoke: 'That one looks like one of the tribunes from Bill Shakespeare's little play they used to call Coriolanus.'

'Health an Safety, innit,' the Tribune said.

Pewter introduced his other two guests as the Mother Figure and the Podiatrist.

At the mention of Podiatrist the medieval scholar raised her head, slowly, from the newspaper and, looking from Pewter to the Podiatrist, edged a leg forward, foot swaying gently, till the shoe began to fall.

'I like the dressing gown,' Madeline said to Pewter.

Just before the reading at Tallaght that afternoon the organizer, a large, bearded man whose name I knew but whom I hadn't met until now, took me aside and, establishing my living arrangements, asked if I was a two-bottle man of Chardonnay a night. Or only a one-bottle man. Then he winked and said that he had preceded me in those rooms, and he knew the form.

Then the penny dropped.

During the introduction, which was a generous one, he said that I inhabited the coldest rooms in all of Trinity; and so he expected a *warm* response, both for and from me, as a result. As he spoke I was formulating a joke, putting forward one of my mother's sayings to the effect that heat and cold are only sensations existing in our minds. (That wasn't really my mother's saying; if anything she believed the opposite; but I like to attribute to her unconventional thoughts I don't quite want to claim myself.) In the end I plumped for something less convoluted.

On the way back to Dublin after the reading I had occasion to reflect on references to my living quarters at Trinity. Earlier – first week in – there had been a reception of graduate students and their tutors, in a splendid room off the SCR. The introduction was rather witty, done by a man from Theatre Studies or Drama; at the end of which he enjoined us to circulate, and to introduce ourselves to at least one stranger. I was introduced to a rather shy, careful man, a philosopher, who congratulated me on my 'sweated sinecure'. Then he hastened to explain that the phrase had been used in one of the Beckett books to describe the condition of fellowship at the College. Beckett was referring to himself, of course, as well as fellows of the past, including Bishop Berkeley, and no doubt preparing me for my fate.

I remembered that there was a portrait of Bishop Berkeley hanging on the stairwell, opposite the one of Queen Elizabeth, said to be the College's founder.

'And Berkeley is the one wearing the dark clothes,' the man who introduced us confirmed.

On my way out I paused to take another look at the Berkeley portrait.

'Careful.'

'Oh, hi!' It was the man from Theatre who had done the introductions earlier. 'If you stare too hard at this fellow, he might *speak* to you.'

I decided to play it safe and not stare too hard at the Bishop; I didn't want to run the risk of his telling me, with his rejection of the reality of the material world, that my rooms in the Rubrics building were not cold or that my bottles of night Chardonnay were figments of my imagination.

The mobile electric radiator made little difference to the temperature of the main room, and the gas heater in the grate didn't work. Decisions, decisions. Better to move the radiator into the little bedroom to defrost it; and get the temperature up to a point where you could read in bed.

I thought back to one of those old Hancock sketches – 1950s sketches where they are all in a room in the middle of winter and no money for the gas meter; Hancock, Sid James and Hattie Jacques, sitting in chairs round a non-existent fire. They are all wrapped up against the cold but it doesn't work. And Hancock has a bright idea. Mind over matter. (A sort of Berkeleyan idea, I now realize: 'To be is to be perceived.') So he puts a piece of brown paper in the grate, and imagines that it's a blazing coal fire. It's not working, so he needs help. So everybody helps now. Stare hard at the brown paper and imagine fire. Within minutes the Berkeleyan idea works so well that Hancock is able to discard his overcoat.

With that in mind, my overcoat still on, the fire in my grate not working – and the need to go to the loo – I formulate a question for Bishop Berkeley.

So there I was later that night, dressing-gowned and contemplative, sitting on the lower staircase in the Rubrics building, a couple of bottles at my side. I had already been discomfited by a man who, as he walked past me up the stairs, pointedly looked at my bottles and gave the thumbs-up sign. This was the man whom I had met on an upper staircase the second night in – the one from which I had slipped and fallen, grazing feet (*oh, my podiatrist!*) and coming down heavily on the right arm. The man had seemed strangely convinced that the college was preparing to install a Tipperary water cooler on his floor, *out of malice*. Tonight, though, he said nothing, just smiled knowingly and continued, with a slow, but surprisingly light, tread that seemed just right for these solid wooden boards that had been scrubbed and worn into service over the last few hundred years.

I had been thinking about Madeline, my minder from the British Council. When she first took me to dinner at an up-market place I can't remember the name of, she had asked me what she called an intimate question: she brought up the business of Hemingway and Fitzgerald in Paris, their flies open, measuring themselves. (That's where I was living now, Paris, coming to Dublin only for the duration of the fellowship.) Madeline's talk of Hemingway and Fitzgerald in the urinal in Paris (or was it in Lyons?) was simply to establish the results of a question we had discussed before, and on which I had promised to do some research: this was an administrative, not a prurient concern. I was reminded that here, as opposed to the Protestants across the water, or in the north, strangers could talk straight about these things. And, in any case, Madeline was a touchy-feely person, admiring my scarf, admiring my hands, not afraid to stroke the scarf, or, for that matter, the hand, in public. I fell for it, of course, and was thinking of writing something savage about all the years of lack of this sort of admiring, of the absence of strangers prompted to stroke scarf and hand.

The following week, at lunchtime, we were sitting on one of the comfortable couches in the hotel round the corner from the Oscar Wilde Centre on Westland Row – and I had the answer to Madeline on my bathroom habits. (Talking of bathroom habits, in Ireland your first impulse is to cite James Joyce as your source; but we didn't need to be coy; this was easy lunchtime chitchat over a toasted whatever sandwich for her and a steak baguette for me, and a glass of red wine.) By then, I had done my research.

I had gone through a similar vetting process with the man in the rooms above me, when we had had an encounter on the stairs. The solution for getting through the night, or for getting up once only in the middle of the night to go to the loo, was in the mind. There he was replaying a disastrous television programme he had done, this time getting the answers right. On another occasion he was imagining world leaders at the negotiating table disguising the state of their health: no popping of pills, no mispronouncing foreign names, no endless trips to the loo. (It didn't work; there he was sitting on the stairs, middle of the night, with his bottle of Chardonnay by his side.)

Nevertheless, it pleased him that I was a two-bottle man. After that we had an inconclusive discussion, bordering on the philosophical or astronomical, about when the 'night' started.

No, I told Madeline; I got up twice, only, in the night, put on my rather distinctive Japanese-y dressing gown –

'Ah, out on the pull.'

Japanese-y dressing gown, bought at Hong Kong airport many years ago, so perhaps it was Chinese-y rather than Japanese-y; and not needing to fumble for the key, which was always left in the door, headed for the downstairs loo with my . . .

'The private fellows' loo.'

'I've got a key.'

'Ah, we know what those private fellows get up to when no one's looking. I see I'll have to keep an eye on you.'

I had chosen the loo-less flat, in my 'Queen Anne' building. I had been rewarded with a key to the fellows' loo one floor down. (Or a graduate students' loo, two floors up.) The *bathroom* was two floors up. It was either that or living off-campus. (On second thought there was no *bathroom* two floors up; there was a loo and, at the other end of the corridor, a plastic shower unit, the sides of which I had crashed into after slipping to retrieve the soap, nearly bringing the whole thing down: *remember those days in apartheid South Africa when black prisoners repeatedly slipped on the soap in the shower, to their death!*)

'So, is it all right?' Madeline felt she had to ask. And I had to say it was all right; and not talk of the nightmares, in which she sometimes featured.

'It must be worth the slight discomfort,' she said, 'to be at the heart of everything. To look out of your window on those lovely Oregon maples that Oregon would kill for. And, on the other side, your very own Doric temple, and cheerful old Sam Beckett, across the way, reminding you that life is no luxury.' Everyone had mentioned the Beckett rooms (the rooms that he had occupied as a student and as a lecturer) with a confirming plaque on the wall. So, with Madeline. And the conversation meandered towards things literary. I recalled the image of Beckett in the foyer of the Usher Library on the other side of my flat. Head and shoulders, in bronze, by someone I can't remember. But the caption reads, 'Head crammed with throttled memories'. And Beckett's expression does, indeed, look fairly throttled. I couldn't help thinking that 'throttled' was the experience of having to restrain yourself from getting up more than once nightly to discharge your Chardonnay, and to play complicated mental games into the bargain. A two-bottle man hinted at urology problems; and a third . . . A third bottle of piss standing in your kitchen overnight would turn the place into a doss-house: this wasn't Dickens country; this wasn't Brendan Behan; this was twenty-first-century, Celtic Tiger Dublin; this was still knowing how to write to your grandmother, living the life of Riley some-where, to tell her that the boy done well.

I was wondering if Madeline's tone would have been different if one was deemed to have been more sexually dangerous, younger. On my upstairs neighbour's recom-mendation, I had just seen a play, a reworking of Rostand's *Cyrano de Bergerac*, an adaptation centring on the love triangle of young man, old man, Cyrano and a woman of thirty-six in the middle. Young man delivers the body

medicine, older man the refinement of feeling (both necessary for the complete satisfaction of the woman) – and I
wasn't ready, yet, to audition for old man Cyrano. Was this
part of the syndrome of uncle-ing one out of the sexual
competition – on the Underground, on the Métro, young
women and middle-aged men giving up their seats for you,
sometimes even offering to carry your bags! Madeline,
twenty years younger, would have no need to get up twice
during the night. She's a woman, too. She had mentioned
Beckett. Beckett had famously said that a cast of women
couldn't play *Godot* because they didn't have prostate problems. (Remember, Vladimir goes to the loo twice during the
play, once just before it opens, and again during the first act.)
Anyway, enough of this. Two bottles of night Chardonnay
was not interesting except as a conceit for a play. And of
course pissing in the sink couldn't be entertained at this
stage of the proceedings; for I would have to use the sink
for washing up. Better, then, to talk about football and . . .
talk about KEYS. Keys seemed a possible subject.

The responsibility of having so many keys, keys to the
flat; keys to the Fellows' loo downstairs; keys to my office
in the Oscar Wilde Centre; special key to the SCR; and then
of course the various codes, codes to get into the building
in Paris, codes to the buildings of friends. Phone numbers
(more codes), mobile phone numbers (impossible-to-
remember codes). Keys and codes and telephone numbers.
I told Madeline the only way of liberating oneself from
these keys was to go homeless – probably on the streets of
Paris, a *clochard*, which is the heaven that tramps go to,
after the hassle of living a tidy life.

'You just want to see how many fairy godmothers
would be queuing up to take you in,' she said.

You couldn't win.

The man on the staircase upstairs was resourceful. He had
so many cures for his urine problem that his life seemed

full. One night he sat there with his bottle of Chardonnay. He had a book beside him, showing the title, a book I knew, but was in no mood to have a chat about it. The game tonight, though, was with nouns. Or was it idioms? It was some sort of linguistic cross-dressing that enabled him to unclench his legs and not suffer embarrassment at the negotiating table. I listened with some interest; this was better than talking about literature. It seemed to be working for him, so I played my part and turned back without going to the loo. Though I nipped downstairs to visit the fellows'.

Back in the flat – some other night; the pattern was the same most nights – relieved of bladder pressure, wide awake, the room cold, you needed activity. I turn on the computer and tap out something about keys. It's the tapping out that matters, for the computer doesn't save; it freezes when you invite it to save, and Neil, the computer man, doesn't seem to know what to do about it. But it serves me well, because what I'm writing about is a character who ends up on the streets of Paris, a *clochard*. The reason he's a *clochard* is that he's lost his best work on the computer. Again and again to the point where he thinks it's some sort of destiny. The trouble is no one on the streets of Paris believes him anyway. They might believe he was some sort of writer; or that he had lost something on the computer; but not convinced that his loss is significant enough to make the difference. So it would be a good symmetry to things that these nightly tappings are lost.

Then one night after Bishop Berkeley's portrait on the SCR spoke to me (not so unusual, after Browning's 'My Last Duchess'), I was quite relieved to be back with the man upstairs and his tested mantra of collective nouns. I wanted to pit my sanity against his: he sat there, on the stairs, middle of the night, distracting himself with chanting an alphabet. It seemed intellectually robust enough to deserve an audience. I allowed myself to be distracted for a few minutes as he went through a catalogue of idioms: an AERIE of hawks and ravens, an ARMY of caterpillars, a BEVY of swans, a BOUQUET of pheasants, a BROOD of small boats, a CANON of laws, a CAST of herrings, a CHAPTER of noble virgins . . . (his eyes were closed, he was swaying slightly, he recited as in a trance) . . . a CHAPTER of noble virgins, a COMMONWEALTH of Africans, a DRIFT of swans, a FAMILY of thieves, a FLOCK of pamphlets, a GANG of Four, a HERD of moose, a LIBRARY of reasons, a MOB of metaphors, a RABBLE of reasons, a SEA of troubles (he opened his eyes and looked at me somewhat sheepishly, and continued), a CONCLAVE of prelates, a PONTIFICATE of prelates, a SYNOD of PRELATES, a PRELACY of prelates . . . (he was losing himself to sleep, it was working; the last thing I heard before I tiptoed back to the flat downstairs was the start of the repeat performance) . . . an AERIE of hawks and ravens . . .

II

I had a secret meeting in the SCR with the man from Philosophy. We chose a time when it was likely to be empty, dinner time in the evening. (There was an ancient man slumped in a large armchair with a newspaper on his lap, but he may have been dead.)

I was a writer, the philosopher said, and would probably know the Yeats poem, the one that mentions Bishop Berkeley.

I had to admit that I didn't. But, overriding my better judgement, remarked on the incident of Dr Johnson kicking the stone in order to refute Berkeley's theory of immaterialism.

He had heard that one too often.

He said, Yeats had Goldsmith, Berkeley and Burke up there on his ancestral stair.

Good people to come to dinner.

It's called 'lyrical'. The poem.

OK.

Yeats was, maybe, wrong about Berkeley.

Ah. I must read the poem.

Beckett, of course, had also mentioned Berkeley.

Ah.

Of course Beckett's tutor at Trinity, A. A. Luce, was a Berkeley scholar.

Ah.

Though Beckett claimed not to have been influenced by Luce.

Quite.

Other commentators on Beckett who single out *Murphy*, *Waiting for Godot* and *Film* as deserving a Berkeley gloss might be mistaken. Those passages probably owe more to Malebranche than to Berkeley.

I see.

Malebranche and Schopenhauer. Than to Berkeley.

And where, pray, is the Vermeer lady with her fallen shoe?

I asked a question which he said was more literary than philosophical: he would need to think about it before venturing an answer.

On a less guilty assignation – this time we were meeting in the Arts Building, sixth floor, Philosophy – we expanded on our intimacy. He had some dialogues of Bishop Berkeley which he thought might interest me. I had a story of Katherine Mansfield which I showed to him.

We agreed that the poor woman had died too young.

We both regretted that neither of us had visited New Zealand.

Though we had friends . . .

But to the story. It's near the start of 'The Daughters of the Late Colonel' where the two girls, Constantia and Josephine, in their bedroom – one giggly, one earnest – are discussing whether the porter should have their late father's hat to wear to funerals. And about their own clothes now.

'Do you think we ought to have our dressing gowns dyed as well?'

'Black?' almost shrieked Josephine.

'Well, what else?' said Constantia. 'I was thinking – it doesn't seem quite sincere, in a way, to wear black out of doors and when we're fully dressed, and then when we're at home –'

'But nobody sees us,' said Josephine. She gave the bedclothes such a twitch that both her feet became uncovered, and she had to creep up the pillows to get them well under again.

'Kate does,' said Constantia. 'And the postman very well might.'

Kate does. And the postman very well might. This passage excited the Berkeleyan professor enough for him to talk about it for the remainder of the session.

III

And then he was packing, at the end of the Fellowship, with all his unanswered questions, and nowhere to put them. Excess books had been posted back to him in Paris; cards had been sent to friends he hadn't managed to see; prints of the Book of Kells had been rolled up and sent off in tubes; he had mentioned the rain in his correspondence: *Where*, he asked his ever-absent mother, *do you put your unanswered questions?*

For he had sued no one for his fall in the shower upstairs, and his forearm still hurt. (*Thanks a lot, Tribune from* Coriolanus.) He must apologize to Madeline from the British Council for using her name in vain, Madeline, loyal to the end, who had agreed to drive him, and his luggage, to the airport.

He had moved lightly through the college and had set down no marker; he had used the seminar room once a week but barely sat in his office upstairs in the Oscar Wilde Building; he had missed the student production in the Beckett Theatre and though he had attended a lecture at the Historical Society had asked the visiting politician no question at the end. No time now to check the achievement of the Nobel-winning chemist whose plaque was on the wall of the Science Building. He had made no headway with the Vermeer woman with the foot fetish in the SCR and had made himself uncomfortable using the students' launderette. (*Launderettes in the town are for losers and solitary old farts; launderettes at the university are for students. Moral: Wash Your Dirty Linen At Home.*)

And he had not, despite nudging and prompting and reading that first dialogue between Hylas and Philonous, got the Bishop to speak sensibly to him.

There was a knock at the door.

12

A House in Provence

I

Mrs Gandhi is sitting on the lawn, reading a magazine; then her husband says something and provokes a response.

The poet in the middle bedroom, the small white room, no distractions with bookshelves, is correcting her proofs. Among random conversation on a terrace some distance away beside the pool, someone explains what is involved in correcting proofs. It is a shame, Mrs Gandhi says, that you have to go through this, through all the hassle of writing the book, only to be saddled at the end with the proof-reading. Then the conversation slides to other things: to the legendary Moors in Spain in the, what? fifteenth century, and a wish to know how they treated their prisoners; and then on to other matters – the nature of inheriting from one generation to the next, whether the claims of blood relations should be rethought; and what about the tug of genes and culture: was 'ethics' something more than being embarrassed by our biology? And why were we programmed to kill one another as if we had no choice; and to blame it on politics? Names from the Balkans are exchanged. Then the conversation reverts to the poet in her room correcting proofs: what, indeed, was a poet? – forget the correcting of proofs. No one knew, really, what a poet was. Putting their heads together – brother, brother, sister-in-law (the sister-in-law is Mrs Gandhi) – they come up with a view that a poet was someone searching for something that was, maybe, pre-human. Unlike a story-teller, say, who just told stories to separate humankind from the ritual of other animals, who didn't tell each other stories, as far as anyone knew. A human urge, was the practice of poetry, like dancing and singing, to separate itself from other animal-kind; though, of course, other animals danced and sang, too. A poet was, in a sense, *pre*-singing: sitting on the lawn, they could imagine a warthog as a poet; but they couldn't imagine a warthog as a novelist, telling a story, with digressions. From time to time the sister-in-law (who was called 'Mrs Gandhi' because she was said to take the moral high ground) turns the pages of the magazine she isn't really reading, a magazine called *Nature*, and reiterates her admiration and protective feelings for the poet up there in the house, correcting her proofs.

This is a slightly disingenuous bringing together of separate scenes at the house, as if they were taking place at the same time; but this distance from the event such fine distinctions seem not to matter much. The house is now part of some other family's cloudy heritage; Pewter can imagine the body floating in the pool there.

So, in this house one man is found dead in the pool. This isn't a dream; it is something that happened and was talked about at the friends' table last night. It happened in a village not far from here, other side of the lake; and Pewter appropriated the event and thought to himself it would fit the place he was returning to. It was good, then, that his mother had never visited the house, the region; for what if she had got it wrong and ended up at the edge of the pool, staring at a man like a giant, bloated frog, face down in the water, flouting hygiene? Even someone living, visiting for the first time, might confuse these villages with unfamiliar names: Bargemon, Clavier, Fayence, Montauroux. (Did *he*, Pewter, make a distinction between one or other of the unvisited 'stans'? – Uzbekistan, Kazakhstan, Turkmenistan – still all the same to him, with no particular shape on the map.) He didn't voice the thought about his mother; it might seem pathetic for a man of his age to be neurotic in this way about his mother, seventeen years dead. If forced again to justify his visit to the house – for the 'rational' explanations had not convinced – he would make a joke of it, he would deflect it with a sort of cultivated eccentricity that he had long cultivated: he would say something like, 'I've come back to check on the flower with the name of a New Zealand cricketer. Y'know, the flower, the plant, whatever, on that lower terrace.'

So, last night, he had listened to the story that his host was telling, of a man, an African, found floating near here, in the pool of a luxury villa, in a village they knew.

Ralph, the story-teller, was an old friend, and had been active in the region for many years, building houses, restoring houses, and now, laid low, made up for this inactivity with the vigour of his story-telling.

So, the man in the pool had been shot several times; he was in uniform; he was a large man, grown larger by the delay of the discovery of the body; etc. It had got into the papers, of course; maybe there was a report of it there among the pile by the grate.

Beatrice, who was French, and felt that the story was being told against the French, interrupted it at some point and brought in the cheese and fresh-cut bread for dessert. She was irritated by the tone of the two men reeling off the list of political criminals – from South Asia and the Middle East to Africa and the Caribbean – who had found a safe haven in this part of France. She had heard enough about the African in the pool; it was not interesting any more, she said.

There was the usual small embarrassment at this, but not of a damaging kind; for they were all friends here, no one had to watch their words. And Pewter was half prepared to read the understatement in relation to the murder as the convenience of someone using her second language, mitigating the slight rebuff to the husband. (And to himself.) In life, this woman had a private cosmology where her own children and the generation of cats in the house and the trees in the garden and the watered plants on her terraces all shared a common something, hard to describe, but something fiercely to be defended. She would not speak lightly of murder.

The dinner conversation veered off into other things: the overbuilding in the region, the problem of water soon to be faced in some villages to sustain the influx of settlers. (Already, there was a town in – was it in Tunisia? – that had run out of water and had to be moved nearer to the coast.) They talked about the water wars to come, in this or that part of the world. There was talk, of course, of the house in Montauroux that Pewter was to rent next day. Reminiscences. Talk of what might have been. Talk of not having regrets. (Coffee or tea?) Then an old game of naming five things about America that you loved, and absolutely not a whisper about the America that you didn't love so much (regime change in Iran and Guatemala and Chile and Grenada and Iraq ruled out), so that you could get to bed not hating the world.

They were sitting in the café next day, the main one in the village, having a drink. Pewter and Beatrice. She was in her new role. She was dressed for work, though the dress was not conspicuously different from the dress she wore at home, cooking, watering the plants; and yet she looked different. He liked that.

They were having a drink before going to see the house

in Montauroux and they were determined not to be awkward about it. She was in her role of letting agents' representative, he of impulse renter of a house he used to own.

He was sort of pleased that the letting price remained high, more than he thought he should spend; but at least this showed that something that was part of his heritage had not deteriorated, had not lost value: it was a thought he would develop, of how moving on didn't mean turning your back on what went before, not ceasing to have responsibility for your past lives: so shouldn't he, even now, employ Madame Roustan, the old help, *femme de ménage*, the prim and proper Madame Roustan, conscious of her status even as she cleaned, to give the place a special once-over, to take a chemical patch, literally, to the telephone, to rid it of the pollution of paying tenants of the past? Or was this now like any other hotel whose necessary contamination you took in your stride? This was now someone else's heritage.

Yet there was no doubting that he was coming here like a thief in the night, no big party for friends, no reunion, no final defiant fling with a poet in her room upstairs correcting proofs. (He thought of her reading *King Lear* or *The Tempest*. Or Wordsworth. As a break from improving a rhyme, rebalancing the stress, shifting a comma or refashioning the *radif* in the *ghazal*.) He must let go – though not fade out – the scene of a brother and his confident wife on a lower terrace being hard on people who wouldn't respect themselves, people who lived the cliché. (Their son had been in the army, had seen things a boy shouldn't be allowed to see. They had paid their dues.) Pewter must not think now of loyalty to old house guests, to friends from Scotland (not Scottish, but from Scotland), Kevin talking architecture as a civic art, urging the necessity to capture the rhythm of a family's living in the shape of the house; Frieda talking of the pleasure of walking in the forest, and of naming the smallest of the flowers found there – ah, this is the environment to help the poet upstairs to know that her corrections made sense. He had a feeling that these and a dozen other mini-scenes that come to mind could only be kept in focus if he still had contact with the house that had engendered them. And yet, to weave all these disparate stories into an always-to-be-referred-to, ready-to-hand, never-to-be-forgotten narrative of possession and loss would be an insult to everyone concerned. A misreading. There was a travel agent, a friend, who had visited: her casual linking of cities by aeroplane helped to shape his own small narratives. So Travel Agent, too, could be the poet-in-waiting who never got to the point of correcting proofs. All of those guests – and the strange man, Emerson, suddenly jostling for attention here, a man from the Caribbean who refused to name his island, his territory – will no doubt be brought into the story before the whole thing faded into a general haze. The alternative is to contract the years into a private glow of anger and resentment. If there was already anger and resentment, he didn't want to embarrass himself by having anyone witness it.

So here he was, in the café, having another drink, ignoring the fact that Beatrice wanted to get on, for she had another call to make before doing a bit of shopping for lunch. There were things, too, on her mind, like the children far away, and a husband not well. The prospect of going through the inventory with Pewter had already lost some of its absurdity for her; it was beginning to be not very interesting. It did cross her mind, though, that the TV in that house was hard to operate. But Pewter would know how to do it; so that was all right.

II

The dead man in the pool was, perhaps, not the worst; the worst being the mass murderers, the kleptomaniacs whose plunder helped to guarantee the living standards of, among others, distant, and unculpable, Swiss pensioners. The worst were the pornographers who employed child soldiers to do their bidding, the callous and pitiless of the world, the Presidents for Life growing sometimes to look like reptiles of blood and lust, whose trick was to blame their obscenities on being victims of history. Many such, living in the region, had been named last night.

And so Pewter had got himself into one of those mad arguments with Beatrice ('Why do they come to France to live?') not in defence of thuggery, but in questioning who had claim to the high ground. ('They're not French, some of them; they speak English. Why don't they go to live in Florida?') What could he say? Years ago, in England, a dinner guest had said to him, 'Why don't they rape their own women?' So the discussion tended to get derailed.

The newspapers at the grate had offered nothing, the reports of the murder being already burnt, but Ralph, at breakfast, was happy to fill in. Apparently, the man, the African, wasn't an ex-head of state, or a military man with a history, but a businessman who had done well out of the army.

Suspicious.

It was a child's army that he had kitted out.

Ah. A warlord!

No, not as anyone could tell. Apparently, he just spotted a gap in the market. Naked children fighting on television didn't look good. So he put the ragged pack into uniform. Gave them a sense of pride in their clothes. Made himself a pile at the same time.

Well, at least that's better than giving them arms and drugs. The children. Putting them in uniform perhaps isn't the worst.

And a uniform might induce a sense of discipline.

To get children to kill more efficiently?

To get the children to kill less randomly.

The man's a war criminal.

Of course. But aren't some war criminals less criminal than others?

He had planned a sort of celebration, something cooling in the fridge downstairs to be opened at the right moment, and shared. If your doctor limits you to three glasses a day, that cut down on frivolous celebration. So you hold back on the occasional toast to Samora Machel of Mozambique. One glass saved. You can ease up on Arsenal and on the woman in your life: Arsenal are depressingly not up to it this year, and the woman in your life needs to be here, to be serenaded in person, not by proxy. So you still have three glasses to spare. There must be so many *positives* to balance the old litany of – Iran in '53, Guatemala '54, Chile '73, Grenada '83, Iraq 2003 . . .

And yes, none of your friends or family has been cut down in the streets in this or that country: crime statistics haven't become *personal*. Drink to that.

'What is cocaine?' That wasn't one of the hard questions sometimes asked in the house. That one was posed by Mrs Gandhi; her questions were easier to deal with. Not that Pewter knew quite what cocaine was. So he waffled. Later, he looked it up on the Net, something he had been meaning to do, anyway, for years; but by then the moment to respond to the question had passed. Mrs Gandhi knew, anyway, what haemophilia was, and had examples of people in history who suffered from it, including ruling families. And Pewter had, earlier, explained to her, apropos of a discussion of American universities, what a sophomore was: Mrs Gandhi hadn't come here to be his student, she had, in part, been flattering him, gracing his territory, reminding herself to be intellectually curious while she was here. (Playing his game, she had cited Janet Reno as a good thing from

America. Reno was Bill Clinton's Attorney General. Mrs Gandhi, who had read a book about Reno, said that Janet's mother, Joan, was a strong, no-nonsense, self-respecting woman; a mother who had empowered her children. Janet, apparently, had built her own house in the Florida swamps, plank by plank. And, of course, the family was integrationist.)

And others, of course, had used the house in their exemplary way. In his absence, a party of paying guests must have discussed French poetry at a level somewhat beyond him, and certainly Théophile Gautier was someone they made erudite jokes about, played literary games with; for there was a collection of his *La Comédie de la Mort et Autres Poèmes* multiply signed and donated to the house, a Latin inscription translated as 'Each hour wounds you, the last one kills you' commented on and, with reference to holidays, food and sex, confirmed, with wit, in three languages. Pewter thought of his poet correcting proofs in the little room and was wounded and enraged by these unknown, temporary users of the house: the joke was against him. So what to do? Middle of the night. Think of five good things about America: *Louis Armstrong. Fred and Ginger. The literary lawyers' firm of Faulkner & Roth*. That's better.

To be alone in the house at night was a mistake. He didn't turn on the television; he read deep into a book by a journalist, a newscaster whose engagement with the world seemed so many lives more productive than his own. (M. L. King had said something about a long and productive life.) He got up and for some reason tiptoed past the silent room where the poet had corrected her proofs. He put on the outside lights, the pool lights, but couldn't summon back vanished guests. Instead, looking down on it all, he was reminded of that scene in the Graham Greene book, in Haiti, where someone looks down from the hotel on a couple making love in the pool in the middle of the night. He should have hung on to this place until this had happened here. On his patch. No wonder his friends had deserted him. They were holiday friends whose lived life was elsewhere. Children growing up with their secrets, secrets associated with a shared room in some unknown town, with the furniture of that house, not with this house, couldn't be claimed; the changing shape of a tree on the lower terrace triggered no impossible longing, no resolve to meet a private target. (And where, pray, among these terraces, was the family pet buried?)

So, to present matters: was the African in the pool villain or merely misguided? A sort of perverted aesthete? Would Pewter have invited him here and challenged him to explain his 'uniform' pornography? For this, too, was a place where the unorthodox could be expressed, where the unthinkable could be thought, where he delighted in playing devil's advocate.

Ah, but the discussion had moved on. With Ralph, in the calm of daylight, they discussed the man in their village called Emerson.

Emerson was a man whom people thought Pewter ought to know because they came originally from the same part of the world; and someone eventually brought Emerson to the house. And, inevitably, they ended up talking cricket. They talked El Salvador, too, but it was said that they talked cricket. They talked boy soldiers, but that may have sounded like cricket.

Pewter must have initiated the subject of child soldiers. Emerson talked of boys taken to the United States as children. By their parents, their guardians. Sometimes illegally. Often by adults whose English was imperfect, who didn't know the ropes, didn't know how the system of the adopted country worked. People, in the main, who simply wanted to lie low. The children sometimes took advantage of the parents' lack of grasp, of authority, to run wild, and fell foul of the law, fell in with the criminal gangs. When they were caught by the police and prosecuted (say, this was in California) – when they were caught they were punished by being deported to the lands of their parents: they are released – these graduates in crime – released on societies not geared to dealing with them, in lands of which they know nothing and to which they have no loyalty. Why are these boy soldiers, Emerson asked, not brought into the discussion when 'boy soldiers' are discussed?

But Pewter would no doubt agree that what he and Emerson had talked was cricket. And he recalled that strand of the one conversation they had, sitting on the side of the pool in the shade, talking cricket. There were a few people around, children of friends in Seillans and their cousins down from Paris, having a barbecue. And as they waited for the *merguez* and whatnot, fish, to be grilled (with two of the young women making the salad), Emerson mentioned to Pewter that listening to the cricket commentaries he had liked a man from New Zealand called Jay Gaboram. The name Jay Gaboram had a certain *oomph* to it. So when Jay Gaboram *biffed* a ball, he, Emerson, had no difficulty in seeing it speeding towards the boundary. And then one day he discovered – he was reading the paper – he discovered that the man was actually called Jacob Oram. Not the same, was it? A Jacob Oram had altogether different associations from a Jay Gaboram; with him the bat struck the ball more diffidently. The listener couldn't see Jacob Oram's ball speeding to the boundary in the same way as the other fellow's; somehow it would be stopped, cut off, by the fielder: what did Pewter make of that?

No one knew what Pewter made of that, because at that point they were called to table: the barbecue was ready. Pewter's eye had fallen on a sort of flower/plant among the thyme and *messugue* dotting the terrace; and as he didn't know the name of it he vaguely thought of christening it the Jay Gaboram, for its unexpected appearance; but the thought soon passed. At the barbecue some wine had been decanted from the bombom in the cave; and the conversation switched to whether that wine, siphoned from Martel's barrel into the bombom and now decanted, tasted any different from the same wine, now sold in bottles with smart labels on the supermarket shelves. They sipped, now from one, now from the other version; they changed their minds; and Pewter was trying privately to gauge how much of this sipping would take him up to his three-glass limit for the day.

Regrets? Ralph asked.

Of course you have regrets. Forget the business of building a house to let and resenting the people who rented it; forget the childishness of having your cake and eating it – even though you're forbidden cake. Forget about wanting your name on something to survive you. This house settled down at the edge of the forest a long time ago; awaiting family. Plan B would have had other houses accompany it; a little square by now. *Place Stapleton.* Grandchildren knowing it was always there. Simpler, perhaps, to write a book. Invent something. To succeed you. Or to discover something. Maybe to be a poet.

And think positive. No one's child had died in the pool here. Some fractured relations have been mended here. A poet has corrected her proofs here. And, to his knowledge, none of the following early forms of life strayed on to these premises: no Richard Perle. No Donald Rumsfeld. No Dick Cheney. No Charlton Heston. Not even the David Koresh of Waco.

III

'The Chinese say if you finish your house, you die.'

Mrs Gandhi, who didn't say that, is sitting on the lawn.

13

Rendezvous at the Supermarket in Montauroux

I

'I have short legs, but I have a long body.'

And he said to me: 'Better to have short legs and a long body than the other way round.'

And that meant, that means, he's celebrating my long body, not my short legs. Even though he went out of his way to praise the things one can do with short legs. And there's so much to admire in a long body. And yes, she had done . . . things with her short legs; and he had praised her for that. And how much of that long body, tonight, smelt of fish? She must smell of fish, despite the shower, despite the special soap, despite asking her friend to take a sniff; but her friend wasn't reliable, her friend was still experiencing grief; her friend wouldn't have minded the smell of fish; that was probably the only aspect of the supermarket of which her friend approved: the woman she was staying with was an old species of French.

But what is the effect of fish on a man of a woman who came to him from hours at the fish counter at the supermarket, despite the soap and oils and the dab of this and that? She knew men who loved women who smelled of sweat, and women who liked the reek of a man being physical. But these were people cleansed from birth (or tolerant to dirt), people who lived in cold countries, and for them fresh male sweat was exotic: she didn't live in a cold country, she couldn't afford to smell of sweat. But fish? We'd all heard of men who refused to allow their women to wash off the (fishy) memory of the day before, the night before, sometimes for days, poor women who couldn't leave the house for shame. Other women, of course, smelt of the hospital where they worked, of the chicken factory. Fish, she determined, wasn't the worst.

She was remembering the rage and passion of this man, the force of his – yes – rage and passion that she had unleashed. Afterwards, he said he felt that his life had been wasted, that he had missed out on the good things of life, not all of the good things, but many of the good things of life. Like a lady with short legs that grew and grew in that room in the house till she was one with the forest. The North Terrace was next to the forest.

And now sitting in the car in the dark, lost, and in defiance wanting to stretch her legs, she thought that act of wilfulness would bring her closer to . . . something or other that she didn't want to try to name. So she got out of the car, and decided not to panic in the dark. As the Germans say: *alles klar.*

II

Earlier that day Pewter had been driving back from the supermarket with his sister. To show that he was functioning in his environment he gently corrected her pronunciation of the name Leclerc. He reached for scraps of information about the Leclerc family and drew comparisons with the Sainsburys in England: people who sold food, but strove to be something other than superior grocers. Into the arts; politics; or even what you might call the ethics of food. He pointed out that Leclerc didn't sell cigarettes in their shops; not in this shop, anyway.

His sister, who was visiting England from the Caribbean and was persuaded to make this detour to France, was prepared to be interested in seeing the sights, the villages, but, keeping her own counsel, couldn't help wondering how a member of the family had ended up here among these foreign hills, speaking a strange language: wasn't this another example of being-in-the-wrong-place, the sort of thing that contributed to her brother's famed insomnia, an affliction that he was now pretending to be proud of? They talked of the confidence, the arrogance, of engineering, of man choosing to live in places where nature was once secure. The brother took that as a compliment, of a man who had outwitted nature. He pointed out a couple of Italian names along the highway, businesses where, two decades ago, he had bought supplies to build where he had built next to the forest. Suddenly she wondered if her brother was corrupt; but she quickly censored the thought.

So they stopped again in a village near to their village, probably even in their village, and bought some postcards so that the sister could show that she was here. She checked again the pronunciation of the village.

That night after supper, he had made a fire in the grate downstairs; it was September and the nights were a little chilly; he decided to sit through the film of *The Da Vinci Code* with his sister and another guest, and then went up to his room to read.

In bed he found himself reading bits of the same page over and over again: this was not working; the super-market incident was still with him – stupid to call it an incident: an incident was what Arthur Miller wrote about in *Incident at Vichy*. An incident was what happened to him a couple of nights ago in nearby Callian. Sunday night, they had run out of wine and bread at the house; his fault for not being a good host. Everything in the village shut, everything on the main road shut; then he comes across this little pizzeria in Callian. Tiny place. Open, but no one about. There is wine on a high counter. He calls. Nothing. But he waits out in the narrow street, knowing somebody must be about. Finally the baker – the proprietor, white apron and all that – appears at the end of the street and sees Pewter standing outside the shop, and makes a show of hurrying. After apologies he confirms that there is wine but no bread. Pewter buys two bottles of wine and expresses his (somewhat theatrical) dismay that there is no bread. As he is about to leave the shop the proprietor holds up a finger and stops him. Maybe there is a solution. He, the proprietor, will go to the restaurant a few doors down and get Pewter a baguette. He does this and they tactfully fold the baguette in two and put it in a carrier bag, as if in a schoolboy sort of pact. *That*, Pewter thinks, is an 'incident'. That is something worth writing up; that is a story worth telling. The village where it happened is Callian; the narrow street is rue de la Ramade, middle of the village, pleasantly flagged, smeared with the minimum of dog shit today; there's a place on the corner where (on a normal day) they sell crêpes; bakery and tiny art gallery on the left. And at the end a restaurant, two restaurants, one opening on to a *place* with a magnificent view of the Callian-Montauroux countryside: 'Like looking out from inside a novel', a friend had said on a previous visit. So, that was an incident. And now, again, what to make of what happened in the Leclerc supermarket where he had seen Fred Belair behind the fish counter?

He had threatened his sister with oysters, and had drifted past the vegetables and the stack with olives and eggs, to the fish counter where he had seen Fred. She had even called to him.

'What's wrong,' she had asked that time, a year ago, 'with wearing your heart on your sleeve?'

It wasn't really a question; they were here in this bedroom, the north bedroom, both distraught, both let down, both seeking consolation: 'What's wrong with wearing your heart on your sleeve?'

'Nothing,' he lied, 'nothing.' And it wasn't a lie. In bed he had got over one awkwardness but not the other, the 'other' being that this might be a one-off, and he minded that, but then he didn't much mind if it proved one-offish, for he saw Fred coming with so much baggage that one needed to be younger, stronger, more optimistic, more . . . full of a sense of possibility not to mind baggage. Though tugging against this old fear was that hour of intimacy, when lowering all your defences, with a woman naked not only of clothes, seemed to indict you for the way you'd lived the rest of your life: he was overcome by Fred's defencelessness and for a while felt adequate to it; and he talked of her short legs, wonderfully short legs displayed here in the north bedroom.

That was a year ago, and he refused to hear voices that didn't exist, refused to see a mirage behind a fish counter, for the woman was thousands of miles away on her island, and would never, anyway, have condescended to work in a supermarket.

So, banishing sleep, he concentrated on practical things. He was revisiting the house they should have sold. He convinced himself he had shed most of the baggage accumulated there; his sister was game for a holiday away from her holiday in England: why not pay one last, last visit before this phase of his life had passed into another person's story. Even if the new owner was not unsympathetic he/she would bring to this two-decades-old project, this living laboratory, this small-pile-in-stone vision first articulated on ruins and villas in small villages in the Var and the Alpes-Maritimes all those youthful years ago, a new perspective. The new tenant of the north bedroom would perhaps glance up from bed, from the novel no longer holding her interest, and cast an eye on the still-pristine chimney flue and wonder why it jutted out at a slight angle, not quite lining up with the floor tiles; and there'd be no one around to explain why. No Pewter. No Muhammad. The new tenants – owners – would gaze at the doors and windows, expertly made by Notto – two brothers, Notto, tucked away somewhere off the main road, in between Montauroux and Callian: were they still in business, were they still alive? So the doors and windows were Notto, superbly crafted, expertly finished; but the cupboard doors were the things you bought from the furniture shop at Mandelieu; no amount of varnishing could bring them up to the Notto workshop standard, the telltale grains in the wood standing out. Was that a fault? But it was behind those cheap cupboard doors that Fred had reached, that night, for one of Pewter's shirts hanging there, not, he suspected, out of modesty, but out of intimacy. That redeemed the cupboard doors: the new owners would see only something cheap, out of keeping with the rest of the house, and perhaps replace them with something nearer to the original Notto.

And so, sleepless, Pewter went mentally round and round the house, pointing out what would never be transferred from one owner (from the founder) to the next stranger with money. He would explain this to his sister over the coming days.

But he had to get a grip. It was the house, coming back, that had made him see Fred in the supermarket, hear her call his name. Physical ailments that he was beginning to have, he could deal with, he could accept, but the mental thing he would not admit just yet: to hear his name called, merely because he happened to be back here – for he had visited the supermarket with Fred when *she* was here; they had had oysters that night; the next day *lentilles* – the mental thing, he stressed, was something he would not admit just yet.

He took up his book, determined to impose his will on this cloudy time.

III

Fred neither accepted nor refused to accept that she was lost. She had been to the house before, of course, the last house before the forest; but she had been a passenger in the car, and not paying attention; and the forest was big, and it was dark. She had driven down three roads that led to the forest and none of them was the right one. So even though she had in her mind tall oaks and pines and lovely terraces with plants and flowers that the man couldn't name, the night wasn't the time to find this hideaway. She had a telephone number but it was maybe an old number, and she had decided not to ring it before setting out. (She didn't have a mobile phone, she was pleased about that.) Because if he had seen her in the supermarket . . .

He had seen her in the supermarket, and she had called his name. If he had not acknowledged her then, it would be too embarrassing now to ring up and say, 'I'm here. Remember? . . . Short legs, long body . . . ?' What could she say over the phone? 'I see you didn't recognize me in my fish garb?' She couldn't put him on the spot and shame him into inviting her over. And he was with a woman; they weren't exactly together, but you could tell that they were together; the shopping in the trolley showed that he was shopping for more than one. And he did look distracted. 'I'm returning the shirt. I've just come to return the shirt. I've washed it.' She could say that.

No, it was better just to turn up, as if she was passing by – at eight o'clock at night? Say she was on her way somewhere else and couldn't stop; maybe just for a drink. Though she was driving . . .

She could say she just wanted to check on those lovely kitchen tiles, those on the counter and draining board, as she was thinking of having something like that put in at home . . .

But she couldn't find the bloody road to the house next to the forest. So many bloody roads into the forest. So she would just have to get back into the car and turn it round and get back to the place with the woman in mourning: it was always easier to get back than to find your way out.

And what would she say when she got back? At least she hadn't let on where she was going; for the woman she was staying with was a friend of the man she couldn't find; so she would say nothing; she would deliver the car keys and say nothing.

But going through the village there was a café open and she stopped for no particular reason; and on the counter there was a menu for pizza. *Pizza à Emporter.* She would take one back and share it with her friend in mourning. *Végétarienne.* She scanned the others: *Marguerite* at 5.50; *Reine* at 6.50; *4 Fromages* at 6.50. *Merguez* and *Thonée* at 7.50, etc. Yes, she'd go for the *Végétarienne* at 6.50, and share it with her new friend. So, the evening wasn't lost after all. *Alles klar.*

IV

The next day Pewter returned to the fish counter at Leclerc. No, he doesn't want to buy fish, but he can't say so. *Je regards seulement.* He doesn't want to ask for Fred and make a fool of himself; but he waits around, just in case;

and so as not to draw attention to himself, he scans the counter, like a prospective customer. Starting on the right, away from the assistants (the oysters are on the left) he notes the *Filet de Lieu Noir* and *Filet de Dorade Sébaste*. On to *Tournedos de Saumon* and *Filet de Sole (Tuaucal)*. Then, there's *Dos de Cabillaud* and *Pavé de Saumon*, *Filet de Rouget Barbet* and *Filet de Loup*. 'Non, Monsieur, on regarde seulement. Merci.' And a quick scan now at the *Filet de Sardine*, *Filet de Truite* and lots of *Crevettes*. Finally — she's coming back, the young woman, now — *Gambas Sauvages*, *Noix de St Jacques*, *Bulots Cuits* and, yes, *Langoustine*. Now: *Excusez-moi, Mademoiselle. Moi, je cherche Madame Belair. Winifred Belair. 'Je ne connais pas elle,'* she says. He should have asked for Fred. Can't hang around the fish counter any longer. No, no, no *pas Tone de Lotte* today. *Merci.*

On the way out of the supermarket, in the large space at the entrance, set out like a promotion, is a cardboard cutout of Ribéry, the footballer, the bad boy of French football. He is in full kit, cradling a ball in his left arm. A filmic scar bloodies his right cheek. For some reason this puts Pewter in mind of the statue of John Lennon at the John Lennon Airport in Liverpool.

Back home Pewter puts Fred Belair out of his mind and sits down at the round table at the front of the house — awning sheltering him from the September sun — to try to do something difficult: he is writing a poem, a sestina.

Fred is on her way to the airport. She is driven there by one of the sons of her friend from Seillans: this is better, for her friend would have tried, still, to persuade her not to go. She will get a ticket at the airport (having pretended to have already done so). She has friends, she has family in this country; she is not a shameless woman chasing a man. Nor a homeless one. She might change her mind and go to

Cannes instead of Nice, to the train station: she has a friend only three hours away. They wouldn't have thought she could do it, come here, a stranger, and just drift into a job in a supermarket, and hold it down for a week, and learn the names of all the fish on offer in two hours flat. At the interview they asked if she was from Martinique and she had said yes. But it was cold behind the ice, the job was not for her. And that brought on the hallucination. Weird that, though she didn't believe in crediting those things: that was the moment to vanish. But here was this boy driving her, she had to be sociable. To entertain him, she rolled out all the names of fish she had learnt; and he seemed impressed. Amused and impressed.

Before he left her at the train station she reminded him to take good care of his mother. (He was only visiting; that was not too much to ask.)

v

Pewter was no longer fascinated by his discoveries. He now knew the difference between a postman and an invoice. The march of French was slow and endless; it was a story that got you there, perhaps, but he wasn't sure what the point of it was. Though occasionally the language hit him like an illegal substance, like his discovery with a woman that *lentille* and *lentilles de contact* had interestingly different meanings. And suddenly there was Fred Belair discarding his shirt: she had earlier discarded her *soutien-gorge* and something else she named and named till he got it right. Like a teacher correcting his pronunciation of *facteur* and *facture*. So he would accept defeat, shrug it all off and do something difficult and mindcleansing; he would write the sestina. He would write a sestina where *facteur* and *facture* would alternate as one of the terminal six nouns. And the dangling breasts of

Fred Belair would be another of the terminal six nouns. And the short legs of Fred Belair would be a third of the terminal nouns. And maybe the statues now of Ribéry, now of John Lennon would be another end noun. And the Leclerc supermarket at Montauroux, of course, would be another. And that left one terminal noun. Oh, yes: *lentilles/ lentilles de contact*; eating one, kissing the space protected by the other. That's it.

14

Her Birthdays

This is not an afterthought, Pewter reassured himself as he headed down to the centre of town, where he was to collect his niece outside the *mairie*. Stupidly, he had got slightly lost again, but not badly; the only way to go was down, down, down; and you were there.

In the car he was revising the notion of the afterthought (that's probably why he missed a turning). What was wrong, after all, with afterthoughts? If you felt good about them they were second thoughts; and second thoughts were better than the original thoughts, usually; unless you were timid. Second thoughts were what saved you from being reckless or silly; but didn't stop you being adventurous – unless you were timid by nature. Or by experience. Or by having lived long. He had been trying to demonstrate, these last years, that he was not timid: he did not feel guilty about having second thoughts: the decision to invite Clara was a good one.

When he got down to the harbour and found a parking place opposite the *mairie*, he glimpsed her across the street. (*Don't mock it*, he said to himself: there were occasions where he had missed the rendezvous.)

Not good to keep the birthday girl waiting; she had got the coach from the airport – her suggestion, to save him the extra drive to Nice; and somehow she had managed it in less than the forty minutes promised. Or had he dawdled?

(Funny word, 'dawdle', never quite sure how to spell it.) Anyway, not to worry. *Ce ne pas la peine.*

He had spent two days shopping for his niece's birthday, anticipating what guests would like; there were oysters for his friend Michelle from Cabris, old now and frail, but someone his niece had met early on, when, as a schoolgirl, she had come out to improve her French. And there were his friends from Seillans, who were in mourning. But a couple of the children from that house were about, people nearer to Clara's age; so that should be OK. And Clara would be bringing a friend.

Seeing Clara on the pedestrian island, he looked around for her friend: gone to the loo, perhaps. (The palm trees looked oddly right today.)

'Where's your friend?' he asked, as he got out of the car and kissed her on both cheeks, and made a show of looking around.

'Oh, she couldn't make it. At such short notice. And then easyJet prices weren't that brilliant.'

He was trying to cancel the echo of one of those old songs in his head, the sort that come to you while you're alone, negotiating the traffic, but not concentrating. Rhyming 'September' with 'remember', sort of thing. 'September' with 'November'. In one of those smoothie voices you used to associate with Americans of a past age. Andy Williams. Mel Tormé. Perry Como. All that. But the new arrival was talking about her friend, who hadn't come. Because of the money?

'Sorry about that,' he said. 'I . . . If I'd known . . . '

She stopped him short from making an offer that no longer mattered.

'Actually, she's, um, she's decided to go on the demonstration instead.'

'Yes?'

'Oh, the Saudi demonstration. The Saudi king and hordes

descending on London for some reason or other. I reckon we should be demonstrating against our own government for inviting those sorts of people to Britain.'

While he was trying to negotiate his way out of the town and on to the A8, his niece filled him in on things in England, and about Saudi Arabia, things that he more or less knew; its corruption and lack of democracy; the arrogance of the endless princelings, women not being allowed to drive, the appalling human rights records, etc. All that. (He refrained from saying that he didn't know things had got that bad in England.) But she updated him on things he *didn't* know. The four hundred planes and eighty-five limousines from Heathrow to ferry the king's party (Or was it the other way round – eighty-five planes and four hundred limousines.) Anyway, hundreds of advisors ensconced in Buckingham Palace; and the arrogance of the absurd king deciding to lecture Britain about terrorism, which, as everyone knew, Saudi Arabia more than anyone in the world was responsible for breeding. Even more than the Americans. (He remembered that his niece's generation were prepared to state their views openly, without worrying about upsetting people, without suffering the curse of political correctness. He liked that.)

Pewter was pleased that she had got all this off her chest right at the start; but was a bit worried, uneasy that his more muted forms of entertainment laid on at the house in Montauroux wouldn't live up to the alternative that Clara had turned her back on in London.

*

Clara had a healthy contempt for her uncle. She didn't wish him harm, of course, she didn't want him to have an unpleasant illness (he probably had those, anyway) or to be humiliated in life. Though she wouldn't mind if he were taken down a peg from time to time. She quite liked his house in the south of France, which she'd visited a couple of times; but she'd been to many other houses in the south – Italy, Spain – equally lovely; and the owners didn't have to go on about it. She was good-looking, she was bright, she'd been to a good university; men (and women) wanted to drape her on their arm. She'd been offered this or that future in Spain, a castle in Germany, even part-ownership of a golf course – for Christ's sake – in Scotland. How could a man, her uncle, who had lived so long, and thought so well of himself, be so blind! (It still rankled that for years he managed to call her Carla rather than Clara; and everyone seemed to find it amusing.)

And it wasn't even her birthday.

*

Pewter told Clara that it was a shame that her friend couldn't come, as he was thinking of selling the house in Montauroux, and there probably wouldn't be many more occasions to meet there. But maybe they could both visit him in Paris some time. (He was thinking that when his friend Milne, an American writer, dropped by last week, the joke was about Nixon. Nixon and Frost. David Frost. There was this new book out of the Frost interviews with Nixon. The 1977 interviews, when the wanting-to-be-with-it ex-president had asked Frost if he had done any fornicating that weekend. Anyway, there's this image on the cover of the hardback book. Just one face, split down the middle, half Nixon, half Frost. And you could barely tell, looking left side, right side, which is Nixon, which is Frost. It's the same face. Milne and Pewter had great fun with that.) Again, Pewter was thinking that another recent visitor to the house, not a writer, had contented himself with complaints against the world in general; the academic and business worlds; but had saved the force of his criticism for the public officials, particularly those who sat at the other end of the telephone, who no longer spoke to you clearly, and reduced you, in effect, to a foreign speaker of your own language. Or to a subspecies of the infirm. Since both Pewter and Milne were somewhat hard of hearing they agreed that that treatment by unseen telephonists was a form of ageist harassment; never mind that it came from the poor quality of education worldwide. Though the Americans, maybe, had to be absolved here: despite their poor public education they still managed to speak clearly. But, yes, this indistinct trend in enunciation was an affront not just to the language, but to speech. What would humans be without speech: we mightn't all rise to the thought process of Socrates or Kant or Wittgenstein, but we're all capable of speech (most of us). *Oh, my Shakespeare, we have dishonoured you.* But now he must turn his attention to the offending Saudis.

(He remembered that Clara had had a friend who had died. Nineteen years old. She wasn't with him at the time; she was far away at university in Dublin. But Pewter never quite knew what it felt like, to have an intimate friend, that age, die violently on the streets of London.)

'So,' he said, trying to lighten the mood, as he hit the autoroute, heading west. 'Half an hour to home and . . . a glass of something to . . . the birthday girl.'

He had had twice as many birthdays as she had, and he couldn't really remember any of them being memorable – when there was nobody about, he ignored them. But he thought it was maybe time to reinstate birthdays. In Russian novels they were always talking about name days, and of course certain Africans, Ghanaians, tagged their birthdays on to their names. Kwame Nkrumah, Kwame meaning (he thought) 'Saturday'. Kofi (for 'Tuesday') Annan. (Or, the critics of the ex-Secretary-General would have it: 'Kofi', equals 'world's-best-paid-bureaucrat', Annan). Pewter had never been present at any of his niece's birthdays, as far as he remembered; and he was suitably guilty; this was overdoing it, he told himself; this wasn't going to work.

Of course it was going to work. So he asked her about the job in London, about her travels elsewhere in the world: they had that in common, a love of travel. (Why didn't his family have a travel agency? The money they'd save. He would write something where a member of the family married into a travel agents' dynasty.)

It's not going to work because remember in that play when the old man in a similar situation sets out a spread for his birthday guests, and waits for them to arrive; and one by one they start to ring up; one had got to the airport at Luton and had forgotten her passport; another one's daughter was taken ill so she had to cancel. Mother and daughter didn't live together and the relationship was strained, but the fact that the daughter suddenly turned to her mother at a time like this meant a thaw in the relationship; so the trip south had to be cancelled. Sorry. And so on and so forth, everyone – in the way of plays – had a credible excuse to decline the party; the old man, in the end, sits down to his sumptuous spread alone. And dies of overeating.

(*Pewter made that last bit up, the dying of overeating.*)

Pewter consoled himself with these facts: he was not an old man, though someone of his niece's age might see him as such. Though the house, the setting for the party, might bear some resemblance to that of the play. (This is the modern gothic, the domestic gothic: see the novels of Lesley Glaister, the Sheffield novelist.) This party wasn't in *his* honour; so the embarrassment of a no-show would be different from the embarrassment incurred at no one showing up at your party.

And of course he had interpreted 'birthday' loosely, a bit like Julius Caesar in that Bernard Shaw play, when he invites Cleopatra to his birthday.

Why did he think that he could strive to be more authentic than the fiction? They had charged him with it, they had accused him. *They.* They had accused him of thinking that he knew it all. They had presented him with the opportunities of fiction and he had declined them – not as being too easy, but as being too convenient. The latest manifestation was in a supermarket in Paris. The Champion, to be exact, in the underground complex at Guy Môquet, not far from his flat, at the corner of Championnet and avenue de St Ouen. He had gone in one Saturday morning – this sort of time, about a year ago, October – to check out the price of a new diary. He was on his way back from Darty, further along the way, with a couple of reams of paper for his printer (really cheap, in Darty) and he called in to the supermarket to see if the '07 diaries were at a price he was prepared to pay; if you hung on for a bit you could get them at another store on the corner for one euro. Today at 3.80 euros he refused to buy. But that was after the incident.

As he went into the shop (with quite a few people about) a yellow-coated attendant – quite a presentable young girl, he had time to determine – was sauntering down the aisle towards him; not particularly eyecatching, at first, but coming along the aisle like . . . And then she got really close and hit him in the stomach.

Well, come on.

Not a glancing blow, but a substantial fist in the stomach. She looked him in the eye, pursed her lips, and continued walking on. (He didn't have a particularly large stomach.)

What do you do? He had fantasized about this sort of thing happening, but here was this young girl knowingly acting it out. She did glance back once, still with that expression.

He thought, to clear his head, he'd press on and find the shelf with the '07 diaries, and when he found they were 3.80 euros, decided not to buy.

He must get her address and invite her out for a drink.

Surely, as in fiction – as in a play – this was the first of three acts. At the end of Act One, i.e., after a coffee at the café on the corner – presumably, during her break – she would agree to meet him at the flat after work. He would hope that she had given him the right telephone number so that if she didn't turn up he could track her down. He would clean the flat, wash up, go to the launderette, tidy the papers, hoover, open the windows to get rid of any cooking smells; and wait. As he waits the curtains would come down on Act One.

Act Two would be the talk scene. She would explain that she really didn't mean to come. It was his scarf and his long coat – somehow un-Parisian – that made her take the chance. Of course she had never done anything of the kind before, never hit a man, never mind a stranger. She just – she didn't know what had come over her: she didn't even calculate whether he would hit her back. She just . . . And now what. 'Now what?' After polite talk about Iraq, and whether Turkey should be allowed to join the EC, now what? Things would be left unresolved at the end of Act Two.

There would be a false start, a misunderstanding; she would leave the flat with neither of them knowing if this was the start of something interesting.

Act Three – after a gap in time – would, of course, take place here, in this house in Montauroux. She would be present at the birthday party for Pewter's niece. She would come down on the train from Paris, and be picked up at Cannes.

And tonight Pewter promised his niece a radical friend from Paris.

*

He knew that his niece didn't think much of him; she was a critic, but at one remove, not hands-on. Y'know, she wasn't like those Baader-Meinhof characters in Germany in the seventies who expressed their frustration with society – with the capitalist system – by turning on their wealthy families, in one case a young woman having her godfather murdered, gunned down in his own house, because he was a banker. *But then again* . . . But no, she wasn't Baader-Meinhof or the Italian Red Brigade, Clara wasn't even an IRA or Muslim bomber; she was a child of West Indian parentage; violent resistance wasn't part of her tradition.

Clara wasn't even like the critic who had had a go at Pewter in public, the one who accused him of pornography because of his supposed obsession with breasts. He had been inclined to brush this aside (killjoys; political correctness) till he chanced to hear a programme on the BBC's *Woman's Hour*. They were dealing with cancer and mainly with breast cancer, with a lot of people who've had the disease coming on to talk about their recovery. Then this woman, very bright and sparky, came on and talked about her double mastectomy, when she was in her early fifties. After the operation the husband was very supportive and moved into the spare room, so as not to disturb her sleep, sort of thing. That was either five years ago or fifteen years ago, and the husband was still sleeping in the spare room, not having touched her sexually since. The woman talked without apparent self-pity, just with a sort of I-hope-I'm-not-exposing-myself-further-with-this-broadcast bafflement. She talked of the erosion of self-confidence as a result, to the point where she could no longer think of herself as a sexual person. In the light of this, Pewter felt ashamed of his focus on breasts in his writing.

*

The house, though, was fine; her friend would have loved it. She chose the middle bedroom because she wasn't sure if this other woman who would be coming down from Paris would be better suited to the master bedroom. She didn't know the state of the woman's relationship with her uncle, whether the woman would be sharing the north bedroom with him.

Also, she decided against taking over the studio, which is where her uncle tended to put people who smoked. Although she smoked, she didn't want him to label her a smoker. He had always called her a Scientist. 'The Scientist in the Family'. Did he know what a scientist was? She didn't want to be put into yet another (family) box that he could dismiss or marginalize. So she opted for the small bedroom in the main house.

*

Even though the table was laid for six or eight people, Pewter took Clara out to the village to dinner. They got appreciative glances from the waiter; it was clear her uncle was showing her off: she didn't mind, particularly; she even had a flicker of sympathy for him: was he as confident and unreachable as he seemed, as he had always seemed? She remembered when she had visited him somewhere in the middle of London when she was little, a part of London where she didn't think members of her family lived, and they looked out of this high window on to the main street below, which was busy, even in the evening; and all she could think to say was: this is the sort of flat where people commit suicide. And he thought that was very funny.

Pewter was trying to disentangle the fact from the fiction. The fiction from the fact. There was this woman in Paris. Right. The woman in Paris was real. Not, of course, the supermarket woman who had punched him in the stomach; that wasn't real; he never saw her again, never had coffee in the café afterwards, etc. But the woman who had stopped him in the street, and had asked some questions, was real. This was in the Marais, an area in Paris where he hoped one day to live. As he emerged from the Métro, from St Paul – he was heading for his favourite bookshop round the corner, the Red Wheelbarrow – as he emerged from the Métro there were these young people doing some sort of street survey, semi-official, with their armbands and clipboards; so he stopped. He stopped because of the woman. Young and pretty and mixed-race. They were concerned about the state of medical provision in France.

But France has the best medical services in Europe. Some say, in the world.

That may be. But look at the people sleeping on the streets.

Yes, the *clochards*, they're a problem. And they talked a bit about the *clochards*.

And visitors to the country, foreigners who lived here, not being registered for treatment.

Ah, that's a . . . that's a big one. Exercising countries other than France.

But something must be done.

Pretty and passionate and young.

A complicated matter, he said.

No, not a complicated matter. We must do something.

Not wanting to be shown up, he promised to think about it; and made his way, sheepishly, to the bookshop a couple of hundred yards away.

And he met her, again, some weeks later; still demonstrating, still pretty and passionate and concerned. You couldn't humiliate yourself by inviting her out. And then he thought. If she was ever in the south of France – for he spent quite a bit of time there these days. If she was ever in the south of France, and she wanted to continue this discussion of how to put the French medical services – and the world – to rights, this is a number she should ring.

And some months later she called the number.

So far Pewter had said little about the woman coming down from Paris.

'So who's this . . . person coming down from Paris, then?'

'Ah! Someone you'll like.'

15

Footprints

(*for Bill Graham*)

I

For all sorts of reasons – taste, distancing, not appearing to tread on tocs, not to appropriate the event – I thought this story should be told in the third person. So, here goes.

Oddly enough, he thought of one of those ads that presidential candidate Reagan ran against his Republican opponent, Bush, in the early days of the 1980 campaign: it was a winter scene and the streets were covered in snow and we had the soundtrack of heavy footsteps squelching through the white vastness; then the camera follows to show that the giant conjured up has left no trace at all in the snow, despite the skis hooked on to the boots: the man (Candidate Bush), who had been director of the CIA, and US ambassador to China and something else of equal magnitude, had left no mark at all in his wake. It was an effective ad and contributed, many think, to Bush losing the Republican nomination that year. This was in Pewter's mind when they went to the clinic to bring Ralph back to the house in Seillans.

You know how it is. There are three of you: your friend who is dying; his (much younger) wife, B, who is accepting of it; and you, not sure whether to put on a show of anger that your friend is missing out. You don't believe in re-incarnation, you don't believe in any kind of afterlife; you are programmed to make the most of this life, and you suspect your friend, who is slipping in and out of con-sciousness – despite the battering of ageing and illness, despite the Irish background, despite the greater long-term certainties of his French (Catholic) wife – would plump for greater fulfilment in this life. (They have three children, a new grandchild; his immortality is secure unless someone chooses to blow up this part of the world; and you have all tried, in your small way, to prevent that happening.)

But there was another sort of immortality that they could point to here, in this (human-scale) world, in this province, and in the neighbouring one. Their friend had built houses. He was an architect who had designed and restored houses in the region and, in that sense, had added something measurable to the landscape. He could claim thirty or forty such mini-monuments over his thirty-five years of building in the region; he had contributed to the, yes, beauty of the French landscape. Prompted a bit by Pewter, but gaining the approval of the wife, the patient agreed to take one last look at some of the structures he had caused to be built. This would, of course, include Pewter's own house of many architects, the house in Montauroux. It was a good deci-sion; our friend perked up; the removal of tubes to parts of his body seemed to have no negative effect.

(This was the sort of compromise that, more or less, satisfied everyone. Pewter privately recalled, some years back, an appearance on British television of the ailing Poet Laureate, John Betjeman, huddled in his wheelchair. What, he was asked, had he missed most in life? He understood the question and smiled shyly. 'Not enough sex,' he said. The interviewer, embarrassed, moved swiftly on to other matters. And now Pewter had a brief and lurid image of golden, firm-bodied youth, lounging around the pool in

Seillans, in Montauroux, and everyone – his friend Ralph, himself, wives and partners – being part of the scene, all in recompense, here, on this earth, for a life underlived. But this was his fantasy, the dream of someone who still felt he had some living to do, some life to catch up on: this probably wasn't the picture of someone who, probably, didn't know they had removed tubes from his arms. This certainly wasn't the image of the young wife who was already beginning to see special signs in the sky – a couple of evenings ago looking out from the terrace of their home, an area where so much of their life was lived [long lunches, dinners, conversation with visitors], looking up and seeing a lone bird flying high overhead, and finding a portent in that. Or in the cloud formations [always in things 'up there'!]. Though sometimes interesting patterns were newly to be observed in the splendid fruit trees in the garden, slowly rearranging themselves. So, looking at splendid dwellings in this or that village, built in materials of earthly substance, materials supplied by entrepreneurs with names like Gaziello and Costamagna, was a good compromise.)

As the day was fine, they drove all the way out to Barge-mon and Claviers, past their own village of Seillans. They stopped for a drink in Bargemon, woke up the patient and suggested a rest in the lovely shaded café in the square, not far from a couple of his architectural triumphs. This was not the old 'tour of inspection'; the buildings were built, occupied, when the owners were in these parts. The days of hanging on to keys, and letting yourself in from time to time to check the property, were over. There was no inten-tion to gain entry, just to take a passing look from the road at something pleasing that he had done, something that had, surely, added to the sum of human pleasure. (The old conversations about violating the landscape, using up the world's resources, putting pressure on the water table, etc., were of the past – or maybe for the future; this was now.) This man's life, then, had made a difference to something more (wider) than family and friends, a difference that didn't strain for metaphysical validation.

At the café, restful – the spaciousness of Bargemon always surprising, pleasantly – they naturally recalled the old times. The village was as unspoilt as ever. A bit too far from the airport, perhaps – though that was partly why it was unspoilt – and from the train station: where would you get off the train for Bargemon? Fréjus? St Raphael? The trains from Paris didn't always stop at these stations, so you might have to push on to Cannes. Or get off somewhere like Toulon. That would be a two-hour drive. As it would be from Cannes. Nevertheless, lovely village, Bargemon. Utrillo-like, in its restfulness. And then – coffee drunk. And chocolate. Water sipped; the water not drunk – how about looking at a villa?

He couldn't shift the mood of – what was it? Lethargy, maybe. It was like reading the big book he was some little way through, and not having the stamina, somehow (the concentration) to push on – all those hundreds of pages to go; and yet it was important to get to the end; indeed, to go through the process with a degree of . . . of renewal and gratitude, yes, as this was better writing than anyone he knew was producing at the moment, and it was brutish to feel that you were doing this out of duty. The sun was shining; he was sitting in his own place; it was a perfect day.

It was stupid to think in terms of betrayal; it was juvenile to talk of a lost opportunity, because his friend had been out of it yesterday, and had spent most of the time in the car asleep; and there would have been no point in bringing him back here to Montauroux to sit beside the pool of a house he might not have recognized. And yet Pewter felt, sitting here, beside the pool, somewhat abandoned.

He was recalling another scene, of another dying man, sitting next to this pool. The man was a distant relative, not someone he was close to. Pewter had offered this treat to the dying man's family as much to put himself in a good light as anything. (This hideaway in the south of France wasn't just for the young and glamorous.) So he could confront that scene with a greater degree of detachment than he felt about his friend, Ralph.

The man must be bloody angry, he remembered saying to himself. Not angry in the normal way; you learn to disguise that: that's part of your socialization. There is a sort of rage that is deeper than anger. Pewter sometimes felt that rage and knew how to disguise it. So as he looked at this dying man, the relative, he was convinced of the rage that refused to declare itself. The features were absolutely without the lift of tension: it took an effort of will to drain your body of that sort of tension. It was like the professional actor (was that what dying in public was?) to relax the muscles, to go with the pull of gravity as if to reverse the fight to evolution. Pewter thought of women and their breasts, which, despite everything, refused to give up the struggle, when signalled otherwise. So he had had another go at reading his guest, the relative: he thought of those old Japanese films of the fifties and sixties where the hero appeared to go with the flow, sometimes for years on end, only to show at the end that the counter-flow was imitating the flow with that posture of acceptance, defeat; the submission was a huge act of mental control. Now, of course, with political correctness, the Japanese are seen to act like everybody else. Enter a young girl in the pool; then observe dying man closely.

Then a light bulb came to the rescue. (It was the middle of the day and the outside light, over the breakfast porch, was on: this is what happens when you're emotionally disturbed and your name isn't Wordsworth: you achieve the opposite of poetry, you descend into banality.) A single light was burning over the long table where, on fine nights, you could assemble up to a dozen guests for supper and put the world to rights. Naturally Pewter thought he had turned off all the outside lights last night. Now he remembered a time, years before, when his friend Ralph had visited, and had noticed that same light burning in the daytime, and had challenged him, in the name of the environment and the conservation of energy, to turn it off. Pewter was pleased with this distraction. He was pleased, too, that this hadn't happened yesterday; if he had brought his friends over; for these things would be read differently. And with B along, small things would acquire significance. He got up, without feelings of guilt, and turned off the light.

*

The trip to Bargemon was not a mistake, for what's a mistake when you're alive, and with friends. The normality of the trip to Bargemon was not a mistake. Parking the car in the main square, Pewter had lingered at the plaque on the wall opposite, the one to Jean Moulin, that he had seen before. Moulin had famously been in the Resistance and had been murdered by the Nazis. Pewter's attempt to resurrect earlier conversations (endlessly at the house in Seillans, round the dining table, or sitting outside on the terrace) excited no interest today. So he did the normal things, went into the little gift shop on the *place*, bought some postcards.

He was himself trying to recover his balance after a most unnerving drive into Bargemon. In the car B, he knew, was not sleeping. They were both in the back. She was not sleeping, but her eyes were closed. You tried not to scan her face in the mirror, for that sort of (healthy) intimacy might seem in bad taste, might suggest that the living were making alliance against someone who . . . Pewter also resisted breaking into her thoughts, for he had no idea what she might be thinking. She was tired, she was exhausted; he suspected it was the sort of exhaustion that precluded sleep. She had nothing to do for a while (she did, afterwards, take the husband to the loo at Bargemon and that took, predictably, a long time) – but her letting go for the duration delivered them both into his hands. That's what the closed eyes signified, that she had let go for a moment, she would be carried along, she would not interfere; she trusted Pewter to drive safely. And yet, and yet . . . how does the mind (it's not blank, it is never blank) – how does the mind not snag on a thought and, despite the owner, hold things up for scrutiny, for reflection?

Is she thinking of the day she had her hair done to visit the clinic? People had remarked on it – as she knew they would. She didn't mean to play the widow before she was a widow. So she made an effort; she had her hair done. Cut, styled and highlighted. The first time in – oh, she didn't know. The response was as she expected, and she didn't trust it. But it made a difference, she could tell, in the way they perceived her husband, related to him, perhaps even the way they treated him. Though he was well treated before that, without that: was she wondering, sitting in the back of the car with her eyes closed, if that had been the right thing to do?

Pewter was conscious of imposing a thought on his passenger; for he suspected that she might be thinking something else; she might be conscious of the tension in his neck and shoulders, however much he tried to disguise it; she must be conscious of his erratic driving; she must be thinking that he was putting them all at risk.

And he was.

*

It was the vertigo thing; he was a sufferer. The down down down descent into this mountain-ravine purgatory seemed to have no end. Even though the tall trees on the precipice side prevented him toppling over, the car stubbornly hugging the middle of the road (thankfully, no traffic coming the other way), this test, by some small god of malice, seemed to have no end. Even with relief at hand – after half an hour? – with a marker saying three km to Bargemon, the downward, winding spiral seemed to go on, terrifyingly, for ever. He was in a panic, of course. His friend was asleep. B, her eyes closed, said nothing. Exhausted? Feeling nothing? Fatalistically, deciding to observe and see what might happen . . . ?

II

Nothing he subsequently said about the experience was right. That you felt as if you were cut off in the middle of a conversation is hardly original. Of course it felt (and feels) like that; but these conversations will be picked up and carried on; and you will adopt the other person's role when it suits you, appropriate his lines, for you own a little bit of him now: maybe that's some form of immortality.

You had been, with him, fond of naming things, which is a game people (maybe men) play. Columbus naming the Indies; Adam naming, naming, naming. On a more localized level, Pewter had been involved in the naming of a university. He had talked about that with his friend – round the dining-room table, or on the terrace outside. They had talked about the naming of the Charles de Gaulle Airport, in Paris; and speculated whether it was wise to have an airport named after someone you admired, because what if a plane crashed there. Joseph Stalin Airport, yes. William Shakespeare Airport, no.

And the friends had disagreed on that, Pewter saying

that the hero should be spared that sort of embarrassment, and should only have his or her name put on something where the failures were less dramatic, longer-term or done by stealth – like a university. So, Marie Curie University, down at the *Ecole de Médecine* (Pierre and Marie Curie); that was OK. But *not* Charles de Gaulle Airport at Roissy; that was not OK.

But these were real conversations, pushed so often to the limits of logic. Airports should be named, yes, after persons, but persons like Jesus Christ and Muhammad. Not that these characters should be held responsible for a possible crash, but that they should be reclaimed by the discourse of logic: if the crash came, there should be no descent into prayer, but the calling up of trained rescue and relief services.

Anyone losing time over prayer would be shot.

(The friends would disagree on this: they often took opposite sides of the argument. One for Aung San Suu Kyi, one for the generals.)

Any bystander at the crash, denying the Enlightenment and confusing the issue with prayer, would be shot. (Another friend, much afflicted, would lay out his pills and medicines, as if they were toy soldiers, next to his half glass of water. There was style in this. Ralph, too, had style, that his friend might emulate.)

Any priest getting in the way of the rescue effort, with prayer, would be shot.

And at some point a lady of the house – B, say – would emerge on the terrace with another bottle of wine, or a pot of coffee, and, playing her part, ask the men not to talk nonsense.

And Pewter must now find another genial layabout to talk nonsense with.

16

Guests

I

'So many people in wheelchairs,' was Nora's greeting on being met in Nice. She'd just come up from Spain, from Andalusia, visiting the sights; but she'd done England prior to that, also visiting family and friends, so Pewter was uncertain whether the wheelchair travellers were located largely in one country, or whether the observation was general. And if so, was there a hint of approval or disapproval in the voice? Pewter couldn't tell; the voice, like the face, gave little away. Anyway, it was good to see her, he said; and he meant it. He complimented her on her (upmarket) bags, hoping he didn't sound patronizing – and he obviously did, because her joke about the bag lady having to demonstrate to the world that she wasn't a bag lady had an edge to it.

So, it was time to head for the hills. 'Unless . . . '

'Is there a problem?'

'Unless you want a snack before . . . It'll be, y'know, the best part of, what, an hour to Montauroux. And something proper. To eat.' (He was thinking ahead; he had overshot the turn-off last time when he had picked up his friends from America who had dropped in after Christmas; and that had added three-quarters of an hour to the journey; not mentioning his embarrassment. The Americans, who claimed to like the diversion, had been good company, bringing the house to life. Nora would be his last guest; he was relieved, for, in reality, Pewter hated these journeys to the airport. So now he must concentrate.)

'I will last,' Nora assured him.

'Good. Because we've got another guest and . . . y'know, dinner together would be . . . It'd be good to have dinner together.'

'I'm like one of those frogs,' Nora was saying, 'that hibernate. Those that go under the ground and hibernate. To conserve the food. The water.'

The image of Nora as something large and froglike momentarily surfaced, and Pewter quickly put it out of his mind. But it persisted. He didn't really know Nora, having met her in the Caribbean, one of the new returnees, on his last visit. She was from Montserrat but living in Dominica at the time; and he liked her style. Like him, she seemed an inveterate traveller, so he had invited her to visit him in France – if she was in the region and he happened to be in residence. It dawned on him now that he didn't really know the woman. So he busied himself with her trolley and headed for the car, which was in the car park.

'You must tell me about Andalusia,' he said.

'Your pronunciation is very good,' she said.

And Pewter thought, This isn't going to be easy.

By the time they got to the Les Adrets turn-off to Montauroux Pewter was ready for it – no veering off to the Esterel today – and Nora, who had dozed off, woke up and apologized: she had stirred during the first stop for the toll, but had settled back to snooze, and Pewter was pleased because he was one of those drivers who preferred not to be distracted by too much conversation while at the wheel.

Pewter assured her there was nothing to see on the autoroute – though it was still light, she hadn't missed anything. But Nora was ready for conversation.

'I think the tolls are a good idea, don't you?' They'd come up against the second lot and Pewter had secured the 50 euros for the dish.

A good idea? Pewter didn't know. They served the pay-as-you-use principle; but then the lorries and vans transporting food also had to pay, adding to the cost of what you bought in the supermarket. In the co-op. He didn't know: he said something to that effect.

And soon he was pointing out the special features of the region, the lake.

'What's it called?'

'St Cassien. Lac de St Cassien.'

Nora repeated the name with something like relish.

And then they came up to the junction, with Montauroux ahead, signposted. (Fayence, etc., to the left, Grasse to the right.)

'Nice-sounding names,' Nora said. 'Montauroux.'

Pewter himself had vaguely liked the sound of Montauroux (though he didn't want to admit too much, as Nora had just come up from Andalusia – Malaga, Cordoba – and might be less impressed with Alpes-Maritimes and Var versions of the exotic than she let on). He suspected that the names, even more than the climate, were part of *his* attraction to the region – a region that, let it be said, voted again and again Front National in presidential (and local) elections. *So was he going to talk now about the aesthetic of names?* In Nora, he seemed to have a fellow 'name fascist': would it affect a child's sense of beauty – of the beauty of creation – if he were, she were, brought up in Mouans-Sartoux, say, rather than in Bridlington? No disrespect to Bridlington, of course.

'Or even Kent.'

Kent? Kent, Pewter didn't know about. Kent put him in mind less of a bland place outside London where bland people are supposed to live, and got their kicks commuting to London – less of that than of a character in *King Lear*. And he was relieved that Nora was too well bred to call him the boring old fart he would have called himself, for coming up with that.

Instead, she asked him about the experience he had had here, some time back, building houses.

'Ah, with the *coopérative*.' He hesitated; people generally asked, but they didn't really want to know. But Nora seemed to be expecting an answer. So he told her about, yes, building in the region.

By now they had gone through the village and were about to turn off into the road that led to the house. He started filling her in on the building of the house, what, eighteen years ago now; but what interested her was the identity of the other house guest.

At the house Simon Hutton was already installed and watching television. That was a slight blow to Pewter's pride, as the television wasn't working when he had left the house, and Simon had clearly got it going. But Pewter was the host, he had to be generous; so he thanked Simon for getting the television going, remembering even to call him Simon, rather than Hutton.

'I take it Roustan didn't come,' he still couldn't help himself asking. Roustan was the man in the village who did odd jobs round the house. He (and his wife) had been doing this since year one, after the first lettings. They, in fact, had had more to do with its general maintenance than Pewter and his partner had.

'No, but . . . I sort of fiddled and . . . somehow, it seemed to get itself going.' He was waiting to greet Nora.

'Nora. Simon.'

'Good trip?' he asked.

'When you're collected at the airport and brought right home, can't complain.'

'I hear you've come up from Seville?'

Before responding to that, Nora generously pointed out a couple of features of the house that struck her; and Simon beamed.

Pewter was pleased they'd hit it off. But he was still miffed by the television. He had been shown how to operate the television by Roustan four or five times, over the years; *but it seemed to get more complicated*. Granted it wasn't the same, original TV set, but the principle was the same, even though now you had *five* sets of controls to service it, *and then you ended up watching Fox News*, if you weren't careful. Nevertheless, Pewter snapped out of it and introduced his guests properly to each other; and then showed Nora to her room upstairs, pointing out the low head-clearance at the turn of the stairs. Then he'd set about heating up the dinner.

They would all be in the main house, occupying the three bedrooms: Nora in the master, with its en suite bathroom; Pewter in the north bedroom at the other end; and Simon in the smaller one in the middle. Simon and Pewter would share the bathroom and (separate) loo. Pewter had thought of assigning Simon to the studio, which was a separate self-contained building, on the other side of the pool: it was spacious, with all the cooking and bathroom facilities, big fridge, etc., only lacking a television. But Pewter thought putting Simon there might be interpreted as isolating his guest, separating him from the main action, so to speak. And Simon's room, though small, was pleasant, with a high ceiling – sloping, but the overall effect was of a high ceiling – and it overlooked the pool. Though, of course, it was too cold for swimming in December. January. Simon had pronounced himself happy with the arrangement. The sensitivity in dealing with Simon Hutton was because this house was originally his; and though invited back early on, he hadn't taken up the offer until now.

Initially, the place had been a ruin, a farmer's cottage; and there were scrapbooks somewhere showing the process of conversion – demolition, renovation, rebuilding. Simon and his business partner had bought the property, constructed the ground-floor unit and then had run out of money. More importantly, perhaps, they had fallen foul of the planning authorities (who had demanded changes in design of a house half-built) *and* had run out of money. Enter Pewter and *his* business partner, with a local Irish architect as go-between. And yes, they did get it for a good price.

So, here was Simon, first time back, second day back, demonstrating to Pewter how to operate a television that had, one way or other, been in Pewter's possession for eighteen years.

That was the second mini-humiliation of the day for Pewter. Earlier, he had made a fool of himself in trying to get to an arts foundation in the region. It was some place he had vaguely wanted to visit and, as it was on Simon's agenda, he had offered to take Simon there. Simon doubted they would be able to do it and leave time for Pewter to get back to go to Nice to pick up Nora: why not go straight to the airport from the arts foundation, which was in the vicinity of Nice? But no, Pewter felt that would be an imposition on Simon: he had his own schedule – and his own hire car; he didn't come here to pick up Pewter's guests.

The point is Pewter had got the location of the foundation wrong, thinking it was just a few kilometres away on the other side of the lake: instead of St Paul en Fôret their destination would be the somewhat more distant St Paul de Vence. So here was Simon, who had no stake still in the region, having a clearer view of its layout than Pewter, who had been paying taxes here for eighteen years. So they decided to put off the trip for later and, better still, take Nora along with them, giving her the option. The men went out to lunch, to a restaurant in the village they both knew, determined to be generous to each other.

There was something about Simon that kept Pewter on his toes, the knowingness of someone who didn't behave as a visitor; even the way Simon picked up local publications in the village, in the *boulangerie*, later to study the contents – poring over the '*petits annonces*' in *ParuVendu* and *Topannonces,* suggesting someone topping off the furnishing of his house rather than a visitor on the lookout for a property. Was he being oversensitive about Simon because other things weren't going smoothly? Last night, for instance, he had been given such a hard time trying to confirm his return – from Paris to London – by Eurostar. Every number he rang was wrong; and when he eventually got through to the right one, they refused to take his Maestro card. Naturally, he declined Simon's offer to use *his* card and settle later. Pewter hoped it was things like that that were making him edgy, rather than a deeper defensiveness about the house. He had prepared a list of things that had gone wrong with the house during the building; maybe a dozen or so things that he felt at some point he would have to own up to because, really, Simon, having initiated it all – and a student of architecture – would be on the lookout for his successors cutting corners.

First of all there was the staircase. It's not that it was a problem; there was no case that he knew of, in all the years that the house had been built, of anyone bumping their head while going up or down the stairs. There was just one point, at the turn, where you had to be careful: you didn't even have to bend your head; you just didn't have to lean back (or forward, if you were coming down) at that point; and then you'd be OK. But, clearly, it was a design fault that should be owned up to. There was a sign, a warning. But it was inelegant. It would have been quaint in an old building. But in a (virtually) new building –

officially, a renovation, nine-tenths new – it was a design fault.

His explanation to people was this: this was 'The House of Many Architects'. Just about everyone around claims to have had a hand in its making. Simon's original design was for a central, spiral staircase, a sweep that, to Pewter's mind, suggested Hollywood of an earlier period; and he wasn't that unhappy to be rid of it. The town planners had, of course, forced the issue. The Irish architect had chipped in with Plan B (Plan B or C or D); and if you were a tall person you'd have to bend your head at one point coming down the stairs. Or going up the stairs. *Would Simon take any responsibility for this design fault?* Last night he had been in a mood to minimize the problem.

Apart from the stairs, what else? There were other minor 'faults' that Pewter would be happy to admit to. The fireplace had tended to smoke before the latest closed-in-by-a-glass-box solution. Not ideal, from Pewter's point of view, but better for the client. Safer, too. The fireplace was built by Muhammad, 'our man from Tunisia', the last thing done, late into the night, the two of them, as Pewter had to return to England next day. Simon knew Muhammad, who had worked with him on the original structure. Muhammad had worked on private projects for the Irish architect, way back since Ralph had left the *coopérative;* Pewter knew him from those days. So Pewter would be careful to take responsibility for the failures of the original fireplace and not implicate Muhammad. Talking of faults, the latest they could blame on France. This was the fencing of the pool, the security fence round the pool. The house (in Simon's time) having fallen foul of the French legal temper, the present owners had no intention of drawing further attention to themselves by ignoring this new ruling designed to protect tenants and their children. Roustan, with the help of Pewter's business partner, had concocted something that, to Pewter's eye, looked rather good. If he had a problem it was in their not taking on the French, as some English residents in neighbouring villages had done; and ignoring the *dictat* from Paris. But the result was fine. The ironwork at the front surrounds, the shallow end, gleamed white and clean, in no sense an eyesore; and the green chicken wire containing the rest could barely be seen against all the greenery of the terraces. So he wasn't going to be defensive about this with Simon. They could blame the French together.

What threw him off guard last night, what made him think that Simon might be playing some sort of game, was Simon's extravagant praising of all the incidental things: the leaf-like metal surrounds on the locks of the main doors, the light fitting in the lounge ceiling – that, after giving him a lecture on the treatment of the white pine in the grounds, oozing some sort of disease. And yes, the light fitting *was* a work of art, why not? Even if it put Simon in mind of this or that installation in some faraway gallery. It didn't escape Pewter that this man was checking up on him.

Nora had had the more obvious response on coming into the house for the first time. She admired the mixture of old and new, the *rustique* stone wall from an older structure incorporated into the new building; the stone 'sculpture' growing out of the floor at the far side of the fireplace, the top chiselled off to make a table; the dramatic back wall arrangement with its alternating working alcoves and light wells and cave set into the exposed rock of the terrace. And lit.

Though the light fitting that Simon flagged *was* tasteful in a minimalist sort of way, and being white against the white ceiling added to its 'clean' look. But Pewter hadn't fitted it; the house had undergone the usual transformations during its eighteen years. So this replacement may have come from his business partner, or from Roustan himself.

Though he doubted whether Roustan would have chosen so tastefully.

So Pewter was wary of Simon. He accepted praise for the light fitting and braced himself for criticisms to come.

He recalled the day they decided to buy the half-finished building. Pewter had been staying with his architect friend in nearby Seillans, and they set out to see the bargain. On the way to Montauroux they ran into Muhammad outside the café in Fayence. He was still on Ralph's books, and was considered a very good builder. Ralph used to say that it was only the usual French racism that had prevented people like Muhammad setting up their own business enterprise. The French wouldn't employ an Arab, however well qualified, to design their villas. But there were lots of foreigners, of course, building in the region.

Anyway, Muhammad had worked on the house in Montauroux, so it would be useful to have him along. It occurred to Pewter that Muhammad didn't look much older than the last time he had seen him, or even than he had done in the seventies, but he censored the thought as racist. In truth Muhammad was bowed; he was always bowed, but now he was definitely more stooped, and Pewter was pleased to register that. Now he could bring back details like the family back in Tunisia, the house built there within view of a college, the proximity of house and college a source of pride.

Muhammad was West Indian in that respect; in island after Caribbean island the 'returnees' would sit on their newly built terraces and point out the surrounding villas owned by 'doctors' and other professionals. But particularly the doctors. He would have to write a play about the doctor as a neighbour, the cries for help coming from the house at night, a woman, women, in distress, and no one intervening, no one *hearing*, because the woman's cries were issuing from the house of a doctor.

But Muhammad was still here in France, his family still in Tunisia (cruel and unusual punishment?): would he have acquired a separate Christian family here in France?

Pewter's fascination with Muhammad began to fade as the builder cheerfully ridiculed the house Pewter was being induced to buy. It was the fault of the owners, he said: they were rich people from England who didn't know what they were about. They kept changing their minds about everything. First they wanted the staircase here, then they wanted it there; then they wanted the ceiling this high, then again they wanted it that high; he was only the builder, he built what they asked him to build, *ce pas grave.*

Pewter, without criticizing Ralph, wanted to know what the architect had been doing all this time. *And* Ralph explained that the owners had had ideas of building the house themselves, and he'd just offered his professional services, to give the whole thing legitimacy. To get past the Circumlocution Office that was French bureaucracy.

Pewter also had ideas about building the house himself, to put his experience of having worked with the *coopéra-tive* to the real test; so he was with the funny foreigners on this one.

They were English people, Muhammad said; they were mad.

So what went wrong?

They went ahead without planning permission and then had planning permission refused.

Ralph confirmed that they were unlucky in that respect. Probably subject to a bit of French xenophobia. As Muhammad said, some English people were innocents in France.

Also, it was two of them, said Muhammad; they had different ideas.

The structure looked raw and wounded. Pewter didn't like the look of it. He said his business partner would have to come down and see it before they could make a decision. You didn't quite trust someone who abandoned a house they were halfway through building. More to the point, you didn't lightly take on a project that had been denied planning permission: it smacked of something any sane person would run a mile from. So why did his friend Ralph think Pewter was mad? Also, he remembered from his time with the *coopérative* how relatively lax building regulations were in France. They, the members, the workers, used to protest about it; they were very idealistic in those days, arguing with the expensive architects from Paris and wherever why this or that German banker or American arms dealer or film-maker couldn't just come here and violate the French landscape. There was an illustration of architectural madness that they witnessed on the road when they went back and forth to Seillans, Ralph's village. Coming back into Fayence you couldn't miss it; it was just above the bend in the road where you had to slow right down; and there above was this huge folly; a near-completed mansion, three, maybe four storeys high, abandoned for what must be ten years now. Why? Because it was built on solid rock (biblical?) and they couldn't put in the septic tank, the loos. The abandoned house in Montauroux began to take on the colour of that image for Pewter. Nevertheless, he agreed to think about it. And talk to his potential business partner back in England.

And they liked to eat, Muhammad said.

Who? What's he talking about?

The mad Englishmen who had abandoned their half-built house. They would make big barbecues in the middle of the day, lots of meat. Or drive into the village and have a sit-down lunch in a restaurant. Naturally, the casual workers didn't like to work when the owners were away, eating. And they didn't speak French; so they got ripped off in the shops. All the suppliers double-charged them for things like sand and cement and *poutrelles*.

And when Pewter had decided to buy and met Simon Hutton in London, the man seemed to confirm everything Muhammad had said. Simon had taken him to a restaurant near his flat in Bayswater. It turned out he was a college lecturer in – was it Kilburn or Willesden? But tonight he was talking food. Food and art, which were not the subjects he taught. He presented himself as a man well travelled, having been to Antigua and Barbados, his pronunciation of Barbados – different from the people who lived there – registering with Pewter. But when he went on talking about travelling in France and Italy it sounded as if he were an architectural groupie. He had done the pilgrimage of the Le Corbusier buildings. But not just Corb. He talked of a famous Sterling building in Stuttgart, features of which he had planned to incorporate into the house in Montauroux. While he talked, Pewter was thinking that Muhammad had got the man right. But, as if sensing something on Pewter's part, Simon brought the conversation smartly down to practicalities. But he gave a promise: just because he couldn't manage to complete the house, it didn't mean he didn't want somebody else to share the vision. His business partner had pulled out; you liked a man, of course, but you couldn't legislate for nerves. *Hélas.* The promise sounded like a warning.

As they worked through the meal (Simon had curried mixed grill, Pewter had prawn and something), and Pewter admitted his own foray into building with the *coopérative* in the Alpes-Maritimes, the conversation turned back to architectural matters, to Le Corbusier: not so much the vaunted Pavillon Suisse, in Paris, which Simon agreed was a little 'picturesque': his favourites were the Maison du Salut in some place that Pewter didn't catch, and the Villa something somewhere.

And here was Simon, eighteen years later, still pulling rank.

He's checking the place out, the bastard. Pewter watched him early this morning, doing the rounds, as if the work was still in progress and he was doing a tour of duty. It was the attitude of a man who would use the phrase 'tour of duty'. He knew Hutton's air of contentment, of playing the appreciative guest last night, was too good to be true. He's only been here a day and has already used up the positives. *The fitting in the lounge ceiling, my arse.* This pose of praising anything but real success of the house extended even to the village. He was impressed at the new aspect of Montauroux, which was much expanded. Instead of the old scattered look, semi-sheltered, the village now imposed itself on the hillside.

'And halfway down. Nearly all the way down.'

'Quite. Smart villas at the bottom, where the caravan site used to be.'

'I'd forgotten about the caravan site,' Pewter admitted.

It now looked, he said, like a village farther south; in Greece, maybe. The white look, all those clean façades. So different from the old Provençal artists' model villages, brown and russet, Cézanne-like. Villages like Cabris over in the Alpes-Maritimes.

And then Hutton had complimented Pewter on the road into the property.

That was ridiculous. The surface was prey to the weather. Early on, a client had complained that the road had done something or other to the sump of his precious car.

But no, Hutton wasn't talking road surface, he was talking design. Landscape design. The new route to the house, he said, making it altogether more cosy, less exposed. Pewter had half forgotten that they had rerouted the road. Originally, you approached the property full on, the front door (set back four or five terraces) lining up with the way in. But they had carved a new road along the lowest terrace – the terrace earmarked for the tennis courts, a plan early abandoned – and planted a hedge of cypress and whatnot for privacy. The hedge had surprised them with its almost indecent growth so that now Roustan had a continuing battle to keep it down. So, yes, the lack of tennis courts was something he had already apologized to Simon for: he had used his standard joke that instead of being in the Var the property (forgetting the pine and oak; and olives) could pass for an accountant's hideaway in darkest Hertfordshire.

So, would he like to see the studio?

But this morning Simon had the air of a man who had done the praise thing, and had decided that he had lost out on the transaction, and was giving himself cause to brood. He stood for a long time at the edge of the pool, contemplating it. Nothing to fault there. Pool, by general consent, one of the most interesting in the region, 'overdesigned' (by Muhammad and Pewter), muttered the architect. It took the contours of the original pond, respecting past usage. So he stood there behind the grille. He had already commended the dwarf palm, planted that first year, still less than a man's height. And yesterday they had agreed that the grille was tasteful; the verticals and diagonals – the spaces in between – making a sort of harmony that even 'Corbusier' Hutton acknowledged to be pleasing. *It was attractive to look at.*

After the pool Hutton took a walk straight down the ground, down the broad terraces, to the non-existent tennis courts. He observed the oliviers and other fruit trees – and the stumps of the tall pines they had had to cut down, because of the disease – and turned round and came back, tour of duty done.

Watching him, Pewter had a sense of his own fall from grace. Standing at his window in the north bedroom, looking down on all this, he's taken back to other scenes. He's in Gloucester Road in the sixties. London. 100 Gloucester Road, just along from the tube station. Top floor. Sharing with two friends, a woman and a man. It's 1968. Maybe 1969. Or 1970. (He's reading Elias Canetti's *Auto-da-Fé* – Canetti has just won the Nobel for literature – *she* (an Australian) is reading Patrick White's *Voss*. And *he* – who knows? He may have been introducing them to decent popular music.)

And one Sunday afternoon she comes to Pewter's room. 'Come and look at this,' she says. He, the other man, has already been summoned. And they go to the kitchen window to look down on a neighbour – a man in his thirties? – looking down on a woman dressing. At her dressing table; her body exposed. The voyeur is in a different building from her. Pewter and company are in a different building from them. It is all so tastefully done. The voyeur is not exactly hiding, but he is discreet. As if he's less embarrassed to be looking on than to be sensitive that *she* should be gazed at in a way that is not sleazy. And the trio looking down from their vantage point in the kitchen, curious and fascinated. And she, the flatmate, says:

'Funny, eh? Here's him seeing it all. And most likely she'll spend all night with *her* guy, preventing him getting a look.' After which the three returned to whatever they were doing.

And here is Pewter, X years later, looking down on Simon Hutton, thinking how to justify himself. And it's intolerable: within minutes Pewter finds some evidence that is actually *damning*. Another little bit of vulgarity thrown in his face. Opening the door from the kitchen area downstairs to the porch reveals, normally, the picture-postcard scene that sets up breakfast: long, highly varnished table under its awning partly framed by a healthy grapevine (in summer); and a giant fig tree, *en face*. The sunshine even in winter allows you to breakfast here. Certainly, to have lunch. A pleasant place to sit all year, casually in touch with people in the pool, etc. At one end is a barbecue and a pizza oven. (So the oven was a mistake, a Roustan addition, substitute for Pewter's original wood oven idea, but that's another argument.)

The new outrage today is the bit of vandalism between the step up to the kitchen and the level of the patio. It wasn't there on Pewter's last visit to the house two years ago. There is a new row of tiles, aslant – as if to make entrance by wheelchair easy? – *in a different colour*. The floor tiles are provincial rust, as are those of the step. The patio tiles are an edge-of-the-pool cream. The new line of tiles linking the two *is a different colour again*, something between the two: *what is the meaning of this?* In addition to this architectural insult, the surface of the new tiles is smooth. Both other surfaces are *grained*. He must apologize, he must apologize to our man from Bayswater, our man from Kilburn.

III

No more Mr Niceguy. Niceguy one word. So no more Mr Niceguy. Dixon's has got to go. Dixon's in Sheffield. Taken out. Vanished. Made to vanish. To disappear. No nonsense. I've had enough of this shit. No namby-pamby liberal nonsense here. This is *personal*. This is an appropriate response to massive anger. *They've* got to go. Granted we're all inhibited after the London bombings. Who can even *think* of blowing things up now. *And I wish you, dear London bombers, the sweetest, slowest tortures in your respective hells. Amen. For ever and ever. Long life to the police.* But to come back to Dixon's. The man who sold me the computer – *some sort of throwback from the sixties, something about him, the runt, bearded* – he can't be allowed to get away with it. So he'll take the building with him when he goes. The morals of a slug. OK, I can't emulate him, must do better: others must be saved. Others of the workforce. The anonymous others. Particularly the woman who helped me, talked me through the machine when I took it back next day. That's always the case, I suppose. There's the old story about Guy Fawkes and Parliament, rumbled when he tried to warn someone the night before from going into Parliament next day. But never mind. The big-arsed girl who helped me must be saved. Not very nice to be referred to as the big-arsed girl, but there it is; that's something we live with: we've all had to live with what biology decrees. And to be a big-arsed girl in Sheffield isn't the worst. And you will be saved, my darling, for taking me through the intricacies of the computer. *What of the ethics of blowing up that unsavoury man and his beard?* my friends will ask. And I ask it, too. I don't need friends to ask it. Forget about the business of collateral damage for a minute. OK, a bit hard to ask that of the people in Chechnya, or the people of Iraq. (What do you make of a country ending in 'q'?) They wouldn't understand that proviso. Forget about collateral damage. What about others of the workforce? Forget about that for the moment and think of the act of violence, violence on that scale. That is, on the scale of the little man beating his wife, his woman, in the torture chamber of a domestic home – on that scale, say, of one to five thousand, *that Dixon act against me is five thousand* . . . And another thing, remember we're all censored. So must we censor ourselves since the London bombings? I say no. Long life to the police.

So what did he do, this throwback from the sixties?

I failed to answer that question satisfactorily once, at a party in Golders Green, in the late 1950s: someone else got the girl. I failed to answer it in various places I should forget, recently, indeed, at Cambridge. Someone else got the fellowship. Don't divert me into confession. Into regret. Let's just say – let's keep it light, let's keep it at the level of revenge and violence: the throwback sold me a computer, a laptop – this one, in fact; I'm using it for the first time. I'm in the north bedroom trying to get something down. It's late. Simon and Nora have gone (separately) to bed. I want to write up something of the day. And what's coming over is not a report of a pleasant outing, but a feeling of incompetence. Of humiliation. Decline of powers. Losing grip. *Rage.* So on top of everything this man, this throwback in Sheffield, sells me a computer as a bargain in the sales (is £500 for a laptop a bargain in the sales?) – sells me *a machine where the disk is not compatible with all my other disks. I am here, away from my desktop machine, here with the forest of Montauroux for company, and my machines are not compatible.* My lives again don't fit, and Dixon will pay for this. For things have consequences.

So Pewter ran through, again, all the things that were wrong with the house. The staircase. The fireplace that used to smoke. The studio beautiful and 'surprisingly spacious, the blue-grey tiling in the bathroom area particularly pleasing', *but* built into the terrace and without enough natural light: so a skylight would do it. The fenced-in pool. Inadequate soundproofing in the main house. (We're not retired people, this isn't a retirement home, *we needn't all go to bed at the same time and turn down the music, etc.*) Overdesign of the pillars in the main house (Hutton). Lack of tennis courts. So Federer won't now visit. *Will we have to settle for Posh Spice?* And, of course, the latest outrage of the nonsense between patio and kitchen area. *Would these things hold up the progress of democracy in China?* He might have a debate on his hands.

*

The trip to the Maeght Foundation had gone well, Simon driving, Nora in front and Pewter behind, a reversal of role of host and guest which seemed to put everyone at ease; for, in a way, the Maeght was Simon's gift, he claiming, even, to be a member of the organization, paying a small annual fee for the privilege. Everyone got into the spirit of the outing, taking out maps, discussing this or that route to St Paul de Vence. It was Nora, looking at an enlarged map of the Grasse area, who remarked on the obvious, the sort of thing that a visitor picks up.

'So many saints.'

And when you looked at the placenames on the map, yes, there they were: St François and St Jacques and St Claude (St *Claude?*). Then there was St Antoine and St Mathieu.

'And up here at the top, St Jean. And look. St Marc.'

Nora decided that France was a Catholic country.

After the Maeght Foundation they decided to do their own thing for the rest of the afternoon. They had had a good lunch in St Paul and when they got back to the house Nora decided to have a rest. (The feature of the lunch at St Paul wasn't so much the meal as the loo. After use, the loo seat revolved while it cleaned itself. Simon was impressed with it, and drew Pewter to have a look – 'like a Chagall joke'. Nora, apparently, had encountered it elsewhere.) Back home Simon and Pewter went their different ways, Simon to look at a ruin in a neighbouring village and Pewter up to Cabris, his favourite hilltop village in the Alpes-Maritimes, where he had lived for a while in the 1970s, to visit an old friend from those days, someone who had seen in the New Year with him and the Americans, in the house. The vague arrangement was that Pewter would be back in time to make dinner – which wouldn't be too early, as they had had a big lunch. But just in case, there was lots of stuff in the fridge.

When he got back from Cabris, a little later than expected, Pewter immediately noticed a change of atmosphere in the house; you could tell that the feeling of buoyancy evident during the trip to St Paul de Vence had vanished. Pewter couldn't imagine what had taken place between his guests. Simon was fiddling with the television controls, switching from programme to programme, still not being able to get past the five or so French channels to the satellite menu. He seemed to be doing this more or less mechanically. (Taking responsibility for things, Pewter confirmed that he had asked a young lad from Seillans, son of the architect, to come and take a look at it tomorrow, because Roustan couldn't work it out.)

Nora was standing at the bookshelf end of the dining area, not really surveying the books, seeming to engage Simon with talk about feet. The terms 'podiatrist' and 'reflexology' were thrown out and commented on, but this was strained, polite dialogue, the sort of thing you associated with an English middle-class domestic scene when everyone is mad at everyone else, but refusing to have a row. The thought did cross his mind that Nora had herself been married into a very middle-class-sounding English family. So was the talk between these two medical or sensual? Had Simon had a go at Nora? Had Nora had a go at Simon? Wasn't Simon reputed to be gay? They were being scrupulously polite and making visitorly chitchat. Pewter decided the thing to do was to play the host and start making supper. He thanked Simon, again, for getting something out of the television. (There was a programme on Mitterrand – ten years after his death – that he would have liked to see, but it was on another channel; never mind.) He suggested that Nora look through the tapes on offer, and put some music on the sound system, while he set about making supper.

There were lots of videotapes to choose from – some

left by previous tenants – the usual films: *The Postman; Howards End; Remains of the Day;* a couple of Jane Austens; *The Merchant of Venice* . . . and, at the other end, *Seven Brides for Seven Brothers; My Stepmother is an Alien; Robin Hood;* etc.

This occasioned enough covering conversation to ease the atmosphere. In the end Nora decided on some music. There were lots of audio discs – maybe a couple of dozen – and she plumped for some Vivaldi (Masters of Classical Music Series), the calm and lightness strangely right for the occasion. Pewter agreed with Simon that the Vivaldi was like a musical equivalent to Utrillo's restful churches and squares. That did the trick. Nora and Simon joined Pewter in the kitchen area, with Simon doing the drinks; and someone initiated random talk about Bush and Blair, while they busied themselves with the cooking.

Over dinner Simon praised the studio.

Pewter said it was built into the terrace to conform with planning laws, the entrance looking like a garage. The first suggestion had been to put it at the bottom of the pool; but the water . . .

Nora said visitors would never know the original site intended. So they accepted a thing where it was.

True, if Paris were X kilometres further north or east, everyone would still accept it as Paris. Athens, the same.

Nora hadn't yet seen the studio but would take a look tomorrow.

Pewter said there was no problem with ventilation, only natural light.

A perfect writer's cabin, Simon said; rather than an artist's studio. Not an *atelier*.

Though some *ateliers* are pretty dark; all those old men carving bowls and whatnot from olive.

During this conversation Pewter was trying to hold in his head a thought sparked earlier by their talk of moving a built object from one place to another; the studio. Paris. What was the city; was it its geography or its history? He would have a go at teasing this out on his computer later.

So what was that all about, then. Pewter thought back to the trip to St Paul de Vence, to the Maeght Foundation. They had got there without mishap, Simon driving. They had taken the route through Grasse (perfume town: Fragonard, Molinard, Galimard; something of the place still smelt of jasmine). Pewter told a story of someone he knew working in the industry, in the 1970s. A 'nose'. The nose was the Napoleon of perfume workers. This young nose was married to the sister of a friend of his in Spéracèdes, over in the Alpes-Maritimes; and one day he walked into the branch office and demanded a 100 per cent rise. So valued is the 'nose' that not only did he get his 100 per cent rise but was promptly transferred to head office in Geneva, where he and his young wife lived sumptuously for maybe a couple of decades before moving on to America and then back home. Nora wanted to know more about the perfume business, the gathering of the jasmine, etc., and Pewter obliged. Though of course, he admitted, all that stuff was in the past. Even in his earlier time down here they'd stopped paying the Arabs a pittance to pick the jasmine, and the perfume was being made up in laboratories in Japan. Or wherever.

So, from Grasse, they had got through to Vence and on to St Paul; the Foundation was well signposted. Everyone had entered into the spirit of the occasion – Simon driving, Pewter telling stories and Nora and Simon swapping tales of Andalusia. And here they were admiring the sculpture garden at the entrance, the Mirós and Arps, and even more the extraordinary monumental figures at the back. Not forgetting the Giacometti garden. Simon talked them knowingly through the visually arresting Braque and Miró lithographs (Pewter noted Simon's pronunciation of Braque, one and a half syllables, so *knowing*), their bright colour and playfulness, the Braque pieces reminding Nora of the pre-Columbian ceramic collection of a friend of hers at home, whose father had been a museum curator.

At one point Simon overreached himself somewhat by pointing out how the floor tiles in the *Salle de Miró* almost echoed, in terracotta, the playful sinuousness of the Miró on the walls. But then they discovered that the tiles were common to all the main rooms, so the others had to protect Simon's feelings after that. Even when Nora made a mild criticism of the endless steps to get about, the lack of consideration for wheelchair users – this was in the village – Simon agreed in good spirit, not thinking his 'place' was being criticized.

So what was the cause of this mood last night? They had done a tour of the village, St Paul, after the Foundation, Pewter noting that James Baldwin had lived here. The village was impressive ('the ultimate Provençal village') but a bit overgentrified for Pewter. He was careful not to criticize what he saw as the plasticky effect of endless art galleries with nothing much in them you'd want to hang on your walls, to put in your house, because everything seemed one stage removed from the 'art', the '*atelier*'. He didn't push the point because both Simon and Nora loved the village – and he loved it too, except it seemed a bit fake. And certainly, by the time they got home, they were still full of their purchases, postcards of some of the Giacometti etchings for Simon, a colourful Maeght carrier bag for Nora (a present from Pewter: she bought postcards for herself) and a book of the Foundation (in English) and a silk scarf to which Pewter treated himself: it had been a successful outing.

And with Simon out of the way, would Nora solve the puzzle? They were having a late breakfast inside. Pewter had done a bit of work on his new computer. Simon had gone off to view something somewhere on the other side of Fayence; and Pewter and Nora were at breakfast. (Nora had to leave next day, so they wanted her to see something more of the region; maybe a trip down to Cannes.)

'So what was that all about? Last night,' he asked.

'It was nothing personal,' Nora said, confirming that it *was* personal.

The story was that Simon had felt marginalized in the house.

Nora stopped Pewter's protests. Pewter repeated that the house was not Simon's house.

It was nothing like that. It was more that Simon felt he had been written out of the story. 'Out of the narrative of the house.' (*What subject did this man teach?*) Then Nora explained. When Pewter had gone off to Cabris yesterday afternoon, Nora and Simon had been looking through bits and pieces of literature that were lying around in the lounge area, including a diary of praise from satisfied customers. Then they'd come across a scrapbook charting the progress of renovation of the house; lots of photos and captions and dates. Pictures of Pewter. Pictures of Pewter's business partner. Pictures of the Irish architect. Pictures of other people, all in photo shots, photo-call-like shots: someone holding a shovel next to a pile of cement; or a trowel against what must be a newly plastered wall; or with a paintbrush and smiling for the camera. Or pushing a wheelbarrow; or posing against a car. Dozens of photos – three books of them. But no Simon, no Muhammad. The pictures were all carefully dated, starting the year after the first bit of the house was built. Simon had left a full photo record of that stage – the first year – of the house; and of that there was no trace. The editing out of that stage of the house – from farmer's low-ceilinged cottage to first floor – was something that had sent Simon into a sudden gloom that Nora had tried to lift him out of.

Pewter hadn't looked at the scrapbooks in years. And when he glanced at them he was surprised at the editing. But then he'd suffered something of the same fate himself. He remembered being here once with his business partners and a couple of their friends; and one of the visitors – a woman he didn't much like because she seemed to have a sense of ownership of the house, having visited it before, and a way of treating *him* as the visitor – indeed, came right out and asked if he was coming here for the first time. His partners didn't have the presence of mind to inform their friends that their holiday was, in part, in Pewter's gift. So, in a sense he could see Simon's point. (As it was, he wasn't the one to put the scrapbook together; but he wouldn't seek to wriggle out of it that way.)

*

They visited Ralph, the architect, in Seillans, together. He was the main architect of the House of Many Architects and, though recently retired, was, in an unofficial way, trying to find an affordable property in the region for Simon. It was good, congenial company, some young people, grown-up children of the house – including the young man who would fix Pewter's television – and their friends.

The conversation was to do with building, yes, but also with painting and travel. Andalusia was much praised; and there was talk of what Europe had missed with the defeat of the Moors in 1492. The name Roustan came up, and Pewter had to admit that he used the term as a sort of composite, or generic Provençal name; and it wasn't the real name of the man who looked after the house. Talking of Roustan, there was their friend, an architect in Seillans (another of the architects of the House of Many Architects) who had unfortunately died. And there was his mother, Madame Roustan, who had been mayor of Montauroux.

There was much talk of other Roustans, unrelated to the Roustans that they knew.

There were lots of people at the table, and during all this talk Pewter could hear Nora having a private conversation with the architect's wife about meditation and yoga. And Simon, restored with talk about art and ruins, seemed back to his old self without need of Pewter's prepared apology for having written him out of the narrative of the house.

Do stories have a coda? There is a moment when tension falls away and complaining stops. And this is the moment, as I sit in the plane at Nice, to Charles de Gaulle. The buoyancy isn't because we are airborne, which we're not yet; though the applause might have something to do with it. We ended up at the wrong terminal and naturally took a wrong turning on the way back to Terminal 2. We get there just in time (too late, really), but seeing our state of dishevelment, the woman at the easyJet counter decides to accept our luggage and warns us that boarding begins now. But we have to return the hire car to Avis. (I have a passenger with me. Not Nora. Not Simon; they've already gone.)

My partner takes the car to the Avis booth and car park. I deal with the bags. I then head for the car park. We have no time to sort out petrol or anything. They've got my address. In Paris. In Sheffield. We *run* back to boarding and are late. (I have a vulgar hope that with our bags on the plane, they might wait a few minutes rather than unload them.) With good-humoured finger-waving they let us through and on to the plane. I hear cheering; it's for my partner gone on ahead.

When I enter the plane I get the same treatment. Three waves of cheers from the entire plane. It's good-humoured, their irony. They have had a good time in the south of

France. Or they are looking forward to Paris without dread. Their generosity: what can I give them in return? I know.

I will let go of my little resentments. I will show that I, too, can be generous. (The mother of a friend of ours, here in this region, near death, called her family together in Seillans and said to them: 'I bequeath you my horizons.' Very French; but who could better that?)

So, yes, I can enter into the spirit of giving. I can say to my bearded man in Sheffield, the man at Dixon's: you are reprieved. All are reprieved. Roustan is reprieved. As are Simon and business partners and the people at Eurostar who wouldn't accept my Maestro card. As this must mean something, not quite all are reprieved. Some world leaders are not reprieved. Child murderers and abusers and wife batterers are not reprieved. The blowers-up of London are not reprieved.

Also unreprieved are those who would make me a stranger in my own home, in any of the places I call home. In this or that house or country. Indeed, in the world. But apart from these small caveats, all are reprieved.

PART THREE

In This or That
House or Country

17

The Brothers Stapleton

I

Eugene-who-has-no-play-written-about-him, unlike the no-hopers like Henry IV (Pirandello), or the Emperor Jones (O'Neill. *Ah. Eugene* O'Neill), or, for that matter, the lesser Shakespeare – King John; Henry VI – Eugene, my brother, didn't ring me on this occasion.

Jennifer, his wife (whose name, today, is Rachael, to conceal her identity), phoned to say she was leaving my brother because of his obsession with Stalin. Well, what was one supposed to say to that? We weren't on that sort of intimate wavelength, Rachael and I; we didn't exchange confidences, particularly; even our visits to each other's homes were sporadic; and that was when I lived in England; so my own visits were – I nearly said hit-and-run: I didn't mean quite that. Of course my first response to Rachael's announcement was – ungenerous, perhaps – my first response was: well, at least, that's not the usual reason people give for breaking off a long-term relationship, for breaking up a long-distance marriage: an obsession with Stalin seemed altogether less banal than, what, an obsession with the floozy, the brazen hussy who performs her own poetry at the floor reading at Torriano's, in Kentish Town, before the named poet comes on. Or with the lonely widow down the street who votes Liberal, because she likes Mr Gladstone. Or, y'know – here's where it's beginning to get silly: how about the jersey-straining school friend of the now-thirty-something-year-old daughter, etc., etc. Naturally, the right sort of instinct rises up to censor these thoughts.

And of course, she wasn't naive, was Rachael, she would know my possible private reaction to the news; this was an opening gambit in her game; and I immediately fell into doubt. I fell into doubt and again into doubt: there were two dubious thoughts chasing me back into a place from which I should never have strayed: now I was thinking of sheep straggling, raggedly messing up the hillside, and the poor dog trying to get them back into line. So that was a third messy thought to cope with. (Maybe the news of your brother and sister-in-law splitting up was supposed to induce such intellectual – or was it emotional? – messiness. But no, I won't spin this out. Back to what was confusing me.) I had reached for the chess metaphor (opening gambit) even though Rachael and I didn't play the game. Not a huge problem, that, but a tiny warning not to do the usual thing and come over as unfeeling. Or 'clever'. Before that – before that thought, after that thought – does it matter? The point is: when thinking of the alternatives to Stalin, I had immediately reached for the 'brazen hussy' and the 'lonely widow', reducing both my brother's options and the available 'talent' out there to the stuff of TV comedy. I must assume that Rachael had half assumed that that would be my response, would be one of my responses; and that she was, securely, being smug at my expense. So (sheep more or less back in the pen), I'll pretend to receive the news afresh.

It wasn't *entirely* a surprise, the news, because my brother had told me before about Stalin. Nothing surprising there, because he had – over the years, the decades – pressed the claims of, well, Charles II of England, for one. Or Napoleon's celebrated map reader (a man called Berthier, who was a genius at map reading, and ended up either a marshal of the empire or a prince). Also, to be considered for dramatization, at various times – we're going back now to the GCE years – there was the Khedive of Egypt, whose name I forget; and various Persian grandees. So, fast forward, no change there; why not Stalin?

We would write the thing together. Years ago, when I was in the theatre, it was a play, keeping pace with Stoppard and company. Then it would be a book, well researched, non-fiction; then an essay, to counter this or that false leader in *The Times*, or wherever. Now, mercifully, it's a short story. (Is it experience of the world, or my own failure to rise [again and again] to the occasion that had caused him to scale down his expectations, to reduce a book, a play, etc. to the dimensions of a story? That's not something I could take as lightly as the couple parting company after endless years of marriage.) So I had not said no to Stalin. I hadn't exactly said yes to Stalin, but I kept the door open (who's on the other side of that door, comrade?) and – as my poor white-haired mother used to say, 'Fuckit'. (Not really: she said something in a foreign language, maybe Russian, which we couldn't translate.)

And my mother wasn't white-haired, at least not in public. And she did have a saying that now came to mind. Things Have Consequences, my mother used to say, this time maybe quoting Plato. Or Lao Tze. And one consequence of 'Stalin' was the call from my sister-in-law.

So the situation was this: my comparative failure in life, he said (for he was an older brother and he could keep alive an image we had of ourselves all those years ago; and was still married, and I was not) – my comparative failure in life was because I had been too ambitious. I had backed myself early on to be original in too many areas, and was of course right to do so, for the assumption we made then was that we were living in a normal society: we misread England then as we did now, though not in the same way; we hadn't realized – *naive, naive* – that this was a society of short cuts. A *short-cut society?* A society of striving to be second best. There was no purchase, no value (except for personal satisfaction and self-respect, which it embarrassed you to have to admit to; for one thing, it brought one too close to those fellows who go around talking about 'honour killings') – there was no value in this society in being original. So, on the phone, now, my brother begged me to eschew originality, go for the short cut and take on Stalin, the research being more or less done. He could help me there, if I liked. (We still used words like 'eschew' to each other, to keep in mind what we used to defend.)

My first thoughts – here we go – my first thoughts were the usual ones. I had, years ago, probably at my brother's suggestion, started to write a blank-verse play about Pliny the Elder. Maybe it wasn't at my brother's suggestion, maybe it came about as a result of one of those adolescent quarrels with Shakespeare, a bit later on: how would *he* have dealt with a great tragedy where there was profound and subtle thought but little action, as with the life of Pliny the Elder? (And make sure it wasn't all soliloquy.) So naturally I had vowed to supply the tragedy missing from that canon. Equally obviously, it didn't get past a few scenes, a bit of which actually got into print. As 'poetry'.

By citing Stalin. Crude fellow, Stalin. Georgian. Spoke Russian with a funny accent. Butt of Trotsky. All that. Killed lots of people as a consequence. *Not* as a consequence; killed lots of people. Caused many more millions to die. No emotional or sexual life that you would credit, or even call interesting. Bleak in a Russian, well, 'Stalinist' sort of way. The worst human being in the world. Worse than Hitler or Saddam or Milosevic. Wasn't my brother actually telling *me* something about myself when he suggested that I give up feeling bad about giving up wrestling with Pliny or Xerxes; or even Charles II and his naked women on the Restoration stage? Give up on all that and settle for a form of Russian depravity? In the light of all this, do I need to worry about whether my imagery concerning the brother's wife and chess quite fits?

And I had done the work. *I have done the work, my brother.* I have read the books, seen the films and made the notes; the failure to produce is the lack of something else that it embarrasses me to go into. Assuming I have the skill to 'go into it'. The last big tome provoked by the subject was Alan Bullock's thousand-*plus*-page doorstopper, *Hitler and Stalin* (over a long summer, interrupting the cricket); and even there Hitler held your interest rather than the man from Georgia. (Interesting, they both had moustaches, as did Saddam – something possible there?) When that weight of murder doesn't drive you frantic to the computer, and instead prompts stale, wearying questions about yourself you're reluctant to probe, why not lie low and bask in the good opinion of people who haven't found you out?

But, of course, you can't say these things to a brother who has (had) high hopes for you.

*

The book that stimulated my brother's interest in Stalin was not a history book as such but one of those 'What If?' books compiled by historians. This one was edited by one of those Identikit fellows who appears regularly on the television, indistinguishable, really, from those boys who used to come out of the Comedy Store; playing his history for laughs. 'What if the Spanish Armada had landed in England in 1588?' sort of thing. 'Napoleon triumphs in Russia'; 'Archduke Franz Ferdinand survives Sarajevo';

'Margaret Thatcher killed at Brighton'; etc. And the one that concerned us was: 'Stalin flees Moscow in 1941'. In this one the little Stalin is presented to us as something vaguely human. 'A tiny figure in boots, and old First World War greatcoat with darned pockets, a fur *shapka* hat with earmuffs . . .' This is at four o'clock in the morning (Friday, 17 October 1941) on a railway siding on the outskirts of Moscow. All that. Twenty-four hours earlier he had admitted to the Politburo that Hitler's push to take Moscow was likely to succeed; that Beria's threat to charge the Soviet Air Force with treason probably wouldn't succeed (Beria, as everybody knows, was the thuggish fellow Georgian and head of Stalin's secret police); and that even summoning the great Georgi Zhukov, hero of Leningrad, to the defence of Moscow probably wouldn't succeed. Also that Stalin's own fall-back plan to make a peace deal with Hitler probably wouldn't succeed, either.

Anyway, the upshot is that Stalin goes (shot in a basement later, his body put in an acid tub). Molotov replaces Stalin, wins the war, ushers in the Cold War with Kennedy and Johnson, invades Afghanistan in 1979 and dies in 1986, aged ninety-six, having outlived most of his chosen successors, Khrushchev, Brezhnev, Andropov and Chernenko. And really, very little changed in the world with Stalin dead in '41. Or with Stalin alive till '53.

This is what my brother and I debated over the weeks that Jennifer – sorry, Rachael – felt there should be less about Stalin in her own home.

And it's outrageous, I think again: it's the middle of the night and I'm thinking it. It's outrageous to spend your time checking the spelling of Fiktionashvili and other lesser forms of life – Poskrebyshev – the sort of creatures you wouldn't ever have to dinner; and now do something trivial with them. As outrageous to be asked to be relaxed about abandoning the soliloquies of Pliny; and before that – or after that – the full portraits of, ah, Darius and Cyrus and . . . whichever of the Persians. (Xenophon, I seem to remember, was more help here than was Plutarch.)

And so, a week or so later, back in England, I made my way to an old flat, in Sheffield, where there was still stuff – books for Oxfam or for the second-hand shop; drawers packed with banking and other 'sensitive' material you're still reluctant to throw out; and boxes of old files from university, long ago: would the drafts of *Pliny the Elder* be in the Plato file or with the (later) *History of the Papacy*? Sorry, it wasn't Pliny, it turned out to have been a Darius play I'd been looking for; a fragment. I said to myself: it's not too late. Who says it's too late? It's never too late. As my mother used to say . . .

When I got down to London I made one of those trips. Put on my long raincoat, so to speak, turned up my collar and turned down the brim of the hat. A scene no one recognizes now, as the concept of shame has gone out of the window. I made it to Highgate, to a man who used to be the butt of my jokes. A dabbler. A pornographer, though not in sex. Why, pray, did you suddenly have to take him seriously? Simple. He's acquired a woman of fame and beauty. A poet, no less. A Persian princess. And his gift to her, this no-hoping, self-dramatizing, inauthentic, self-pitying, plagiarizing gentleman who still walked with a limp from some early (fake) accident, was to dust off my Persian play and present it to her as his own.

Actually, that's a fantasy. I ran into this man more or less by accident and he irritated me in exactly the same way he used to do in the days when we talked drama together, thirty years ago.

Now it was the French thing that grated; who was to be accorded ownership of France, sort of thing. After which I had to meet my brother, and be careful about discussing

Stalin. (Stalin was never among the books that we had abandoned in St Caesare, decades ago, to take flight for England; and though I had tried to recreate our library, the brother couldn't blame me for missing out, there, on Stalin.) Again, I had talked – we had talked – of doing something for my mother; of breaking into her thoughts: we trusted her, it was safe to break into her thoughts; there would be no unpleasant surprises. What were her thoughts as she sat at the upstairs window in the house in Ladbroke Grove? As she sat looking out on a street that didn't suggest any of the Englands in our minds. I had done some lines for her in blank verse, but had rejected them, for they were located in the Caribbean, in the past; and I didn't want her to seem a refugee, an alien; ethnic. And I knew there was a better way, and that I would find it; but I fear that my brother was giving up on me ('we not getting any younger'); had given up on me.

He had given up on me because I had once done the 'crowd' to his satisfaction, and he expected great things from that. That early scene that elevated (and damned) me comes back to mind: I was not yet eleven years old and hence was confined to rattling along in a large house in the country with my grandmother. My brothers and sister, older, were at the grammar school in town, and looked after by my mother. They came home at weekends, and during the holidays. The scene I have in mind is this. My brother, keen on showing off his Shakespeare, enlisted me as his 'extra'. That day he decided to act out a scene from *Julius Caesar*. *The* scene. He is standing halfway up the stairs (facing down) between dining and drawing rooms, reciting Antony's funeral oration to Caesar; and I am commanded, standing at the bottom of the stairs (looking up), to play 'the crowd'. At the end, he pronounced my 'crowd' OK. Later on, in England, when these occasions were referred to, my brother recalled that my crowd had been 'brilliant'. Even later, when I was writing 'dialogue' (and reading Ancient History) he (reading more modern history) made suggestions of what members of the 'crowd' might say. Had he given up on me now?

Jennifer (the joke's gone stale, call her by her name), Jennifer was present, so we talked of, among other things, Bertrand Russell. First we talked about the cricket in India, and of the tactics of Greg Chappell, the Australian manager of the Indian team; and my brother seemed unusually put out that I had confused Greg Chappell with Mark Waugh, another Australian managing another Asian team. Jennifer encouraged the brotherly bantering to the point of recalling some of the old 'brother' jokes; and soon we were citing the African brothers Ian Smith and Robert Mugabe and again, the English brothers Robert Maxwell and Richard Branson. That sort of thing.

Then it settled down: we were saying comforting things about getting old – even though it was good to be still here to regret the fact that we were getting old. And my brother reminded us, apropos of nothing, that Napoleon didn't know his limitations. I privately put that down to one of my mother's old sayings, though I have no idea whether she thought Napoleon knew his limitations or not, whether the thought (looking out of that window, in Ladbroke Grove) had ever exercised her. And after an animated discussion of various Persian heroes from school days, I then decided to do something for my brother. I reminded them that Bertrand Russell had written a story about Stalin. This was really for Jennifer's benefit; she had become passionate about Xenophon quoting from memory a passage where the boy Cyrus is pulled from his horse when, charged by a she-bear, and showing no fear despite the wounds on his body, he kills the animal, in heroic style. She was passionate, was Jennifer, she was *beautiful*. (My sister-in-law was a schoolteacher in west London and her specialist knowledge of the classics was never called on, professionally.) So I introduced Russell as a way of broadening – elevating, you might say – my brother's interest in Stalin. I had to explain that the Russell piece wasn't a proper story, just one of those little sketches tossed off ('tosser', my mother says, from her Ladbroke Grove window) late in life. He had called the series *Nightmares of Eminent Persons*; with Stalin and Eisenhower and, I think, someone like the Queen of Sheba on display. In the Stalin story, Russell has Stalin, the war criminal, falling in among the Quakers in America, determined to rehabilitate him with an excess of love and goodliness – and mugs of cocoa last thing at night. The Quakers all have those *Pilgrim's Progress*-y names, like Goodbye and Thinkright; and Stalin's punishment of love and understanding enrages him to a degree that all the free hot chocolate on offer can't restore his calm. The subtext here is that the Nuremberg trials generated too much sympathy for the old Nazi killers, so now the victors must do it differently. The absurdity of the scenario made Stalin a little bit less threatening to my sister-in-law.

My brother nearly spoilt it by saying how odd it was that Stalin – this is the Stalin from What Might Have Been, *What If . . . ?* – Stalin, while waiting to be executed, is discovered reading a Chekhov short story, and hence must be assumed to have some redeeming qualities.

And then my irritation with him resurfaced. Eugene was determined to pull this back from nonsense, from farce. What to make, then, of his hints that *I* give up on the old agenda, the one that involved Pliny and Cyrus? Or my mother. When he had suggested to me, recently, that I write something about France, where I now lived (*please, not about the riots*), I had politely fended it off, not wanting to associate my brother with the clown in Highgate

who thought that being able to boast the difference between *pain complet* and *pain campagne* (or, as the joker
would have it, *pain de campagne*) was somehow knowing
about France. He boasted his French disability card – he
walked with a limp – which entitled him to jump the
queue in the supermarket or at the post office. Highgate
man also always took the opportunity to correct my pronunciation of my French address because he, living in
England, with minimal French, knew better than *all of us
who lived at that address*, how it should be pronounced.
And shouldn't the 'r' in '*rue*' of street names not be capit-
alized! I had the feeling that my brother had already given
up on me as someone who could still resist the Short-
cut Society; who had given up new ways of playing the
'crowd'. (It was revealing, I reflected after the meeting,
that in the days when we really discussed brothers we
were less inclined to cite Smith and Mugabe, to dust
down, say, from our Ancient History bookshelf, old Gaius
and Tiberius, the Gracchi boys [whose mother was not
unlike our mother] promoting their agricultural reforms
that had made us wonder, then, whether we shouldn't
switch from the dead language to something postwar and
environmental, and become farmers in, maybe, darkest
Somerset.) Fragments of a Gracchus speech survive, scenes
in a play. My brother; my brother I haven't given up yet.

*

But certain things *are* more interesting than you thought.
Could you get past the fact that at the time of his impend-
ing murder in Moscow, according to the 'What If . . . ?'
book, the Little Monster was reading Chekhov? Why
didn't something in Chekhov disturb him, shame him, make
him weep (much more than the idiocy of the Quakers in
America, serving him cocoa or chocolate, whatever, to
keep him calm). Why didn't reading Chekhov make Stalin

more human? (Though I suppose you can't rule out the possibility that it *may* have done, that without that Chekhov short story Stalin would have been *worse*: he may have killed the domestic animals as well as the people.) If that were the case it would be quite interesting to imagine the creature sans Chekhov? Surely he would not have been able to stand upright on two legs! Yes, it was a truism, among those who knew Russian, of which I plead ignorance, that Chekhov was not a stylist: non-judgemental, open-ended, curious about people, modest about self, but not a stylist. A new thought: what if Chekhov, secretly, *were* a stylist but had forebodings about Russia; and his way of signalling that was to abjure the style thing – perpetrating a deeply political act. With that in mind I would have to read other people differently. People closer to home. The likes of Updike, say, a smoothie. I would have to understand more fully the secret code of John 'never-to-have-written-a-bad-sentence' Updike. Up you, Updike, as my mother . . . And, on our side of the pond, someone like young Julian Barnes. Another smoothie. Like those fancy drinks on the supermarket shelf. And at the airports and train stations. I'll have the Strawberry and Apple, please. My mother will have . . .

And by now I was thinking of myself as somebody else; something not yet seduced by the gloss put on things, by the *spin* of language, by the velvety skin of the syntax; and saw myself driven to defend a position that my brother felt I had ceded. Here am I standing in front of the headquarters of our favourite smoothie store. Prime site on the High Street. Barnes and Updike. *Barnes & Updike*. BARNES & UPDIKE. I am a bearded man with something threatening in my hand. I charge you, Barnes & Updike, I charge you, B & U, with frivolity and self-love. WITH THE FRIVOLITY OF SELF-LOVE. I charge you with never knowingly having destroyed your own products once they have met your full, ah, satisfactions. It gives me little pleasure, etc. (The rest of this is unwritten, *censored*.)

And things intervene. Inevitably. You have no idea what's likely to be important, except that you register that the death of someone known to you means something that must change your life a little bit. As much as, if not more than, discovering that a bit of human dirt, in Highgate, posing as a man, also known to you, has managed to get off with someone you would not hesitate to describe as a higher form of life. (So, come back, Stalin.) But the incident that comes to mind now might not relate to anything, except that I can't detach it from other things I'm trying to think about. It is of a woman in a fish shop, *at* a fish stall. This was in France, but it could have been in Bridlington, or . . . Elderly woman. Blank. Very little animation. She was at the head of the queue so I didn't pay attention to what was going on. I was some way down the line. Then after some time she turned to go on her way, served – or not served, as the case may be. At which point the assistant behind the counter (who, presumably, had served her) called after her. He called twice. Three times. Loudly. Others took up the call. To no effect: the woman was deaf. The attendant, aproned and wet and somewhat bloody, large fish-knife in hand, then pursued the woman to attract her attention. Finally he managed it, just as she turned into the street. The action wasn't hostile, but as he caught up with her he had the knife an inch from her face. And she stopped and turned, and re-engaged with him, showing *not* the slightest fear and surprise of the knife. *I* was frightened: so this is what it must have been like living under Stalin.

In the 'What If . . . ?' book, the sketch was written by someone called Simon Sebag Montefiore. (A made-up name, probably, with a mini-biography to match: Cambridge. Print journalism and some such nonsense. Written a novel.

Has daughters with implausible literary names . . .) The point is this man has Stalin reading a story by Chekhov just before he is brought out to be executed. And if you believe this, you must believe, I suppose, that he had something in common with Xerxes and the Gracchi. And maybe even with Pliny. And my mother.

So I rang my brother to say he had provoked me to action; and I had Plan B worked out, in case Jennifer answered the phone.

18

Poetry & Pancakes

The doctor looks up from his computer and says:
'Well, Mr Stapleton, there's good news and bad news.'

And there's a pause. And the doctor continues:

'You'll have to give up pancakes . . . But you can keep up with the poetry. Sestina three times daily.'

'So which is the good news?' Stapleton asks the doctor.

And the wit, the wit in the English department to whom the story is recounted, says:

'This sestina taken three times a day. Is it before or after meals?'

So Pewter was relieved to shift this little scene from England to America – from Sheffield to Boston – where he could just take out his gun and shoot the doctor, without being upstaged by a jobbing academic.

*

Pewter was in Boston, officially recruiting students (at £7,000 a time) for the MA course at City. Taking coals to Newcastle, they had said; but each year they'd managed to snag high-quality American students, and Pewter liked to think his visits to East Coast institutions – rather than the Internet – was what did the trick. Unofficially, the poetry readings he'd managed to arrange for himself over there did him no harm at all, financially. But suddenly he felt as if he had been summoned home, mission un-accomplished.

Pewter was staying at a guesthouse that he knew in Cambridge, the Irving House round the corner from Harvard Square; he'd stayed there last time, a couple of years ago: they ran a couple of establishments, so there was usually a room. He had friends or acquaintances round about but liked, on these short trips, to be independent; and though the Irving House was on the pricey side, it was convenient, and a good address from which to have people phone you back: it made him feel, paradoxically, as if he were not a stranger to America (who either had to stay with friends or to settle for an anonymous hotel): his America was a place he'd been visiting for twenty years.

From the Irving House he phoned a friend in London, a poet; and she asked him to describe his room: how do you describe a hotel room?

S'orite.

No, really.

Oh . . . ridiculous hotel room. All right, all right. Top floor. Low-rise, y'know, it's only a guesthouse, three floors. Room three-oh-three. I so much hate it I prefer to read it backwards. Y'know, not three-oh-three. But three-oh-three. Backwards, not forwards. Sorry, I'm . . . What's it called? Palindrome. If numbers have palindromes. No, I'm OK, really. Got to do a bit of work, bring some money into the university, in the shape of young, well-fed Americans with good teeth and . . . who read Hemingway. What?

What? *Describe it? What? The room?*

Well, how does one describe a hotel room to someone who's never seen one? This is a *single* (that is, for one person) room. Right. Small for America.

Quite small, actually. Yes, bathroom and . . . oh, what else, dunno, hang on, let me have a look: *this is exciting*.

I've had a look. Right; you there? Well, now I'm at my

desk, little wooden . . . fold-out. No, not plastic. Wood. Old wood. (*Knock on wood*.) Old wood, nicely polished. Don't mind paying the price for this. And, yes, instructions for the phone and breakfast. Breakfast from seven to ten. And that's it, really.

End of the game; but the self-consciousness persisted. It was quite warm for November. So he opened the window. He went to the bathroom and noticed it was nice and clean; everything as it should be. *Six* towels on the towel rack. Assorted sizes. All white. With a roll of loo paper on top. Rather spoiling the effect, that. And over the loo, a little sign:

THIS IS A LOW
WATER USAGE
TOILET PLEASE
USE PAPER
SPARINGLY AND/OR
FLUSH AT REGULAR
INTERVALS TO
PREVENT
CLOGGING AND
OVERFLOWING

THANK YOU

He'd like to think this was in the interests of the environment (six towels?) rather than just skimping on water, though, in a sense, that might come to the same thing. A bit dubious, though, aesthetically, the sign over the loo, a card, dark letters on a white background, edged in blue – with a picture of a loo at the top. *Was this cause to change hotel?* He wouldn't even bother to steal sachets of shampoo and soap, never mind shower cap made in China.

Ah, but this was displacement activity following the news – it was his fault for checking his e-mails – that he was scheduled to give his inaugural lecture the day after he returned from America. He hadn't written the lecture; hadn't thought about it. He may have thought about it, but he had as yet no idea what form it would take: you just didn't spring this sort of thing on someone; suddenly his old resentment at the accountants who ran the university re-surfaced. *For the inaugural he'd deliver an open letter of complaint, a J'accuse sort of letter against the accountants who ran the university.* They had a feeling that as a poet one would probably just turn up on the night and give a poetry reading, and that that would serve as an inaugural lecture. He vowed not to give a poetry reading, but to do a proper lecture. But on what subject? Poetry, of course. A meditation in the tradition of Philip Sidney and the boys following him down the ages – Eliot and Heaney & Co. He had two weeks really to think about it.

He was thinking of having misled his friend in London, the poet, about the number of his room. The number on the key was 305, not 303, no palindrome. You don't ring London back to say you'd made a mistake about the palindrome. Unless you could make it witty: *he would write her a sestina, in contrition, with light and suggestive 'terminal nouns'.* He was thinking of ways to make it witty when he got lost going to the bookshop (bookstore). *The bookstore was on Massachusetts Avenue: how could you get lost going to the bookstore on Massachusetts Avenue that you knew so well?*

Along whatsitsname, through Harvard, then out on Massachusetts Avenue. And left.

Ah, always a little bit further along than you remembered. Then, on the other side, the old Orson Welles cinema, now a Chinese something. Pointedly, Pewter would refrain from checking the shelves of the bookstore for his latest publication.

Oh, hi. After you, *please*.

(Polite. Nice.)

This brought back an earlier incident, walking through the Yard. Better than polite. Gracious. *Gracious*. He was beginning to reflect on *change* in this country, which he'd known for twenty years, a country that had provided him with a partner for some years. He was wearing his splendid long coat, about which that poet in London had written a poem; he was fitting in. Two days later he was still feeling as if he were reclaiming old territory. If he had six months to the inaugural he might give a lecture on *change* in this country.

*

A poetry reading would make sense, nevertheless, for the inaugural.

He might reinstate that. He had wanted to aim at something more ambitious than a poetry reading; a disquisition, say, on Spelling, Grammar, Reading & the Aesthetics of Speech. Or . . . The Process of Recreation of a Lost Shakespeare Play, *Pliny the Elder*, for instance – to show the academic boys (and girls) that his business was 'reconstruction' rather than 'deconstruction'. But he mustn't get carried away. That way self-parody lies. He had read an interview recently with a poet he admired; she had talked, not with anger but with some wistfulness, about being a writer in 'this age of celebrity'. Even poets who picked up prizes caused barely a ripple in the public consciousness: what to do, what to do, while resisting the lure of being something strange to capture the attention of the media, the interviewee concluded that the poet's real rewards were intangible, a sort of sense of personal satisfaction, like catching a butterfly. Nice image. Put Pewter in mind of Nabokov. But he wouldn't let Nabokov's oddity spoil the image. So Pewter thought he might call the inaugural

'Catching a Butterfly'. Unless that would play into the hands of the academic hit men, who would find it suitably safe and quaint. Unthreateningly 'other'?

An *illustrated* poetry reading might just do it, like the ones he gave anyway. He saw performance as a bit of theatre, the readings as 'closet' theatre events; the Little Theatre of Poetry Readings, he would describe them as, each poem part of building a theme (arguing with it, contesting it); and framed by anecdote. He had looked through his old reading programmes with a view to teasing out some sort of pattern, and he wondered if these mini-lectures, tailored to the occasion, could be woven into a larger pattern of transcending their original time and place. But that was a six-week job, at least.

He really wasn't concentrating; he caught himself humming a tune, as if in harmony with the Harvard Yard. Something about waking up in the night, problematically, to the sound of music; and he was wondering what sort of music he would like to wake up to, and then that led him on to *Desert Island Discs* and . . . He had to take hold of himself, remind himself of the history of this place. Not so much now of the African Americans who were flexing their muscles, but of the Indians that history had abandoned: what was this yard called when it belonged to the owners? It was a Beatles song he was humming. He suddenly had a vision about America and the English language. Lucky he was to be part of this colonizing force, with no need for translation. All these 'others' swapping their idiom for it. The farming Swedes and Danes in the middle of the country, the swindling others elsewhere, all speaking the clearest English, making America familiar to him, in its strangeness. Maybe he could explicate a Shakespearean sonnet to his invited audience back at City. Pay homage. Treat them to a 'close reading' master class. Though someone from Linguistics could probably do it just as well as he.

Of course, the Beatles song in his head reminded him of the fate of John Lennon in this country.

What would his opposite number do as an inaugural? He wasn't thinking of the *academic* opposite numbers, who would probably treat you to a bit of literary archaeology, with in-jokes by the spadeful. He was thinking of his real opposite number, making music. A few years back he had been writer in residence at a university in Ireland and his opposite number at the nearby university, a musician, was composer in residence. This man had his own string quartet, had composed music for a Bruce Chatwin opera about Rimbaud and had consulted Pewter about the appropriateness of some of the lyrics set in the Ethiopian desert, through which the French poet had travelled. Pewter, knowing nothing about Ethiopian music, thought the request vaguely racist.

But he was aware that this man, his opposite number at the university, had set the bar at a level that he should attempt.

*

Henry Louis Gates Jr. (a man on Pewter's visiting list), in his book *Thirteen Ways of Looking at a Black Man* (how many ways of looking at a black woman?), did some revealing profiles of eight black, or blackish, Americans. Writing about Colin Powell, Gates declares that part of the general's popularity rests on the fact that he is not threatening to white folk. To a non-American like Pewter, this raises interesting questions for discussion: why is a black military man so easily neutralized? Does it mean that *all* high-profile black men, in order to gain status and popularity (outside the entertainment and sports worlds) must be neutralized? Why shouldn't a black general, responsible for armies, for Desert Storm, etc. be *dangerous*? Is this evidence of racism?

Out and about – walking through Harvard Yard: *When I find myself in times of trouble/Mother Mary comes to me* . . . Pewter, too, receives due deference: it surprises him slightly to be called Sir – at the bookshop; by the woman on the street he'd bumped into on his way to the bookshop; even – a couple of days earlier – the taxi driver from Logan. Not just politeness, surely. *There again*: the man sitting at the desk at the entrance to the periodicals library (even though he's telling Pewter he has to go next door to fill out the visitor's card). The same from the woman upstairs when he seeks assistance to photocopy. There he was thinking everyone was so accommodating, now he realized he just wasn't threatening. (He was a certain age; he was wearing an expensive coat of which someone had written a poem; he was wearing scholarly glasses; it was broad daylight . . .)

He had thought, for some reason, that black people might be *feared*, what with all the high-profile cases, the aftermath of Rodney King. O. J. Simpson. All this racist gunning down of black children and the inevitable backlash; yesterday he'd read of just such an incident, in the *Boston Globe*: had white Americans come to see themselves as Louis Farrakhan's 'blue-eyed devils' and were trying to atone? No, no.

That 'no' was reinforced when he found himself looking into a mirror in the Barker's Building on Quincy Street. He had an appointment to make an appointment and he brought along not only his latest book but bits and pieces about the writing programme at City. He got to the second floor a bit too soon for comfort, passively spurred on by someone at the bottom who clearly found it odd that he should think of waiting for the lift. (Was he misreading yet again?) And he wasn't really waiting for the lift, the elevator, just getting his bearings; but nevertheless it gave the impression that he was slow on the uptake that the second floor was only one floor up; and he hated giving the impression that he was new to America. So he was unready to face his double at the top of the stairs, at the entrance to the Du Bois Institute. Not that it was an exact fit; the other man was fairer-skinned, more bearded, perhaps more restful in countenance, more settled in . . . *arrival*. But out in the street, or in the Memorial Library, or restaurant or bookshop, etc., they would be seen as identical, they would be *twins*.

His twin was gracious, soft-voiced and courteous; unhurried courteous, not ingratiating courteous: could he help?

This package to the secretary of the director . . .

She may not be in, but . . . if you'll follow me this way . . .

The brothers walked off in the direction of the secretary's room, deciding not to make small talk.

Then: I take it Professor Gates isn't in.

No, I'm afraid Dr Gates isn't in.

(Those in the inner circle called the man 'Skip'. These brothers weren't close.)

The secretary isn't in. May I put this in her pigeonhole for you?

Yes, these were two tame niggers in Cambridge: why would anyone want to keep them out of libraries, out of the academy, or, for that matter, off the streets?

A feeling of depression descended on Pewter; ah, it was all too humiliating; he would move out of Irving House, head back home early and prepare for his inaugural.

*

That was after the visit to Grolier's, his favourite bookstore on the Square, its chaos and mess putting him in mind of something European, Shakespeare & Company in Paris. And good women who took themselves extremely seriously in attendance. He had bought a ticket there for a

Mark Strand reading. No refund. No shit, as they say: *that's the way to do it – an idea for City? Sell tickets for readings and master classes in advance. Charge for them.* There he picked up a massive James Merrill collection (highly recommended by Harold Bloom et al.) and three or four University of Michigan volumes of *Poets on Poetry*, the sorts of essays and memoirs and interviews that the Americans do better than the Brits: enough ideas there for the inaugural. He wasn't really enjoying this.

*

'Poetry & Pancakes' seemed not a bad idea to resurrect for the occasion. This was a nostalgic look at early-1970s Shepherd's Bush, where Pewter lived at the time. As a scribbler you were anxious to seek out places to read your work. The two that you tended to return to were the Troubadour café in Earls Court and a private house called Avatar, behind Gloucester Road, in Kensington. There was a Sunday lunchtime session at the Troubadour, devoted to agitprop; raw and passionate, visitors talking about oppression in their various countries, the odd American accompanying himself on the piano to *We Shall Overcome*. Singing beautifully. The Monday night sessions were less openly campaigning in the sense that there was as much literary homage paid to Yeats and Plath as to Neruda and Dennis Brutus.

Avatar was presided over by an ancient lady (indeed, a Lady) in what must have been a converted church. The Lady sometimes opened the sessions (but didn't sit through the proceedings), which included fairly unprepossessing men with impressive names – Sir John Waller among them – thought to have long died out. The convener was a young-ish man called Oliver Cox who, too, claimed to live in a converted church, in Suffolk.

The musical interlude was provided by young men from Cambridge, with witty snatches of song: they called themselves Instant Sunshine. One night Oliver Cox, unusually, read out a poem of his own, quite a fierce one; and this prompted comment. It was his birthday, he said; this made him angry, and that anger provoked the poem. Pewter wondered now, here in America, if he was angry. (So the lecture would be pitched between the anger of Oliver Cox's birthday poem and the acceptance of the Beatles lyric.)

But, talking of poetry and pancakes, not to be outdone back then, Pewter and Lindsay, his American partner from New Haven, also a poet, had started their own weekly poetry sessions in their Shepherd's Bush upstairs room, which, with the large landing and kitchen serving others on that floor, wasn't particularly cramped. They advertised in *Time Out* (and maybe also in *City Limits*), and people struggled in on a Thursday night with their poems. One factor in its popularity was the offer of refreshment: the sessions were advertised as 'Poetry & Pancakes'. Coffee was served and, in the interval, pancakes. (When Pewter had phoned Lindsay, now living in Maine, the day before, she had talked nostalgically about poetry and pancakes, and their time in Shepherd's Bush. Pewter was surprised that the memory was so positive, so untainted.)

That experience – something like it: poetry outside the Academy, the democratization of art, the demystification of the process; the providing of a collective watchdog of practitioners to maintain the standards of their art – that might form the core of the inaugural.

He did eventually attend the Mark Strand poetry reading in Cambridge; it was good value. That night he dipped into the Merrill book, and found a fun sestina where the six 'terminal words' are 'one' to 'six', Merrill managing to rhyme 'six' with 'Sikhs' and 'classics'; 'two' with '*tu*' and 'Timbuctoo', etc. Nonsense, but fun.

*

When Pewter got to DC – no, he wasn't going to cut his trip short to get home to prepare for the inaugural: he had done Amherst, four of the five colleges, he was earning his keep – when he got to DC he found that there was a demonstration at Maryland University scheduled for the night of his reading. It had been on the news for the last couple of days. Someone had written letters to 'black leaders' at the university threatening physical harm; and antiracist groups were organizing a protest march. The local radio had been updating progress every half hour or so – from the night before and all morning. His hosts, a good southern white-skinned couple of academics, said Pewter probably shouldn't overreact to the incident.

*

Pewter was staying with Bill and Evelyn, whom he had first met in the south of France. Bill had been around the village of Spéracèdes in the Alpes-Maritimes in the early 1970s, when Pewter had had a spell with a building co-operative there, restoring houses. Bill had been getting on with writing his novels and stories. Then he had gone off to places like Drake and Des Moines in the Chicago area (Drake probably was in Des Moines) as writer in residence, and then on to Colorado and now Maryland.

But Bill was pulling rank now, exercising that strain of pessimism that Americans are supposed not to have; had given up on fiction ('I just can't compete with those fellows in Congress and the White House in creating the stuff'), and had switched to teaching academic courses on Pound and Melville. Bill and Evelyn lived just round the corner from the Library of Congress and each day for lunch, the men sloped off to sample the fare at one of Bill's favourite restaurants round the Eastern Market area: there was a particular Louisiana establishment that Bill liked. (He came originally from the South.) It was usually the men; Evelyn, who taught at one of the universities in the Georgetown area, seemed always pressed for work. One of Bill's academic friends sometimes joined them for lunch.

One day at lunch they got to talking about Pewter's projected book about the *coopérative* in *Spéracèdes*. At the table was Bill's academic friend, whose name Pewter couldn't remember.

'I hope it's not a novel,' Bill cautioned.

Everyone agreed that the world didn't need another novel.

'I can't write novels any more,' Bill said. 'The damn things take too long to read. I can't remember the bits I've already written. Now, I end up hiding from my friends who're writing novels.'

'But you must know lots of people writing novels.'

'They get this look when they see you, you know. They've got this . . . I guess it's what the missionaries used to have; they pull up on the kerb, like these gangers in the films; and then they bolt across the road to block off your escape.'

'They're gonna cross that road, traffic or no traffic,' the other man said.

'With just one thing on their mind.'

'Not sex.'

'Sex. That wouldn't be so bad. One thing on their mind: *have you read my book*. I'm afraid of those guys. I hide when I seen them coming. If there's no place to hide, I run.'

'Nice one,' said the other man, whose name was Peterson. 'Seeing you run.'

'When I see the crazed author coming, I run. How'd you like the catfish?' This last was directed at Pewter.

'I still like the idea of you running from those guys.'

'If you saw those guys coming, you'd run. How's the catfish?'

'Catfish is fine.'

'Better to eat than to look at,' said Peterson.

'Catfish is a scavenger. Down there lying on the bottom, scavenging. Not a pretty fish to look at.'

After the catfish talk Pewter admitted that he was thinking of doing a master class on the sestina for his inaugural. The men set about naming their favourite sestinas in the language; and all agreed that there were fewer than a dozen decent ones written in all the years since Phillip Sidney four hundred *plus* years ago. They urged Pewter to rise to the challenge. (Peterson was surprisingly well-informed on the sestina.)

*

When I find myself in times of trouble . . .

He comes back to that opening line of the song. The openness of the 'I'. He's thinking of his own production, all those 'you's, as if in disguise, in hiding, a protective shield against accepting the logic, the nakedness of the lyric. As if he's in a relationship and trying to cover up an affair, as if he's gay and not wanting to come out.

And then *in times of trouble*, assuming times of trouble, already casting off the juvenile belief that things will go well for ever because you're in the right place with the right person (no one close to you is terminally ill, your country is well governed, and you're living at a good time in history). So the maturity of 'times of trouble' strikes home. And what of 'trouble' itself? An inclusive term, not something only likely to target the unlucky; it's a more all-embracing (though not really embracing) word than 'danger' or 'hardship'; not melodramatic like 'abandonment' or 'catastrophe'; just 'trouble'. 'Trouble' is domestic violence, 'trouble' is the loss of faith, of optimism. (And Mother Mary isn't a visitation; she doesn't startle: first she comes, then she speaks, giving you time to adjust. Mother Mary could be your long-dead grandmother, alive in dream.)

The nakedness of the 'I' takes him back to Poetry & Pancakes in Shepherd's Bush in the early seventies – or was it Lindsay's unclouded memory triggering his own? He remembers one young lad, bearded, sitting cross-legged on the floor, reading a Denise Levertov poem, checking first with American Lindsay on the pronunciation of 'Levertov' – who, in fact, had been born in Britain. At the end of the Levertov poem somebody said: how do we respond to that poem? And the lad who had read it said, 'It makes me want to dance.' So *the inaugural should end with a dance*, a fitting metaphor for Pewter's introduction of creative writing into the academy: the rigour, the emphasis on exploring key texts, the formal disciplines relentlessly practised, the endless revision – all ending in a *dance* by the invited audience. Not unlike the ending of that Shakespearean comedy, really. (But before that he'd spend twenty minutes on workshopping a sestina, to show how impossible it was to write a sestina; to catch that butterfly.)

And then the dance.

*

It was the day before returning to England; so it was time to do the tourist thing. A friend who had a friend who worked for Janet Reno, the attorney general, offered to get Pewter a ticket to the White House. He didn't want that, he'd do it the tourist way; he'd go down to wherever and queue like everyone else and get his ticket, as if there was nothing else on his mind.

Out of the house by just after seven, he decided to walk, to take in early America, past the Library of Congress buildings, past the Capitol Building, the building that some thought impressive and others vulgar, views which, in an earlier conversation, had threatened to expose a racial divide among people at Maryland University. So his walk took him down through the park to the monument, and right. Straight on. And on and on and on, like British Tory governments of recent times; isolated people huddled on the wide, clean pavements, wrapped in blankets, their possessions in plastic bags, occupying benches or curled round the vents in the sidewalk emitting steam. Some of them women. Some of them youngish. He thought of his family governing this state. It wouldn't matter what their politics were; pride wouldn't let them permit this to happen; his mother would pronounce it a disgrace. His grandmother would have provided jobs for those sleeping rough: hoeing land, picking cotton (picking cotton: *would American black people be content to pick cotton in 1999?*). There had been a little discussion at Maryland the other night, not of busing but of buses taking students to the university. Apparently, the buses were overcrowded, people bunched up at the front, a lot of black students, elegantly attired. (Rich daddies? Is the American black daddy maligned?) In order to make room on the bus, to get more students on, the white bus driver asked those at the front to move towards the back: *was the man for real?* Or was he on the other side of racism, no longer traumatized by Rosa Parks? So, naturally, the students had refused to shift; the driver had been reported, and a protest was now being organized to get him reprimanded or sacked. When this was confirmed, among a racially mixed crowd, Pewter was relieved he was British. That he was West Indian. Relieved that he was thinking of his inaugural.

He was glad he didn't take the subway, the subway to Federal Triangle, nearest station to the White House. In this atmosphere Federal Triangle somehow suggested Monica Lewinsky in the Oval Office, something he tried to put out of his mind. So he was content to walk along Independence Avenue. Funny how many buildings – two or three – looked like the White House: he wondered how many tourists, Japanese and otherwise, had got it wrong and had the pictures – here are we next to the rose garden – to prove it?

Americans were clearly into the business of buying into heritage early in the game: outside the civic-styled Archives of the United States building, a couple of classical-looking statues on plinths, male and female, displaying open books on their laps, were captions: 'What's Past Is Prologue' (female) and 'Study the Past'. Further along the road, on the opposite side of the street, the National Theatre was spelt the English way.

As it happens, you didn't need a ticket to visit the White House, not on a Saturday in November. So at the Information Center he collected the map of DC, watched the displays of various presidents with advisers attending to crises – lots of people on telephones – and he bought a collection of presidential inaugural speeches in the bookshop. Getting stuck in the White House slow-moving queue at half past ten, Pewter was prone to a burst of hallucination. He was looking at Abe Lincoln but he was hearing a Beatles song. The woman *whispers* words of wisdom, whispers like the silken sheets of reassurance in the darkness; then there's the 'Yeah' as in an orgasm, as in the youthful joy of devilry and possibility, as in – why not? – Danny the Red at Nanterre, in '68, as in . . .

And when the night is cloudy, 'cloudy' as cataracts on the eyes are cloudy, as cloudy as the fear of what lay behind cataracts on the eyes . . . No no no. Better to get back to the script, to the book of presidential inaugural speeches in your hand.

And *my hour of darkness* is bearable; it's not a *time* of darkness, not an *eternity* of darkness; the hour is a measurable unit. (Oh, my Egyptians of long ago who are said to have invented the twenty-four-hour day.) An hour (of darkness) is a long time; but it's not such a long time.

And yes, here in the queue, Pewter is intrigued to discover (something he knew, really) just how dedicated Abraham Lincoln had been to the continuation of slavery and how explicit he had been in the first inaugural address in reassuring the slave owners that he would not seek to deprive them of redress for their runaway property, etc.

He rather liked the White House – in which he was propositioned. (Maybe it was the place, not the incumbent, that did it.)

*

The rejected topics for the inaugural were:

Catching a Butterfly
Poetry & Pancakes
Letter From America
Master Class on the Sestina

He was thinking of something new; even as he prepared to deliver his poetry reading.

19

The Food Taster

It was the Nazi on the autoroute to the south of France in '72 who tried to poison us.

But she disagreed. It wasn't the Nazi, it was the nice man in Oslo, in the Volvo, who had invited us to share his pizza; *he* was the villain of the piece.

Odd that we should disagree over something as obvious as that. But then a lot had happened in our separate lives since then. Lindsay had gone back home to the US and married, and I, back to England; we were both divorced now; thirty-five years had passed, Nixon was no longer in the White House, Pompidou no longer president of France. (I couldn't, for the minute, remember what was happening in Britain: probably Elton John and Cliff Richard in the hit parade.) So, really, did it matter who had tried to poison us, in whatever country, all those years ago?

I was reminded of that old film, a televised thing, of what had been the Robert Graves book, the scene where the stammering Emperor Claudius is sitting at dinner directing his food taster to sample this or that bit on the platter. I remembered thinking at the time: who would want a job as food taster to an emperor who was likely to be poisoned – unless they had Food Poisoning Slaves? (Pliny the Elder had Writing Slaves trailing after him, taking down his thoughts.) But you would need to be a desperate man to apply for the job as food taster. (Man or woman: have a woman food taster and start the feminist movement right there in first-century Rome.)

But then if you were an emperor would you want any old bit of riff-raff sitting next to you, sharing your plate? You'd want someone washed and oiled, just come from the baths, not too bad-looking, good teeth, etc., so that the breath wouldn't be offensive at dinner. And, surely, someone you could talk to, if the mood took you; so not a foreigner who couldn't speak the language: the fellow would have to know his Latin. So your food taster is likely to be someone from your community, if not quite of your class, someone in touch with it enough to pick up references to things going on in the empire – if not actually at the court in Rome; and that person would, presumably, have a discreet line to the kitchens, to get them to hold off on the poison. So, really, the choosing of the food taster would almost be enough to guarantee that the main eater wasn't poisoned. (Of course, Claudius' wife, Agrippina, was successful in the end, in poisoning Claudius. Allegedly.) But this is a long way from the business concerning Lindsay and myself wandering round Europe in 1972.

Everything would point to the Nazi. And yet . . . It was early evening, I remember. We must have been travelling for . . . two days. Setting out from London, we stopped off in Paris and were put up overnight by a friend, who warned us against trying to hitch with so much luggage. But, you know how it is: the prospect of coming south to the sun and sampling a new life – for who knows how long? – meant that after you'd parked away books and records on more or less willing friends, you really needed to take with you as much as you could manage on the road. We had, I seem to remember, seven or eight bits of luggage between us.

This was evening of day two, the light failing. We were well south, certainly south of Lyons, but exactly where I can't remember, and we took the wrong turn-off (after the last lift) and ended up back on the autoroute. And then this man – we didn't know, then, that he was a Nazi – in an ancient, small car, pulled up. The first sign of unease was that he made Lindsay sit in front, something she was vaguely reluctant to do; but he had the car and we were hitching. How to make conversation: he knew no English, we knew no Nazi (or whatever language he spoke); so then it was French. Oh good, Lindsay was better at the language than I was. Though his interest in the *noir* and the *blanche* travelling together seemed intrusive. When he reached into the glove compartment I was already calculating how swiftly we could escape from the car with how much of our luggage. We could disable him, unless it was a gun. He was an old man. Already I was tensing my right hand, fingers ramrod straight, ready to chop, to give the karate chop from behind, back of the neck, the way they did it in the films. He was driving very slowly, we wouldn't crash, I could grab the wheel from behind; or Lindsay could. And then . . .

It wasn't a gun, it was sandwiches; we had to share his sandwiches, and, having shared his sandwiches, he put us out, with our seven or eight pieces of luggage, in the middle of the autoroute. (Much later, telling the story, we imagined that the sandwiches had been poisoned by the man's views.) By now it was dark. Later that night, Lindsay was sick. In sympathy with Lindsay, I was sick. (It was too late, after all these years, to be clear on this – I had tried in a half-hearted way before and had failed – it was too late to explain, to confess that I was only sick that night, in sympathy with Lindsay, and not because I had been poisoned by the Nazi with his sandwiches.)

Why did the Nazi insist that we share his sandwiches – *which he didn't eat himself* – unless he wanted to do us harm? *Who knows the mind of a Nazi?*

Good question. But then I recalled, years ago, in student years, in South Wales, being picked up by an old man in an ancient American-type car; again, an old crock – we hitched everywhere, then; the university scarf helped. And as he crawled along the whatever it was, A40, between somewhere and Cardiff, or maybe somewhere and Newport, the man reached into the glove compartment and brought out the pictures. (Has any social study or psychological profile been done on the relationship between the sad driver and his glove compartment?) Anyway, this Welshman extracted his porno pictures from the glove compartment showing men being friendly to one another. I was relieved, then subsequently pleased at my psychological handling of that one. This isn't to say that men in cars who wish to abuse stray passengers are pathetic creatures more or less easily dealt with. Countless raped and dismembered women and boys would give the lie to that. The man in Oslo, Lindsay's man, was not pathetic. He drove a shiny Mercedes.

He drove a Mercedes, spotless, sparkling, plush. (Lindsay remembers it as a Volvo, but it was a Mercedes, a black one; though I must say neither Lindsay nor I was into cars); and yes, he invited us to a restaurant, a pizza restaurant, but an up-market one, where we shared a pizza. He ate his share of the pizza; so far so good. He wasn't actually Norwegian, either from Sweden or Denmark; but he lived in Oslo; and the slight surprise was that when the large pizza that he had ordered was brought to the table, he was taken aback by its size, and asked if we minded sharing, while he set about cancelling our order.

In the ensuing small talk he said he was very careful what he ate these days because he was having difficulty at home and his wife was trying to kill him: the wife was a chemist and he suspected that she might resort to a sophisticated slow-working poison, not easy to detect; but he still ate what she put on the table before him, so as not to demonize the woman he had married. (Another warning sign: too good to be true.) But the anxiety had taken away his appetite and affected his business; that's why he couldn't manage such a big pizza on his own, even out of the house.

It was clear that Lindsay didn't trust him: the story about his wife was a way of upstaging us, to minimize our own tales of what might have befallen us on the road. I agreed that that showed a man somewhat self-obsessed. Though yet again that might just be the sensitivity of someone, *in place*, trying to spare us the indignity of having to be 'colourful' because we were travelling on the cheap.

But, yes, we both smelt something fishy there; and we probably shouldn't have accepted his invitation to give us a bed for the night; but it was late, we had no money, Oslo seemed a safe place to be. (Who had ever heard of people being murdered and dismembered in Oslo – a little sleepy capital with only four letters to its name?) And he was a businessman driving a sparkling new Mercedes (or Volvo): he wouldn't do anything to put himself behind bars. So we accepted the invitation.

*

When I did get serious food poisoning it was in Sheffield, many years later, and I – in a sense – blamed Lindsay, because I'd just come back from America, having visited her. It's true that the poison was identified as out-of-date yoghurt that I had left in the fridge maybe three weeks earlier, before departing for America; and feeling thirsty and somewhat groggy after the hassle of the flight back and the trip up from London (either up from London or across from Manchester), I opened the fridge and gorged on the out-of-date yoghurt, and ended up in hospital next day. That experience, long ago now as it was, I don't even want to recall. (I prefer to recount not the agony of the food poisoning, but the benign menace of – what would you call them? – the two giants sent up to the flat to get me down to the waiting ambulance.)

Though the odd thing is I did begin to feel queasy the moment I boarded the plane at Logan, was sick in the loo at thirty thousand feet, had an unspeakable flight over, and then compounded it with the yoghurt. As I tell Lindsay when I get the chance, my *real* food-poisoning drama is associated in my mind with that last meal we had together in Boston before my flight, when Reagan was still the president. Or maybe it was Clinton: *so why did she want to kill me now?* She was pleased about that; she was perfectly OK after the meal – I was sick, she was OK – that made us even. Fair enough.

*

My play about food poisoning failed to get on to the stage, or to be done as radio: so, what was new? Obviously, you fictionalize things. It was clear that you had in mind, while setting down to the play, the Nazi on the autoroute in the south of France all those years ago; and the man in the Mercedes in Oslo; but you were also interested in the – what was it? – psychology of your being taken ill on that last night back from Boston *before* poisoning yourself with the out-of-date yoghurt. That was background to the play, which was set in the south of France and in ancient Rome. I wanted it to be a different south of France from the south of France visitors and tourists know, and Rome to be different from the Blackadder version. There is this old man who lives there . . .

In another version the pile in France (built in the shape of a Roman villa) belongs to the food taster, who had come through years, through a lifetime as a professional food taster, and now wants to look at things from the other side. He would put aside the humiliations of the job and not bear resentments: in one situation he had – in addition to eating stray bits at his master's whim – had to sleep with a brutal president's wife, on demand. Not easy: if she were not satisfied, he might be dismissed, if he performed the job too enthusiastically, he might be executed. But that was a long time ago. And far away. Now he resolved to treat his dinner guests as food tasters, his sort of house theme. Unfortunately, on this occasion, one of his guests has a stomach upset in the middle of the night; and dies.

*

It was good to be living in Sheffield and not in ancient Rome at the time. For by then I had looked up the record of poisoners in ancient Rome, and it was a thriving industry: I felt very protective of the food taster. By then the poisoners had discovered arsenic and it was so pervasive that you couldn't understand how anyone who wasn't a slave, and forced to do it, would consent to be a food taster. Food poisoning was so rife, an Internet wit said, that, later on, it pushed Christianity hard for prime position as the state religion. (If only that woman had managed to poison Constantine . . . !) And, of course, we haven't given up on poisoning down the ages. Hitler. Saddam. But in the play I tried to treat this, if not in a lighter, in a more manageable way. I preferred to make stray references to poisoners of a domestic kind, the local Croydon poisonings in the 1920s (arsenic), etc. And even slipped in references to those generations of women in the Caribbean who used the cassava juice (cyanide) to get their own back on the men who had abused and betrayed them: indeed, they had got it to such a point of perfection that hardly anyone was ever prosecuted.

But really my play was about contrasting that evening in Sheffield when, struck down by yoghurt, I waited, writhing in agony, neither able to lie nor sit, kneeling the only option (oh, if there was a god of poisoning!) until rescue came in the shape of those two slow-moving giants – contrasting that with the celebrated poisoning merchants at work in ancient Rome. *In Sheffield, I am in my dressing gown, for decency. The men come up the stairs, past the two bookcases on the lower landings, past the stairwell, choked, piled high with books, up to the top landing – another bookcase – where I'm sitting, trying to ease my body into a shape that's bearable; and the first giant pauses and picks a book at random from the stairwell and flicks through it, taking his time.*

'I see you like to read,' he says.

Downstairs, I'm got into the ambulance – first time in an ambulance; the hospital is maybe two hundred yards away, but I am to be taken there by ambulance. In the end I see maybe seven doctors and nurses, have a private room for the night, and lie on my back with a drip in my left arm, unable to sleep. Bored with this, I reach for the reading matter in the bedside cupboard. A Bible. I want to write something. I throw caution to the winds and ring for the night nurse and ask for pen and paper. Intrigued, she brings me a red ballpoint and a tiny sheet of (A5) paper. It's OK writing with one hand (in red ink) with the other rigged up to the hospital contraption; I feel the need to confess. Inevitably – I may have been thinking of this happening to me in Claudius' Rome, or Nero's Rome – I cover both sides of the A5. What to do: you can't be a bore and ask for more paper; the nursing staff have things to do. And should you annoy them, might they not . . . ?

But a solution is at hand. The Gideon Bible has lots and lots of pristine white pages at the back. Next day, a moral decision: do you steal the Bible with your latest gospel (on food poisoning) at the back; or do you rip the pages out and try to market them separately from the Good Book?

This is where the play ends.

*

So in the end I come back to Lindsay's view (if Plan A doesn't work, try Plan B) that we were poisoned by the man in Oslo, and I don't even mind if he was driving that fictional Volvo. He was clearly up to no good, and we were lucky to escape with our life. (And did we collude with his little bit of pornography, demonizing his wife, the chemist?) In the revised play I bring him over to England. (No nonsense with EasyJet, this is a *play*.) I bring him to England and make him the manager of the Somerfield supermarket in Sheffield, the Broomhill branch, at the top of the road where I used to live, because I want to tie it in with my yoghurt poisoning and my night with the doctors and nurses at the Hallamshire Hospital. Someone said I might be sued by Somerfield if the story ever came to light, and you have no idea about these characters – the sorts of people who run Somerfield's and Asda (must check, really, on this: are they all high-achieving Tory Archie Normans and do-gooding Labour Lords Sainsbury, or what?). So that would be a neat tie-up, globalization/environmental risk. Supermarkets – capitalism – too much food here, too little food over there – sort of thing. Or, if you like, the obvious point that mobility across Europe is not limited to the economic migrants and people-smugglers from the Balkans, but includes an upright, Mercedes-driving, poisoner from Oslo running one of our top supermarkets, etc.

The Blackadder scenes had to go. The turn-on scenes of Agrippina, in Roman dress, had to be sacrificed. (Oh, yes, they had their plates and dishes galore, the Romans, even though archaeologists tend to play down their finds.) In the end I went for the man from Oslo as the poisoner, for reasons aesthetic. This is my play, my book, my story; I won't give a Nazi prominence in this space which I consider mine. Even if it's to condemn him. (How dare a Nazi take a space that might properly belong, say, to my grandmother [who, as far as I know, was not a poisoner]?). So, the presentable businessman in Oslo it is, in whatever car he chooses to drive. That offends my sensibilities less, even though he was unconvincing that night in the pizza restaurant; even though he subtly demonized his wife, the chemist (whose nibbles didn't hurt us); and even though he's now come over to England and a well-paying job in a top supermarket: the Grenadian smartarse who maybe was pressured to apply for that job might not be qualified. Don't get excited about it.

Yes, I agree, Oslo Man was the poisoner. (And Lindsay *did* say she had had a bad reaction to the pizza that night.)

20

The Tailor in Amsterdam

I

In the films, the stalker is a man, usually – though not always a loner, or after sex. And women have devised sophisticated ways, over the years – by becoming older, maybe. Or less trophy-like. Even by giving the man at home more sex rather than let him loose on the streets to threaten and molest the unsuspecting. All this, she says – my muse, my lover, my fantasy, the woman who stalks me – all this physical and emotional labour is performed largely in silence, is invisibilized.

Yes, maybe. But why, I ask myself, is she telling me this, is she stalking *me*?

I met her at a publishers' party, and – sensing something – we were careful not to challenge each other; and I moved on, eventually, with relief, to someone with whom conversation was easier.

And now, again, in Amsterdam; she is here, I know it: *who's the Moroccan she's obsessed with?* I don't know. *The fellow who delivered pizzas to his friends in jail and then murdered somebody.* Yes, I sort of know. But, really, I don't know.

*

The last time in Amsterdam I was headed for the Rijks-museum, to give myself a break, a little treat. First, I remember going to the Van Gogh Museum to take a look round, and then I ran into these Americans, two young women from California, I think – youngish women – one of whom had done Peace Corps duty in South Africa; so we talked a bit about southern Africa, and I was surprised to find that I was somewhat more optimistic than she was, even as we ran through the headings that Africa watchers go through as they disagree over whether the continent was moving forwards or back: which country deserved what used to be called Brownie points for dealing with AIDS and child soldiers, which for fair treatment of women; and the old one of weaning themselves away from Presidents for Life. In the end I cited Mozambique and then went back to my hotel, alone.

You're always left feeling vaguely unsettled by these encounters, foolish and dissatisfied: chance conversations in restaurants lack nuance. I should have said *this*; I should have admitted *that*; I should have said: what's a good-looking woman like you . . . ? Though she did mention her husband – the one who had worked in South Africa, in the Cape. My friends in Johannesburg had always promised me the Cape, and here was someone who had done the Cape, and didn't really think much of it.

We were in the Indonesian restaurant just round the corner from the Rijksmuseum, where I'd spent another couple of hours that day. I had had lunch in the restaurant the day before and another American had struck up a conversation, a man this time: you put it down to the American way with strangers. More pronounced now that they were feeling a bit unloved as a nation. The man had heard me talking to the waiter and wanted to know where I was from.

'Britain.'

As I say, these conversations lack nuance.

Back here now (this is the last trip we're talking about, not this one) in the evening, to sample the famous curried goat, only to find they didn't do curried goat. But you're here, might as well stay and have something. The place is packed, up-market couples, yes, but single men, too, at their own tables, each surrounded by a dozen dishes, tiny portions set out on most of them. Men without partners; maybe not so odd here. So I was sitting at the edge of the high counter; and the two American women appeared on the other side, facing, one complaining of jet lag. During the conversation – before Africa? after Africa? – I was asked if I was an art dealer. (I had mentioned going to the Rijksmuseum to see the Vermeers and planning a trip down to Delft to have a look at the Vermeer country.) Are you an art dealer? That's the way of fiction, isn't it? Some-one plants something in your head, and then you become it. Or you seek to become it. Chance meeting in a restaur-ant in Amsterdam, two presentable young Americans, one, lying or otherwise about a husband, talking of Africa, making the running; the other asking if I am an art dealer. So this is where I come clean – they could be my students, after all – and admit to my relative ignorance about art. Enthusiasm for, yes, hence this Easter visit to, y'know . . . Slight disappointment that the Rijksmuseum is being reno-vated, scaffolding all round, only one wing open to the public, featuring The Masterpieces. And that, in a way, was enough, the Vermeers, Rembrandt's *Night Watch* – never could get over that little man in the white fancy dress at the front. That and . . . Hals and de Hooch, etc. (Over twenty characters in *The Night Watch*: if the man were a calculating *contemporary* he would have got twenty separate pictures out of it.)

No art dealer, me; as a shrewd businesswoman in Kilburn, who knew about the art business, could testify.

The next day I was back at the museum, before going down to Delft, curious to see the lay of the land, even though there were no Vermeers in Delft. The *View of Delft* was said to be in The Hague, next door. As was, yes, *Girl with a Pearl Earring*. Fifteen minutes on the train between Delft and The Hague. An hour – less than an hour – from Amsterdam. Things seem so *manageable* in a small country.

So I was back at the Rijksmuseum. This time I didn't bother with the headphones and skimpy commentary but went straight for the painting that intrigued me. No, not the Rembrandt, not even the Vermeers, but something on the ground floor, on the left as you enter, in the corner of the room facing the entrance; and I couldn't help but be disturbed by the memory of a painter on a small island in the Caribbean.

I remembered doing the quick tour of The Masters upstairs, just to check on the odd detail, to get certain things right should I chance to run into the American women again and decide to play my art-dealer role. So, note, again, *The Syndics of the Drapers' Guild* dominating one wall, the five soberly robed and hatted cloth inspectors at their table (the table draped, naturally, in rich cloth: *they are cloth inspectors, these 'Syndics'*) with their hatless servant standing in attendance. Naturally, one would point out to the girls (the Americans would be in their early thirties, maybe) – point out Rembrandt's genius in varying the *line* of the row of heads by having one inspector in the process of standing – either of standing or sitting – raising the head and torso of that figure above the others, to the line of the servant *standing* behind. *The convention, remember, is that these guys should be painted sitting.* So, all that done, I returned downstairs to the painting that puzzled me.

The painting was *The Tailor's Workshop*, and it was by someone called Quiringh van Brekelenkam. Fun name. ('Oi, darling, I'm van Brekelenkam, the butcher.' 'You what? Getoff. Back to yer offal.' *But* 'Ah, Madam, I'm van

Brekelenkam, the *painter*.' 'You don't say. Tell me more. Would you like to paint my buxom daughter?') His dates are 1613–1675. And I suddenly knew why the picture disturbed me. *It's of my mother!* Of course van Brekelenkam didn't paint my mother, another man with a fake name did that – three hundred-odd years later. Leon da Firenze had somehow copied this picture, substituted my mother in place of the visitor to the tailor's workshop, and vandalized her image. Why? I couldn't of course ask him because he was dead.

So this was, by association, a *family* painting. And it made a sort of sense. Here, the Master Tailor is in discussion with his woman visitor. The Master Tailor is sitting flat on the workbench with his legs drawn up, the knees spread. This is on the right side of the picture. He is well-fed and prosperous; he's wearing a beautiful, white, maybe silk scarf showing off a (clean?) brown coat; his long, flowing hair (brown, like the coat) and neat cap suggestive of a man well-groomed. His expression is benign and sober as he explains something to the woman standing (imposingly) at the edge of the table. Note the palm of the tailor's right hand, facing upwards! The garment under discussion is rich and heavy, a coat of some sort, yellow, all very well lit from the natural light streaming through the massive double windows on the left. Now, to the woman, the visitor. *My mother.*

There's that woman, isn't there, Somalia . . . Somalian-Dutch. One of those statuesque models – you could see her as a Frans Hals figure. Discreetly superior. Of course her life is at risk. Speaking out against Islam. Bodyguards; the lot. Her name . . .

OK, how about the guy whom they call Mohammed B, Mohammed Bouyeri. Twenty-six-year-old Moroccan-Dutchman. On the day in question, this creature was dressed in a grey raincoat and a prayer hat. Then he shot the man. The man was Theo van Gogh who was riding a bicycle somewhere in Amsterdam. Theo van Gogh was a film-maker and TV personality. A controversial figure. The killer also had a machete – a curved weapon – and a knife. After shooting the film-maker the Mohammed B character cuts the fallen man's throat with the machete [urrgh] and then sticks the knife in the man's body, pinning in place a piece of paper on which something is written.

'At least I got an urrgh *out of you,' she says, a glass of white wine in her hand. I can hear her. Still at the function.*

I have a glass of red wine in my hand, red for my condition. Do I talk dirty about my condition?

She has a glass of white wine in her hand; she's got a different condition. We move away to avoid confrontation: this is a party. But before we move away she whispers something. I imagine she whispers something – for your ears only.

So this, now, in a way, is my act of resistance, thinking of that portrait of my mother in the Rijksmuseum. She is middle-aged, yes, but only just; hair pulled back in a bun and her figure richly dressed, the dark top edged with white, her orange skirt – lots of colour – also edged. Neat shoes. Made in Holland. Though she's carrying something odd. Hooked over her left arm, is a metal thing (shines like aluminium: was aluminium processed in 1601, the date of the painting?) – a metal bucket instead of a handbag. And she's wearing what might be a pearl earring. (*Ah! Vermeer: what were Vermeer's dates? Seventeenth century, of course. Died young. Lots of children; only thirty-odd paintings; couldn't do hands.*) Anyway, behind this Brekelenkam woman in the tailor's workshop there are things hanging on the wall, belts, maybe, a sort of fabric bag with a long strap; clothes on a plank, one end set into the wall, the other held up by a belt fixed to the ceiling.

I went back to the gallery day after day, partly because it was just across the street from the hotel, and also because I was on my own. Anyway, I went back, *I come back*, to the woman in the picture, to her face, her posture: she's not especially pretty, none of these women is pretty, except, perhaps, Vermeer's girl with the pearl earring, but they have what we would call good Dutch seventeenth-century faces. By the time we get down to our own island version (the one I saw, a decade ago in a studio in Kilburn, and didn't recognize) my mother has lost her face: why? Why did the artificial man, da Firenze, who perversely painted my mother – a good-looking woman to the end – not give her a face? That night, at the hotel, I had nightmares; not your image of an Easter break in Amsterdam to wind down after the teaching, with Tracy Chevalier's *Girl With a Pearl Earring* in mind. Anyway, back to da Firenze (who killed himself in the end): it's true that in one phase of his work he didn't do faces; but sometimes he did faces, perfectly good and recognizable West Indian faces. When he chose to paint eggs for faces – particularly on the thing they call his *Triptych* – he was making some sort of statement that might be interesting to discuss. But when he just blanked out the face – as he had done with my mother – what *was* the point?

He must have done this picture late on, in the 1970s, when he was in England on some sort of fellowship, and had access to my mother's place in London: I remember talk of his copying some of the 'Old Masters' at the National Portrait Gallery, one of which was the massive portrait of *Members of the Anti-Slavery Society* by someone I forget. The point he was making, I seem to remember, was that this society painting sported only about three dark-skinned faces among the sea of white – though there *was* a prominent black man at the front, with his back to us. Da Firenze would 'revise' the history; he would paint in some more black faces, starting with my mother. (She was coyly flattered by that. Though slightly alarmed at being labelled 'black'. So how do we get from that – this from a guest to the house responding with good manners – from that to the tailor's workshop in Amsterdam?)

And now I'm embarrassed to be playing the art critic: but if you don't make these connections, who will? So bear with me – on the left of the Master Tailor (i.e., our left, the picture's right) are the two young apprentices, also sitting in a relaxed position on the workbench, facing each other. The one facing us, bathed in angelic light from the big window (leading on the panels), has a profusion of hair falling both sides of his little cap, like a girl, and is wearing a light-coloured costume, head bowed, intent on his mending. There's a pincushion and some huge scissors in the foreground. The other apprentice, dressed in a darker, muddy brown, has his back to us, and is sitting on a cushion (light brown, contrasting with the dark brown costume). The brown belt gives the loose-fitting lower garment a roguish semblance of style, and he's wearing an extravagant broad-brimmed hat, with long, brown, curly hair flowing down his back. This master, you think, is indulgent to his apprentices.

The other bits and pieces aren't so interesting: a barrel under the workbench – which, incidentally, is high off the ground – a barrel with a spill of cloth over the edge – also bits of cloth on the floor – cuttings; as well as a sturdy chair. Wicker seat but solid frame, a bit askew to the worktable. On the lower right side of the picture (apart from the lower half of the woman visitor) virtually nothing. Good job at handling the cloth, though, this painter; convincing folds. A large bright patch of pocket on the woman's skirt.

II

I'm attempting not to – if you like – overpaint this canvas with the picture of a man on a bicycle, murdered, lying on the ground, his throat cut, a knife stuck into his stomach, with that message from the Koran. That would be an affront to my mother. I should be ashamed of myself for this obsession with family history; of wanting urgently to go back to Kilburn to see the woman who had a stack of her cousin's paintings, one of which was of my mother. Instead, when I get the chance I must read up on the impact of Moroccans in Holland, on the circumstances that made both Theo van Gogh and, more famously, Pim Fortuyn before him, notorious, disturbing. Two murdered men.

So, no cute identification of the picture called *The Bicycle Race* – and the city of Amsterdam. It was a calm picture – da Firenze's were usually 'calm', so his 'frenzy' of having walked out of the shelter in St Caesare during the '89 hurricane, presumably to commit suicide, was an unresolved puzzle. Anyway, the beauty of *that* picture – which must have been inspired, too, by Amsterdam – the beauty of this picture, the wit, really, is that there is no obvious race. Five cyclists moving along a flat stretch of road – puts you in mind of Surinam, too. Moving in a leisurely way – no trailing or billowing cloth, no frenzied pedalling, body language relaxed. One cyclist might be pedalling, a lawyer, maybe, or a priest, someone in a gown – a graduate showing off? But even he is doing it without apparent effort. One cycle bearing the entire family: man in the seat, wife sitting behind (not holding on), child in the basket in front. Asian-looking. Indeed, the group presents an interesting racial type, racial mix (the Caribbean, at a pinch).

That time, standing outside the Indonesian restaurant in Amsterdam, I observed the various cyclists, people of all ages, classes, unhurried; men riding ladies'-frame bicycles – almost like a lost world. All these people on bicycles on their way to work or wherever; to the restaurant, to the concert; men in suits, women: *these women must have strong legs!* So these office workers and schoolteachers and hospital attendants get to work sweaty. Shower on arrival? Water wouldn't be a problem in this country. Imagine a similar situation in England, the directors of our national galleries cycling to work: Nicholas Serota at Tate Modern. Dame Esteve-Coll, who used to be at the V&A. Pedalling away. Then into the obliging shower.

Then I think of an incident that sours everything. Not a particularly ugly incident; but not unconnected with the pursuit of art here in Amsterdam. Just between the hotel and the Rijksmuseum is a fish stall. All very health conscious, you might think. A substantial enough business, this; two, three tables inside to sit down, and grilles and shutters to secure it all after hours. So what's the story? This establishment is presided over by a Viking of a man. He already has a couple of drop-in customers, a youngish woman and her child, both blond, *all blond*. As I come in he welcomes me in a slightly noisy way. I indicate that I'm just looking. His attitude – and something of his smile – freezes. He continues to urge me to sample his fare, and the rather forced, complicit smiles of mother and young daughter help me to translate. In the end I withdraw with a little bow, puzzled again that people little realize how much you give to them – are tolerant of them – moment to moment.

III

The polka-dot dress, and the way she carried the handbag, was your cue: you recognized that, but more as authentic period detail than as the person: that dress would have been handed down to a maid, though the maid wouldn't have carried her handbag quite in that way. It was a *composite* of the time. Though the tailor was definitely not our old Maas Croggins. Croggins was the only tailor in the village, the man who had made our new clothes for the journey to England in '56; and was regularly visited by me from time to time, these last weeks, as I checked on the progress of the suit.

So here she was, in the painting, remonstrating with him. What made me slow on the uptake, perhaps, was the odd composition of the figures, all three men virtually squatting on the workbench; we'd never seen that arrangement in the Caribbean. *What was this man saying to us?*

It made me angry that my mother didn't have a face in the painting. *Why this departure from . . . why this failure of nerve?* On entering the museum in Amsterdam you're greeted by this huge canvas, which is the civil guard at their banquet. What a mass of faces, some looking this way, some that way, some full on. Good, solid citizens, showing off their bourgeois dress; but clearly proud of their seventeenth-century faces, not a mole or scar or birthmark among them; and we're talking of what, twenty-five people, including the landlord and his wife. Why have the Dutch, I ask myself, so many faces and we, in the paintings of a man from a small island, so few?

I was thinking anew of the difficulties that people in the islands, particularly in those days, had with portrait representation: this person wanted to be fairer-skinned than she was, that one wanted to have straighter hair or a differently shaped nose. Or – understandably – the goitre de-emphasized, the rolls of fat tactfully reduced. They wanted, in fact, what patrons of paintings always wanted, to be idealized. Except the islands had no patrons of the arts; each picture was almost a sort of calling card: if it didn't flatter, the painter was turned away, didn't get invited back to the house. So if you were painting for your supper, you had to make sure your painting got you supper. So the clever man had painted eggs for faces in order not to offend.

Theo van Gogh's nasty little film offended and he was killed in Amsterdam.

Must visit the house, yes – Pim Fortuyn's house-museum – in Rotterdam, the Palazzo di Pietro, and do the tour, pay tribute to the high priest of camp; to Dutch kitsch.

Ayaan Hirsi Ali, too – that was her name, the Somali-Dutch beauty in the news. Ayaan Hirsi Ali's outspoken challenge to the medieval practices of present-day Islam has earned her death threats and a permanent bodyguard. (You don't take death threats lightly after the murders of Fortuyn and van Gogh.) (She escaped to safety in America.)

And no, I haven't yet visited those 'dish cities' critics talk about, in the Moroccan-Turkish parts of Amsterdam.

The stalker – will she come to the hotel tonight? – who had whispered something in my ear at the party, at the publishers' party, is in the city; I know it. *So it's scribble scribble more notes about Amsterdam.*

21

For a Brother

(Joe: WSGM 1932–2007)

I

A man is dying in a hospice; this unknown part of town is now the focus of attention of those close to him.

But before we get ahead of ourselves, the man is in bed, in his own room, gazing at the television; he is said by those who visit to want the television on, perhaps – this is speculation – perhaps to exert a little control over the bedside conversation, where reference to the familiar day-time quiz might be less taxing than other types of mental probing. If the man in bed can't summon the energy to respond to these feelers it doesn't matter much; all can agree that the TV-induced subject is trivial.

Is his voice clear; is he still speaking in sentences?

The answers are contradictory.

Someone comes in to prove a point; there is some conversation; it is better than no conversation.

He is comfortable; he is not complaining about not being comfortable; the tension in his face mustn't be over-interpreted.

It must be good to have a familiar voice (familiar voices) around you; and he appreciates having his feet massaged. By a concerned niece.

It is confirmed; he likes to have his feet massaged.

Someone else, a brother, is on the way to the hospice. Like everyone else, he has forebodings about the term. 'Hospice' has never formed a sentence structure with 'family' before. So this is a challenge larger than an individual's fate, this is a greyness signalling that something like summer is over. And yet, don't play to the mood, try to be specific and not be emotionally lazy; is this an endgame, an end-of-line time, a terminus where the buses and trains stop their journey? This brother is threatening to become something beyond that, like a parent you hadn't yet prepared yourself for being without.

This is, literally, beyond where the train terminates. End of Northern Line. Morden. First time this far out. After the train there is a bus, and fringes of unfamiliar country that is London: it is this sense of being ushered out of the city, past where the train stops, that most unsettles the visiting brother, confirming the superstition of 'hospice' as a point of no return.

The prospect of an elder brother dying before you is unsettling in a subtle way, for though it is more or less expected, that is a security not to be trusted. And this elder brother has lived an altogether safer life than the other has. The elder brother's going first assumes a logic of something somewhat more mysterious and arbitrary than reason: only the childlike or unimaginative welcome life's tidiness in these areas. So the predictability of this must have been a small weight for the elder brother to bear; not consciously, of course, not something pressing enough to warrant articulation, but something that might have appeared from time to time, a shadow at the edge of vision, before vanishing. (He must have defeated death on occasion, glancingly, unheroically, in the lottery of his own living and that, too, must have communicated a sense of . . . journeys not cut short. If so, how to repay the thoughtfulness without reminding others of it. The brothers have never discussed this, of course: so is this the time for the younger to show appreciation that the other is prepared to play this old-fashioned ritual that makes no real sense any more?) Enough. Enough of this bus-passenger talk.

He's got the daily paper, the younger brother. (There are some papers his brother will not read; he likes that.) He will go through items of interest in a paper that his brother reads. Then, perhaps, turn to the sport. (News on the radio is altogether too heavy, nothing but disorder in the world, and obscenity.) They've had fifty years at railing against it and no one has listened. Now, a man of calm and benign temper would not want to go out to a world still given over to prejudice and violence and genocide. So it'll be better to talk about sport. (Though not of the interview with Clive Lloyd, recently heard on the World Service, of the West Indies touring Zimbabwe. The great man seemed curiously uncensorious of the Mugabe government: would he be comparing Mugabe's stewardship favourably with Ian Smith's, say, or with the earlier rapacious brother, Leopold of the Belgians?) So an upbeat and heartiest review of the sports comedy on the back pages might be the right tone for the hospice.

In a room at the hospice – the visitors' holding room, so to speak – family and friends gather, get updates, review the situation and visit the sickroom in rota, so as not to crowd the sickbed. It is a Sunday; there is a whiff of church in the air.

The patient's wife and daughter have pride of place. Their body language, their attentiveness to guests, etc., indicate this is already home from home; they are in residence. The wife, too, is not well; her medical history recounted in some detail shows her as being stubbornly heroic; the daughter is, understandably, suffering. The obsessive reference in 'the silent killer' strikes a note of acceptance.

A young priest comes to pay respects; and someone – two people – from the lodge to which the man in question belongs. Friends and relatives from far away make light of their journeying. The priest is female and pretty; she talks of dignity, of how difficult to be deprived of it, particularly when one is as dignified as the patient in question, his name on everyone's lips, surprisingly, a diminutive not used by the family: this then, this church, this lodge, these friends, constitute another family. Affection and warmth emanate from this family. Later, in the sickroom, the nurse, too, is warm and tactile. The visiting brother's prepared reservations begin to fall away, and yes, in an ideal life he could commend both nurse and priest to his brother's service; they are unselfishly on the case.

He has an odd conversation with a man from the church whom he tries not to place in other – more theatrical – company. They disagree on the meaning of life and death, but with politeness and courtesy. They probe each other with light name-dropping. They share a joke about 'Creation' – a trade name stencilled on the metal frame of the patient's hospital bed. They end, like wary boxers, circling each other with a Bishop Berkeley reference; they end by being quietly pleased with themselves.

Waking up. Waking up in the middle of the night without a brother. Waking up in a strange flat in the south of London in the middle of the night without a brother . . . This is a first. You have woken in panic before, in consternation, but the loss of a manuscript, or of a partner, has proved, on reflection, to be something in which you were complicit. You could resolve, in time, to play a better hand. To play the hand differently. But to wake up to the loss of a brother strikes as something elemental. Making yourself a cup of tea won't do it. Scribbling a few lines on your notepad won't do it. Resolving to be a better listener/

correspondent/linguist, etc. won't do it; it's not in your hands.

So you reach for foolish analogies. Like waking up with one leg missing. Like . . . in the end you settle for being in a country where you don't speak the language. This has happened to you, often. Recently even. The humiliations at this or that national bank of language where you are overdrawn and the manager pitiless – most recently at Alliance Française – is instructive. The brother is a source of that bank of language.

But there's the night to think it through, to mull things over, in a strange house, in an unaccustomed part of London. A small accident occurs here, in Balham; but it's not significant. Also, he has a dream, which makes him uneasy.

*

The next day the brother repeats the journey; gets the train from Balham to Morden and then the 93 bus to the hospice. It's the bus ride that disconcerts him today, as it moves out of the city, London being left behind again. St Pancras, where he came in yesterday, is already a distant place. Theatre-land with lights and crowds and buzz . . . the river . . . Arsenal . . . these have to be abandoned like tittle-tattle among the healthy; this is the suburb of a city in the process of disowning you.

Another thing – this is what happens when, despite yourself, the gloom sets in. Another thing: this 93 bus is going to North Cheam. Is this real? In the 1950s, on a Sunday afternoon, the brothers, back in Ladbroke Grove, would listen to *Hancock's Half Hour* on the radio, the references to East Cheam making the programme slightly amusing, as East Cheam was assumed to be a made-up name. A no-place. And now, fifty years later, this 93 bus to the hospice is heading for North Cheam. There is a feeling of a light mockery in the air. This seems the opposite of dignity that the clergyperson spoke about yesterday.

Talking of dignity: does the brother know where he is? (Kidnapped prisoners in shuttered rooms come to mind. The visiting brother has been reading Alan Johnston's book describing the experience of being abducted in Gaza.) The elder brother's road map of London, so laboriously set out in fifty years, has been snatched away, crumpled and binned; he's set down in a foreign place with only church-persons and lodge members for guides. Members of the family had inspected the hospice prior to the residence, but he would not have done so: do the family have the strength to creolize this new part of London? Yesterday the nurse had asked if the patient had anything specific in mind that he would like to discuss. Or any questions he wanted to ask: he had apparently said no. Which was not surprising, as there were about six people crowded in the room at the time. And an appropriate answer to that sort of question needed, if not to be scripted, if not some pre-paration, at least some privacy. (Though it could be argued that he had had preparation: something the brother and the priest had put in a different construction on the day before, and then shook hands on it.)

So the visiting brother had made a half-hearted attempt, overnight, to 'script' some possible 'issues' on the patient's mind, if for nothing else, not to cede the terms of the 'debate' to others. This sadly had nothing to do with the patient.

So, of the hundred or so things that seemed relevant last night to ask when someone next invited questions from the deathbed, he had mentally crossed them out by the morning, along with the old favourites like 'Why me?' He must get closer to the brother's temperament, to his spirit. What was 'bothering/puzzling/baffling' him might be nothing new or different: *What's a black hole? Is Saturn nearer to the earth than, say, Jupiter . . . ?*

'Will I now never get to do this thing that I've never spelt out, even to the most intimate among friends?'

Surely, there's a better thought forming as he lies there listening to the recording of a Cornish choir rendering what were said to be his favourite hymns; as he appears to sing along, and then accepts the prayer that visitors bring as a gift.

There is mild controversy in the holding space, the visitors' anteroom, as a niece holds the hospital treatment of her uncle (not the hospice's) up to scrutiny. But other visitors preach acceptance. In the sickroom the church members, the lodge members, call both for a miracle and for acceptance.

In truth, the patient *had* said something in answer to the nurse. He had always been polite. Also, not to answer would indicate that you were more ill than you would like others to realize. And what he said was interpreted by those who heard in . . . in ways to reassure themselves. So there was no point in the supplementary list of questions. Or, *was* there an urgent need for a supplementary list of questions?

The brother, who lived abroad, was conscious that he shouldn't muscle past the guard of others who were near at hand, in case his concern might seem proprietorial. Among other things, he was late on the scene.

Family and friends fully understood that he had a cold ('French flu') – a cough and cold – and it would have been thoughtless to come sooner and bring a cough and cold to the sickroom. But he is welcomed to the gathering, adopted, even, by more than one person, as someone who sounds like his brother, a form of welcome. He is mildly surprised at this, but not unhappy. Maybe, at an opportune moment, he might risk ventriloquizing the odd saying or two, à la brother.

In the anteroom the talk is of miracles, miracles symbolized by present company cheating death. Just about everyone over a certain age seems to have survived despite the logic of science and predictions of doctors. So who knows? The visiting brother is both uncomfortable and reassured by this elastic stretch of the term 'miracle'.

(On the phone, later, to a more secular friend, he is able to agree that someone dying in this undramatic way is, perhaps, not the worst. The melodrama of deaths on the TV, say, or in the theatre, invite the audience to pose more credible alternatives. The pornography of death [mass death] on the evening news, or that encountered violently, alone, in the street from a thug with an attitude would rightly be the spur to rage and anger. So the tone of death in the hospice, showing respect for the living as well as to the dying, is perhaps right.)

II

THE LIFE & THE ART OF IT

There has to be a personal note between brother and brother, a special look, correctly interpreted. If not, it would have to be invented. *I missed a few of your birthdays: do I make up for it now with a dozen birthday cards, all at once, in compensation? I imagine the hospice festooned with gifts that the neglectful feel they can unload on to the sick. But that's to assume that acts of omission can be righted by a last-minute rush of contribution.* Like a deathbed confession of the not-yet-dying.

MAKE ME WELL, the note will say.

He's ill, but he hasn't lost his mind; he knows I'm not a doctor.

The note slipped under the bed sheet while no one is looking will say something else.

Neither brother is able to devise that text at the moment.

The visiting, younger brother, long thought to be ambitious, secretly feared for because of the ambition, always in need of a steadying hand, still needs what you might call parenting. His brother, in bed, prone, is trying to transmit some thoughts that might help. *I will soon vacate that place at the edge of the precipice that prevents you hurtling over. Think of your books toppling off the shelf, without a book-stop. I drive within the speed limits to prevent you crashing, or to minimize the effect of the crash. I know you understand me. I am from a small island and know the lack of hinterland and know that the border of the land is sea: you're no swimmer, where are your Olympic medals for swimming? . . . I taught you to swim, remember! And you didn't learn to swim; not in the sea; you feared the sea. You learnt to swim, much later, in a pool at the Swiss Cottage Library: funny that a library should have a swimming-pool. None of us can explore land that isn't there. We are not God. None of us can swim seas that are built for boats; that are crossed by aircraft. And they crash. Boats sink and aeroplanes crash. Accept your limitations, my brother, and live within the resources of the family.*

Or – to use another analogy, as you would say: *That picture, that landscape that you paint, with the family, of the family at its most ambitious, of possible imagined families, it needs a frame. We are lost in the vastness of that landscape; we don't recognize it as our own. You must start reminding yourself now that there are limits to ambition. You must understand the foolishness of vanity; you must not fear death.*

The visiting brother is thinking: it may be time to swap cosmologies. If the Elder has pencilled in heaven and hosannas, the Younger could offer a more earthly road map.

'This is where I find myself today', sort of thing; my compass, my point of orientation. Here is my *Atlantic Monthly*. There is the *Paris Review*; it's taken I don't know how many journeys to get here. Now I'm preparing to meet my *New Yorker*. Which journey will lead to a fool's paradise need not be openly discussed; the brothers will have communicated. Other things can be brought up to pass the time.

What other things might be discussed?

Their long residence in this country might be discussed; they are not *new* Londoners. Did you know, for instance, that Bethnal Green Railway Station in the East End and Bethnal Green Underground are different stations, maybe ten minutes' walk apart? Well, then, that wouldn't be in a book for visitors to London. Even the new Londoners, from Poland and elsewhere, wouldn't know that. The brothers have a lived life in London in common, even though one of them no longer lives here. They have close to a hundred years of knowledge of London living in common. *And we're not even taxi drivers?* Add the rest of the family, and they go back into history; they have provenance.

But he won't pursue the conceit.

A picture of the family comes to mind. Literally, a picture of the family; now lost. One that the older brother claims not to know. In it the older brothers are wearing sharp suits (they'd be about thirteen and fourteen). White suits as for church. They are standing on either side of their mother, seated on a chair at the bottom of the front steps of the family home. The mother is wearing a polka-dot dress, and has on her rings, her bracelet, her earrings and a brooch. Just a few months ago the not-yet-diagnosed brother contested this; thought it historically incorrect that the brothers would be wearing jackets at that age. The younger brother had the photo in his possession, courtesy of his mother. Twenty years ago he had given lectures on it, on its circumstances, in the highlands of New Guinea, largely to demonstrate to folk there how this family, on the other side of the world, dressed in the mid-1940s. This part of the family history is stored in the younger brother's archive; so he must not lose his mind.

III

PREPARING FOR THE EULOGY

Back home in Paris after the second trip to London in two weeks. (Eurostar is thriving at his expense.) Important to be grounded, to sleep in your own bed. It's Sunday. Back in London on Thursday for the funeral. Must write the eulogy tomorrow and then check with people giving tributes that there's no unnecessary doubling up. There's a time limit on the proceedings.

Up very early in the morning, Monday, feeling refreshed, but not yet ready to attack the eulogy. Did the washing yesterday, went to the launderette; if not, would have used this, today, as an acceptable displacement activity. So, better have some breakfast; it's still only seven o'clock.

The obvious thing is to start rearranging the library, the bookshelves. The library is not a fixed thing, the books have never been placed in alphabetical order; more in terms of genre. Poetry and France in the sitting room. Art, Drama and Short Stories pride of place in the corridor – with Biography and Africa. Everything else – the bulk of the library – in the bedroom. This is the Writer's Room, should the *Guardian* choose to call: the writing desk and computer and everything else here where this writer lives.

So – at seven o'clock in the morning – books are being quietly pulled off shelves. Big Art Books taken down from a top shelf, making use of the stepladder, *l'escabeau* (masculine). They'll be put on a large bottom shelf below Short Stories. He recently came across a man, a writer, who boasted about the number of short-story collections on his shelf. Slightly depressed by this form of vulgarity, he is seeking ways to limit his short-story selection, not to get rid of the books, but to make them less visible, less *countable*. So he'll keep the four corridor shelves of short stories for quality collections, and stock the other stories somewhere, in an old bookcase at the opposite end of the corridor. (That means displacing Military History [mainly Napoleon] and Language Texts from that bookcase; these can go in the large overflow cupboard, to join books parked there four years ago. In the end – after two hours – the reassembled library gives one a feeling of – not quite lift, but – of resettling.)

Books are possessions, of course, to be left behind unless some university could be persuaded to take them. But this act of reshuffling makes them still seem like part of the living experience – you can't just reach for a book on the shelf knowing that it is always in the same place – and that makes them seem less crudely possessions, trophies. (Of course there's the famous Foyles postcard produced during the war, a huge pile of sandbags outside the store, being added to by a couple of middle-aged Foyles workers. The caption: 'Books made good filling for the sandbags during the war. Meanwhile, up on the roof, copies of *Mein Kampf* were protecting the building against German bombs'. He'd settle for that: a use for books, both English and German.)

The eulogy must strike a balance between respect for the memory of the dead and care for the feelings (and prejudices) of the living – each member of the family expecting a different emphasis.

There's also the thing of acknowledging the reality of the majority, the family, who are staunchly Christian; the church, who gave impressive support; the lodge – all the things inimical to the person giving the eulogy. So, some balance must be struck there. (*Must check on the real meaning of 'staunch'.*) But, the thing must be done; and done today.

How trivial to think that a missed conversation with a brother is the old one of what to do with the books after you're gone. Not even rising to the interesting level of the debate now being conducted between librarians and the illiberal Right in America, the militants of the Patriot Act (passed after 9/11) against those representing the Office of Intellectual Freedom. The order sent out to librarians demanding what certain 'suspects' are reading; the gagging order on librarians accompanying this is an issue this brother will have to shelve till he has occasion to talk to someone else about 'democracy'.

So he will recall talk about libraries in the old way. The fact that universities don't want them. That the children (assuming you have children) don't want them. A pathetic display of human vanity would be burying them with you, Pharaoh-like, and have later generations – who can no longer be relied on to read – puzzling over the gesture.

IV

EULOGY

Delivered at Upper Tooting Methodist Church,
Balham High Road, 13 December 2007

I have an image of one brother holding his brother's hand, as they crossed the road on their way to school. These are my brothers, Joe and Norman, nearly seventy years ago, in faraway Aruba, where the parents lived for a time. The one who held the other's hand, who guided him safely across the road, was Joe – William, better known to some of you here as Bill.

It's true to say that a few days ago, in Paris, where I live, on my way over to London to give what support I could to the family, I had a curious sensation of needing that guiding hand. As I went out of the front door into the main street, I had a strange feeling of being newly exposed, of needing that protective hand that the loss of a brother had removed from us.

Joe – Bill – had always been that protective presence. It wasn't a smothering or oppressive kind of protection, it was one that you might expect of a caring parent; indeed, of an older brother; a big brother.

But we're here today – I remind myself – to celebrate the life of someone who was important to us – important in some of the ways I'll try to articulate.

While we acknowledge that all life is important, in all its forms, from the least evolved to its most complex, which is, as far as we know, human, it's a special privilege to be able to celebrate the life of someone in whom those special human qualities of tolerance and gentleness, of selflessness and modesty, predominated – qualities that earned my brother the love and respect of family, of extended family, of friends and neighbours, of fellow members of the church and lodge, of people at his various places of work over the years – many of whom are happily (unhappily) here today. To the above qualities we must add a sense of duty.

For the record; and to remind us of the reality behind the sentiment: Joe was born William Sylvester Gurney Markham on the twentieth of June, 1932, in Harris, Montserrat, an outpost of the British Empire. His parents were Linda Anne Eliza Markham (née Lee) and Alexander Sylvester Markham of Bethel, later to be a Very Reverend in Canada. Joe was the eldest of four children – Norman, Julie and my humble self.

Joe attended the Montserrat Secondary School, and is still remembered by contemporaries as a fine grammar school athlete. He came to England in 1954, at the age of twenty-one; and, nine years later, in 1963 (the second of May), married Lydia Humphrey, from a Montserrat family, like the Markhams, long prominent in the Methodist Church. Lydia played the organ at church. (She had been a schoolteacher and also cashier in the Royal Bank of Canada on the island.) Later in life, as a mature student in England, Joe attended the Open University and gained himself a degree in sociology.

Of the marriage it was said – with Lydia's facility at the organ, and with Joe's fine tenor singing voice – that there was every prospect of musical harmony in the new Markham household. Their daughter, Glenda Elise, born in 1964 (on the second of May), has inherited something of her mother's musical gifts. Joe's earlier daughter, Gloria Miriam Herbert, has been a valued addition to the family.

But back to the text. Joe was, for me, something of a role model, against which I measured some of the qualities that I personally lack. Modestly, he would emphasize my own achievements instead of his own, and never take credit for the part he played in them. Modestly, he was quick to accept his limitations, and not fret about disappointment. He was not self-obsessed; he was not a prima donna; he did not rail against destiny; he was of a most equable temper, of a mature wisdom. (It pains me to speak of him in the past tense.)

Resolute and selfless. An interesting combination. As a boy, just out of his teens, Joe was dispatched on that long sea voyage to England that some of us remember with unease: did the fact that his father, and before that, a cousin, Reggie Osborne, had volunteered to fight in Europe's two great wars in the first half of the last century, make the welcome in postwar England easier? Don't bet on it.

Nevertheless, Joe succeeded in creating for us (with the help of his mother and his mother's family) the conditions where the family could resettle in a spirit of dignity, without ever having to accept the hosts' careless valuation of us.

My niece recently said to me – I have four nieces and they're all wonderful. I have a nephew, Jimmy, and he's wonderful. My niece Gwen has just played an important part in this celebration. Gwen strives hard to educate us into healthy eating (and we try to do what Gwen says, because she's a solicitor by profession, and we can't afford litigation). My niece Glenda has been, as you would expect, her mother's support at this time. My niece Yvette was being kind when she said she thought of me as a free spirit. It is an ambition, certainly. Yet, we know, don't we, that some spirits are allowed to be free only because others put in the work on their behalf. In contemplating the loss of something nebulous in our translation from Montserrat to England in the mid-1950s I later wrote a story entitled 'Taking a Drawing Room through Customs', hoping to suggest that this family was part of the nuance and texture of sophisticated living, before England. That was the free-spirit approach. Meanwhile, my brother Joe and his brother Norman, and my sister Julie – and, yes, my mother – played their part in establishing that physical space – that emotional hinterland – to make the *idea* of taking the drawing room through customs real. Joe was instrumental in producing that labour, in the process putting his own ambitions on hold. For that, my brother, much thanks.

I underline his selflessness. To the end he refused to take credit for the lifeline that he threw to us all when we needed it. I mentioned his sense of duty. This went beyond the familial to the civic. For decades he was a member of the TA (the Territorial Army).

I've mentioned his modesty. To the end he persisted in thinking that my going to university at the right time, with family support, was a more significant achievement than his own long-striven-for, hard-fought-for, well-earned Open University degree when he was of more mature years. I wish more of us had had his modesty.

And he was tolerant. We had a different world view: well – *he lived in south London, innit; I lived years north of the river*. But no, we had sometimes different views of how the world works; we had different views, even, of how life ends. While disagreeing, he was always tolerant of mine. For that grace, for that lack of dogmatism, I thank you, my brother.

So this is a life that it honours me to celebrate; and though my brother left us in a frame of mind that was positive, I have to admit that one of our last conversations was bordering on the gloomy. It had to do with some young people not fully respecting themselves. Eleven young people in particular. They sometimes dress up in white clothing and take to a field and pretend to be West Indian cricketers. Need I say more? But the point I wish to make is this. Even then, with that extreme form of provocation, reducing the rest of us to anger and despair, my brother found it in his heart to be generous. No, he said to me, the boys should not be punished in the medieval ways I suggested, for dishonouring us; instead, they should be pitied. Even at that late stage in his life, Joe found it in his heart to be generous.

So, I still see a man with his family, a man and his extended family; a man and his friends; a man and his church; a man whose life has made a difference; a man who urged us not to bear ill-will; an exemplary son brother husband father uncle, friend; a role model that I, as a writer, would have invented if he hadn't existed. Joe – Bill – William Sylvester Gurney – will surely live on in our hearts as a good, as a very good thing, as a part of our lives that will endure. Amen.

The crisp December day, sharp but bright, seemed right for the occasion. Thoughts about the statement being made, the responses provoked on this busy early afternoon, as the too-smart cars nose their way through streets of shoppers who try not to stare, must be put aside. The packed church was an answer to your own private anxieties. The tributes told you things about your brother you didn't know, all of which gave greater social depth to his life than you knew. The Reverend's 'Address' was well-crafted, well-balanced and devoid of private coding. (Reverends work harder than you realize. The emotional range to the job must make it strangely fulfilling, like being a nurse or a doctor; or maybe like the challenge of writing poems and stories for a living.) So why carp at the sentiments in some of the hymns, at the invitation to 'join our friends above'; at all this 'crossing' to . . . 'the heavenly land'. This is part of the ritual, the imagery, however unpalatable, of the brother's world; and in *Amazing Grace*, sung at the graveyard, the resonance of 'grace' serves, as ever, to free us from a too-narrow interpretation of the lines.

(*Why is the cemetery so large?* you ask – beautiful in its spaciousness; tasteful in its layout, tidy clusters of gravestones in white and black marble. A hint of something ethnic – the Jews to one side, the Poles over here. The Jewish dead in raised tombs. The brother's body placed in a spot that might make it hard to find without help of the caretakers. [A clump of trees here, a low building a couple of hundred yards outside the fence, to the left: neighbours are SYDNEY J. WATSON & GLADYS WATSON.] The ritual seems at its most appropriate here, a large group of well-dressed people facing the direction of the coffin, people wrapped up against the cold, not minding the mud on best shoes, singing in memory, in respect, for someone soon to be buried. (A tiny flare of rage escapes at those brutes in power in countries all over the world, disposing of humans without ceremony and respect.)

And, yes, you are happy to accept this gentler ritual, without reservation.

At the reception – an upstairs hall in Streatham – everyone gathers. Friends from the other side of London, from outside London, from abroad. One woman has a limp, but no one seriously disabled, so the lack of dis-ability access not an issue. The clergyperson pops up (new change of clothing) to bless the meal.

Lots of older people. Older people are generally under-employed and have (perhaps) limited social contacts; so funerals are a useful outing. Also, if you are a certain age ('I'm ten years older than you, my friend; do I look it?') there must be a certain sense of reassurance in having outlived another contemporary: so this is gently preening time, as well as the other thing. People talk at slight cross-purposes; but that's all right. The talk is pitched some-where between dialogue and soliloquy; and everyone present seems to have done better than might be imagined. (So where are the real no-hopers?) One answer is that attending funerals is expensive. You have to travel, some-times far distances (a couple here are over from America). But before that you have to make yourself presentable. A new suit or coat. New shoes and whatever. The down-and-out going to the library or the betting shop for warmth couldn't afford this outlay. The seriously ill would be too ashamed to attend. So this gathering is something of the quality end of the market.

A second small accident takes place at Balham, outside the Underground. This is number two. Then there was that dream. None of this is significant, yet to gloss over them might give the wrong impression. Take the dream:

In the dream, he, the visiting brother, is back at the university he has vacated. There seems to be some public event in progress, lots of visitors. Colleagues, dressed for the occasion, help to make up the audience. Some are standing in the wide corridor. Able to follow the lecture in the lecture theatre, which is open-plan. The visitor, at the microphone, seems to be enjoying himself. But the day-to-day work of the university continues; all the seminar rooms on that side of the corridor are in session. His own short-story class is gathered in a room at the end; he is late. He squeezes along the crowded corridor to his class. An ex-student, a young woman, high on stilts, calls his name as he goes by, and bends down to shake his hand. (In the confusion he forgets her name.)

He comes to the short-story class and apologizes for being late. (He is not very late.) He immediately sets the students to work, realizing he hasn't pushed them hard enough in the past . . . Let's start, he says, by making a note for a story that can't be written. First, convince yourself that it can't be written. And before the end of the session we will write it together. Now, he says, make another note, of a story that your reader, your listener, already knows as well as you. You've got five minutes.

He disappears. He returns after ten minutes.

Now, he says, how are we going to tell that story to someone who knows it as well as we do? Any suggestions?

VI

ANOTHER EARTH

The hymns, the givers of tributes, the clergyperson, all promise a place beyond this earth. A brother would certainly have bought this. And a response that is not self-centred needs to be found to engage with this.

So you start by saying that we are all reasonable people, not extremists, not fanatics, you can come to maybe a compromise, certainly an accommodation . . .

Recently, listening to the radio, following the talks on climate change in Bali, a useful image cropped up. In order to dramatize the issue, one delegate (from England) said that we were using up the world's resources with a wantonness and at a pace as if we had another two worlds standing by to supply us when this one was depleted. A useful image.

The image of parallel worlds seemed altogether more *sane* than a world down here and another *up there*. That was where the brothers' cosmologies could meet. In a parallel earth. A parallel world. It's largely fanciful, and yet the little we know of astronomy doesn't rule it out. (*Star Wars* seems as interesting a point of reference, in this context, as a Bible or a Koran.)

Already there are worlds – constituencies – familiar to one brother that the other would know little about.

The worlds of church and lodge on this side; the library added to on that side . . .

The Gospels taken literally on this side; the Gospels as imaginative literature on that side . . .

London and Paris, two big cities in common. But London and Paris, worlds apart, etc.

And back to earth. South London with its new mix of population – a babel of eastern Europe and the Middle East – seems full of new possibility. That Italian restaurant on Balham High Road was excellent, the young waitress respectful of an older man. The Afghan minicab driver to St Pancras knew the way. He probably knows already that Bethnal Green railway and Underground stations are a little way apart, and no problem to get you to either.

22

Back Home from Kathmandu

I

A small relief, always, as the key works. A welcome shelter from the rain. Anyone at home? No one at home. Some mail, but of little interest. Bills, of course. No let-up. And yet a sense of relief mixed with the disappointment. Go to the office, then, for the mail; the e-mail. Glad that it's raining.

It was raining when I left: did it let up? Not as haunting as at the start of that Dickens book . . . but atmospheric, nonetheless. You get bad dreams when it rains.

II

Rain would have been better than this drizzle; the grey is like your eyesight after the operation. Before the operation, for that matter. Never a good idea to come back, they say. (I recall a Tory MP jumping up in the Commons to welcome the Prime Minister back from abroad, from a fairly extensive world tour. The MP, playing to his own gallery, welcomed the Prime Minister on his visit to Britain: *wah wah wah*.) Did I, on this latest trip, give useful examples of the English sense of humour? The world makes it difficult, increasingly, for you to tell your jokes. Though a stab at cricket is always possible. England v. Australia.

I wouldn't care to live in these damp, sad houses any more; wouldn't want her to be waiting up for me in one of these houses. So, next time it'll have to be Rio, Provence . . . Sydney? Friends in Sydney have a sense of humour; they'll be sitting round the kitchen table in Balmain making jokes about John Howard. But those kitchen-table conversations were long ago. Twenty years, maybe. Older now, ravaged by, what, two big fires and grown-up children – the Sydney Olympics long gone. After all that, and the business of immigration – asylum seekers – my friends in Balmain will be sitting round the dining-room table explaining why, reluctantly, they must vote for John Howard. So then it must be Rio, Montauroux and – some place yet to be identified.

III

The mail is disappointing. No surprises. (It would have been something of a challenge if it were in the wrong language.) No one seems to have noticed that you've been away. Not quite true, perhaps, but no one registers that it matters that you've been away. Everything here can wait for a response. (Urgent mail still absent. On one of his Italian campaigns, Napoleon – instructing all bad news to be brought to him forthwith, any hour of the day or night – ordered his *chef de bureau*, Bourrienne, to leave all mere letters unopened for three weeks; and then predicted how much of the correspondence would resolve itself without his having to attend to it.) So no need for frantic phone calls and apologies on a Saturday. Make yourself a cup of tea, then. A light thought of not quite guilt passes as I move to the kitchen, conscious of not having contributed 'coffee money'.

Milk from the fridge feels safe. People I know rag me for spending so much time in hotels, having meals there:

think of the opportunities of hotel staff hanky-panky, putting *things* into your food. The moral? Be good to hotel staff. Not quite Aristotle or Pascal, but a sensible self-protective attitude. If, still, they spit in your soup, that won't kill you; they're into self-protection – and the fear of Hercule Poirot and Lieutenant Columbo, in his raincoat. So, spitting in your soup isn't the worst that can happen.

No need to brood on these matters, despite the rain. Go to your own rooms *status status* and read the e-mail.

IV

The computer doesn't work. The computer was 'fixed' before I went away; now it doesn't work: whom to blame? The newspaper headlines this week are to blame. A pre-palaeolithic geological blast that reshaped geography was to blame. The collapse of the West? Or a man (give him a name, call him Roy; later, call him Neil), the technician. My room, e-mail threatens to plunge me into a professional victim's state of rage. Till I think that this is an environment (university) where things are thought through: we pride ourselves on it. So, think this through.

It's a Saturday. Saturday is spelt with a capital S. Like a country. Or a person's name, if that person isn't a criminal. A criminal should have to forgo the right to capitalize his name, her name. Surely, this refinement to the criminal code will, in time, appeal to someone in the Home Office, capital H, capital O.

On Saturdays, then, men and women of good faith are at home with the family. Or out with the family. So no need for the office computer to work. Don't push this insight to the point of Moral Rearmament or religious fundamentalism. And the rage is subsiding. Pity to lose the energy of that balloon of rage, the air seeping out. Trap what's left of it into something. A story. Write a story.

V

THE STORY

I'm passing through a warm place. It is not st caesare in the caribbean or maputo in mozambique (OK, I'll restore capitals to the world. Maputo in Mozambique); let's just say I have a wad of rupees in my pocket, so will try to find the right country for rupees. When Robert Maxwell, the Fat Man, was finally discovered living in an unguarded villa in St Caesare after the volcano – where he went for a swim in the sea every day – I took no particular credit in having predicted it. What was more interesting was the vengeance the people of St Caesare took, blaming the volcano that destroyed the island and disturbed the graves on the Fat Man's presence there. They were, I'm told – the good people of St Caesare – unhappy about the way I wrote up that story.

Concerning Maputo, the same: my love of the Mozambique capital (and of the country) is undiminished. I remain a loyalist of its revolutionary past and celebrate its two (alas, assassinated) Great Men, Eduardo Mondlane and Samora Machel. I wrote something to this effect, which produced a response I hadn't anticipated. So I must back off for a while. Till then, it's back to Rio, Montauroux and . . . some place to be decided for a safe address. I want a different location for the story.

VI

No point in hanging around the office. Computer still not working; can't check or send e-mails. (*Wreck the joint!*) So, might as well wreck the joint. Or call the porters to lock up. Mission unaccomplished, then. I know: write up the story. A new story now of the porter refusing to come and lock up. (Instead, when you ring, he promptly recites the opening of Act II, Scene 3 of the Scottish play.) Anyway, he's a big man with a family and grown-up daughters whom he probably doesn't molest; and though he doesn't mind working at weekends, it *is* a Saturday: *Arsenal Liverpool Man United*. ARSENAL 23 – UNITED 0. Saturday. Got to separate himself, anyway, from those poor bastards in some foreign country, slaving in tourists' hotels, sweeping up the forecourt after the hoi polloi, what! This image of the porter gives me an idea for a story.

VII

THE STORY (CONTINUED)

Back at the house I fall asleep and have a bad dream.

(*Forward, to the revised version.*)

Back at the house I fell asleep and had a bad dream. That house was always an unlucky house for dreaming. That's why no one else is around. Maybe the dream was inevitable, as I was conscious of letting myself in without squaring it with anyone. And when I dreamt of my partner with a new partner, a man whom I knew vaguely and was on smoulderingly polite terms with, I had to distract myself with a story.

So, in this story I am on my way back from Kathmandu. (Ah! Rio, Montauroux. Kathmandu.) So I'm changing planes at, where, Doha; that's Qatar. Qatar Airlines, then, safer than BA with all this terrorism about. Better than BA or Mr Branson's Flying Machine. (Mr Branson is said, at the university, by someone who uses his trains, to be the old Robert Maxwell in disguise. The beard, you see, doing the trick. That, and a slimming machine. *Also, he swims.* But this last bit isn't in the story.)

So, as we were saying: on the way back from Kathmandu we change planes at Doha. A detail might be the sight of orderly lines of white-clad pilgrims queuing up at the airport (it is Ramadan). They're all so spotless that in the story I'll have some of the ambitious restaurateurs in the city turn their business into laundries during Ramadan.

VIII

The conversation in the airline queue, conversation among the white-clad pilgrims, is about the invention of aircraft.

The A300 is the newest one off the Doha factory lines.

This information is *classified*; a closely guarded secret among the pilgrims. If it gets out the West will appropriate the technology, or steal it and simply rebrand the aircraft as a 747 or a 742, or perpetrate some similar outrage. The pilgrims fall silent as I go past, as I am not to be trusted.

About the Kathmandu story, the scene would be a café in the city, discreet on local colour.

I am with a Nepalese friend.

We are conversing easily in English; and I make the odd note, shamelessly, in my notebook, that we are not talking about temples and trekking and climbing Everest. And, of course, *nothing* about the Gurkhas. (Lower-class people, you know, those Gurkha, and dark-skinned. Good at taking orders.)

Despite everything, the local colour intrudes. *The square, the temples, the statues of* . . . So I suspend the note-taking and close the book. The conversation is similar to those I hope to have (or imagined I've had) in Rio and Montauroux.

IX

The joke about England and Australia is easily understood, as cricket is a coming sport in Nepal.

Though I can't finish the *story* without a bit of name-dropping. (All right, I've visited Durbar Square and Pashupatinath – Hindu holy place, temples, cremation ghats, ritual bathers, half-naked sadhus . . .) In my book I'm sitting here with Salil, a writer, whose father is a poet. Sitting here high up on the balcony of the Café Nyatapole, looking down on the square. (There's a broad, low platform for ritual and performance. I could use that. For ritual and performance.)

OK, the place is Bhaktapur. Taumadi Square. How's that, then?

Acknowledgements

The publishers of this collection, and particularly
Alan Mahar, Publishing Director, would like to thank
the executors of the estate of E. A. Markham;
the Markham family; and Archie's many friends
for all their kindness and help in the publication
of this book, at a time when the loss of our author
and friend was still raw.

Some of the stories in this collection have been
previously published in other publications.
Particular thanks are due to Peepal Tree Press,
publishers of the memoir of the '50s, *Against the Grain*,
published 2008, where a slightly different version
of 'For a Brother' first appeared. Two stories
have also been published in *Stand* and *Wasifiri*.

Fiction by E. A. Markham